SUNFALL: Season Two
(Episodes 7-12)

International Standard Book Number (ISBN): 978-1523770557

Printed in the United States of America

Other Works

TIM MEYER

Demon Blood: Enlightenment
Demon Blood: Gateways
In the House of Mirrors
The Thin Veil
Less Than Human
Worlds Between My Teeth
The Organ Harvest (An October John Novella)

PETE DRAPER

Sacrifice & Surrender (A Short Story)

TIM MEYER, CHAD SCANLON, & PETE DRAPER

SUNFALL: SEASON ONE
SUNFALL: SEASON TWO

SPECIAL THANKS:

A huge "thank you" to authors Natalie Carlisle and DS Ullery for taking the time to read and provide feedback. Season Two is better for it.

CONTENTS:

On Terrible Things
& Other Such Occurrences

(A Foreword)

It came without warning, as most terrible things do. Without discernible motives or clear intentions, the sun fell from the sky and scorched humanity to the brink of extinction, leaving little in its wake, and substantially less than there had been before. Some things have changed while others have ended, and the line between such subtleties has blurred indefinitely, perhaps forever erased. What remains is what the few survivors make of it, if they choose to make anything of it at all.

The most significant of tragedies strike unexpectedly. In worlds both fantastic and factual, that much can be certain. And even when their occurrence is foreseen and anticipated, there is often very little which can be accomplished to deter or prevent their arrival. Hearts are broken, lives are shattered, and all too frequently are we left with the fragments of the past, wondering how can a future be built on what *was* and never will *be* again.

As Sam, Soren, and the others are beginning to realize, the moments following the aftermath of such terrible occurrences is vital. In those times there are many decisions to be made, some less questionable than others. With regard to those more complicated matters, while the resolution to such may be apparent, it is often the means to achieve that end which receives considerably more scrutiny, especially in dire circumstances. This is what my fellow coauthors and I find most fascinating about the world portrayed in *Sunfall*. Individually and collectively, all of the characters have experienced some sort of tragedy, whether foreseeable or unexpected, and certainly some more personal than others. Nevertheless, despite their extensive collection of experience, none of them have ever faced the challenges which lay before them subsequent to the events of The Big Burn. Accordingly, the most important question is not what decisions will they make, but rather, who will be the one to make them.

If history has shown us anything, it is that we as a society rely upon those who demonstrate strength and courage in times of desperation and despair. In those darkest hours, those men and women who rise and lead their communities, cities, or nations to better tomorrows shine the brightest. This prompts yet another question: who will rise and shine? Sam or Soren? Both or neither? The best answer we are able to offer is this: Patience.

One may argue that patience is something which neither Sam nor Soren can afford, especially under the circumstances which they currently find themselves. Perhaps there is some truth to that logic, but there remains much in need of exploration, and thus, it is essential that our characters be given every opportunity to rise, so that they may shine their brightest. Or perhaps you, faithful reader, advise that you yourself have not the time for patience. We are well aware of this, and on behalf of Tim and Chad, I thank you for your exercise in perseverance through the delay between Season One and Season Two. It is no easy task to be asked to stay vigilant and tolerant, and left wondering and waiting, but we thank you for continuing on this journey with us. Much like our characters, an opportunity was needed to rise so that we too, as authors, could shine our brightest. We hope we have not lost any luster on the way to creating what we believe is an exciting second season.

Much has been said about the unexpected tragedies that come and go in all worlds of differentiating shapes, sizes, and schemes. But what cannot go unmentioned is that much like terrible things, great and wonderful things tend reveal themselves unexpectedly as well. It is the unexpectedness of these great things that make them even more romantic and worthwhile than imagined. We are not always told or forewarned of these joyful occasions or possibilities; they simply happen, with or without our permission. They come without warning, as most wonderful things do.

Thank you for your patience and continuing on this journey with us, faithful reader. May you too find your moment to shine.

Pete Draper

SUNFALL
SEASON TWO
(Episodes 7-12)

When he closes his eyes, all he sees are ghosts:

January 22ⁿᵈ, 1985

The man in the glass reflection pushes his hair back in place. He dusts off his lab coat, sending a chalky powder airborne. He sighs deeply and places his hand on the security pad next to the door. The glass panels spread, giving way to a long white hallway. It looks like Heaven, but this place is far from divine. Truth be told, a demon lives here, and his name is Elias Wheeler.

This place is Hell, he thinks as he approaches two guards. They're blocking the entrance to Wheeler's lair.

Stop, one guard says.

I've been sent for, the man responds. He shows them his beeper with the boss's number scrolling across the screen.

We weren't aware Mr. Wheeler had a meeting this afternoon.

The man smiles. Feel free to consult with him. I'll wait.

Your name?

Sandborough.

San.. San... San...

The guard runs his finger down a list. Nothing, he spits. According to my record, you're only a Level 5 clearance. I doubt Mr. Wheeler would request a meeting with someone from your sector. His nostrils flare like a bull.

Very well, the man says. I'll be on my way.

Hold it right there, Sandborough. The voice comes through the speaker next to the door. It booms like thunder. Boys, you can let Mr. Sandborough through. I apologize I didn't inform you of our meeting earlier. Things were quite busy.

No problem at all, Mr. Wheeler.

The guards push the doors open manually and Sandborough steps inside, his feet heavy with uncertainty. The doors hiss shut as he enters the loft. The room is big and open, unlike the facility beneath them.

Elias Wheeler rises from his desk, removing his nose from a small mound of cocaine. His arms are outstretched, like he means to wrap them around the world. He wants to embrace Sandborough, but the last thing Sandborough wants is a close encounter with a demon. As Wheeler strolls across the room, Sandborough notices the book on his desk; Fear and Trembling *by Soren Kierkegaard.*

We did it, Alan, Wheeler says, a child's grin growing across his face. We fucking did it.

Did what, exactly?

The demon's grin concerns Sandborough. It doesn't look natural.

Ignoring him, Wheeler pointed to his desk. Care for a bump?

Sandborough shakes his head. I'll stick with cigarettes, he says, pulling one from his pocket.

Wheeler makes his way to the minibar. He's quiet when he fixes himself a drink. The silence is unsettling. He didn't come thinking Wheeler had invited him here to celebrate. He thought Wheeler summoned him to terminate his employment. Or relocate him elsewhere, which—if the rumors were true—was worse than getting fired. Remember Bobby Egbert?

Maybe I will take that drink, Sandborough says.

Excellent!

Joe and I are making headway with A61Z, he says, trying to fill the silence.

That's great news. He spins with two drinks in hand. He extends one to Sandborough, who takes it reluctantly. But I have better.

Please tell.

The United States Government is extending our contract through the year 2000.

Sandborough's eyes widen. That is great news. Fifteen years is a long time.

That means job security for you.

Sandborough laughs. Dr. Wheeler, I'm just a research analyst. I'm a dime a dozen.

Not anymore you're not. You're being promoted.

Promoted? To what?

Head research analyst.

What about Joe and A61Z?

You'll be overseeing that project. Among many others.

Dr. Wheeler, I don't know what to say.

Say yes. And call me Elias.

OK, Elias.

Elias Wheeler turns to the long window behind him. It overlooks the snowy Alaskan landscape. In the distance, an endless mountain range stands in the purple glow of the afternoon sun. It's beautiful, Sandborough thinks. He's only seen beauty like this on postcards and dreams. He closes his eyes and wishes she was next to him, enjoying nature's gorgeous statues. But she can't be and he knows it. She does too.

Is it lonely down there, in The Dish? Wheeler asks.

Sandborough shrugs. Sometimes, he lies.

It's quite lonely up here.

You have your wife.

Wheeler doesn't flinch and continues to gaze into the vast white terrain. Kyra, he speaks softly.

Hearing her name fills Sandborough with joy. He hides his delight behind a cloud of cigarette smoke.

The door to Wheeler's domain whooshes open and as if on cue, she enters. Both men turn, her presence draping smiles across their faces. She doesn't expect Sandborough to be there and seems startled by his appearance, if only for a second.

Dr. Sandborough, she says. What brings you out of The Dish?

Me, Wheeler says.

Kyra forces a smile and sidles next to her husband. She pecks him on the cheek. Sandborough clenches his fist at his side.

I've offered Alan a job.

A job?

Yes. Head Analyst.

Oh.

Isn't that great news?

Absolutely, she says, turning to Sandborough. Guess that means we'll be seeing less of each other.

Much less, Sandborough thinks. But isn't that the point?

Has my wife told you the good news?
Sandborough, in a daze, shakes his head.
Kyra's pregnant.
The world spins, but Sandborough is able to keep his balance.
Embarrassed, she looks at Sandborough coyly. *I thought Aldo would have told you. Didn't my brother tell you?*
Sandborough, now a practiced actor, puts on a smile even he mistakes as genuine.
No, Aldo has been hush on the subject. But congratulations! I'm very happy for you. Boy or girl?
Too early to tell, Kyra says. She looks like she wants to cry. *But my instincts tell me—girl.*
Congratulations, he says again, unable to think of something more original.
You look pale, Wheeler comments. *Can I fetch you a glass of water?*
No, Sandborough says. *But I'll have another Scotch.*

The past is a graveyard, and the ghosts are active:

September 19th, 1985 – *Of that day, he remembers the blood the most. Hers. Puddles of red in the white hallway. Her hand over her stomach, catching crimson. Her mouth stretched to scream, but the world is mute and no sounds are heard; not her, not the commotion of the moving crowd, not the encroaching army, not the trampled innocents. Joe tugs him under his arms, helping him to his feet. Traitor Joe. Aldo is waving him on through the chaos. People screaming. Running. When he closes his eyes, he can still hear the echo of their feet clanking against the white marble floor. So much blood. Dripping from her. Not one life lost, but two.*

February 3rd, 1985 – *The cells underneath the microscope stir. The blue cells invade the pink cells' territory and the pink cells react violently. A swirling frenzy of blue and pink. The blue cells advance on the pink coagulants and the pinks fight their best battle*

13

yet. It's not long before they're overtaken and eliminated from the slide.

And? Joe Nava asks.

Sandborough looks up from the microscope. Joe looks like a clown minus the makeup and Sandborough has always found this funny. But today Sandborough isn't laughing.

A61Z is a failure, Sandborough says. He slams his fist on the table. Everything shakes.

We'll get there, Joe assures him.

He believes Joe. In that moment, they're friends. They talk about things beyond their work, mostly over beers. That's before the revolution. Before things go south. Before the demon crowns himself king of Hell and turns Heaven upside down. Before the white room becomes red. Before—

December 2nd, 1984 *– She's on top; he's beneath her. There's lots of sweat. She's grunting, pains of pleasure, but he can barely hear her over her beauty. Before he knows it, it's over and she's dismounting him, falling on the bed next to him. She's trying to catch her breath while calling his name. Alan. Alan. Alan, that was amazing. He turns to Kyra, wanting to tell her the same when—*

March 15th, 1985 *– Remember Bobby Egbert? He stares at Aldo Hood, watches him rub his caterpillar mustache. What about him? Aldo asks.*

He defied Elias once. Then disappeared.

He's living in North Carolina. Retired.

How do you know?

I have sources outside of The Dish. I told you.

Right.

Trust me.

Elias is a monster, he says. Your sister is in danger. Don't you care?

Of course I care.

I've seen the bruises, cigar burns. The scars.

Aldo sighs. He's an asshole. Not a mass-murdering psychopath.

How do you know?

I see it in his eyes.

You're paranoid, Sandborough.

He has to be stopped.

And who's going to stop him. You?

Maybe.

It's too dangerous. He's too powerful. And if you bring him down, you'll bring the whole Dish down with him.

Maybe not.

Oh no?

The government owns this facility now. They'll replace him with someone else.

Maybe they replace him with someone worse.

Maybe your sister will be safe.

Aldo slaps his forehead. You're putting me in a terrible position here.

You're not going to help me carry out my plan?

It's dangerous.

Yes.

You need a Plan B.

It'll work.

You're not Clint Eastwood. You need a Plan B.

My plan will work.

You need a Plan—

—More blood. Lots of it. On the floor. On the walls. Red footprints cover the floor, impossible to follow with his eyes. When he thinks of the last time he saw her, he sees her stomach and the hole the laser rifle created. He thinks he sees the unborn baby inside, trying to slither its way out of the womb, but that's not a memory, but a horrible snippet from a nightmare he once had. In the nightmare, the baby lives and crawls out of his lover's stomach, toward him, asking questions, like what happened to my mother, and Sandborough can only cry and—

—B. Don't you understand?
What does Joe think?
Joe agrees with me. Thinks your bat-shit crazy. You'll never pull it off.
You don't know me that well.
I know you well enough.
You think you do.
You love my sister?
More than anything.
Then don't do this. At least not without a Plan B.
What if Elias pushes the button?
He won't.
You don't think he's capable of activating one of them? Quakefall? Sun—

—Round two. He's on top this time, thrusting rhythmically. She cries out his name—Alan, Alan, Alan—and he whispers—I love you—into her ear and for the moment they're one, inseparable, until it's over and they're two again and—

—there's blood on his hands. He thrashes wildly. Two guards are carrying him, holding him up by his arms. Sandborough's shouting, calling for his release, but the guards only grip him tighter. He sees Aldo ahead. Aldo turns. There are tears in his eyes. His sister's blood stains his jacket. He faces Sandborough and stabs him in the neck with a long needle. He says welcome to Plan B and he's sorry and—

—The smell of cow shit is strong. He awakes in darkness, hears something that sounds like thunder, as light floods his eyes. Straining, he looks past the sun and stares out across the American landscape. Cows graze on grass greener than Irish hills. Wild horses run amok across the never-ending stretch of field, purple snow-capped mountains behind them standing proudly.
Hell?

No, not Hell, a portly man jotting down notes responds. But close. South Dakota. At least I think it is. This part of the country all looks the same to me.

Can't be.

Look, pal. Could be worse. Could be New Jersey.

Sandborough crawls his way out of the train car. He dangles his feet over the edge, taking in the sights, sounds, and smells of life outside The Dish.

I was instructed to give you this, the man says.

From him, Sandborough takes the newspaper and reads the headline. ESTIMATED 10,000 DEAD IN MEXICO CITY EARTHQUAKE.

By whom?

Some guy. Deep voice. Sounded like Satan.

Satan?

I think he was using one of those voice-changing thingy-ma-jigs. The man laughs heartily. The shit they come up with nowadays. Soon we'll all be talking through computers and flying cars like in Back to the Future.

Back to the what?

Back to the Future? The movie? Never seen it?

I don't go to the movies.

VHS guy. I gotcha.

The man hands Sandborough a large yellow envelope. Wanting answers, he quickly tears the envelope open. A picture ID tumbles out. It's a driver's license, New Jersey issued, belonging to someone named Soren Nygaard. A social security card with the same name.

Who's Soren Nygaard?

You are, the man said.

That's not my name.

Is now. The portly man smiles. Made it up. Got it from that book.

Sandborough follows his fat finger to the corner of the train car. Fear and Trembling *by Soren Kierkegaard rests on a small bale of hay. He turns back to the man. Did Aldo put you up to this? Are you his man on the outside?*

The man scratches his head. Man, I don't know whose idea this is, but someone loves you. They're giving you a new life. Not a cheap purchase, I can tell you that much.

Sandborough digs through the rest of the envelope. A MasterCard. A birth certificate with a raised seal. Legit. Genuine to the touch. The last item is most important.

Any questions.

Just one. Sandborough plucks a cigarette from the new pack, pops it into his mouth. Got a light?

When he opens his eyes, all he sees are ghosts—

"EXODUS: PART TWO"

EPISODE SEVEN

-1-

NOW

"Are you listening to me?"

Soren Nygaard peered through the smoke of his cigarette and saw Susan glaring back at him, her eyes resting above her librarian glasses. The wrinkles in her mouth twitched even after she spoke. She was about the same age as him, but in the dim light provided by the camper's lantern she looked much older. She sat down on the rock across from him and threw one leg over the other like she intended on staying a while.

"Yes," he replied, tapping his cigarette. Ash fell to the earth and landed like a gray, shriveled worm.

"It looked like you were daydreaming again," she said. "Where do you go in that mind of yours?"

"Where do I go?"

"Yes. It sure isn't on planet Earth with us."

He bit down on his tongue. "What is it you want to tell me, Susan? You have some pertinent information to relay? Because if you don't, I prefer to be alone with my thoughts."

She pretended to laugh, but she wasn't fooling him. Folding her arms, she pretended his attitude didn't bother her.

"I think we should talk about the group."

"What about them?"

"Well... where do I start?" She put a finger between her teeth and chewed her nail. "Two days ago, we left with forty people. We're down to almost half that."

Soren nodded. She wasn't telling him anything he didn't know. Their numbers had dwindled rapidly. Unforeseen accidents had taken place, which tallied a few deaths. Wendy Forester, a

19

school aide before The Burn, went for "a walk" the first night on the road and never returned. No one ever saw her again, but would have, had they traveled a good mile into the forest and found the small lake where she drowned herself. The one they called Mouth found Ted Banks, a retired construction worker, deep in the woods, hanging from rope pilfered from Costbusters. Dan Treadrow, a one-time investment banker turned freelance financial adviser, was found not too far from Ted, hanging from a branch of his own. These were good people. Smart people. People Soren assumed would make it to the end. No one was safe from the new world's unique effect. The sun had more than one way of eradicating life.

"I count about twenty-five," Susan said.

Hearing the number, Soren winced. He set the Dan Brown book down on the ground. Susan scoffed at the title.

"Problem?" Soren asked.

"That book is preposterous and—for the lack of a better term —stupid. A man of God like yourself shouldn't read such filth."

He shrugged. Instead of arguing with the intolerable woman, he chose to keep his mouth closed on the subject. He suspected she knew his intentions were not of a Holy directive. This was not a pilgrimage to God's promised land. God was as much behind Soren as Santa Claus. He didn't know how, but she saw past his deceit, all his untruths. She had grown suspicious of him the entire walk, her judgmental eyes suffocating him like a scorned lover's pillow.

Admittedly, she had been impressed when he walked into the sunlight and didn't combust. He had seen it on her face, the still expression of shock and awe. The same reaction was present from the rest of the survivors. But Susan's was different. Now he no longer mystified her. Now her face contained doubt, too much for his liking. Plus, she was clever—too clever—and that would not do. He could no longer manage her expectations, her thoughts, her beliefs. She would always question him. Forever skeptical from here on out. Such skepticism, he thought, was unacceptable— intolerable—especially when it could tarnish the loyalty he earned from the others. Nothing was going to change that. Not even the unwarranted skepticism of some doubting bitch.

"I thought you came here to talk about the group. Not about my literary preferences."

Susan nodded. "Yes. Of course." She composed herself, staring at him weirdly, like their meeting were a poker game and she couldn't read his tell. He would hint at nothing and returned her awkward glare. "In addition to the suicides and the missing, others have reported that some want to return to their homes. Back north."

"So?"

"So... they left. Mort said—"

"Who is Mort?" Soren asked.

"You know him as Mouth. But I think nicknames are bit juvenile. Don't you?"

Disgusted, Soren cleared his throat. "Oh, that fool."

"Yes, well I can't say I care for him either. But he's been useful at keeping the others motivated, at least when it comes to the Wright girls. He seems to be watching over them very closely. If I didn't know any better, I'd say Sam put him up to it."

Soren nodded.

"Anyway, several people have abandoned our... *mission.*"

"Why do you say it like that?" he asked.

"I don't know how else to say it. You haven't exactly been transparent with us, Mr. Nygaard. It's one of the reasons I think some of the survivors changed their minds about Alaska. They're frightened of you."

"And what of the twenty-five remaining?"

She paused. "Honestly, I think they're scared of you, too."

"But it's not the same kind of fear, is it?"

"No." She continued to chew her finger, squinting, still trying to get a read. "I can't figure you out. You're leading these people across country to a place that—for all we know—may not exist, but who are you?"

"Who am I? I'm the one who saved everyone from a band of killers. That's who I am."

"No..." A sly smile wormed its way across her face. "No, that's what you did. That's not who you are." She bit her lip as creases formed on her forehead. "You're not the second coming of

Christ, that's for sure."

"I beg to differ."

"You may have spewed that religious zealot crap to the rest of them, but not to me. I'm a real Christian, mister."

"Is that right?" Soren asked, amused. The game was starting to become fun for him.

"Yes, I am."

Placing a hand over his mouth to hide his growing amusement, he almost laughed.

"So who are you really?" Susan asked again.

"Who I am..." Soren said, "is of no concern to you. All that matters is the temple beneath the Alaskan tundra. It's where we can survive for the rest of our lives, free from whatever is happening out here."

"And what exactly is happening?"

"How the hell should I know?"

"Because you seem to be the only person who's immune to it."

"I can't explain my anomaly any more than a zebra can explain his own stripes."

She looked at him dubiously, not believing a word.

"Don't take me as a fool. That would be unwise."

"Whatever you say, dear."

"There's a few more matters at hand," she said, getting back on subject. "The group is tired. You've pushed them hard these first two nights. They need rest."

"Four hours will suffice."

She shook her head. "We found a nice safe place here; it's off the highway and the trees provide extra protection from direct sunlight."

"I told you we can stop anywhere we please. The tents are adequate protection."

"They are paper thin."

"They are adequate."

"Please, let them rest the entire day." She was begging now, and he could see how much she hated it. "At this rate, they all might quit on you."

Uncaring, Soren shrugged. "They won't."

"Well, you sure have a strange way of seeing things."

"Will there be anything else? I'd very much like to be alone now."

"One more thing," she said as if *he* were the annoying one. "Shondra."

"What about her?"

"I don't trust her."

"I'm finding trust to be a common theme with you."

"I think she's plotting something. She's always staring at you. At me. She's always whispering in people's ears. I don't like a thing about her."

"So... what are you going to do about it?" Soren asked.

"I was hoping you could tell me."

-2-

With a hunting knife he'd taken from Costbusters, Brian Waters whittled a fallen tree branch into a spear. He paused and whistled at Shondra Wilson, who was inflating an air mattress the old-fashioned way. Breathless, she glanced up at him. He nodded and she looked over at the woman she once compared to a desert buzzard entering Soren's tent.

"What do you think they're plotting?" he asked.

"Ways to kill us off."

"I don't think they need much help with that." He glanced around the camp, taking a quick census of the remaining party. "Vicki and Armando left before sunup and never came back."

"Maybe they went looking for Wendy."

He rubbed the blade against the branch more furiously with each stroke. "I think it's safe to say Wendy is not coming back. Neither are Vicki and Armando."

"Think we'll find them hanging from a tree?"

Shondra's question went unanswered as he continued to forge his weapon.

"You think he's using us, don't you?" Shondra asked, changing the subject.

Brian winced. The blade slipped off the end of the branch and nearly sliced across his leg. "I think Soren's up to something, yes. What it is? Anyone's guess at this point. If Alaska is where he's truly setting his sights on, then he's not going to make it there alone. It would benefit him to keep a few of us around. The useful ones."

"And the not-so-useful ones?"

He stared at her. "Notice how upset he is about the suicides?"

"Good point." Shondra huffed. "That bastard. Wish we could do something."

"No point trying anything now." He touched the end of the branch. It was sharp, but it wouldn't pierce the flesh of a small animal unless the distance was short. He shaved the branch over and over again, eventually reaching his desired result. "Soren's got enough of these idiots thinking he's the second coming of Christ with that little magic trick he pulled. I'm willing to bet they won't let you within six feet of his tent. But here's a real scary thought: some of them might actually kill for him. Protect him at all costs. Those are the people I'm guessing he'll want to keep around."

"Like that old buzzard in there."

Brian chuckled softly. "Yeah. Like Susan. Soren has proven himself to be a great manipulator. Look what he did to Sam."

"God, I hope he's all right."

She turned and saw Becky and Dana arguing over who got the last inflatable mattress. As they were beginning to shout, Mouth cut between them, telling them to "shut their pie-holes", that they'll have to take turns. Becky threw her hands up and stormed off, while Dana stuck her tongue out. Mouth said something about Becky having her "blood buddy" and Dana laughed, asking him to elaborate on his comment, knowing perfectly well what he meant. He stammered and told her to never mind. Smirking, Shondra shook her head. "Well, at least they're in good hands. I think."

Finally comfortable with the penetrating ability of his spear, he tapped his pointer finger on the tip and yanked his hand back immediately, shaking it in the air. A small blood bubble formed and he stuck his finger in his mouth, sucking on the coppery taste and spitting it out.

"Christ on a crusty cracker," Mouth said, approaching with his hands on his hips, his head swinging back and forth like an old porch door. "If anyone knows how to prevent two teenage sisters from clawing their eyes out, I'm all fuckin' ears."

"I had a fifteen year old niece. It's not the most pleasant experience," Brian said.

"You *have*," Shondra corrected, giving him those *you-know-better* eyes.

He nodded. "Yes. I *have.*"

"Well, any time you two want to pitch in and give me a break, feel free. I'm about to tear what little hair I have left right the fuck out," Mouth said.

"You're doing a great job, Mouth," Shondra said, patting his back. "Sam would be proud."

25

"Well that sumbitch better get his stubborn ass back here pronto, or Mort is going to have a major fucking meltdown."

"Please refrain from using your name in the third person, Mouth," Brian said, grinning. "It's weird when someone calls you something other than Mouth."

"Sorry, fuckface. One of my many bad habits, which I'm probably never going to break, so go fuck yerself stupid."

For the first time in three days, the three of them shared a laugh.

"What the hell are you all talking about anyway?" Mouth asked. "I saw you two staring down Miss Pissy-Pants before I had to break up the cat fight, so I assume it's nothing good."

Brian looked over his shoulder, ensuring he was out of earshot from Soren's more faithful followers. There were a few close by, pretending not to look in their direction, but in the moment Brian glanced at them, he caught their shifting eyes. He turned back to Shondra and Mouth and shook his head, subtly nodding in their direction. Shondra took the clue and went back to inflating her bed. It took a moment for the hint to register with Mouth. As he understood, he rolled his eyes and pretended to yawn.

"Oh fer fuckhole's sake," Mouth said. "You two!" He pointed at the two eavesdroppers and watched their eyes drift toward him. They didn't respond; they stood like statues, waiting for Mouth to continue. "Yeah, you two knuckle-fuckers! Don't you have something better to do than eye-bang the shit out of us? I mean, I know I'm working on a pretty healthy set of man tits over here, but come on."

They regarded him like bad gas and shuffled on. Mouth found their disgust the highest form of flattery and released a series of thunderous laughs, causing his beer belly to shake. His outburst cut through an otherwise quiet camp, turning the heads of Soren's closest lackeys.

"Fuckin' chumps."

Brian squinted. Mouth was treading a fine line. The leftovers from Sam's side were clearly outnumbered. They were, for the lack of a better term, "guests" in Soren's house. If they became too much of a liability or a hindrance of any kind, there were trees waiting with their names on them.

"Mouth, as much as I appreciate your peculiar sense of humor, you might want to crank things down a notch," Brian told him.

"What? Fuck those geese-feeders. Not like we're trying to make friends here."

"That's my point."

Mouth shook his head. "What? You want me to play nice-nice with these boneheads?"

"You don't have to offer them a back rub or cook them dinner, but pissing them off probably isn't in our best interest."

"He's right," Shondra agreed. "There's more of them than us. What's going to happen when they decide they don't need us?"

"Look, I know this crazy sumbitch is our best shot at surviving this goddamn debacle," Mouth said. "But just because the sun's melting everyone's skin off except his, doesn't mean I have to get on my knees and suck his—"

Brian put up his hand and stopped him. "Like I said. We don't have to be friendly. We just have to co-exist and convince them we're worth keeping around. If we can't make Soren think we're useful, he'll have no problem feeding us to the sun."

Shondra placed her hands on her hips and drew in a slow breath.

They turned to Mouth, hoping he'd go along with their plan.

He threw his hands up in the air. "Yeah, fine. I'll do my fuckin' best."

Shondra squeezed Mouth's shoulder, thanking him.

Mouth smirked. "Guess that means I should go retrieve that small bag of deer shit I left outside of Susan's tent."

-3-

3 DAYS AGO

He read the words for the four-hundredth time. *Headed to Alaska.* Each time he waited for them to change, to reveal their true identity. *Headed just up the road* or *we'll be waiting for you at X.* Something attainable, something real. *Heading to Alaska* didn't seem real to him. The words were an illusion and Samuel Wright thought the longer he stared at them, the sooner they'd show the truth beyond the dried ink.

Alaska, he thought. *Fucking Alaska.*

He knew Becky would leave out of spite. Alaska was the last thing he would have agreed with. Anywhere but there. He'd pick the 7-11 on Maple Street over a cross-country venture ending with a scenic trip through the treacherous Alaskan terrain. And where in Alaska were they headed? He was no Geography scholar, but he knew Alaska was vast and all nature. What would they do once they got there? Stumble around the forests and trek across the tundra until they found each other? He started thinking the note wasn't even written by Becky, but by someone else. Just as the thought passed, he sensed a presence looking over his shoulder.

"Have they changed yet?" a woman's voice asked.

Sam turned and saw his ex-wife staring at him, fixed in that annoying, passive-aggressive pose she perfected over the years. "What?"

"The words? You've been staring at them for an hour," Brenda said. "They haven't changed. Have they?"

"What's your point?"

She reached for the paper, but Sam moved it out of her grasp.

"Point is, maybe you should put it down and figure out where my children are."

He shoved the note in her face, practically rubbing her nose in it.

"Read it," he said. "Not clear enough for you?"

"I haven't spent the last four months with them. You have. As

28

with the rest of these people. If anyone has any idea where to find them, it's you."

"Alaska. That's where they're headed. The man leading them is hellbent on some sanctuary there. Says there's enough food and water to last a lifetime."

"Sounds great," she said. "But how the hell are we supposed to find it? Don't suppose this man left you a map."

"No, he didn't leave us map," Sam said. His anger rose, heating his skin. He didn't want to instigate another argument; he had little strength and their fights usually exhausted more energy than any aerobic workout. "If he left us a map, I wouldn't be staring at this fucking note."

"All right," she said, putting her hands up. "No need to get your balls in a knot. I was just asking a question."

Stuffing the hateful words begging to be spoken back into his throat, Sam nodded. It would have been easy to unload his feelings on her in a series of expletives and reminders of how much she fucked up the past, and how if she hadn't been such a stuck-up bitch during their marriage they'd still be together and ninety percent of this mess never would have happened, but Sam didn't give in to his urges. He kept his mouth shut and started to formulate a plan in his mind, something attainable, something real.

"Okay, everyone!" he said, stepping past her and into the center of the small group who, until this point, stood around speechless, examining the massacre that had happened before their arrival. They counted themselves lucky they hadn't been there. Trails of blood and evidence of brutal violence turned most of them pale. "We need to move. And soon. We don't know exactly what happened here, but I think we can all agree it wasn't very good. And we don't know if the cannibals are coming back or..."

He paused, considering the possibility the cannibals were still out there, lurking about.

"Anyway," he continued. "I suggest we hurry. Let's gather as many supplies as we can. There are camping bags in aisle eighteen if we—"

"Aisle eighteen has been picked pretty clean," Tina said,

emerging from the aisle. She held two hiking backpacks in her hands. "These were the only ones left."

Soren, he thought.

"Okay, they'll have to do. Why don't we help Tina gather as many things as we can. See what we have in the way of knives, rope, tents, apparel, and water. Especially water."

The group of ten dispersed. Some went more willingly than others. Matty nodded at his father, then waved Lilah on. She followed, but her pace wasn't brisk enough for Sam's liking. Bob's enthusiasm was lackluster at best. He stared at Sam for several seconds as if he had a better way to proceed, but advised himself against speaking out. He took Brenda by her arm and whisked her away before Sam could put his confrontation mask back on. Sam watched the people he had released from the cages head down the aisles. Most of the people they had freed from Malek's human zoo fled on their own and he refused to talk them out of it. If they wanted to take their own chances, so be it. As far as he was concerned, he was done trying to save people who didn't want to be saved. He wasn't Jesus. He wasn't Mother Theresa. He wasn't fucking Gandhi. He was Sam Wright, Store Manager of Costbusters Store 0635, father of three smart, beautiful children, your average American man. He had watched those scared survivors run for their lives, knowing they were as good as dead without his guidance, and didn't care. Instead, he led the people who wanted to survive, who wanted to live life the way the universe intended humans to live; back to Costbusters to start over again, to succeed where he had previously failed.

Sam turned and almost bumped into two others he had sprung from the cages. The one who had introduced himself as Jarvis and a shorter man Sam didn't know.

"What are you two doing?" he asked.

"Um, chilling," the short man replied.

"Well, how's about instead of 'chilling', you help grab some supplies. Why don't you head over to aisle twelve and grab some snacks. There's beef jerky, roasted peanuts, granola bars—"

"Um, dude, I know you helped save us and all, but I don't

work for you."

"Excuse me?"

Jarvis slapped his friend on the shoulder. "I think what my compadrè Chuck is trying to say is, we'll be more than happy to grab your nuts." He yanked Chuck along by the collar of his shirt. "Aisle twelve?"

Sam nodded.

The two men shuffled down the aisle and disappeared.

Great, he thought, rubbing his forehead. *These are the people I'm supposed to depend on.*

He made his way down the aisle and found Brenda staring at a depleted bay of potato chips. There really wasn't much left; Joel and Craig had an addiction to the crunchy treats Lays and Doritos provided. He was surprised the two hadn't stocked up for their long journey.

If they survived, he thought. He hadn't made his way back to the truck bay to find their dismembered remains, and would never get the chance.

"Those chips aren't going to pack themselves, Brenda," he said.

She suddenly snapped out of her distant reverie. "Relax, Sam."

"We need to hurry. The longer we stand around looking at the pretty packaging, the farther our children are going to get away from us."

"Well, maybe we wouldn't have to look for them if you kept an eye on them for a change," Brenda snapped back.

Sam felt a twinge in his neck. "Maybe if you didn't let them do whatever the hell they wanted, they wouldn't be so goddamn rebellious."

"Oh, yeah," Brenda said, making her sour face. "Like Dana is so rebellious. She's twelve for Christ's sake and still sleeps with teddy bears. Get to know your children, Sam. It's not that difficult. Even you could handle that."

"I'm not talking about Dana."

"Oh get over it, Sam. Becky's eighteen now. She's not your

little girl anymore. She never really was to begin with so I don't know why you're pulling this shit with me. Now of all—"

"What's that supposed to mean?"

Brenda glared at him. "You really want to do this? Now?"

"Yes." His collar was drenched in sweat. "Tell me what you meant."

"You know what I meant. You were never there for her! Not once. You missed birthday parties, soccer games, dance recitals—"

"I was working to support—"

"Whoa!" Bob intervened. "What seems to be the issue here?"

Doctor Bob to the rescue.

"Thanks for the concern there, Robert," Sam said, enjoying the face Bob made when he heard his birth name. "But how's about you stay out of this and go find a back to adjust. I'm sure one of your cage-mates could use a good rub down."

Beyond Bob and Brenda, Sam saw Tina watching closely from the end of the aisle. He could tell she wasn't trying very hard to stay undetected. She shook her head, warning him to tread lightly.

"Come on, Sam. There's no need to act childish. We are all in this together," Bob said, gazing at him with that same old concerned look, which always brought Sam's blood to a turbulent bubble. "Why don't you have a seat over there in the corner and we'll talk things out. Man to man. Let Brenda get back to gathering supplies."

Sam watched Tina disappear behind some racking and he knew she wouldn't come to his rescue. He understood; he had dug himself a hole and he was responsible for digging himself out. He turned to Bob and bit down on his lip.

"Fuck you, Robert," he said. "Fuck you and the lame horse you rode in on."

"Sam, please. I know you have a lot of pent up frustration and your head isn't in the best of places right now, but this is not the time to fall off track. These people need you. Your children need you."

Sam lashed out and stretched for Bob's throat. Brenda screamed, sounding like a crow cawing over a fresh meal, and jumped between them. He stopped himself and stood chest to chest with his ex. Bob, no longer feeling threatened and dropping his defensive position, placed his hands on his wife's shoulders.

"You know what I wished this whole time," Sam said, pointing his finger in Brenda's face. "I hoped you two were playing tennis the day of The Burn. Or going for a jog. Or sunbathing. Something outdoorsy. I prayed for it."

The slap was heard from several aisles over. It stung like a bad sunburn. Her open hand was a blur and Sam had zero time to react. He pressed his palm against the sting and felt his hot, pulsing flesh and nodded.

"How dare you speak to me that way," Brenda said. "I could've buried you in the divorce, but I didn't."

"Hon," Bob said, grabbing her shoulder.

She brushed him away. "But I didn't, you understand?" Spittle drizzled from her mouth as she spoke. "Because, even after all your faults and fuck ups, deep down, you were still a great guy. A good human being. Someone my children could look up to and idolize."

"Hon, I think we better—"

"But not anymore. No way. You've become something else. You've become... I don't even know the word for it."

Sam nodded. He turned and walked down the aisle. Looking over his shoulder, he said, "Just grab whatever you can and bring it up front. We're leaving."

-4-

The dreaded walk across the campground felt like an hour long journey rather than a few short minutes. Mouth received many sour glances, expressions he had been accustomed to for the better part of his life. He had always rubbed people the wrong way, ever since his youth. Teachers, parents, friends, colleagues, bosses, neighbors, and the general population he interacted with daily. It wasn't intentional; that's just how he was. He tried to fix his behavior, and so had his parents. They sent him to summer camps and week-long getaways through a local church organization, even sent him to a month-long military camp the summer between eighth and ninth grade. Nothing worked. Finally, his mother resigned to the fact that God forgot to give her Morty a filter for his mouth. He was blessed with the gift of the four-letter adjective.

Passing the other survivors, Mouth tried eavesdropping on their conversations. He caught whispers of this and that, but he couldn't string more than a few words together. They weren't talking about him. They weren't talking about Brian or Shondra, Becky or Dana. Most of the conversations contained the name "Soren." He caught glimpses of them praying every half hour or so, as if Soren's tent were a temple and he were the god inside. Mouth couldn't help but laugh. He wasn't sure what he had witnessed back at Costbusters, but it damn sure wasn't the handiwork of a demigod. He'd seen too much death to believe in gods, or any spiritual influence, for that matter.

Becky was on the outskirts of camp, staring into the woods, perhaps pondering whether running away would be the best course of action. He stood next to her and she pretended to ignore him. Glancing at her, he wondered how the conversation should start to avoid sparking the teenager's inner angst. He opened his mouth, but for the first time in a long time, he had nothing to say.

"What?" Becky said.

"Nothing," he replied, facing the woods. "Nice view, huh?"

"It's woods. What's so nice about it?"

Mouth shrugged. "You're the one staring at it. You tell me."

A subtle smirk grabbed her lips. "What do you want, Mouth?"

"Just wanted to see how yer holding up." He turned back to her, examining her figure. When they first met a few days after The Burn, Becky had been skinny. Now she was all bones, looking like an anorexic fashion model. "Er... how are you holding up?"

"Fine," she said, her features expressionless.

"You sure?"

"Yeah."

"Not sad about whats-his-face?"

She whipped her head toward him. Her face dared him to speak another word, and Mouth was never one to back down from such a challenge.

"Christopher."

"*Chris,*" she corrected.

"Christopher and Chris are the same name, darlin'."

"It was just 'Chris' and you didn't know him so don't you dare talk about him like you did."

Mouth raised his hands. "Fine. You got it." He stopped and for a second, he had convinced himself he wouldn't push the topic any further. But alas, he was who he was. "If you ever want to talk about anything, I'm here for you."

She shook her head. "What the hell would you know about losing someone you love?"

"Ohhh, a thing or two." He brushed away a wet eyelash. "Maybe even three."

"Well, I'm not the one who needs counseling." Becky turned, facing the camp. Mouth followed her gaze. She nodded past some of the survivors kneeling in prayer. Near Soren's tent, Dana sat, dragging a stick in the dirt. Every few seconds she looked up, staring at the tent as if she expected him to emerge. "What do you think?"

Mouth nodded. "Oh, goddammit."

"I know my father put you up to this—the whole 'protect my daughters' speech he probably gave you."

"Ah-em, I don't know what you're—"

"But one of the things my father never noticed was I'm not a little girl anymore. I can take care of myself." She nodded at her sister. "But Dana needs someone to look after her and I trust Soren less than you do."

"Pssh, doubt it."

"I don't know what game he's playing," Becky said, "but I don't think he's the good Samaritan he has some folks believing."

"Has anyone ever told you you're smarter than you look?" Mouth asked, grinning. He failed to evoke any emotion from the teenage girl. He kept up his smile. "What do you suggest?"

"I don't know," Becky said. "But she won't listen to me. She needs someone to guide her. Please try?"

Without waiting for an answer, Becky walked away.

Mouth grumbled to himself as he trekked toward Dana, dragging his feet the whole way.

-5-

While most of the survivors made their way outside, Sam remained inside, raiding aisle three of everything he could stuff into a rubber storage crate. Canned veggies, bags of rice, and an assortment of soups were cleared off the shelf with one arm. Once he packed the tote to a manageable weight, he stood up and lugged it up front.

The door had been opened and in the distance he could see the rest of the group standing in the parking lot under the guidance of the pale moon. He dropped the tote on the concrete and the sound of the rubber smacking against the ground grabbed their attention.

"I thought I said to grab as much as you can," Sam said, feeling fire in his eyes that wasn't the result of the poisonous atmosphere. "What are you people doing out here?"

Bob stepped forward. Brenda grabbed his arm, but he smiled, telling her it was okay. She listened and put her arm around Matty, pulling him close.

"We've packed what we could, Sam," Bob said. "But we need supplies that your store doesn't have. I think maybe we should split up for a few hours and try to find operational vehicles—"

"You know what? I'll just do it all myself," Sam growled. He headed back inside while the others called his name, telling him to leave it alone, that he was wasting valuable time.

"I'll get him," Tina said. "I think I can talk some sense into him."

Brenda eyed her warily. "Good luck. The only person I've ever known to talk sense into Sam Wright was Sam Wright."

Tina gave half a smile and jogged toward the store. Once she disappeared down the main aisle, Bob turned to the rest of the group. They immediately began whispering amongst each other, discussing the next course of action. Some of them suggested a hotel room, somewhere to hide out; the sun was due up shortly and no one wanted to be scrambling for last-minute refuge.

"We have approximately two hours and forty-six minutes before sunup," Matty announced. "I say we head down Route 70 West. Judging from this map I found inside," Matty traced his finger along a stretch of highway, "I believe this is the only road our friends could have taken. They may have a head start but we can make ground if we travel during the day. We can—"

"I'm sorry," Jarvis lamented, "but did Doogie Howser just say travel by day?"

Matty nodded. "I've done a few experiments. I'm very confident only direct sunlight causes the chemical reaction on our skin. We just have to stay covered. Sweatshirts, hats, goggles, masks, anything we can find to cover ourselves up."

"Very confident?" Jarvis asked.

"Extremely confident."

"Forgive me if I sound brash, but you won't mind if I ignore the advice of a twelve year old."

"I'm fifteen," Matty corrected. "And I'm fully prepared to prove my theory."

"That's great, kid. But I think we should stick to a more practical approach. Like, I know the moon is my friend and he's not going to burn my face off, so I'll stick to the vampire lifestyle I've grown accustomed to."

"Say the word *vampire* again, dude," Chuck said, "and I'll kill you."

"Guys, please," Bob said. "Matty, I of all people appreciate your advice, but Jarvis has a point. We don't need to take any unnecessary risks."

"But it's not—" Matty started to say, but Bob waved him off.

"We'll travel by night, seek refuge during the day. A hotel is a great idea, if we can find one. We'll stick to the map and see if we can catch up to the rest of the group."

"Sorry, pal," Chuck said. "But I have no skin in this game, so I think we're better off not setting off on a wild goose chase. None of us are Indian trackers, right? Unless they left us a trail of bread crumbs, finding them will be like trying to hit a bullseye blindfolded."

"It's imperative we find Dana and Becky," Bob said. "I understand it's not *your* number one priority and no one is forcing you to come along. But I should warn you there is safety in numbers and you might find surviving alone challenging."

Chuck opened his mouth to speak, but couldn't find the words. Bob was right; there *was* safety in numbers. If he hadn't been alone when Malek and his crew of crazy assholes came knocking on his door, then maybe they wouldn't have abducted him so easily.

"I'm in," Jarvis said. "You guys helped me out back there. I'm all yours. I'm just not too keen on this whole afternoon stroll idea."

The others agreed.

"No one is traveling by day. Although I'm sure Matthew has good evidence to back up his claim, we're not going to risk anyone's life."

Matty looked like he wanted to speak, but Lilah grabbed his hand and squeezed. He looked at her and she smiled at him. She mouthed the words, "I believe you" and for the moment it eased him. He cupped his hands over his mouth and leaned toward her. She met him halfway and he whispered in her ear, "I want to show you something."

As the rest of the group discussed their journey, Matty led Lilah away, back toward the store.

-6-

The moment dusk settled, Soren emerged from his tent and informed his followers the time had come to move on. The group packed their belongings quickly, but Brian, Shondra, Mouth, and the girls were slow to follow. When the group set off, they lingered, hanging back so they could discuss certain topics without having one of Soren's many ears eavesdrop.

"We need to find out what his end game is," Shondra said. "What he's hiding from us."

Brian shook his head. "He can't hide it forever. The truth will come out soon enough. Be patient."

"Why don't you go ask the almighty fuck yerself, Shondra?" Mouth asked. "Either that or close your mouth-hole because you sound like a broken record. Plus, all this Soren talk is giving me one hell of a headache."

Brian spotted Susan up ahead. She looked over her shoulder and whispered to another one of Soren's disciples. A few more heads rotated in their direction. He stared back at them, making sure they knew he didn't care for their secrets. His stern glare awarded him their phony smiles.

"We can't talk to Soren," Brian said, ignoring Mouth's request. "But maybe we can corner Susan. She's not as strong as she thinks she is. I can crack her."

Mouth nodded. "Boy, if you want to hear a fucking sermon or the gospel according to Soren's left testicle, you go right on ahead and strike up a conversation with that crazy broad. As for me, I think I'll pass. I'd rather stick my manhood in a wood chipper than to converse cordially with that nut job."

"Thanks for your blessing, Mouth," Brian said.

"No problemo. That's what I'm here for, sassy-pants."

"I'll do it," Shondra said. Slinging her survival pack over her shoulder, she started forward. "The bitch doesn't scare me."

Hours passed before the group finally stopped to rest. They

40

had reached a convenience store, a place called Melvin's Food Mart, and Soren demanded his disciples scope the place out in case cannibals or other crazed individuals were hiding inside. The small place took less than a minute to comb and the team returned with good news and bad news. The place being free from weirdos and flesh-eating maniacs was the good news; the bad news—the place had already been raided for supplies, water, and every other useful item.

Susan told Soren she'd be right back. Although she didn't mention it, she couldn't hold her bladder any longer. Jogging into the woods, she located the first tree she could find, one with enough privacy from the others. Unzipping her dirty jeans, she squatted and rested her back against the tree. She sighed as her bladder leaked.

"It's not safe on your own."

At first, her heart plummeted. She remained still as the last few drops left her. Once emptied, she stood up and yanked her pants over her hips. She fiddled with her button as the crunching of leaves grew louder.

"Next time, I suggest bringing a bathroom buddy."

"What do you want?" she asked the shadow as it stepped into the small sliver of moonlight between the trees.

Shondra chuckled casually. "Just to talk. Privately. Thought we could iron out a few details on the down low."

Susan eyed her like stranger candy. "I have nothing to say to you."

"Just listen then." She folded her arms across her chest. "I've taken notice to your overall displeasure for my friends and I. I don't like it—neither do they—and I don't expect much to change, but I have to ask—what the hell is up with Soren? Since you're the only one going in and out of his tent, I thought maybe you could shed a little light on all the mystery."

Susan, clearly amused, vibrated as a soft chuckle clung to the inside of her mouth. "Isn't it obvious?"

"If it was, we wouldn't be having this conversation."

"This is the End of Days, child. This is Hell on Earth. God has turned the one thing that keeps this planet spinning against us.

41

And Soren—he can't be burned by God's touch. So, what does that make him?"

Shondra shook her head incredulously. "You don't believe that, do you? That Soren is some chosen one?"

"He's not just *some* chosen one. He's *the* chosen one."

Snickering, Shondra waved her hand in the air. "That's what I thought."

"It's easy to ridicule something you know nothing about it. Are you frightened? You should be. God can be scary, but He is good too. Maybe not to a sinner such as yourself."

"A sinner such as myself?"

Susan narrowed her eyes. To Shondra, she looked like a wolf approaching wounded prey.

"Before he foolishly sacrificed himself, Clay Burrows said something very hateful to you, didn't he?"

Shondra recalled the memory to her mind. She often wished she could go back to that moment and kick the shit out of Clay for the way he spoke to her. She never wished death on anyone, and certainly hadn't when it came to Clay, but she didn't miss the prejudice bastard either.

"What's your point?" Shondra asked.

"Was he right?"

"About..."

"Do you keep your hair short like that because you're a dike?" Susan asked.

Shondra ground her teeth together. She almost fell prey to her instinctual reaction to rush the delusional woman and rip her throat out, but she knew nothing good would come of it. If Susan didn't return the same way she left, a war would start, and Shondra and the rest of her squad were greatly outnumbered. Instead, she submerged her anger and closed her eyes.

"That word bother you? Dike?"

Shondra shook her head, but she knew Susan saw that it had.

"Homosexuality is a sin, Shondra. God punishes sinners. The gays will burn in the sun along with the murderers, thieves, dope fiends, and perverts. You'll see. God has a plan for you and your kind. A plan you will not enjoy. So I suggest, instead of sticking your nose in other people's business, to look in the mirror and ask yourself a few questions."

Shondra had dealt with her type before; equal rights parades, rallies, the celebration at town hall when the state of New Jersey passed the Same-Sex Marriage Bill. Susan was the dark cloud hanging over those sunny days, a fraction of the crowd holding up signs that read "God hates fags" and "Gays will burn for this." She was the type of hate monger who had probably organized those rallies, using God's wrath to fuel her misguided rage. Shondra had no time or patience for these people. They didn't understand what it was like to be different. All they understood was their own simple-minded hatred and how to spread it to anyone willing to listen.

"Well, this has been a lovely talk," Shondra said through gritted teeth. "But I think it's time we head back to camp. Wouldn't want anyone to think we're fucking out here, would we?"

Susan curled her lower lip. "You're a vile woman."

"Funny," Shondra said, brushing past her, "I was thinking the same thing about you."

Brian held his arms out, reading Shondra's expression. "No good?"

"That lady is a fucking crackpot."

"What the hell did I tell you, woman?" Mouth said. "Did she tell you to say ten *Hail Marys* and five *Our Fathers*?"

"Not quite."

Brian nodded. "Did you get a vibe from her? Like she knows what's happening with Soren?"

"I don't think she knows, but I still don't trust her, or the others. We're better off on our own."

"No way," Mouth said, shaking his head. He pointed at Becky. In the near distance, she kicked rocks into a small pond. "I promised Sam I'd look after his kids, and that's exactly what I'm going to do. I go where they go."

"Bring them with us. Hell, we'll go find Sam and the others."

"And where exactly do we find them?" Brian asked. "We have no idea where Sam is. If he's even alive. And I'll be damned if we head back to Costbusters. We don't know how many of the cannibals are still out there. We can't head back. Becky left a note letting him know where we're headed. If he's alive, he'll head west. Eventually..."

"Eventually what?" Shondra asked. "Do you know the likelihood we'll find each other again? Do you know how big the United States is? He'll never find us."

"He'll find us," Brian said.

Shondra shook her head. "It'll be a miracle."

Brian winked at her. "Trust me. He'll. Find. Us."

It took a minute to register, but she understood. "Okay."

Mouth shook his head. "Look, whatever you two are blathering about, I don't really give two tits. But that," he said, pointing to Dana walking side-by-side with Soren, "is an issue."

The three of them watched as Soren put a fatherly hand on Dana's shoulder.

-7-

A few hours later, a rural town replaced the trees and stretches of forest on either side of the highway. They turned off Route 70 and walked along Main Street. Small shops and eateries stood vacant since the day the world ended. Above, a three-quarter moon provided additional light, their lanterns and flashlights aiding them in the good fight against the black sky. Four of the group's biggest men took the perimeter, keeping lookout for potential hazards; mostly desperate people seeking easy prey. No life had been met along the highway, which surprised many. They had found a few bodies, some charred to a blackened crisp, others just dead, murdered, stuffed in the backseats of abandoned vehicles or strewn haphazardly along the side of the road. Some were riddled with bullet holes, while others had so many stab wounds they looked as if they'd been dragged across a cheese grater.

Soren kept his position at the point. Dana followed closely behind him, while Susan and the other disciples lagged behind her. The rest of the group followed, too afraid to explore other options. In less than six months, the world had changed forever, and most weren't ready to change with it.

Brian, Shondra, Mouth, and Becky took up the rear, moving along at a pace suggesting they didn't really care if they ever got to where they were going. Shondra shook her head as she stared at the scene in front of her. Mouth noticed what she was looking at, and did what Mouth did best when things were uncomfortably quiet.

"Probably just small talk," Mouth said, watching Dana and Soren converse with each other like old pals catching up on past times. "You know. *How was your morning, Soren?"* he asked, mimicking a child's voice. *"Pretty good, little girl. How about yours?"* he said, deepening his tone.

"Small talk with a twelve year old?" Becky inquired, leery-eyed. "Somehow I doubt it."

"Well, what the hell do you think it is? Think he's shaping her into the next Hitler?"

Shondra and Brian glanced at each other, sharing their own

bit of skepticism.

"I hate to say it," Shondra said, "but Dana seems addicted to the Soren Kool-Punch."

Although they all shared the thought, Becky didn't like hearing it aloud. The comment stung; here she was, solely responsible for her sister's well-being, without any parental guidance, and she couldn't even get her to walk with them. They had never been exactly close—the six-year age difference being the big factor—but Becky had expected to fit into the caretaker role in the absence of her mother better than she had. If this were a college exam, Becky would have failed.

"Sorry," Shondra said. "Just pointing out the obvious."

"Thanks for that," Becky said sharply.

"Do you think you can talk some sense into her?"

She rolled her eyes. "Don't you think I tried already?"

"Maybe you should try harder."

"Maybe you should mind your own business."

Mouth jumped between them. "Okay, ladies. Pipe down. No sense tearing our own throats out now."

A few neutral parties spun their heads, wondering if the quiet argument would escalate. Both women listened to Mouth and ended their tiff, the curious onlookers' hopes of further confrontation squashed.

Mouth parted his lips to ridicule the nosy bastards, but advised himself against it. He amazed himself with his own self-control. He started to chuckle when he noticed a pair of staring eyes, a wry smile resting beneath them.

Susan narrowed her eyes to slits and blew Mouth a subtle kiss.

Soren waved the group off Main Street, down Fox Trot Lane. They walked two more miles until they reached a retirement village. Soren led his group underneath the metal arm manufactured to keep unwanted cars from trespassing, though he never met one that could keep a speeding vehicle at bay. One by one, the group limboed under the gate and continued on, passing houses identical to each other, save for different siding and shutter colors. Lawns, once mowed bi-weekly, sat long and unruly, diseased with weeds and yellow dandelion heads. The street, once filled with the scent of freshly baked fruit pies, now basked in a moldy, wood-smoke odor.

A few of his followers whispered complaints behind him, but he chose ignorance over confrontation. Each time they spoke a little louder, and he could tell they wanted him to hear. Still, he did nothing and pushed on.

Canterbury Lane, the sign to his right read. Soren made the turn and in that moment, the crowd knew he was guiding them somewhere very specific.

"Where the hell are we going?" someone shouted behind him, in a tone that couldn't be ignored.

"What is this place?" another asked.

"Are we going to stay here the night?"

"I think I see people in these houses."

"Do you think they have running water? I could sure use a bath!"

Soren abruptly turned to his followers. They stopped in their tracks. Fear took hold of the majority, like they expected their leader to set them ablaze with one wave of his finger, a dangerous display of his wizard-like abilities. They didn't know much beyond what they had witnessed, and the unknown frightened them. He knew it, and he would play that hand until they found a way to beat it.

"We are here for something very specific. I cannot disclose all the information at this point, but I need you to trust me. I haven't let you down, have I? No? Good. Then keeping following and silence yourselves. Do not look at the people inside these houses. If they come out, do not talk to them. Do not acknowledge them. For all you know, these people are ghosts. Treat them as such."

Soren spun forward and quickened his pace. His destination was on the right, a few houses down, standing much like the rest; a single family ranch, covered in white asbestos shingles, black shutters around seven windows, and gray roof shingles, curled and shoddy and needing repairs. It was the place all right, and Soren eagerly strode toward it, unable to contain his excitement for what was inside.

Susan was about to put her hand on Soren's shoulder, hoping he'd let her in on the secrets he hid from the rest of them, but as if he expected it, he turned, raised his hand, told her, "wait here," and trudged ahead, leaving the group to entertain themselves in the street.

-8-

Tina followed the sounds of an angry man packing for a cross-country journey. Something metal clinked rhythmically somewhere ahead. A can of tomatoes rolled across the aisle. Sam shouted, "Motherfucker!" and she sprinted the rest of the way.

She turned the corner and found him sucking his thumb. He removed his finger from his mouth, then flapped his hand in the air with furious strokes. While doing so, he spotted Tina and rolled his eyes.

"Having fun?" she asked.

"Cut my finger," he replied, placing his thumb back in his mouth.

"Not supposed to do that." She strolled down the aisle, chuckling softly. "You sure get hurt a lot. Bet you had some insurance policy before The Burn."

"If you're trying to be cute, you're not doing a very good job."

"You can be a real dick sometimes." She was still smiling, but Sam knew she meant what she said. She walked toward him and attempted to throw her arm around his shoulder. He recoiled as if she were a snake lashing out with venomous fangs. "Whoa. I'm just here to help."

"I don't need help."

Tina sighed and took a seat on a crate of propane tanks. She threw one leg over the other and propped her hands on her knees. "Sammy, Sammy, Sam-Sam. When are you going to listen to me?"

He shook his head, rolling his eyes like a scolded teenager too smart to heed parental advice.

"You'll come around," she continued. "I can see the kind of man you are. I think this place has warped you. You've lost a bit of yourself in here. Leaving this place behind will be good for you."

"What do you mean? Leaving it behind?"

Tina narrowed her eyes and scratched her chin. "What do *you* mean? Once you've realized this place isn't the answer—"

"This place *is* the answer. It's always been the answer. Can't you understand that? Why doesn't anyone else see it?"

49

"Sam, no," Tina said. "We tried it your way and this..." She waved her finger in circles. "This is where your way got us. I hate to say it, but Soren was right. It was only a matter of time before this place finished serving its purpose. Even Rome fell, Sam."

He grabbed his hair and for a second Tina thought he was going to rip the clumps right out of his skull.

"You're blind like the rest of them. You don't want to follow me anymore? So be it. Anyone who wants to go astray and die at the hands of flesh-eating maniacs and whatever else is out there, more power to you. I'm not gonna stop you. Not anymore."

"Sam..."

"Don't." He bent down and grabbed the bags packed with plenty of goodies to keep his body fueled. "If you're not with me, you're against me."

"No one is against you." *What the hell is this guy talking about!* she wanted to scream. In the short amount of time they knew each other, he never acted like this much of an asshole. Stubborn, sure. Firm in his beliefs, yes. But now that the evidence was right in front of him, Costbusters reduced from a perfect sanctuary to a bloody battlefield, he could not allow himself to consider other options. *He can't be that nuts,* she thought. *He's a normal guy in an abnormal situation. He's not thinking clearly. He'll come around.* She had her doubts about the last bit; she had seen men pushed over the edge and attempt the impossible climb back up. It seldom ended well. "Go outside, and talk to the group. Be level-headed about this."

"If the others don't have a solid plan to get my children back, then I have no interest in what they have to say." He stormed off down the aisle and disappeared around the bend.

Tina shook her head. Part of her wanted to cry, but there was no time for tears. Not today. She stood up and stared at the propane tanks, debating whether to waste another second trying to convince Sam that his dream was dead.

-9-

THREE DAYS BEFORE THE BIG BURN

The shed reeked of cigarette smoke, just the way he liked it. He lit another, exhaling a rolling cloud as he cleared the tools littering his workbench. After the bench stood uncluttered, he rested on the small couch in the corner of the room, savoring the ashy taste on his lips. Taking another drag deep into his lungs, he wondered if this was truly how he'd spend the rest of his life: cleaning other people's messes, patching up their mistakes, replacing dead light bulbs, and pleasing that shithead principal. How could a man with no understanding of the theory of relativity and zero comprehension of probability density plots ensure society's youth was properly educated? Soren had grown tired of working for people less intelligent than him. Also, he was bored. Something needed to change. There was an injustice taking place, no further explanation required.

It's all part of the plan, he reminded himself. What that plan was, he didn't know. *The world needs a sharper tool in the shed, a bulb without a flicker. And when the time comes, they'll see. All will be clear again.*

Soren stared at the corkboard above his workbench. Sticky notes and a small itinerary for the next several days practically covered every square inch, but something was out of place. A pink note the size of an index card was tacked to the center, covering mundane notes about which florescent bulbs were awaiting replacement in the faculty room. He never used pink notes. Always white or yellow. The only time he saw notes in that color were from the teachers' desks.

Stubbing out his smoke in the ashtray next to the couch, Soren stood up, stretching his painfully-tight muscles. He ambled back over to the workbench, his curiosity piqued. The words were small and written in cursive, barely legible. Soren squinted and read:

AS QUAKES HAVE FALLEN, SO SHALL THE SUN. ROOM D8. LUNCH.

Rattled, the rest of the day dragged. He couldn't concentrate. A few times he felt dizzy, disoriented, as if lost in a desert for days without water. The hallways of B-wing tilted, the science lab spun, and the mop wouldn't go in the direction he wanted no matter how hard he tried. People spoke to him, but he barely answered. His inarticulate responses were met with curious glances, but he didn't care about them or the people who gave them.

He passed Principal Reynolds in the hallway. The boss man stopped, muttered something, but Soren continued walking. Reynolds shook his head and walked away, rambling on about how he needed to "clean house", but Soren didn't hear that bit either. His eyes remained focused on the clock and the fast approaching lunch hour.

The clock struck eleven and Soren stood outside of room D8. Pushing the door open, he stepped inside. The door closed behind him as he stared at the man sitting at the desk, his face hidden behind the paperback cover of Stephen King's *The Stand*. At the click of the door latching into place, the stranger rested the book down and greeted him with an expressionless nod.

Soren's chest tightened and his hands trembled into fists. Clenching his teeth, his jaw flexed. When he was ready to breathe again, he uttered one word.

"You."

"Hello, old friend," the substitute teacher replied.

Waving his forefinger in the air, Soren shook his head and stepped forward. "Understand this: we are not friends."

The man rolled his eyes. "Spare me the dramatics, Alan. At least this once. There is much to discuss, all of which concerns you greatly." He paused and reached into the desk drawer. "But if you really don't care for what I have to say," he continued, tossing a pair of scissors at Soren's feet, "then feel free to cut out the messenger's tongue."

Staring at the scissors on the floor, Soren dropped his hands at his sides and relaxed his shoulders. It took everything he had not to act out his impulses. His eyes moved on from the shiny shears to the aged bastard staring back at him.

"I'm only asking for ninety seconds."

"Okay, Joseph. Speak."

"Look, I'm sorry about what happened in Alaska. I truly am. No one meant for things to turn out the way they did."

"You should have listened to me from day one. You and Aldo. But no, you had to have your Plan B."

"It wasn't meant to play out that way, Alan, I swear it," Joe reiterated. "But, if it's any consolation, you were right."

"About what?"

"About Elias Wheeler needing to be stopped."

Soren almost laughed.

Joe glared at him as if he had swallowed something rotten. "You don't understand. Things in The Dish are bad, worse than ever. I wish I saw it before like you had, but I was blind. We wanted a plan in case you failed, but in truth, I was a coward, looking after my own skin. I should have been more on your side. Things should have been different."

"Yes. They should have."

"I could spend all day apologizing to you," Joe said.

"Please don't. It's boring and doesn't suit you." Staring at his old friend, Soren fought to subdue years of bottled aggression. "What is it you want, Joe? I know you didn't come here to apologize."

"After the Mexico City event, the government cracked down on Elias. Hard. For years we had daily visits from mouth-breathing bureaucrats. Then they wanted their own people in on 'Special Projects', wanted to know exactly what was happening and when, basically turning Elias into a fucking company man. And you know Elias. He doesn't respond well to taking orders. He fought with them for decades, but not enough to where they pulled the plug on the whole operation. He figured he needed them as much as they needed him, with all the bullshit overseas. Every decade had its problems and the government kept paying Elias to figure out how to solve them."

"Time's up, Joe," Soren said, glancing down at the scissors.

Ignoring him, Joe continued. "Secretly, the United States saved the world on more than one occasion. Elias had come close to pushing the button several times. He became this loose cannon, and the only thing that stopped him from firing was intense government oversight and... *her.*"

"Who?"

Joe's eyes shifted from side to side.

"Who?"

"Look," Joe said, his eyes fixed on the clock, "lunch is almost —" The bell rang. "Over. I have three more classes to sub for, then I'm all yours. I can meet you in the shed after class, okay? I'll explain everything. In the meantime, take these." Joe tossed him a cloth bag, small enough to fit inside his breast pocket, next to his cigarettes. "It took me a long time, but I've finally perfected it."

Soren peeked inside. He immediately looked at Joe, his eyes bulging. "A61Z?" he asked.

"Something like that. We we're close back then, but not close enough." Proudly, Joe reissued his famous shit-eating grin. "After school. Your shed. I'll explain everything."

Joe knocked on the shed door. Silence. He knocked for a second time, then a third, and finally a fourth. Pushing open the door, he let himself inside, expecting to find Alan waiting for him with a baseball bat or that pair of scissors. He could tell Sandborough hated him; the man's scornful gaze couldn't be ignored. And Joe couldn't blame him much either. But the past was the past and neither one of them could change it. The future, however, was in their capable hands.

The shed stunk of cigarettes and another toxic stench his nose couldn't decipher. *Thirty years of a gram-a-day coke habit will do that to you,* he thought, looking over the shed's décor. Empty soda cans, heaping ashtrays, decaying fruit, and trash weeks old greeted him in the dim light.

What felt like hours passed and Sandborough never showed. Joe decided he was halfway to Texas with the thought he'd been sent to kill Alan, not liberate him. He went back to his car, parked in the teacher's lot, a special corner reserved for substitutes and other visitors. By the time Joe reached the lot, most of the cars had disembarked on their journey home. He set his eyes on his 87' Blazer, put the school behind him, and never looked back.

He had tried to give Sandborough the opportunity he never got thirty years ago. He had tried to make amends, but Alan was stubborn. *Same old Sandborough.* He sat in the Blazer's front seat and sighed. He hated New Jersey and the past few months spent in that dumb retirement village. Nothing depressed him more than watching ambulances carry away the deceased elderly every other day. Aldo's "connection" said that was the best he could do with short notice and Aldo had told him to "suck it up."

Fuck you, Aldo. He wasn't the one who had to deal with inquisitive old folks with nothing better to do than knock on his door, wanting to meet the newest resident of Pleasant Gardens.

Joe slipped the key into the ignition and cranked the engine to life. He shifted into gear and adjusted the rearview mirror. As he drove from the parking lot, he thought a lot about the future, what might happen if the worst really were to happen. Luckily, he had plenty of A61Z to keep him safe, a whole stash no one in the world would find; unless they were told.

A few miles down the road, Joe noticed the Blazer's tank was just about empty. The next gas station wasn't for a few miles and he had a hankering for sushi. Although gas station sushi was as safe as juggling dynamite, the craving could not be ignored. His mouth began to water just thinking about it.

Something latched around his throat and his nervous system jumped, lifting him off the seat. The Blazer swerved, and if someone had been barreling down the opposing lane, a nasty head-on collision would have ensued. Joe put one hand to his throat and felt leather. The belt constricted and his eyes bulged. Slamming the brakes, he took both hands off the wheel, attempting to loosen the belt's grip around his neck. Rubber screeched beneath him and the Blazer skidded to a complete stop in the middle of the empty road.

He watched the man in the backseat lose his seat. The belt became loose and Joe used the opportunity to free himself. He started choking, his windpipe nearly crushed. Instinctively, he opened the door and stumbled to the road. He tried to run into the nearby field, but his legs gave out and he tumbled to the pavement.

A shadow fell over him.

Sandborough looked down at him, belt in hand.

"Please... *stop,* " Joe croaked. "Don't.... ma... stake."

"I've made many mistakes," Soren said, "but this won't be one of them."

"Not... jus... sun... fall."

He wrapped the belt around Joe's neck, slipped it through the buckle, and pulled with every ounce of strength he could muster. He watched intently as Joe's face went from red to purple in the matter of seconds. He pulled harder; Joe's eyes nearly exploded from their sockets. A minute later, his body went limp, but Soren kept the pressure on until he heard the audible break of the man's neck.

Then he let go, allowing the lifeless body to fall freely.

Soren searched Joe's pockets. He found another pouch of A61Z—two vials inside—and a wallet. He opened the wallet, stripped the cash, and examined the license. The name was fake. Frank Wieser. The address? 616 Canterbury Lane.

What did he want to tell me?

Soren would never know.

Probably more lies.

There was plenty of time to investigate and plenty of stones to kick over. He'd get to the bottom of it—what was happening at The Dish—one way or another. Why Joe came bearing precious gifts, he had no idea. It raised many questions.

He said "her."

Yes, but that was a lie. Kyra was dead. He was sure of it. He had watched her die.

But...

No "buts." Dead was dead, and Soren remembered the red as it poured from her body.

But it's possible.

He needed to investigate. But first, there was a body to dispose of.

-10-

He considered picking the solid red brick off the porch and chucking it through the window, but the front door was cracked open. With two fingers, Soren pushed the steel six-panel door in, cringing when the old barrier's hinges squealed in protest. A smell suffocated his nostrils, something of the old world; leftover Chinese and skunky beer.

Soren set one foot on the dull green carpet, soggy beneath his boot. He peered to the right and left, shining his battery-operated lantern in both directions. He didn't know exactly what to expect; he wouldn't be surprised if a two-headed monster with long fangs jumped out, or nothing at all.

Surveying the living room, he couldn't overlook the mess. Garbage littered the floor like an episode of *Hoarders*. Empty cases of beer covered the coffee table, leaving no spot for weary feet. Empty boxes of TV dinners were piled on the couch, surrounding the impression of a grown man's body. Things looked more or less the same in the kitchen. The island had no visible counter space left; old newspapers and magazines were bundled several feet tall. Used paper plates were scattered across the rest of the counters. The dishes in the sink were stacked so high they blocked the window looking out into the backyard. Rats scurried between the walls, gleefully chattering to each other as they enjoyed the freedom provided by a non-existent homeowner.

He shone the light to the right, down a lengthy hallway. Quietly he stepped forward, passing a room on his right and looked inside. It had been an exercise room, but the treadmill had turned into a clothes rack, the weight racks converted into a magazine stand, and the padded mat on the floor a surface for dirty laundry. Soren thought he heard rustling farther down the hall and directed his lantern toward the commotion.

Continuing down the hall, he concentrated on the last room and the movement he heard inside. Drawing the blade from his pocket, he kicked open the door. A shadow jumped, turning away from the far wall. It shoved its hands in the air and dropped something on the floor. Soren looked down at two familiar vials. He glanced back at the shadow and found a face he didn't recognize.

"W-what t-the f-fuck!" the shadow shouted.

"Who are you?" Soren asked, holding the knife out.

The shadow, belonging to a frightened teenager, backed himself into the corner of the room, tripping over more crap the previous owner had left behind. Trying to speak, he stammered several times. Soren approached him and the kid's eyes followed the sharp dagger in his hand.

"Are you from The Dish?" Soren asked. "Did Elias send you?"

"Elias?" the kid asked, confused. "Naw, man. I'm Braiden. Patty Worchester's grandson? From Ellsbury Street." He pointed as if Soren knew where he was talking about.

He stared at the boy as if he were lying. "Are you sure?"

"Fuck yes, I'm sure. What the fuck? You don't think I know who I am?" the kid asked, his eyes watering.

"What are you doing here, Braiden?" he asked. "A little ways from Ellsbury Street."

"The man who lived here hasn't been around since... you know." He pointed to the sky. "Thought maybe he wouldn't mind if I took a look around. Being dead and all. Figured he wouldn't care."

"And how do you know he's dead?"

The kid's eyes widened. "I just assumed. If you haven't noticed, mister, a lot of people are dead."

"Yes. Yes they are." Soren tapped the knife's sharp point with his finger.

"Please don't kill me, mister."

He didn't answer. "What were you looking for?"

Braiden swallowed. "Food? Water? Anything I could find. We raided most of the nearby stores. Not much left. Figured we'd start raiding homes."

"And what were you doing with that?" Soren asked, pointing to the two vials on the floor.

"Nothing..." Catching a look in the armed man's eyes, Braiden waved his hands in the air. "Honest."

"Honest?" Soren stepped forward. "Son, I'll carve the honest right out of you."

"Oh, God."

"Tell me the truth and we'll get through this and go on with our lives."

Braiden began crying. "Promise?"

"Swear on my life."

"She always told me the guy who lived here was a bit of a weirdo. She thought he was a drug addict or something. So... I came looking..."

"For drugs?"

Braiden nodded. "Please don't tell her."

"Is there more of this stuff?"

"The bag on the dresser is full of it."

Soren glanced over his shoulder and stared at the small leather pouch like buried treasure. He turned back to the kid, catching him inch toward the door.

"Are you sure you don't know who Elias Wheeler is?" Soren asked one more time, his lips curling into a smile that weakened the kid's knees.

"No. I swear."

"Not much of a liar, are you?"

The kid took off as Soren lunged forward, the knife slicing through air and flesh.

Mouth paced in circles. He looked over at Dana every few seconds, watching her sit on the curb outside 616 Canterbury Lane. He didn't know what Soren was doing in there and what was taking so goddamn long. People began to appear in the windows of their homes, looking at the group of survivors as if they were traveling apparitions.

As the minutes ticked, the staring competition between the inhabitants and the newcomers intensified. Becky muttered, "This is fucking creepy" over and over again, under her breath.

Shondra added, "I'm getting chills."

Brian told them both to keep calm, that everything would be okay, but when Shondra asked if he had dreamed about this moment, he shook his head and turned away.

Just when Mouth planned on strolling over to Dana and whisking her away from this potentially dangerous environment, Susan took the curb next to her. Dana didn't look happy about her presence, and Mouth smiled.

Thatta girl, he thought. *Smack that bitch across the face while yer at it, honey.*

Dana rested her chin on her knees and pretended to ignore Susan's presence. Inside, Mouth danced happily. It was when Susan draped her arm around Dana's neck and she didn't shrug her off that his demeanor changed. He felt his flesh warm like a bright summer morning. Rolling up his sleeves, he announced, "That's it" and charged across the street.

Shondra slapped her forehead and whispered, "Oh, here we go" under her breath.

"Okay, crazy-pants," Mouth yelled, shoving his finger in her face. "You and me need to have ourselves a talk!"

Susan glanced up at him with that irritating smile pasted on her face. She looked back to Dana. The girl avoided eye contact with her at all costs, her gaze fixed on the pavement. Susan and her heinous smile turned back to Mouth. She glanced up at him, the twinkle of the moon in her eyes making them look black and soulless, like a demon from the deepest pits of Hell.

"What can I help you with, Mort?" she asked.

"What the fuck is your problem?" Mouth yelled. An ordinary woman would flinch at the loud outburst, but Susan remained calm as if she expected this verbal battle. "How dare you try to manipulate a twelve-year old girl! You should be goddamned ashamed of yerself, you... you..."

"What?" she asked. "What is it you want to call me, Mort?"

For once, he couldn't come up with the proper insult. Perhaps there was none in the English language suitable for the Susans of the world.

"A bitch?" Susan asked. "A cunt? What is it? I've heard them all before so make it a good one."

Mouth stammered. "Well, you know... Yer all of those things, but that's not why I wanted to talk, so don't try to change the subject on me, Miss Jesus-Christ-Superstar." He jabbed his finger in her face. "This is about you and that innocent little girl sitting over there. See, when her father comes back and I tell him all about how you tried to fuck—"

"Sam won't be joining us in Soren's paradise."

"Yeah, well that's what you think. He'll catch up—"

"No, you don't understand. Soren won't let him in."

"Okay, crazy-pants, I've had enough—"

"Just because you've denied Soren as our Lord and Savior, doesn't mean you have to squander the opportunity for the others."

Mouth shook his head. The conversation was getting him nowhere. He glanced over at Dana and wondered what was going on in that young, impressionable mind of hers.

"Yer a fucking screwball," he muttered. "And if you utter another goddamn word to Dana, I'll snap yer fucking neck, woman."

"I'm sorry you see it that way, Mort, but here's some advice to you and your friends; you're only here because you provide some value to us," she said in a whisper only he could hear. "Once you stop providing whatever it is Soren sees in you, you're out. You understand?" It wasn't much of a question. She glared at him through haunted sunken eyes, which raised the hairs on his neck.

"Oh yeah? What if I find a nice tree to dangle from?"

Susan's grin stretched. "Then I'll be more than happy to find you a reliable rope." She pressed her finger on Mouth's chest. "And I find it curious that a grown man has taken such interest in a little girl."

Mouth twisted his lips into a snarl. "Hey now. I'm just trying to help—"

"Hm. I wonder how the rest of the group will see it when I tell them I saw you trying to grab her in the most inappropriate places."

He wanted to separate her jaw from her skull with his

knuckles, but the rest of the group was watching. He opened his mouth to tell her what a vulgar woman she was, and if there was a God, He likely hated her. But she opened her mouth first.

"Don't mess with me, Mort. And everything will be A-O-kay."

Wiping the blade clean with a dish towel, Soren stepped through the open patio door and onto the small deck. Once he rubbed the metal spotless, he tossed the towel into the nearby shrubbery. He bounded the stairs two at a time until his feet found the patio. Soren searched the immediate area, knowing he needed something else, something the long trip would require. He had searched every square inch of the house for the item and came away with nothing. He dug beneath the crap littering the floors, looked inside every cabinet, even searched the attic and old boxes of worthless junk; found nothing but bugs, alive and dead. Joe wouldn't make it easy for any person that came looking. Soren needed a sign, something that would clue him into its whereabouts.

Think goddammit, think.

Soren rubbed his cheek while scanning the backyard. Rows of shoulder-high bushes acted as gates, surrounding the entire property. There wasn't much else in the yard save for a small shed and a tiny garden ruled by weeds and dandelion heads. He thought about searching the shed when something in the garden caught his eye. A lone cluster of flowers. In the center of the bed of dead vegetation, the vine containing baby blue petals with yellow pistils stood out like a clean diamond on a dirty beach. Soren's eyes immediately fell on the flower and he began to migrate toward it.

Forget Me Nots, he thought. He recognized them instantly. *Of course. Joe, you son of a bitch.*

Forget Me Nots—Myosotis alpestris—were the Alaskan State flower. Soren jogged over to the cluster of flowers and felt his lungs resist.

Immediately, he dropped to his knees and began digging. Shoveling the dirt aside, he silently commended Joe for his artful thinking. He should have expected such given their lengthy discussions on molecular phylogenetics and advanced biochemistry, but Soren never viewed Joe as someone who could orchestrate a strategic plan such as this. He never struck Soren as anything other than "book smart."

His fingers struck something and he stopped digging. For a moment he stared into the dirt as if it were divulging secrets, filling his ears with answers to every question he had asked himself over the past few months.

Turning his attention away from his thoughts, Soren reached the object and plucked it from the earth. He held the palm-sized item in one hand while using the other to brush the dust away. Once cleaned and free from dirt, he grabbed the item with two fingers and held it so the moonlight could do its job. A metallic shine glinted off the key's backside. He tucked the key in his back pocket and started to rise when something in the dirt caught his attention. Peeking out of the soil, a folded sheet of paper containing an "X" on it looked up at him.

"What in fuck-nut city took you so long?" Mouth asked as Soren emerged from around the corner of the house. "You better have found some good news in there and not spent all that time whackin' the ol' weasel."

Bemused, Soren pushed past him, not even giving him the courtesy of a lie. He strode into the center of the street, unable to ignore the stares of the senior residents, their eyes watching him warily from their windows, just as they had upon his arrival.

"I'm going to speak and everyone will listen," Soren said, "then you will do exactly as I say, no questions asked." He glanced at Mouth and repeated, "No questions."

The crowd shifted uncomfortably, as if they expected him to ask something immoral of them. There was something unsettling in the way he spoke. His words lacked the same confidence they had come to expect.

"I want you to knock on these doors and see if anyone has keys to the cars in these driveways. We'll take as many as we can get."

"Take?" Shondra asked.

Soren and the group turned to her. Every eye shared a similar, eerie quality. Even Brian stared at her oddly, but for a different reason than the rest.

"What if they refuse?"

He spit on the ground, then popped a cigarette into his mouth. "Then ask again. More convincingly perhaps."

He brushed past her, walked up the closest driveway, and knocked on the front door. An elderly woman answered a few seconds later. The woman shook her head, but let Soren inside anyway. A minute later, he emerged from the house, alone and jingling a set of keys.

-11-

"Maybe we should head back," Lilah said, stopping near the door leading into the back stockroom. "Maybe it's not safe in there."

Matty shook his head. "We'll be okay."

"No, Matty. You don't understand." She pointed toward a bloody trail on the pavement. It disappeared under the door. "You probably won't like what you see in there."

"I can handle it."

"That's not the point," she said. "Why see something horrible if you don't have to?"

Although he understood her perfectly, he disagreed with her logic. The world had changed and was bound to show him atrocities beyond his most imaginative thoughts. Why hide from it? Savagery had become the standard. Humans were no better than animals surviving the perilous wild. Many textbooks taught him animals either adapted to their environment or perished, and Matty had no intention of leaving the world behind. Not when there was so much left to see and do.

Like getting laid, he thought to himself. He felt embarrassed just thinking about it.

"I'm not a kid," he argued. "I'm fifteen. Almost sixteen."

"I know that. I'm not saying you *can't* handle it. I'm saying why have to?"

"I just thought... you know..."

"I won't think any less of you," she said, flashing a sleek grin. "Come on. Let's head back and—" She grabbed her stomach and hunched over. She gagged and Matty dashed to her side. "Oh shit."

"You okay?"

"Yeah," she said, rubbing her stomach. "I don't know. I feel weird."

"I'll go get my stepfather," Matty said. "Maybe he can help."

"Thought you said he was a chiropractor?" She laughed, struggling to maintain her calm. "I have a stomach ache, not an outta-whack vertebrae."

"Okay..." Matty said. "Still, I should get someone. You don't look well."

She waved him off, forcing the smile wider. "I'm fine. I'll head back to the rest of the group." She looked him in the eyes, but less like a friend, and more like his parent. "You should come too."

"But what if there are people alive in there? Maybe we can save them."

Lilah shook his head. "Trust me. There's no one left." She turned and began walking back the way they came.

Matty watched her. Part of him wanted to follow, the other part of him wanted to go inside, check the place out for himself. Running his fingers across the closed cut Malek had left on his cheek, he knew he could handle just about anything. *I'm a man now,* he told himself. *I need to start acting like one.*

Matty closed his eyes, gathering himself. Once he was calm and his heartbeat simmered, he walked over to the back door and let himself inside.

"Glad to see everyone's getting along," Sam said, walking past the group, toward the other end of the parking lot. The keys to the Jeep jingled in his pocket. "Keep up the good work."

They couldn't tell if he was serious or not, but his recent behavior suggested the latter. Bob placed his hands on his hips. He opened his mouth like he had something to say, but closed it and saved his breath.

"Where are you going?" Brenda asked, reading her husband's mind. Bob placed his hand on her shoulder and rubbed gently. She clasped her hand over his and squeezed. "Sam, I asked you a question."

Sam stopped as if hitting an invisible wall. "I'm going to find our kids. What the hell do you think I'm doing?"

"Don't you think we should discuss this as a group?"

He closed his eyes and envisioned her standing behind him, hands gripping her hips, tapping her foot, her lower lip twitching as she quelled the creeping rage. Sam shuffled his feet, turning toward them. When he opened his eyes, she wasn't in her usual angry pose, but hugging Bob as if she were dangling from a cliff and he were the only thing keeping her from falling. She rested her head on his chest and stared at him, her eyes on the verge of producing tears. Sam felt something twang inside him, starting in his chest and working its way down his arm. At first, he thought his was having a minor heart attack, but he ignored the funny feeling and tightened his jaw. "What is there to discuss? Anyone who wants to come with me, come. Anyone who doesn't, can go eat a turd sandwich for all I care."

"You're kind of a dick, bro," Chuck said. "These people are trying to help you."

Sam glared at the newcomer. "I don't need you." He pointed at Jarvis. "I don't need you." He found Lilah, approaching the group from behind. "Or you." He swung his angry finger at Bob. "Or you." Brenda watched his finger find her and stop. "And I sure as hell don't need you and your fucking bullshit attitude."

"Sam, please stop," Brenda said. "For our daughters' sake. If we're going to find them, then we need to be smart. You need to drop the I-hate-the-whole-fucking-world act and start working with us, not against us." She narrowed her eyes, an innocent expression Sam saw as an act of war. "What the hell has gotten into you? I know we've had our disagreements in the past, but... fuck, Sam, what the hell happened to you? You used to be logical. You used to use your brain, at least."

He felt the last shred of composure leave him. Balling his fists, he rushed forward, unable to control himself any longer.

"That's it—"

A thunderous bang interrupted his words, killing the thoughts that followed. At first, he didn't know how to react. His eyes followed the noise and found Costbusters. A giant fireball rushed toward the sky, black smoke following in its wake. Another explosion sounded and the glass doors exploded outward, shattering into a seemingly infinite number of shards. The rest of the windows busted out in the next fiery bang. The concrete exterior crumbled in parts, and when the next explosion went off, most of Costbusters' face tumbled into the parking lot, pieces of building raining from above. Another clamorous eruption thundered throughout the night sky. Fragments of concrete and other debris shot toward the group, landing before their feet. They covered their faces, protecting their eyes from the falling rubble.

Sam sank to his knees. He felt the life being sucked out of him through his pores. His legs went rubbery, his arms and hands tingling with numbness.

This can't be happening, he thought, *not now.*

He had promised a different outcome the second time around. Costbusters would be the answer he knew all along, the one others couldn't see. He had promised to make them see his vision for a future, a sustainable system in place inside the giant retail warehouse. Now that vision crumbled before him, surrounded in flames and unfurling towers of black smoke.

"Ohmygod," someone said from behind him, their voice dying in a whisper. "Matty."

Sam turned toward the voice. *Lilah.* She paced back and forth, throwing her hands over her mouth. She repeated "Ohmygod" several times, closing her eyes. "Matty," she said, breaking her tune. "He was inside."

"No," Brenda whispered. The color in her face matched the glow of the moon. "He was just here."

Sam frantically scanned the area, his son nowhere to be found. He ignored the weakness plaguing his knees and jumped to his feet. With the acrid smell of destruction stinging his nostrils, he took off toward the store.

"Sam!" he heard to his right. He turned and spotted Tina limping his way. Matty was with her, his arm draped over her shoulder. He couldn't tell who was supporting who; both of them looked ruffled, their clothes slightly torn, their faces painted with black ash.

Sam sprinted toward them, reaching Matty first. Scooping his son into his arms, he began to weep. He squeezed harder and Matty squeezed back, nowhere near as firm.

"I'm okay, Dad," he said quietly, his voice trembling.

Sam pulled back and stared at Matty, tears running from both of their eyes now.

"I thought..." He shook his head. "I thought I lost you." He took the moment in, fixating on his son's face, hoping he'd never feel the way he just had for the rest of his life. Once the moment was over and reality settled back in, Sam looked to Tina. "What the hell happened?"

She shook her head. "No idea, Sam."

Tasting something rotten, Sam writhed his lips. "The cannibals?"

Tina shrugged, furrowing her brow. "My best guess. What do you think, Matty?"

Matty nodded in agreement.

"Bastards," Sam grunted, surveying the damage. Flames spit above the rubble, tendrils of smoke reaching for the cloudy black sky. He let go of Matty and faced the store. Dropping to his knees, he began sobbing.

Tina glared at him, a look of pity and wonder crossing her features. She glanced over to Matty and Matty shrugged. The rest of the group watched from the distance as Sam continued to cry, everything he had come to believe in destroyed before his eyes. Tina let him carry on for a few minutes, hesitant to intrude. Finally, she approached him the same way she would sneak past a sleeping bear. Gently, she placed her palm on his shoulder.

"Sam..." she whispered. She bent down on one knee. "Sam, are you okay? Maybe you should step back and relax a little. Come talk to the rest of the group."

Talk and *group* were the only words he heard clearly. A few yards away lay a sign that read, "Welcome to Costbusters. How can we help you today?" The sign had been hanging on the front door, a staple of the establishment since day one. *How can we help you? How had he helped them?* Sam turned back to the rest of the group, finally feeling their eyes on the back of his neck. Their sympathetic glances dug into him. *What the hell have I done?*

The entire few months played itself back. The decision to fortify Costbusters and turn it into a safe haven, a place where people could go about their lives after the sun ruined the day, weighed heavily on his conscience. *I failed these people.* In many ways he had. *They trusted me and I failed them.*

"I fucked us," Sam said quietly so only Tina could hear.

"Don't worry about that—"

"Every decision I made endangered us." He shook his head furiously, over and over again. "I nearly got us all killed."

Tina thought about arguing, telling him it wasn't his fault, that he did the best he could, but she would've been lying. Instead, she remained silent and let him figure the rest out for himself.

"Soren was right."

Sam felt a hand on his shoulder. He looked up, expecting to find Tina's comforting face, but was met with Brenda's concerned, watery eyes. She had her other arm around Matty, resting her cheek on the top of his head.

Tina narrowed her eyes and stepped away slowly, receding into a corner of the parking lot void of moonlight.

Sam placed his hand on his ex-wife's, a comforting sensation rolling over him.

"I was such a fool," he said, struggling to get to his feet. Brenda and Matty helped him as the rest of the group ambled forward, watching the flames dance in spastic waves behind them. Hanging his head, Sam turned to them, wiping away the last of his tears. "I was convinced this place was the answer, that we could build a life for ourselves here. But I was wrong. I took things too far and for that, I am sorry."

Brenda patted his shoulder while the others nodded, accepting his apology.

Sam shrugged. "I guess the only question is... where do we go now?"

"Judging from the amount of cars left here," Bob said, "I'd say the others are probably on foot. Would that be safe to assume?" he asked Sam.

"Yeah," Sam said, shrugging. "The parking lot looks about

how I left it."

"I think they headed out on 70 west," Matty said, reiterating an earlier point. "I found this about one hundred yards away." From his small knapsack, he retrieved a foot-long Barbie doll that appeared to have been dragged across the blacktop or trampled on, perhaps a little of both. Matty held it up for the group to see.

"That's nice that you like to play with Barbies, kid," Jarvis said. "But what does that have to do with what direction we're taking?"

"Dana said something about Susan trying to give her a doll. She found it pretty weird," Matty said. "Anyway, it must have fallen out of one of their packs, and where I found it suggests they are headed that way."

"Are we really listening to a fifteen year old right now?" Chuck asked. "I mean, no offense, dude, but come on. Let's get serious."

Bob sighed and looked at the sky. A sliver of bright blue just over the horizon began to cut into the night. They didn't have time to argue about which way to travel *and* search for cover from the sun.

"Chuck..." Bob said, sounding disappointed.

"Yeah?"

"You don't have to come with us, you know."

Chuck didn't respond.

"But I happen to think Matty is right. If this Alaska business is true and that's where they're headed, I'm sure they headed west. It's only logical."

Chuck shrugged. "Whatever, dude. Just throwing in my two cents."

"Well next time be a little more polite about it," Bob said, smiling. "I say we take a few vehicles and follow 70 until we either reach the others, or we don't." Bob shrugged. "Either way we know where they are headed."

"Finding them will be impossible," Jarvis chimed in. "Like a needle in a fucking haystack."

"We have to try," Brenda said. "My babies are out there.

Without me." Her voice wavered as she spoke.

Sam took hold of her hand and squeezed. "They'll be okay," he said. "They're with some good people. Brian is with them." He remembered Mouth and the promise he made. "They're fine."

She nodded. "God, I hope so."

"Then 70 west it is," Bob said. "Anyone in disagreement, speak now."

No one argued. Chuck hung his head and kicked a few pebbles around. Jarvis shrugged, having no better suggestions. Brenda nodded, agreeing with her husband. Matty smiled. Lilah hung back, rubbing her stomach, trying to fight off the spinning sensation plaguing her equilibrium. Tina paced back and forth, her arms folded across her chest; she pretended like she wasn't listening, but Bob knew she had heard every word. He turned to Sam, expecting him to speak.

"Sam?" Bob asked. "Do you agree?"

He drew in a deep breath, taking in the smoky odor hanging heavy in the atmosphere. He snapped his fingers at Bob like Elvis. "Whatever you say, amigo."

"DOPESICK"

EPISODE EIGHT

-1-

The moon was not enough. Its sliver of silvery-white light provided no hope of chasing the shadows back to where they came. Flashlights helped, but their range of guidance was limited. Batteries drained, they became taxed beyond their limits much like their carriers.

I can't believe I sold these to people, Sam thought, repeatedly pressing the hand-held beacon's power button. *Absolute garbage.*

Besides the issue of visibility, things had stabilized. The food was rationed accordingly, and it had lasted. Tina had trapped enough rainwater, purified a few gallons by boiling, and refilled the empty water bottles. They had weeks before needing to worry about running short on food and water.

Sam tried not to worry about those things. Ever since the cars ran out of gas three days ago, things had looked grim. Chris Atkins's Charger was the first to run dry, the motor coughing itself into seizures from which it could never recover. They had debated cramming everyone into the Jeep, but it was physically impossible to seat everyone comfortably. The Jeep was running low on gas too, and judging from the scenery, gas was unobtainable. Plus, they had bled the local stations dry on their midnight excursions.

Walking made Sam nervous. Bob too. Although he never spent any quality time with his ex-wife's husband, he had a good read on Bob and how he operated, a gift Sam often utilized, the main reason retail came so naturally to him. He could see into people and understand the core of them after a few short exchanges. He could tell Chris Atkins was a dipshit within the first few moments of his interview (Brian had lobbied to hire him), and Sherry would be the best damn cashier Costbusters ever had (she won the Costbusters Cashier Olympics three years in a row), and that Soren Nygaard would bring everything he had worked hard for to an end. Sam knew people, knew what made them... *them.*

Bob was a planner. A strategist. His mind constantly targeted on the future, mulling over each possible scenario, examining every potential outcome diligently, not taking anything off the table until carefully analyzed. Sam figured Bob would have been a world-champion chess player if he hadn't practiced cracking backs. Always ahead of the curve, seeing the moves before they happen, Bob was a visionary in his own unique way, and Sam finally knew who should really be leading them along. It was a bitter fact to swallow, but Sam took the truth pill without any struggle.

Maybe it'll be nice, he thought, *NOT being responsible for once.* Indeed, it eased him, relinquishing his responsibilities. He was calm. His chest felt lighter. The storm in his stomach settled. Despite the blisters on his feet, he felt impeccable. This was the feeling he longed for. This sense of internal peace.

Even in the dark, the world looked brighter.

-2-

A little voice urged him to grab her hand, but something else insisted he bail. *What if she doesn't grab back? What if she gets mad? What if she doesn't talk to me ever again?* These questions came as fast as machine-gun fire. Other questions came without allowing the previous to be answered. *What if Mom sees? What if Dad sees? What if he's compelled to give me 'The Talk' again?*

Six years ago, his father tried giving him the dreaded "Talk." It didn't go well. He started off with the typical birds and bees analogy, which had been botched past the point of saving; Matty questioned whether birds and bees "got it on" as it was so eloquently put. The whole conversation had been a disaster, full of half-spoken sentences from both parties and lots of stuttering and the worst description of the female anatomy one could come up with (like a little pretty flower, his father had said). It was a traumatizing experience in Matty's life and being nine didn't help matters.

He had learned much about girls over the last six years, the Internet proving most informative. Anyone who could hack Bob's childproof passwords had unlimited access to the Web's filthiest secrets, and hacking was something Matty had practiced like an art. He learned a lot from Becky, too. The wall between their rooms was thin and unable to contain her gossip. He was careful not to listen too much—things got uncomfortably weird after a while. The Internet and the neighboring lunch table at school supplied him with plenty of knowledge on the subject. Not that it mattered much; he accepted the fact he was too ugly and too nerdy to get a girl to talk to him let alone take her to bed.

Just take her hand.

Her hand was so close, yet so far. His brain said yes, but his nerves said no. They fought the battle for minutes. A few times she glanced over at him and he concealed his fear behind weak smiles. She giggled and he felt dumb. He couldn't appear more inadequate if he tried. And worse, Matty knew she could see through him like an open window. He wasn't fooling anyone. Especially Lilah

Carpenter.

Stop being such a pussy and do it!

Something grabbed his hand and his heart cartwheeled in his chest. He traced the hand back to Lilah, and he couldn't stop his eyes from growing. An invisible butterfly fluttered within his stomach. She smiled and his knees lost their strength.

He heard Jarvis and Chuck whisper to themselves (something about "young love") but he ignored them. They were teasing him, Matty figured, because they were jealous.

Of course they are, he mused. *Anyone would kill to be with someone as hot as her.*

As they walked, Matty became more comfortable. Her hand felt oddly cold for a rather warm fall night. He found himself caught in the moment, and although the bliss would pass, he found solace he never knew existed. Even when his mother turned to check on her son he didn't let go. There was no harm in holding hands. It wasn't like he jammed his tongue down her throat.

As they walked hand in hand, Matty overheard Bob and his father talking. His stepfather had stumbled upon several mining lamps left behind from Soren's ransacking of Costbusters. Sam replied with a sigh, mixed with both relief and frustration, and further commented on how fortunate they were to discover such a find. He knocked the flickering flashlight against his palm to emphasize his point. Bob mumbled something Matty could not discern and Sam wisely steered the conversation toward a new issue.

"We cleaned most of the neighboring towns out of food and water," Sam told Bob. "Whatever we didn't get to, the cannibals did."

"There will be other towns on the way. Maybe some stores haven't been hit yet. Especially the bigger towns."

"Bigger towns mean more people. And more people means..."

Matty could tell his father wanted to continue. But he paused. Silence was progress.

"Nevermind. I'm sure you're right."

Bob continued leading the way, light beaming from his

forehead.

"Bigger towns may provide us with more opportunities for shelter."

"Good point, Bob," Sam said.

Bob? Matty's jaw dropped. He started to question his father's newfound outlook as Lilah's hand slipped from his grasp. He immediately turned to her. Her eyes were slipping under their lids, losing consciousness. Matty reached out and grabbed her. Her eyes perked and she clenched his wrist, her palms icy and greasy with sweat.

"Are you okay?" he asked in a whisper.

She nodded.

"Are you sure?" Matty noted her pale complexion, strikingly similar to the moon's shiny aura above. "You look sick."

"I'm fine," she said firmly. "I'm probably hungry."

Dipping into his shoulder bag, he offered her turkey jerky. She raised her palm in the air, covering her mouth with the other.

"I never want to eat another piece of meat again," she said, wanting to vomit.

"Going vegetarian?" he asked. "I've thought about that myself. Could never pull the trigger though. There's pros and cons to the Western Diet—and I love chicken. But who doesn't?"

"Matty, stop," she said, looking like she had swallowed spoiled milk. "I'm literally two seconds away from barfing."

Gently taking her hand, he did as she asked.

Her pores exhaled heat as if ablaze.

It was Chuck who found Matty and Lilah holding hands humorous. Jarvis considered it sweet, somewhat refreshing. The past months had been filled with bloodshed, burnt bodies, and the unveiling of true human nature under social unrest, mankind's ultimate calamity. The sight of an innocent exchange between young lovers had been as relieving as a cool breeze on a blistering summer day. Chuck giggled behind his palm while Jarvis smiled, reminiscing about his own youthful indiscretions. The last one had been Christi and she was a tall blonde who loved puppies, grunge rock, and crystal meth.

"So I guess this makes us, like, the seventh wheel," Jarvis noted.

Chuck continued to snicker quietly. "Well I sure as shit ain't holding your hand."

Jarvis smiled, continuing to think of Christi and how she had once held his hand. How good it was to be loved. To be wanted. Needed.

High...

Jarvis shook away his thoughts. Chuck was sticking his forefinger through the circle he made with his other forefinger and thumb, winking while he pulled out and pushed in, over and over again until Jarvis got the joke and forced his new friend to stop.

"Don't be an ass," Jarvis said.

"What? You know they're gonna bang."

"Yeah, and so what? I think it's kind of nice."

"Nice? What are you, fucking Shakespeare?" Chuck laughed. "You wanna write them a love poem while you're at it?"

Chuck wasn't the kind of guy Jarvis found irritating, but he wasn't someone he'd pal around with unless the world ended. He was more like the idiot stepbrother Jarvis never had.

"Look around," Jarvis told him. "What do you see?"

Chuck glanced at the dark empty streets, a late September chill crawling down his spine. Street lights hung over them, dead as the bodies they had passed not more than a few miles back. The bodies, killed elsewhere, were dumped on the side of the road, their guts spilling through the wide gashes in their abdomens. It was a grisly sight Chuck wished he hadn't seen and hoped his fellow travelers missed him retching into a patch of overgrown grass.

"This isn't a trick question, Chuckster," Jarvis said. "What do you see?"

He rolled his eyes. "I don't know. Not much."

"Would you say our surroundings are jovial? You finding much to get excited about lately?"

Chuck furrowed his brow and looked at his new buddy as if

he had spoken an alien language. "No. What's your point?"

Jarvis swept his hand across his body, palm up. "Now look at that. Two kids. Holding hands. You're witnessing a budding romance, unfolding right before your very eyes."

Chuck's eyes were wide with wonder. "Man, you're a pretty weird guy. I liked it better when we were in the cage and you weren't talking. Can we have *that* Jarvis back?"

Jarvis patted him on the back. "I'm serious. If you can't appreciate something like that, then you're not human."

"Trust me. I'm human. And my humanity is telling me if I don't get a double-bacon cheeseburger inside me soon I'm going to Tasmanian Devil myself to the nearest Burger King."

"You're hopeless."

As they continued, Jarvis watched Matty and Lilah closely. The way Lilah walked captivated him, not their budding romance. The subtle stumble triggered it. She walked it off like no one had noticed. Jarvis continued his observation, eyeing her movements; every little twitch, every fine detail. Moonlight glistened off her sleek skin; she was sweating a lot for the middle of fall, when the temperature barely dropped below sixty. Matty leaned in, whispered something in her ear. Jarvis read his lips: *Are you okay?* She told him she was fine. A few more exchanges, nothing informative. Small talk. She was dodging the subject, diverting the topic elsewhere. *Rookie move, sweetheart. Real novice shit.* As if the pale sweaty flesh and the struggle with gravity wasn't enough, her actions told the rest of the story.

Gotcha, girl, Jarvis thought.

The chick was dopesick.

-3-

Twelve Years Ago

Curled up like a lazy dog on a hot afternoon, twenty-two year old Jarvis Mott fought the chills, sweats, and surging pain all at once. He battled hard but the sickness was all too much, breaking him down minute by minute, hour by hour, until he wanted to gnaw on his own brain. His skin froze like a sheet of ice, yet the blood beneath burned like a dragon spitting fire into his veins. His heart hammered like in the middle of a rigorous fuck, but Jarvis hadn't been lucky, not since Christi broke things off and eloped with his best friend to Texas, or Arkansas, or some other state where they wore cowboy hats and herded cattle. Apparently she got clean and found Jesus. *Great for her.*

Fuck it, Jarvis thought as he squirmed beneath the sweat-soaked bed sheets, dying. If it were one symptom, he could have endured. But all three? No way Jose. Not the big three. He figured it wouldn't be much longer until he opened his wrists with the box cutter he had "borrowed" from work. The bastard gleamed at him from the corner of his nightstand. He wondered which cut would bleed out fastest: horizontal or vertical. He'd heard arguments from both sides, but never had the balls to see for himself.

He managed to remove the sheets away from his face. His joints ached and burned while goose-flesh populated on his sweaty arms. He closed his eyes, hoping the nightmare would end. When he opened them, another nightmare appeared, this one taking the shape of a concerned mother, *his* mother, the one who volunteered at the local church, never missed a Sunday service in the last forty-nine years, and watched Mel Gibson's *The Passion of Christ* at least once a month. She peered over her thin-rimmed glasses, panic assuming control of her face.

"Jarvey?" she asked. Hearing the childish nickname, he wanted to hide. Jarvis thought they'd all call him Jarvey in Hell, one of the main reasons he hadn't ended his suffering. The other was—deep down—he wanted to live, wanted to see himself clean again.

The Big Three tested reason two. "Jarvey, sweet Lord in Heaven, are you okay?"

"Y-yeah, Mom," he said, teeth chattering. "F-fine. Thanks f-for asking."

"You look like death," she said bluntly.

Feel like it, too, you wench.

He didn't hate his mother, but she annoyed the living piss out of him. Pops too, although he could talk baseball with the old man when he wasn't reading Bible passages or watching that Joel Osteen character give squinty-eyed sermons on the boob tube. It seemed the only thing mother wanted to talk about was how many cans of soup she donated to Father Scandrick's monthly food drive.

"Did you call out of work today?" she asked.

"Yup." Speaking hurt. So did existing at this point, but the box cutter seemed like a mile away and it had lost its charm.

Mother put her hand on Jarvis's forehead, retracted it immediately like she had burnt it on the stove.

"Oh Jesus and the Gospels, you're burning up!"

Don't be so dramatic, he opened his mouth to say, but the words came out garbled, an unintelligible mess.

"What?" she asked.

He waved her off like a king to his plebeian jester.

"Oh, is that the thanks I get for being a concerned mother?" she asked, expecting an immediate answer. Instead, she received the usual eye roll. "Well, this is the second time this month you've gotten the flu, and it's not even flu season yet." She squinted, suspicious of something foul. It was an odd, unfamiliar look and it hit him where it hurt the most.

Does she know? How could she? I've been so careful...

"Something you want to tell me, Mister?"

Go away...

"A mother knows when something is wrong with her baby..."

Get the fuck outta my room!

"Just sick, ma," he said. "Something's..." A few coughs for dramatic effect, "going around the office."

She flared her nostrils, catching a whiff of bullshit. Standing up, she shrugged in defeat.

"If you ever need to talk," she said, making her way slowly toward the door, "I'm here. I'm your mother, remember? You can tell me anything."

She offered him a way out and the smart thing would have been to take it. But he couldn't. He wouldn't take it. There were consequences. Always consequences. He'd done too many awful things over the years. Telling her such meant facing those consequences to the end. He'd confess to everything—the stolen cash from work, the unexplained shortages from the family vacation jar, the robbery of the Drive-N-Dine Christi and he pulled last month—and all for what? A chance at redemption? No. Forgiveness? Of course not. Truth be told, there was no way out. Only consequences. Some worse than others. Now he had to decide which consequences he'd rather endure.

"I'm fine..." he said. Cough, cough to seal the deal.

She turned down the hall.

The next ten minutes dragged like Sunday morning mass. Joints ached. Muscles burned. And the hunger for methamphetamine jumped his bones.

Fuck it.

That's what it came down to.

Fuck it.

The only conclusion Jarvis could draw.

Fuck it all.

It was time to feel good again.

FUCK IT.

He scraped himself together, dressed for success (a hoodie and jeans), stumbled down the hallway and into mother's room, raided her jewelry chest, and booked it to the nearest pawn shop.

-4-

They paused to rest and regroup near the highway overpass. Below, many cars littered the streets, forging a trail away from a small town, where many had attempted to flee. A nearby sign read "Mooreville", a place no one in the group had heard of. Minutes later, the sound of commotion coming from within reached them. They listened to the shouting. *People*. The faint sound of harsh words carried in a soft breeze. *Fighting*. The wind further revealed the severity of such. *Killing*. The echo of gunfire fell upon their ears.

Without hesitation, Sam sprinted forward. By the time Tina and Bob took hold of him, he already had one leg over the guardrail, determining which vehicle to break his fall on.

"Sam!" Tina shouted as she wrapped her arms around his shoulders.

He swung his other leg over the edge. "Let go of me!"

"Not happening," Bob said. He took a firm hold of Sam's left arm.

"That could be them! They could be down there!"

The others considered the possibility amongst themselves while Bob and Tina brought Sam back. More gunshots rang out in the distance.

"You're going to get us killed," Brenda snapped as she rejoined them.

Bob stepped between them before more fireworks launched. "Everyone calm down."

Matty crept over the guardrail, peering out.

"It's not them," Matty said.

"How do you know?" his father asked.

"They'd be much farther by now."

"You don't know when they left. They could be there. In trouble."

Matty closed his eyes, shaking his head for the second time. "We know approximately when they left. And unless they crawled, they'd be much farther. At least two days. I know we've been pushing hard, but if I had to guess, Soren's been pushing them harder. We're nowhere close."

Sam gazed upon the rooftops and listened. The gunfire was fading. He moved closer and strained his eyes. A yellowy-orange glow danced from one residence to the next. Within minutes, black smoke billowed out from the town's four corners. His view became obscured as the group raced in front of him to witness the inferno. Slowly, he found a seat on the pavement and rested his head against the concrete barrier. He had seen enough.

"I'm fine," Lilah said in a low whisper, as soft as a breath.

"You're not fine," the group heard Jarvis tell her. "You're sick. Really sick. And it will only get worse."

She rolled her eyes and turned her back.

"Hey!" he said, reaching for her shoulder.

Before he could lay a finger on her, Matty was between them, brow furrowed and ready for answers.

"Whoa, little man," Jarvis said. "I'm concerned about your girlfriend here."

"She's not my girlfriend," Matty said. "And what's the matter with her?"

Lilah tugged on his sleeve. "Come on, Matty. The guy is talking out of his ass. Don't listen to him."

"I know what's going with you. You do too. Don't pretend like it's not happening," Jarvis said. "That would be unwise."

"Will it be unwise when I put my foot up your ass, bro?" Lilah asked.

"Nice mouth, girl," Chuck said, applauding her.

"Shut it, Chuck," Jarvis said. "I'm serious, Lilah. You need help."

"Fuck you!" she screamed and turned away.

Matty took off after her, but not before shooting Jarvis a nasty look.

"What the hell was that all about?" Chuck asked.

The group faced Jarvis, awaiting an explanation. He hung his head and rolled a few rocks beneath his sneaker.

"Forget it."

Although they were quiet, the expressions on their faces clearly made it known they wouldn't. As they turned from him, Jarvis reached down and grabbed a stone with a sharp edge. He walked over to the sign and scraped the stone against the metal. The ear-pulling screech startled the group.

"What the hell are you doing?" Chuck asked.

Jarvis stepped back and tossed the rock aside.

NO

MOOREVILLE

the sign now read.

No one disagreed.

"Wait!" Matty said, running after her. "Lilah, wait!"

She stopped at the end of the overpass. She turned around and he abruptly stopped. He bent over and put his hands on his knees, catching his breath.

"What was that all about?"

"He's a dick."

Matty tilted his head. "Come on. You can't fool me."

She knew he was right. She couldn't fool him, nor could she trick the rest of the group. And it would only get worse. Much worse. She couldn't deny what Jarvis suspected, not forever.

"I don't want to talk about it. Please," she smiled, although it looked more like a painful wince.

"Okay. What should we talk about?"

Lilah shrugged, dropping her smile and all other emotion.

"What's your favorite movie?" Matty asked.

"My favorite movie?"

"Sure. Mine is *The Day After Tomorrow.* I know it's not, like, the best in terms of story structure and the writing is kind of iffy in some parts, but it's fun. I can watch it over and over again and not get bored. So what's yours?"

Lilah thought about it, glancing up at the moon and the trillion stars crammed into the midnight sky. "I don't know. *Seven,* I guess."

"The one with Brad Pitt?"

"That surprise you or something?"

Matty cackled. "I thought you'd say *The Notebook* or something."

She squinted as if trying to spot a distant object. "Listen, mister—growing up with two brothers didn't allow me to have many girly hobbies. So wipe the smirk off your face if you know what's good for you."

"Listen, I love *Seven.* Classic movie. Doesn't get enough attention as it should. Plus, the ending? Come on. Perfect. Absolute —"

"And Chimichangas from Bienvenido's. Love them."

"Huh?"

Lilah jerked her head back and forth. "You know what I mean? The best."

"Lilah..."

Her eyes shifted. Her mouth twitched.

"You don't smell that?" she asked. "That's crazy! We used to eat there all the time when we were kids and God it smells like salsa, the sweet and spicy kind."

She lost her balance and stumbled sideways, but she caught herself before Matty reached her. He grabbed her shoulder, and she squeezed his.

"Carp..." she said.

"Carp?"

"Why'd you let him touch me, Carp." Tears filled her eyes, dribbling from the corners. A drop ran down her cheek, leaving a wet trail in its wake. The moon made the path sparkle. "Why did you let him touch me, Carp. Goddammit, *why did you let him?"*

She stumbled to one knee. Matty called for help, but the group was already running toward them.

"You're going to be okay, Lilah," Matty promised. "We'll get you help."

Puke exploded from her mouth, and splashed the pavement.

"I really did like the pink dress better, Daddy," she said, her pupils lolling before disappearing behind her fluttering eyelids.

Matty wrapped both hands around her body as she convulsed. The violent seizures continued as he corralled her head against his chest and screamed into the night.

-5-

ELEVEN YEARS AGO

"**Careful, skinny-boy,**" the juice-head on the couch warned. "Dat some good-ass shit."

Jarvis, wearing sunglasses and a hoodie in a dim room with no air-conditioning in the middle of July, looked at Juice-Head sideways. He tossed him the money and looked down at the bag of crystals. They had a purple hue to them, and Jarvis wasn't sure if it was the way the drugs were manufactured or the odd light of the room. *Could be some good-ass shit*, he thought, *or it could be bath salts.*

"Better be careful," Juice-Head said again. "Dat's dat good shit. Fuck you all up. Make you see stars, the moon, Jupiter and Uranus, you know."

"Yeah," Jarvis said, "I know."

"Good, now get the fuck outta here."

Juice-Head went back to weighing his inventory and appropriating them into little clear baggies. When Jarvis didn't move, he looked up, continuing on with his daily duty.

"Did I fucking stutter, skinny-boy?"

"No, sir. Just thought you could tell me how to get the fuck out of here. Not from Newark. Wouldn't know one street from another."

"Do I look like a fucking map to you, motherfucker?"

No, you look like a big bald, no-dick, steroid-abusing motherfucker, motherfucker.

"No, from here you don't look like a map."

"Good. Then you heard me. Get the fuck out. You paid, now get the fuck out."

Jarvis turned and headed for the door. A few minutes later he was on the streets of Newark, after dark and in the wrong neighborhood. Hoodlums on the corner pretended to hold a knife fight, stabbing the air between themselves, calling each other names like, "Young Blood" and "Young Crip" and other monikers Jarvis had heard before and never understood. He knew getting his suburban white-boy ass out of there was paramount. He hustled down the street, feeling the hoodlums' eyes following him. They called to him, said something like, "Hey, yo, white boy! You forgot something!"

He took off running and found his car a few blocks down. He didn't know if the hoodlums were following him because he never looked. He ran. And fast. As quickly as his under-worked legs would carry him.

He slipped the car key into the lock and popped open the door. The hoodlums were seconds behind him. One of them reached for something in his shorts and Jarvis was sure it wasn't anything pleasant. Jarvis ducked into his rusty Oldsmobile and cranked the engine. He expected the bitch to fail. That's usually how things went in Jarvis's fucked, shitty life, but the bitch roared and he threw her in gear instantly, peeling out of the parking space. He waved his middle finger to the hoodlums and they fired shots in reply, which hit nothing as far as Jarvis could tell.

Before he reached a safe, comfortable road he had been familiar with, Jarvis opened the baggie on his lap. He surveyed the side streets for cops, but cops rarely patrolled those streets unless called. Driving with his knees, he packed his pipe full of crystal and and put his lighter to it.

"Good shit," he mumbled to himself, his eyes shifting back and forth between the road and his hot pipe. "That's all these fuckers say anymore. My shit is good. This shit is good. Fucking heard it once, I've heard it a thousand times. This stuff be the hotness and all that whack bullshit—fucking assholes."

Smoke curled before him and Jarvis placed his lips on the glass and inhaled. He closed his eyes and the smoke grabbed his lungs. Much to his surprise, the dealer was right. *Dat's good shit!*

"I'll be dammed." He blew the smoke out, a cloud appearing before him, fogging the windshield. "Motherfucker was right. That was some good-ass shit." He didn't wait long to take another pull. The second time around was even better than the first.

He navigated through the ghetto fine, honking at pedestrians and laughing because they looked like characters from the *Candyland* board game he played as a child. At some point the road turned into a rainbow and the apartment buildings towering on both sides of the road took the form of giant gumdrops. He laughed and returned to the pipe for thirds. Thirds were better than firsts and seconds combined.

He laughed some more.

As the drug turned on him, he slowly realized something was amiss. The shit was *too good,* and Jarvis considered the grave possibility that Juice-Head laced his bag with something he didn't pay for. When no semblance of the real world remained and all he could see was gumdrop mountains, candy corn hookers, and gingerbread death machines, he knew it was time to pull over and ride it out. But here? In the middle of downtown *Candyland?* The gummy bear people and candy cane animals would rip his skinny-white ass apart and eat him alive. No, he had to press on. Muscle his way through this. Follow the Rainbow Road and get the fuck home where he could ride this nightmare out in the safety of his own bed.

He convinced himself he'd make it when three Twizzlers appeared before him, screaming and throwing up their red licorice arms. Jarvis knew if he stopped, the Twizzlers would tear him to Reese's Pieces. So instead he hammered the gas pedal and drove through them. The licorice liquefied on his windshield and Jarvis drove a few more feet blind, until his car hit something solid. His head smashed against the steering wheel and the light of the world blinked.

Seconds later, Jarvis found himself handcuffed to a hospital bed. Two police detectives were staring down at him, asking him some basic questions—like who he was, how old he was, and if he drove a black Oldsmobile. He answered slowly, but truthfully, confused about what was happening, but also glad the *Candyland* nightmare had ended.

He wasn't so glad when the two detectives told him the licorice he hit weren't licorice, but a woman and her two daughters.

-6-

"Lilah!" Matty screamed for the third time. The first two times didn't work, and neither did the third attempt. Lilah was unconscious and wheezing laborious breaths. Foam bubbled on her lips.

Jesus, what's wrong with her?

A chill cut through her veins, sending her body into convulsions. Beads of sweat covered her arms, forehead, and upper lip. Matty looked up and saw Bob and his mother standing over them. They struggled for air, but being in excellent shape, the sprint across the bridge didn't seem to bother them much.

"What's wrong with her?" Matty cried out.

The worrisome expression on his face sliced through Brenda. Bob kept a stone-cold appearance, dropping to one knee beside his stepson.

"Let me see," Bob said.

Reluctantly, Matty handed her over. He hated to let her go, but he knew there was nothing he could do for her. He didn't think there was anything Bob could do either, but he was an adult, and adults usually handled these situations better than petrified fifteen-year olds.

Brenda placed her hand on her son's shoulder. Matty closed his eyes in attempt to block the tears from coming through. He failed and the wetness streaked down his cheeks.

"Put her on the ground," Jarvis told Bob. "She's having another seizure."

Bob glanced up, giving Jarvis a *who-the-hell-are-you* look. When Lilah thrashed in his arms, he listened. Carefully, Bob placed the girl on the ground. She continued with her fit, foam spilling from her mouth and running down her cheeks.

"There's nothing you can do for her," Jarvis told Matty.

He kid looked on in horror as she sprawled out on the road, experiencing a series of spastic convulsions. He wanted to help her, hold her, *kiss her.*

For a brief moment, he thought she might die. In this new

world, it'd be nearly impossible to find a magic pill for whatever was wrong with her. And what was wrong exactly? Matty didn't know. Despite being the smartest kid in his freshman class, in that moment, he felt dumb.

And helpless.

He craned his head toward his father. Sam stood a good distance away from the group, his hand resting over his mouth. Matty never saw his father like that before. He looked... *uncomfortable.* Sam watched on, his eyes narrowing to slits. Matty stared, hoping to make eye contact with him. He needed his father, needed him to confirm that everything was okay. He received no such comfort. In fact, Sam continued to stare on, unable to move or express himself in any way.

Things are falling apart.

For the first time since the world had ended, despair touched him. Standing on the overpass near a city full of raucous marauders with his first girlfriend in dire need of medical assistance, and his father staring off like a mindless robot, all seemed lost. Matty wanted to blink and wake up in his bed, the nightmare over and nothing but a distant memory. But no such thing would happen. This was reality. And reality sucked. Big time.

Lilah's pupils rolled, turned white, and reappeared a moment later. He stared, seeing no semblance of her in them. She looked dead. Maybe she was. Stretched beyond his limits, he couldn't take it anymore.

"Somebody help her!" Matty shouted. When no one responded, his skin grew hot. "Somebody help her!"

No one came to her side.

Jarvis put a hand on his shoulder. "Can't do anything about it, little man. Gotta let it ride out."

Matty balled his hands into fists. He'd never hit anyone before, but then again, he'd never been so angry. So... *useless.* His mind kept reciting the word, *useless.* He couldn't look at himself any other way. If he was stronger, maybe he could have helped her. *Stronger.* Smarter? *If I was smarter, I'd know what to do.*

"This..." Matty said, clenching his teeth, "this is bullshit!"

No one argued with him. His mother shed a tear, unable to handle her own emotions. Bob looked at his stepson, commiserating with his helplessness. Staring off into the distance, taking time to reflect, Sam remained still and silent. Tina watched Matty fall apart. She knew Jarvis was right; nothing could be done. *Ride it out* had been the best advice anyone had come up with since they left Costbusters. Jarvis reached for the kid's shoulder again, but thought better of it. Chuck stood behind them, trying to keep out of the way and doing a good job of it.

Jarvis ripped the leather belt off his waist with one strong tug. He knelt next to the sick girl and went to place the belt in her mouth.

Bob grabbed his arm.

"I don't want her to bite off her tongue," he stated.

Bob shot him a dubious look.

"Please, man. I've seen it happen before. It ain't pretty."

Bob let go and Jarvis slipped the belt between her chattering teeth.

"Now what?"

"Now we ride it out."

They rode it out. Although it seemed longer, it took less than a minute for her body to stop quivering spastically.

Matty fell beside her, dropping to his knees. He placed his hand over her forehead. *Freezing.* He looked to Bob, the next closest person, the only fatherly figure not stuck in a dreamlike trance. Bob grabbed her by the back of the neck and lifted her, aligning her on an incline. More foam bubbled from her mouth and seeped from her lips, dribbling down her chin. He didn't want her choking.

"Is it over?" Matty asked.

Lightly, Bob tapped her on the cheek. "Lilah," he said. "Lilah, honey?"

No answer.

"She'll wake up," Jarvis told them. "Give her a few minutes."

Bob held her and waited. He read the impatience in his stepson's eyes like *Chiropractor for Dummies*. Jarvis seemed to know a lot about what was happening. He didn't give off the doctor vibe, although they did come in all shapes and sizes. However, Jarvis was a little too...

What's the word I'm looking for?

Street? He couldn't find a better word. *Street.* Like maybe he had come from a rough neighborhood, grew up on the wrong side of town. Bob didn't think any less of him; it was merely an observation. Jarvis didn't seem like a bad guy. He figured he came from a poor family, maybe lived in some urban city—like Newark or Jersey City—and listened to too much hip-hop growing up. But the guy appeared decent, concerned, and willing to help.

"Lilah?" Bob repeated. "Come on, Lilah. Wake up."

As if she heard him, her eyes fluttered and cracked open.

Matty's mood sparkled. "Lilah!"

She frowned.

"Wha..." Matty said, noticing something about her had changed. "What's the matter?"

She cocked her head to the side. Blinking rapidly, she asked, "Who are you people? Where the hell am I?"

95

-7-

TEN YEARS AGO

Jarvis sat in the semi-circle, surveying the two dozen faces, all of whom looked as uninterested to be there as he was. He didn't listen when they spoke; didn't have to. This wasn't his first rodeo, and it damn sure wouldn't be the last. He had heard the stories before, all of them more or less the same. *Blah, blah, blah* was all he heard from their mouths, and after a while, he stopped paying attention altogether. The floral-pattern walls of the small recreation center held more interest and where he focused his attention.

"Jarvis?" called Mike Braxton, the ring leader of this snooze-fest of a circus. Mike was all right in Jarvis's book. At times the man was too preachy, but he understood things. He had been through some shit, which he had shared on a weekly basis. It wasn't his fault the weekly meetings were boring as all hell. If Mike had the floor for the entire hour, Jarvis might have paid more attention. "Anything you want to share?"

He peeled his eyes away from the wallpaper and focused on the sixty-year old hippy who had once dropped so much acid he'd been stuck on a bad trip for two weeks, which ended after he jumped from the third story of an office building and broke both legs landing in the parking lot. Every now and then he experienced a flashback and revisited those awful times. Mr. Mike never shared what the trip entailed, but Jarvis could tell by the way he spoke about it, the event had been traumatizing.

"You've been here—what's it been—eighteen months?" Mike asked. "I understand you might be in line to head to the county correctional facility at the end of the month. Do you think it's time to open up to the group?"

He chewed his gum, which had replaced his pack-a-day smoking habit. Now he smoked about two cigarettes a day. Some days, only one. He stared at Mr. Mike, pretending the thought of sharing pissed him off.

"Come on, Jarvis," Mike said, winking. "I know you got a

story in you waiting to pour out."

Jarvis shook his head.

"Are you sure? You might find it somewhat liberating."

He surveyed the faces around him, those sad, hopeless faces. Pretenders, he thought. *They share their feelings and shit because no one else will listen to them. No one else cares.* But Jarvis had people who did care about him. His parents. They visited every other day, sometimes every day, depending on his father's work schedule and his mother's church schedule. He talked. They listened. They gave him good advice. *Do well here,* they told him, *and maybe we can get you out early on good behavior.* The chances were slim. He had killed one person, seriously injured two. One of the little girls hadn't survived; the best doctors in the tri-state area had given their all. After almost twelve hours of surgery, the girl had died on the operating table. Her mother and sister spent a week in the ICU, another three in a hospital bed before being discharged.

"Unburden your soul, man," Mike said. He encouraged the group to inspire Jarvis, and they did as their ringleader asked.

"Come on, Jarvis!" a woman with one eye said. She had lost it in a knife fight in North Philly during a drug deal gone bad.

"Yeah, Jarvis, you can do it!" A long-haired man of fifty said. He had crashed his eighteen-wheeler into a gas station convenience store while high as a fucking kite. Cops found two pounds of weed and six kilos of cocaine in his cargo.

"Hey, man, it's not so bad," said a nineteen year-old kid. His name was Marlo and he was the closest thing Jarvis had to a friend in this joint. They talked about the Sixers and attempted to settle the great debate of who was better, east or west coast hip-hop. Jarvis argued Biggie and Tupac crushed Dre and Snoop lyrically and musically, and Marlo told him he was a "Trippin' Fool" who knew nothing of good rap music. "You can do it, white-boy. I got faith."

"All right. Fine."

The group clapped, loudly, but silenced themselves as he started speaking.

"So what's on my mind..." he said. "What's on my mind? I'll tell you what: I'm scared. Pretty fucking scared that's for sure. And anxious. Confused. Angry. Ashamed. I want to control what's going to happen, but I can't. I realize that." He paused. A few members nodded in agreement.

Jarvis sighed. "Not a day goes by I don't think about what happened. The crash. I mean, I was so fucked up I barely remember any of it. It's like I dreamed it. A nightmare. It's like I woke up and had to pay for stuff I did within a dream. It wasn't me who crashed that car and killed that little girl. I feel like it wasn't me at all. It was this *other* me. It was like someone else took over my body and did all this fucked up shit."

Mr. Mike squinted. "I think it *was* you, Jarvis."

"No. It wasn't. I'm not a bad person."

"I'm sure you're not," Mr. Mike said. "However, we are only as good as the decisions we make."

Jarvis glared at him. "It was the drugs. Not me."

"And who opted to take those drugs? Was that someone else? Did someone else put a crack pipe in your mouth?"

"No, that's what I'm saying, Mr. Mike. It was this *other* me. I couldn't help myself."

Mike winced. "You're not understanding. You *chose* to take those drugs. You *chose* to get behind a wheel that day. You *chose* to use while operating a vehicle. Those were decisions *you* made; the drugs had nothing to do with that. The disease had nothing to do with that."

Jarvis slunk in his seat. He now had a different opinion of Mike Braxton.

"I leave for Rahway in seventeen days. State prison," Jarvis said, his voice wavering. "Lookin' at possibly seven years for vehicular homicide. I'm scared. Scared I'll want to use. But more scared of what's going to happen to me. I mean... in case you haven't noticed, I ain't exactly big. I'm afraid..." Tears blurred his vision. "Well, fuck. You all know what I'm afraid of."

No one said anything. They didn't need to.

"I killed... killed that little girl," he sobbed. *"Fuck."*

He wiped his face with his forearm, but a second later it was wet again.

"There's a chance I can get out of it, but I dunno. Not looking too great right now." He breathed deeply and collected himself. Every eye in the room turned on him, their collective gaze burning his face, but he didn't care anymore. Mike was right; better to get it all out, to purge his emotions. "That's all I got."

An hour after his speech, Jarvis caught up with Mr. Mike outside of his office.

"You wanted to see me?"

Mike waved him inside and told him to have a seat. The second he entered the office a wave of negativity washed over him. Whatever he brought him in for couldn't be good.

"What's up?" Jarvis asked. He was tapping his foot on the carpet, a nervous tic he had recently developed since getting clean.

Mike sat down and at first, said nothing. He rested his elbows on his desk and placed his chin on his hands. He stared at Jarvis and each passing second amplified the awkwardness.

"Jarvis, I'm afraid I've got some bad news."

Jarvis's stomach plummeted. The room spun, the air heavy with negative vibes. He found breathing difficult.

"I just got off the phone with Judge Ruggerio, from the Appellate Division. Your Excessive Sentence Appeal was denied. The court felt with your history of theft and the damage you caused your family, I mean—we couldn't even get your parents to write a letter supporting you, and then there's the accident. She said, well... she said some other unflattering things I don't wish to repeat."

"What do you mean they wouldn't write a supporting letter?" he asked, confused. "They visit me almost every day."

"Yes, well. Not writing the letter doesn't mean they don't love you, I'm sure... my best guess is they're trying to teach you a lesson here."

"What fucking lesson? That it's okay to let your children go to prison and get ass raped?" His anger rose more quickly than he anticipated. Mr. Mike put his hand up to stop him before he reached the dangerous level he was capable of. "What fucking lesson?"

"Jarvis, please." His somber tone didn't do much to curb Jarvis's temper. "I know this isn't what you wanted to hear. I know you got your hopes up and thought we'd be able to get you a longer stay here, but... you can handle what's coming. You're stronger than you know, you just don't know it yet. This is your chance to learn. You gotta suit up, show up, and man up, and it'll be over before you know it."

"Fuck you!" Jarvis said, jumping out of his seat. His chair fell back and skidded across the carpet. He pounded the desk with clenched fists, causing pens, a notepad, and a stapler to jump. Mike pushed away and Jarvis could see the fear in his eyes; he thought Jarvis was going to hit him. "Your old hippy ass doesn't know shit!"

Jarvis stormed out of the office and Mike Braxton let him go, and the two of them never spoke again.

-8-

Lilah sat on the curb. Matty held her hair back while she unloaded her stomach on the street. He looked away, the sounds of her retching twirling his own stomach, thinking he might join her if he listened any longer.

The others watched from a good distance. They whispered to each other, everyone throwing in their own take on what to do next, how to proceed with this seemingly delicate situation. Matty knew what they were discussing and ignored them. Instead, he tried to make small talk.

"How's the memory?"

"Better," she said between dry heaves. There wasn't anything solid left to disgorge. "I remember some names."

"That's good," Matty said, wrinkling his nose at the smell. The air was heavy and solid with an acidy stench. It reminded him of the time he left a carton of milk in his mother's car and what it smelled like when they discovered his mistake three days later.

Lilah had awoken confused and unable to remember much. The look on her face had scared Matty; there wasn't a single hint of recognition, like someone had pressed a reset button in her mind.

As time advanced, she was able to remember. Relieved, Matty couldn't imagine how he'd explain everything that happened. And not only the crazy sequence of events, but their relationship. *What is our relationship?* He didn't even understand it, and if *he* didn't, how was he supposed to explain it to someone who had forgotten who he was? Fortunately, she remembered him.

He stayed with her until she was done and helped her to her feet. Gave her a hair tie his mother had given him. She couldn't stand on her own power, so he threw her right arm over his shoulder and walked her over to the rest of the group. He knew there would be questions to answer and decisions to make, some wrinkles in need of a good iron—Lilah being the biggest wrinkle of them all.

"Are you feeling better, honey?" Brenda asked.

"Yes. I think so."

"You look like absolute shit," Chuck said. He wasn't joking.

101

She looked horrible. To Matty she was beautiful, the goddess of his dreams. To everyone else she was a heroin addict badly in need of a fix.

Lilah pretended like Chuck didn't exist, and Matty followed her lead. He looked to his mother for guidance, but she was barely holding her own shit together. Bob seemed concerned, but not overly attentive. His mind had wandered elsewhere, perhaps toward the troubles ahead. Tina hung in the background, stalking around the perimeter of the group. She had a different look about her since Costbusters met its demise. He knew why, but kept his concerns to himself. No need to complicate an already complicated situation. Matty turned to his father last. He stared toward the burning city in the backdrop, scratching the beginnings of a bushy beard.

Jarvis looked worried, the only one in the entire group. He hovered over Lilah, checking her pulse without her permission. She shot him a glance, and he put his hands up to show he meant no harm.

"She needs a doctor," Brenda said.

Sam laughed through his nose, and the group turned to him, surprised he had been paying attention this whole time. "Let's call and make an appointment."

"Dude has a point," Chuck said. "I haven't seen too many places open for business."

"Honey," Bob said to her, "the odds of us finding a doctor—a real doctor—is..."

"Absolute shit," Chuck added. "Looks like you're gonna have to ride it out, little girl."

"Who are you calling little girl?" Lilah asked. She jumped to her feet, which was not the best idea. Her world spun and she lost her balance. Matty caught her before she fell, wrapping her in his arms, tight against his chest.

"You should sit," Matty suggested in her ear.

She listened and he helped her back to the curb.

"Not a little girl," she whispered over and over again, like some personal mantra. *"Not a little girl."*

Her eyelids fluttered like butterfly wings and her head swayed back and forth like a tree in a hurricane. Matty knew it was only a matter of time before she passed out again, or worse—suffered another seizure.

"You need to rest," he said, stroking her hair.

They sat huddled together, Lilah resting her head on Matty's shoulder. Poor hygiene had gotten the better of her and an odd, not overly pungent, smell found his nostrils. In the background, Matty could still hear the occasional gunshots coming from the city, accompanied by intermittent screams. Children crying. Maniacs laughing. The world had gone to Hell.

"Not a little girl."

"She needs medical attention," Jarvis said, loud enough for everyone to hear. "Or else this is only going to happen again. Worse next time. What she really needs is medicine."

Bob squeezed his forehead. "I don't understand. What medicine? For seizures? You think she's epileptic?"

Jarvis waved his finger in the air. "No, no. Flumazenil. Romazicon. Or some other receptor antagonist."

Bob stiffened his back. He recognized the titles, but couldn't put his finger on their purpose. "What are you saying?"

"He's saying the girl has a drug problem," Sam replied. "Isn't that right?"

Jarvis told them, "Yes."

"Whoa, dude," Chuck said. "Who are you? Dr. House?"

Lilah shivered in Matty's arms and he gripped her tightly, wanting to never let her go.

-9-

The aurora lit the horizon, casting faint shadows across the road. The group was on the move; a power walk had turned into a light jog. Sunlight crept up behind them faster than they had predicted. Matty meant to stay tuned to these sorts of things, but the sick girl occupied his mind. They had less than an hour to find shelter, and the road ahead didn't exactly promise them hope.

"This isn't going to work," Sam said to Tina. She was jogging next to him. The two had fallen back, farther behind Matty and Lilah. The poor girl couldn't keep the pace much longer. Sam could see she was minutes away from another episode. "We're not going to find what he's looking for at the local Rite Aid."

"No?"

"No," Sam confirmed.

"Well, look on the bright side. At least if it all goes to shit, you won't be the responsible one."

He chuckled even though he didn't feel like laughing. "I guess."

"What do you think of Jarvis?" she asked, keeping her voice down, making sure no one else could hear them.

"I don't know. He's all right, I guess." Sam had agreed with the man on two things: one, Lilah needed help and two, she needed it now. It was only a matter of time before she'd seizure again.

"I can't put my finger on him," Tina said. "I don't know if he's a doctor or a drug dealer."

"You mean *was. Was* a doctor or a drug dealer."

Tina glanced at him, wrinkling her lips and narrowing her eyes. "Semantics, mister."

"We need to get used to 'was' and forget 'is'," Sam told her. "We're not who we were."

"You've become quite the philosopher Costbusters."

Sam glared at her.

"Sorry. I know it still hurts."

He glanced at the ground. "I really thought that was it for us. That Costbusters was the end all be all."

"Still think that?"

Sam thought about it. *How could it be?* "No, I don't think it is."

"You mean 'was'?" she asked, jabbing him with her elbow.

"Aren't you the ball-buster tonight?" he said, a faint grin finding its way onto his features. "It *was* the answer. It's not anymore. Happy?"

"Very."

"So Jarvis?"

"What about him?"

"You don't like him?"

"I didn't say that."

"Well, you didn't say you did."

Tina rolled her eyes. "God, what is it with you?"

"What?"

"I don't know what to make of him. He seems like he knows too much about this withdrawal stuff."

"He didn't really go into detail about how he knows this stuff. Did he?"

"No. I find it weird now that you mention it."

Jarvis had told Bob and Sam how the medication would work, how it would help Lilah. Sam couldn't remember too much about the medication he had studied once upon a time ago, and took the man's word for it. Bob, much in the dark about these sorts of prescriptions, nodded his head and said "sure" a lot. Jarvis also told them what he learned being an animal in Malek's zoo. *Blood*, the drug-infused cocktail a former meth cook named Rollins manufactured, had been given to all his disciples, especially those closest to him. Malek had used the drug in many fashions, mostly injecting the drug into the "meat" or the cooked parts of their victims. The drug was also given as a reward. If one of Malek's followers brought home some good "meat" or reaped important materials from neighboring towns, he rewarded them with a small vial of *Blood*. "It was like some super speed, only there was a moment of—what I'd call downtime—where you're all chill," Jarvis had told him. "Totally fucked up, whatever was in it." Chuck corroborated all of this, claiming the two had overheard many conversations between Malek and his followers. They had also seen Blood in full effect. They didn't elaborate on some of the things they had seen, but Jarvis told them the drug had made the cannibals "hungry." Jarvis went on to say what he *thought* Rollins had put in it, and rattled off the list of medications that would battle the horrible withdrawal symptoms Lilah was experiencing. He told them she was acting like someone dependent on benzodiazepines, almost to the letter. He recalled Rollins saying something about being low on clonazepam, a benzo used for coping with panic attacks, seizures (ironically), and anxiety, a solid concoction for keeping calm and controlled.

"I guess we shouldn't jump to conclusions," Sam said.

"Guess not. We've been wrong about people before," Tina said, nodding ahead. She was talking about Lilah of course, another one of *old* Sam's highlights. She liked *new* Sam a lot better so far. Although it had only been a few days, *new* Sam made far less mistakes.

"Well, if we left it up to Soren, he would have tortured the girl."

"Maybe things would've turned out better."

Sam glanced at her dubiously. "Maybe they would have turned out worse."

Tina smiled. "I like the way things played out. They look cute together."

"It's something all right."

"What? Poppa doesn't approve?"

Sam stared at his son and his first... *girlfriend?* He didn't know what else to call her.

"I don't know..."

"Talk to me."

"Matty isn't..."

"What?"

"He's not..."

"Spit it out, man."

"He's not a lady-killer."

"A lady-killer?" She cracked up, an unexpected high-pitched squeal. "That's the best you could come up with?"

"You know what I mean."

"Is he a virgin?"

"How am I supposed to know?"

"That's a yes." Tina laughed again, this time she covered her mouth.

"I'm glad you're enjoying this."

"I am. Have you given him the talk yet?"

"Of course." Sam cracked a faint smile. "I'm not *that* bad of a father."

"No," Tina said. "You're not."

Sam's smile quickly faded. "You mean it?"

"Yeah," she said, sounding unconvinced. "I do."

"Well, thanks."

"No problem."

They stared at each other, exchanging comforting smiles.

Twenty minutes until sunrise:

Purple light soaked the forked road ahead. Behind them, dawn waged war against the sky, conquering the horizon, golden tones stabbing against the black receding night. No one in the group was comfortable with their situation, being close to sunrise with no destination in sight; no one knew at exactly what point the harmless golden glow would turn heinous, when the human barbecue would begin. They had to think and act fast, or else join the ranks of corpses they had passed along the highway, the blackened bodies they had found melted into the seats of their vehicles.

A sign they had seen miles back stated Philadelphia was only ten miles away. They had avoided Camden, hearing more terrible sounds resonating from the notorious city. The plan was to find the nearest pharmacy and find Lilah the drugs she needed to get well. But the direction away from the city led them down roads with no stores of any kind. Nothing but trees and open fields, nothing that provided them with adequate shelter and the tools to help Lilah through her sickness. They came to a fork, and each choice looked less promising than the other. The road on their left led straight into darkness, away from the small glow creeping over the horizon. Choice number one seemed like it would buy them more time, but no places of refuge appeared visible. Illuminated by solar-powered streetlights, the road to their right looked promising. It seemed a little more lively, and up ahead in the far distance, they could barely make out the shape of what appeared to be a building. Maybe it was a small town. Maybe it was one lone building. But whatever it was, it was better than walking to their fiery deaths.

Bob led the group down the promising path, his arm resting on his wife's shoulder. Sam eyed them with a smidgen of jealousy; this had been the first time he'd seen the two together for more than a few minutes. Seeing Brenda in his arms, happy—the way she used to be with him—stirred past memories, reminded him of the good times they had, even though they were few and far between.

He glanced over at Tina, who only paid attention to the road ahead, mindful of potential hazards that could emerge from the woods on either side of them. She had mentioned packs of wild dogs more than once, and how a large pack could overtake them with ease. Sam didn't give much thought to it. Maybe dogs died the same way humans did when exposed to the sun's almighty rays. Would animals know what's going on? Would they know traveling by day was no longer acceptable? It was an interesting thought and he suddenly realized there was much to learn about this new world. Even though the climate refused to change—fall still felt like fall—the ecosystem surely would as soon as species began to die out. *If they are effected*, he thought. Birdsong of variety whistled from the trees to his right and he wondered what the winged creatures were saying to each other. Were they warning each other of the impending dawn? Or instinctively, did they already know?

A small town formed on the horizon. A wave of relief washed over him, as with the rest of the group. Tina concentrated on the woods as if expecting the trees to sprout arms and grab at them. Sam touched her shoulder and she whipped her head toward him.

"What's the matter?" he asked in a low whisper.

She ignored him, returning her attention on the trees.

Weird...

Everyone was tense and on edge, except Sam who relished his newfound attitude, inviting the numb in. Even when Lilah was on the ground, twitching like a fish on a dock, he felt nothing, no sense of urgency, no desire to help. He couldn't put a finger on his emotions. Had the destruction of Costbusters destroyed a piece of him? It was the only logical explanation for his dull spirit. A piece of him died in that explosion, he was sure of it. He didn't know if he'd ever feel like himself again.

Or maybe you feel guilty, he thought. *Everything that happened was your fault. Wasn't it?*

Maybe. Maybe that's why taking a backseat and letting someone else drive had been so easy. He had caused everything to fall apart. He was responsible for keeping those people safe, protected from the dangers outside.

And he had failed.

Some of them had been slaughtered like farm cattle. The rest had been forced to travel with Soren, what Sam considered a trip toward certain death. He thought about Becky and Dana, wishing he was next to them, holding them like when they were his little girls. He hoped they were safe. If anything happened to them, he only had one person to blame and it wouldn't be Mouth. He thought about what he might do to himself if they found his daughters' charred corpses like they had so many others. He was barely able to live with himself now and he couldn't imagine what guilt of that magnitude would bring.

The group pushed on, the small unnamed town becoming clearer in the dusk. Most of night had been kicked aside by the impending morning light. It was only a matter of minutes before the sun was upon them.

"Hurry!" Bob said, breaking into a sprint.

The rest of the group followed, picking up their pace. Tina rushed to Matty's side and helped him with Lilah. The girl did the best she could, but it wasn't fast enough for Tina's liking. She threw Lilah's other arm over her shoulder and the two of them lifted her toward the finish line. Sam bustled in tow, his mind dodging in a thousand different directions. He ignored the rumbling in his belly, realizing he hadn't eaten anything in almost a day. Lightheaded and dizzy, he retrieved a bottle of water from his pack. He swallowed the last few ounces in a few short swigs and tossed the empty plastic bottle on the side of the road.

"Look!" he heard Jarvis yell. "A pharmacy!"

Sam followed the man's finger and located the building, a simple construction no different than the other small businesses on the long stretch of road. The road they had traveled intersected the downtown area, doctor and law offices surrounding both sides. They were shaped like small ranches, and if Sam hadn't noticed the signs out front shouting out their business, he would've suspected they had stumbled upon a suburban neighborhood. Past the business houses, a few higher buildings stood, no taller than four-stories. Their concrete facades with wrap-around windows differed from the ranches, which had matching vinyl siding and louvered shutters, each with their own unique coordinating colors. A grocery and a pet store neighbored the pharmacy.

The group went directly for the pharmacy, but Sam stopped to have a look through the pet store window. The place was dark, but he could make out the long rows of empty cages. Unlikely they had escaped on their own. Someone had sprung the animals loose.

"Are you coming?" Tina asked, holding the door open. Everyone else headed inside.

Sam turned away from the window and walked toward the pharmacy. As he ducked inside with Tina following closely behind, he couldn't ignore the intense heat crawling over his exposed flesh.

"Anything left?" Bob asked as Jarvis rifled through the long rows of prescription medications.

"Nothing that does us any good. Found a shitload of Viagra, not likely to help anyone though."

"Must be an old people's community nearby," Chuck joked. He held up a box of diapers targeted for the elderly.

110

Ignoring Chuck, Bob turned back to Jarvis. "Looks like you were right."

"I hate to say I told you so," he said, "but I told you so."

Sam tossed a bag on the cashier's counter. "Found a bunch of pain meds. Might come in handy down the road. Couldn't find much of anything else."

"This place has been picked clean," Jarvis added. "Not that they would have had what we needed anyway."

"So where do we go from here?"

Jarvis cracked his knuckles. "You're not going to like it," he said, and told them their next move.

Matty held onto Lilah tightly, fearing she would forever slip away if he let go. Stroking her long, greasy hair, he listened to Jarvis and the others speak about what to do next. Whatever the case was, they needed to find Lilah the proper medication and quickly. The girl did not look well; her eyes grew dark circles around them, her flesh was moist and clammy, and she shivered despite complaining about how hot she was. Heat radiated from her forehead, sweat bubbling from every pore. None of them smelled good, but the stench coming from Lilah rose above the others. Matty figured it was the traces of vomit on her clothing. He hated seeing her like this.

"There's a methadone clinic close to Philadelphia, just outside the city," Jarvis told the group. "I work there. *Worked.* There are detox centers all over the city, but this one is close. We'll have to backtrack a bit, but I'm fairly certain we can get there and back before dawn."

"We'll have to wait for sundown obviously," Bob said.

Matty raised his finger. "We can travel by day. We have to protect ourselves—"

"Matty, that's enough." Bob shot his stepson an uneasy glance. "We discussed this already. It's not safe."

"But Lilah is dying!"

Jarvis winced at this. "I know it sucks, little man, and yes—

there's a possibility she might be in real danger soon—but, she can hold out another day." He had a lot of practice telling important lies, and this one rolled off his tongue gently. He almost convinced himself. "We'll get what she needs and she'll be better. Okay?"

Matty glared at him. "Promise?"

Jarvis turned his eyes away. "Yeah, I do."

"Good," Bob said. "We'll leave as soon as dusk settles."

"Hold on there," Sam said. "I think I should go."

"All right," Bob said. "I think we'll need a few of us to go."

"I think you should stay here, Robert."

Bob cringed at the sound of his full name. "Sam, that's quite all—"

"They need you here," he whispered to him. "Please."

Bob wanted to argue, but he thought better of it and folded his arms across his chest. "Any other volunteers?"

Chuck's hand shot up in the air. "I don't like being cooped up in this place. It's small and smells like my grandparents. I'll go."

"I think three is more than enough," Sam said. "What do you think?"

Before Bob could agree, Tina wedged herself between them. "I'm coming," she said as if it weren't up for debate.

Sam smiled like she had told a lighthearted joke. "I think you should stay here."

"It's dangerous out there."

"Yes. It is. But I think you're better off protecting the people inside here."

"You can't stop me," she said, daring him to try.

"I know I can't. But, please. Stay. For me."

She kicked the idea around. "For you?"

"And for them."

"Fine. But you'll be sorry you didn't bring a woman along."

"I already am," Sam said, turning to Matty. He knelt next to his son and examined Lilah. She was sleeping now, her head resting on Matty's lap. Sam placed the back of his hand on her forehead. The fever burned through her, remaining strong, and he knew waiting until nightfall was cutting it close, if not pointless.

"How is she?" Matty asked.

"She'll be fine," he lied. "Jarvis knows what he's doing."

"He's a stranger. You haven't even known him a week. Since when did you become so trusting?"

It wasn't a terrible question. He knew Matty was in a bad place. The situation had taken a toll on him. Like everyone else, he had surpassed his limits.

"I've turned over a new leaf, Matty."

"Why?"

"Because. Life is much better this way."

"What if you're wrong?"

Sam stretched to ruffle his son's hair, but Matty dodged his hand.

"What if you're wrong?" Matty repeated.

He noticed a change in Matty as well. *Maturity.* His kid had grown up over night, and Sam had missed it. *Love will do that.* It was crazy to think his son was in love with a girl who once ate people. Nevertheless, love was love, and who was Samuel Wright to change his mind? Not the girl Sam would have picked for his middle child to take to the prom, but these were strange times, and strange times brought strange circumstances.

"Well?" Anger mingled with Matty's words. Frustration mounted in his eyes, taking the form of tears.

"I don't know, son."

"Not good enough."

"Listen. You don't understand—"

"No," Matty said. "You listen." He practically growled. What happened to his sweet little boy? "I promised her I wouldn't let anything bad happen." Tears spilled down his face, dripping like summer sweat. "I promised," he rasped through his teeth.

"Take it from a guy who has broken many promises—they aren't always easy to keep."

He grabbed his son's shoulder and stared at him directly in the eyes. Matty returned his father's intense gaze, but his eyes eventually shifted to the unconscious girl on his lap, and remained there until his own eyes grew heavy and carried him off to the land of dreamless slumber.

The trip took longer than Jarvis predicted, which he blamed on a poor memory and five years of heavy drug addiction. They questioned if he knew where he was going when they got lost the first time. Chuck had been more vocal than Sam. Jarvis sensed neither cared much about Lilah nor if she received the proper meds. Chuck seemed too self-centered to care about anyone other than himself, and Sam—well, Jarvis could see how relaxed he was since the destruction of the giant retail warehouse. Jarvis figured he was the only one who cared, the only one who could relate to what the girl was going through.

"I thought you said you lived in Philly, man," Chuck said.

The Ben Franklin Bridge and the City of Brotherly Love stood in the distance. A few lights remained on in office buildings, but not many. It would only be a matter of time before gas generators became invaluable and darkness ruled. In the future, moonless nights would not be easy.

Chuck threw his hands up in the air. "I mean, where the fuck are we?"

"I didn't live *in* Philly. I lived near it. Just give me a minute." Jarvis scanned the map, running his finger down the road they had traveled. "Here. We're here. I think."

"You think?" Chuck said. "Fuckin' great."

"I don't need your negativity, Chuckalicious." Jarvis glared at him. "Curb your attitude."

Chuck muttered something under his breath and turned away.

Another half hour, and Jarvis found the road he'd been familiar with, the one he had taken to work everyday.

"It's up ahead," Jarvis promised them.

Within an hour they arrived at the clinic, the carved wooden sign out front welcoming them to New Beginnings Detox and Rehabilitation Center. Chuck took the lead, hitting the handicap ramp before Sam and Jarvis. He jogged up the ramp and stopped when he got to the front door. He turned the handle, but it was locked. Peering inside, he cursed. Too dark to see. The lights had gone out some time ago and never returned.

"We're screwed," he said.

Jarvis smirked. He bent down and ran his fingers along the brick exterior, making sure to touch each individual brick.

"The hell?" Chuck said, looking down at him. He glanced over at Sam, who could only offer a shrug of confusion.

Jarvis continued examining each brick, tapping them with two fingers. Finally, one moved. Removing the loose brick with both hands, he carefully set it down on the wood planks like a baby in its crib. He placed his hand in the dark cavity in the rehabilitation center's exterior. Digging around, he reached farther and farther until his eyes shot open, remaining that way until he extracted a small object.

"What is it?" Chuck asked eagerly.

Jarvis removed his hand and held up a metallic object as it glistened in the moonlight. A brass key. He stood up and inserted the key in the door handle, turned, and pushed the barrier open. A moldy, musty smell greeted them. He led, and Sam and Chuck followed, their eyes slowly adjusting to the dark inside.

"You know what you're looking for, right?"

Jarvis ignored his companion, a habit beginning to form. He headed straight to the back of the building, passing offices and common rooms as he went. He never looked side to side, never hesitated. He found the room where the good drugs were hidden, locked away so the recovering addicts couldn't abuse them. Locked. Jarvis remembered how he once held a key to that door, but Malek and his gang of trolls had stolen it along with every other key he owned. Didn't matter though. Jarvis knew how to break in. The door was rustic and not in an aesthetically-pleasing way. Its flush luan face was cheap and flimsy and a few forceful kicks later it became a broken piece of garbage with hinges. The jamb broke and the door swung inward, the hinges groaning like the spiral stairs in your favorite haunted house. He smiled at his two companions, pleased with his handiwork. He entered first.

Jarvis checked each desk drawer in the small office, looking for flashlights. He found a small one, no bigger than his middle finger. It didn't brighten the room much, but at least the others could see where they were going. He handed it to Sam. Jarvis didn't need light to see where he was going; the streaks of moonlight beaming between the window blinds were more than enough. He continued making his way around the office, heading to the back where a giant cage stood from the floor to the ceiling. The cage was unlocked, as the workers left it most of the time. He noticed the gate was shut, a good thing. It meant the contents went untouched since The Burn, or the looters had good manners. Jarvis thought the latter was unlikely.

Standing in front of the cage reminded him of both bad and good times. He remembered Mike Braxton and the opportunities Mr. Mike gave him to succeed, and how he pissed it down the drain on many occasions. Relapsing was easy. Getting clean had been difficult. He remembered the day he raided the drug closet, stole every pain killer his pocket could fit, and how he nearly overdosed in the New Beginnings parking lot. A co-worker had found him later that day, half-hanging out his car, his eyes glazed over, and his hands twitching erratically.

Relapsing is easy, he thought, his mouth watering as he scanned the cage and the labels within. *Staying clean is hard.*

He popped open the latch on the cage's gate and the chain-link barrier swung inward, its ancient hinges squealing like rusty shackles. Jarvis stepped inside, immediately grabbing the contents on the middle rack. He stuffed what he could in his pockets until they were full. He turned to Chuck and said, "Grab a bag, if you can find one." Chuck left and returned a minute later with a woman's brown leather purse. He dumped its contents on a nearby desk and offered the handbag to Jarvis.

"It's all I could find," Chuck told him. "Take it or leave it."

Sam smiled behind his hand.

Jarvis grabbed the purse, stuffing the necessary medicine inside.

"Do we really need that much?" Sam asked.

"You never know," Jarvis said. "Besides, it's not all for Lilah.

There are some other useful stuff in here. Coagulants—typically used for the wrist cutters. They help coagulate the blood—"

"I know what it is," Sam said.

"Are we good to go?" Chuck asked. "This place is starting to freak me out, and I don't know if that's the wind outside, or someone's car."

Matty paced in circles, his nerves swimming like a school of frightened fish. Brenda watched from the corner of the pharmacy as he followed the same pattern over and over again, staring down at his feet as if they held answers to the greatest secrets in the universe. She could see his mind was far from home; she could tell. Good mothers could, and Brenda was the best.

Am I?

Being without her children for over three months had practically killed her. Bob had done his best to comfort her, and saw her through those frequent panic attacks when the world spun too fast and her equilibrium couldn't catch up. He told her there was medicine for that, but Brenda would hear none of it. *I need my children,* she had said, *that's all the medicine I need.* And who was Bob to argue?

There had been dreams. Bad dreams. Dreams where Becky was hanging from meat hooks inside a butcher's freezer. This occurred after Malek had taken her hostage, when her world tilted off its axis and her mind constantly spun. The dreams didn't stop there. Once she dreamed Dana was being eaten by wolves. In the dream, Brenda could only watch and look on in horror as they tore her little girl limb from limb, until there was nothing left but blood and bones. In another, Matty was running from her, toward the edge of a cliff. The drop led to an endless black abyss. Matty had been laughing, but she didn't think the game was funny. She couldn't remember what her dream-self had been yelling, but it didn't matter. He reached the edge of the cliff, looked back, smiled, said something like "Don't worry, Mama", something the real Matty Wright would never say, and jumped to his death. She remembered looking down at his broken body before the dream cut out and the image of Matty's limbs twisted and gnarled in unnatural ways haunted her more than Dana and the wolves.

The pacing ate at her sanity. She had never seen him like this. She knew her son had a pure soul and would care for a fly if it landed before him, broken and dying. Matty was compassionate, determined, devoted to whatever the cause. He put all his effort into things, never accomplished anything half-assed like his sister Becky. *He got that from Sam,* Brenda thought. Her ex-husband had put all his effort into things; too bad it was always the *wrong* thing. If he had spent half the amount of effort on things that mattered like family and their marriage instead of work, maybe things would have turned out differently. But she couldn't think about "what ifs."

"Matty?" she said. "Why don't you come sit down?"

He looked up from his feet and found his mother's concerned eyes. She tapped the empty spot on the floor next to her. Matty looked back to Lilah, examined her sleeping body, and figured it was safe to take a break from panicking. He shuffled toward his mother, watching the smile spread across her face with each step. Sitting down next to her, he couldn't stop his eyes from wandering back to Lilah. She lay motionless and Matty hoped her dreams were better than this real-life nightmare.

"Oh, Matty," his mother said, throwing an arm around him and pulling him close. She rested her chin on top of his head and closed her eyes. She wanted to cry, but wouldn't; she'd have to stay strong for him. His body trembled as if a January chill passed through him. She hugged him closer. "You really like this girl?"

"Yes."

"I know it's killing you inside," Brenda continued. "But your father will come back with the others and they'll have what she needs to get better."

Doubt cramped his smile.

"It's okay to be afraid," she told him. "It's okay to show it."

He looked up, tears quickly filling his eyes. "I want her to be okay. I want her to get better, but there's nothing I can do to help. All I can do is wait."

Brenda pushed his shaggy hair away from his face, pressing her lips against his forehead.

"You know," she said, forcing her eyes dry, "when you and your sisters were little, one of you was always sick. If it wasn't you, it was Becky. If it wasn't Becky, it was Dana. And there wasn't a whole lot I could do about it. I felt helpless, too."

Matty said he understood, but she wasn't convinced.

"She'll be okay," Brenda said and hugged her son again.

"I hope so," he said, and cried into her shoulder.

-10-

Bob watched Brenda and Matty from the corner of the pharmacy, holding back tears of his own. He loved Matty as if he were his own son, and hated seeing him like this. He'd feel the same way if it had been Becky or Dana hurting. Bob had no kids of his own; his ex-wife had been unable to carry his seed to term and although they had discussed adoption, nothing ever came of it, which ended up being a good thing. Procreating with that wretched woman would have meant communicating with her after the divorce, and Bob relished in the fact he'd never have to see her face again.

Matty's tears tugged Bob's heart. He wished there was something he could do or say. He was fairly confident that Sam and the others would retrieve the proper medication and save the day. Call it *a feeling,* but Bob had positive vibes and his intuitions usually proved themselves correct. He was right about finding the kids again. *Well, one-third right.* Becky and Dana were still out there somewhere. The world was large, but he continued to promise Brenda they'd find them.

He almost believed it himself.

An idea came to him as he watched Matty and his wife end their embrace. They were still sitting close together, making small talk, and avoiding what really occupied their minds. He walked over to them, unaware of the smile slowly spreading across his face.

"Hey, guys," he said, waving at them. "How is everyone holding up?"

Matty didn't care to answer. Brenda shot him a look: *how-do-you-think-genius?*

"Right," Bob said. He knelt next to Matty and clasped his hand on his stepson's shoulder. "I'm really sorry this is happening, buddy. It upsets me, too. I know you can't help her right now by getting medicine and all, but maybe you can help in a different way." Matty raised his head. "Help all of us, I mean. Once we're ready to push on."

"What?" Matty asked. The tears had slowed.

"I noticed a sporting goods store when we first got to town. Figured maybe we could use more supplies. What do you say?"

Matty looked to his mother for permission, which she gave in silence. Matty looked back to Bob.

"Okay. Sure..."

"Great. It'll be good to get out and get your mind off things." Bob ruffled Matty's hair. "I'll get ready—"

"Maybe she should go with him," Brenda said, nodding to Tina, who was down the aisle, standing in front of a rack stocked with sappy romance novels and beauty magazines. She was glancing at the back jacket of a western romance, the front cover displaying a stock photo of a half-naked cowboy sporting sculpted abs and a lasso wrapped around his bare shoulder. "Tina."

"Her?" Bob asked. He didn't understand.

"Well, she has a gun and she used to be a cop. Maybe it'd be better if she went. And you stayed here. With me."

Bob mulled it over for a minute. "Sure. Yeah. He'll be safer with her."

Brenda smiled and pinched her husband's cheek. "I ever tell you how adorable you are?"

Matty made a puking noise and got to his feet. "I'm outta here."

The light blinded them. Jarvis put his hands over his eyes and stopped walking. Chuck muttered, "What the fuck?" and Sam turned away. The red and blue ambiance Jarvis was familiar with cloaked the front of New Beginnings.

"HANDS WHERE I CAN SEE THEM!" a voice blared through a speaker system.

Keeping the purse over his shoulder, Jarvis pointed toward the sky. Sam and Chuck reluctantly obeyed, their eyes slowly adjusting to the light.

"Please turn off the light!" Sam shouted.

"DROP THE BAG, MISTER!" the voice boomed again.

Jarvis didn't react immediately; he kept his arms raised, and looked to Sam.

"DROP THE BAG!"

Sam didn't move. He kept frozen, looking away from the blinding spotlight. Jarvis slowly reached for the strap on his shoulder. He let the bag fall on the concrete landing.

A tall figure appeared in the light. Bending down to grab the bag, the man said, "Good."

Jarvis fought against the urge to bash the man in the head and take off with the drugs. Maybe it was the man's tall presence. Maybe it was his bulky, intimidating figure. Maybe it was the .38 in his left hand, the one pointed directly at Jarvis's chest.

"Good," the figure repeated, digging through the bag and examining its contents. His Jersey accent was deep and thick and reminded Jarvis of Tony Soprano. "My my. What do we have here? Looking to open up your own pharmacy?" The figure cocked his head back and laughed, a sinister howl making the hairs on Sam's arm stand. "Keep your hands up," he barked. The figure hustled back to the squad car and killed the spotlight. This time the darkness blinded them. It took a minute for their eyes to readjust. "Looks like I got yous for Breaking and Entering. And we'll add Jaywalking to the charges," the cop said. Once their eyes adjusted to the night, they could see the cop clearly. He wore a brown campaign hat displaying a shiny silver star. His cream-colored uniform looked perfectly ironed and clean, save for the little white dusting around his collar which had fallen off a delicious doughnut. With astounding clarity, Jarvis could make out his own reflection in the cop's Big-Texas sunglasses. A wiry handle-bar mustache that took a decade to grow and groom twitched as he spoke. The ends were slightly curled and Jarvis could tell the man twisted them using a super-hold styling product. "Yup, Jaywalking is a huge problem around these parts."

Chuck let his arms fall to his sides and laughed hysterically, so loud and obnoxious it sounded phony. "Jaywalking!" he yelled. "Oh, man. That's a good one!"

The cop rushed forward and bashed Chuck in the mouth with his .38. He dropped to the ground, blood spurting from his mouth. A bloody tooth skipped across the concrete and rolled down the handicap ramp.

"Motherfucker!" Chuck roared, rolling on the ground. He placed a hand over his mouth; blood seeped through his fingers and ran down his hand. "Fuck is wrong with you, man!" The words died behind his hand, but everyone understood what he had said.

Jarvis and Sam rushed forward to help their friend, but Officer Quick-Draw aimed his weapon on them.

"You fuckers stay exactly where you are and don't move a muscle unless you want to eat a bullet. Don't recommend it myself. Metal taste like shit."

Still holding the gun on them, the cop removed the cuffs from his hip and knelt. He rolled Chuck over, who surprisingly enough, went willingly. The officer cuffed him and yanked him to his feet with one hand.

The brute waved his weapon in the air like a baton. "Turn around. Hands against the building."

Sam and Jarvis exchanged uncomfortable glances.

"I said do it!" Officer Friendly bellowed, his voice thunderous.

Slowly, they turned. Jarvis pressed his palms against the rough exterior of his old workplace. Sam did the same with an equal amount of reluctance.

The two of them were cuffed and being escorted to the cruiser. Officer Friendly opened the back door and waved them on. Jarvis went first, Sam next, and the burly policeman tossed Chuck next to them like luggage.

Before they took off, the cop pushed a CD into the disc player and cranked it to MAX volume. The opening to AC/DC's "Highway to Hell" blared through the speakers, so loud no one could hear themselves think. The crunchy guitars Sam ordinarily enjoyed rubbed against his eardrums like sandpaper. The crash symbols needled the center of his brain. Sweat leaked from every pore. A lump rose in his throat.

Highway to Hell. As the cruiser sped down the dark road, Sam wondered if Hell was coming to them.

An hour later, the cop turned off the highway and pulled down a service road, overgrown foliage running its leafy arms across the windows. Springsteen's "Born to Run" played through the speakers and Sam knew what he had to do: RUN. It was the only thing he could think about. He played the scene out over and over again, examining each possible scenario. He imagined himself barreling into the cop as soon as the door opened, knocking him over, and running as far as his legs would take him. However, there were a few problems with that dream: the major being sunrise taking over the horizon, an orange glow beginning to eat away at the night sky. He might be able to hide from Officer Friendly but the sun would eventually find him. The man was armed and clearly not afraid to use his weapon.

The road gave way to an open area, a small municipal building standing in the center. A few cars were parked out front and Sam wondered if the cop had friends and if they were as crazy as him.

"We're here," the cop said, turning Bruce down.

"Officer, this is unnecessary," Sam said.

The cop jammed on the brakes and the cruiser skidded to a stop. Chuck surged forward and slammed his head against the clear bullet-proof divider. He cursed as an egg started to farm on his forehead. Jarvis swallowed hard. The cop craned his whole body toward them, his lips pursed, his eyebrows rising over the gold frames of his aviators.

"Unnecessary?" he asked like it hurt to speak. "Unnecessary?"

"Sir, with all due respect," Jarvis said. "We really don't have time for this."

Sam saw anger flash across the cop's face and jumped in before Jarvis could make matters worse. "I think what Jarvis meant was we know we might have broken the law."

"You *did* break the law," the cop grumbled, his mustache dancing above his lip.

"We did break the law," Sam admitted. "But we have to get back to the pharmacy in Havencrest. The medicine is for a teenage girl who is dying."

"Possession of narcotics," the cop mumbled.

Unable to fathom what was happening, Jarvis covered his mouth with his hand.

"Do you understand?" Sam asked, his voice growing louder. The cop didn't care for his tone and let him know by wriggling his mustache. "A girl is dying. If you don't let us go, then she will die!"

The cop stared at him, his expression remaining the same.

"Don't worry, cupcake," he told them. "You boys will be in and out. Guarantee it."

The cop threw open his door and stepped out, immediately going for the passenger's door. He escorted his prisoners out, the opposite order in which they entered.

Twelve streetlights stood around them, circling the parking lot. A single rope had been tied to the top of each pole. Chuck saw what hung from them first. Jarvis muttered, "Holy shit" before Sam exited the cruiser. When Sam looked up, he spotted them swaying in the strong fall breeze. Twelve charred bodies dangled, one from each pole. Around their necks, the corpses donned necklaced placards that read "GUILTY" in red letters. As the wind blew, the stench of their burnt remains found their nostrils.

The cop smiled. "In and out. Guaranteed."

"TUNNELS"

EPISODE NINE

-1-

A city of rats.

The sun hidden behind ripped tarps. Beams of light shooting down from the sky. People huddled in the streets. Dirty wanderers. Nothing but rats scurrying about, carrying filth and transmitting disease. A woman feeds her small child a slice of stale bread. Now she feeds her a rat, cooked of course, but the meat is squishy and rancid in her mouth. The girl's face twists as she eats but she continues to chew because it's the rat or go hungry. It's eat or die here. Eat or die.

A man with a knife stalks the streets. Papers tumble across the pavement as the wind kicks up. There's a deep chill in the air. Winter is coming. The man with the knife smiles. The dreamer has seen this face before. He's the man who searches for the BAD LITTLE BOYS, the one who keeps them locked in cages; who teaches them lessons by stripping the flesh off their backs. He's a bad man and he must be avoided. But the dreamer can't warn the little girl eating the rat. The dreamer has no voice, only eyes. Scared watchful eyes.

People shuffle past, but the dreamer pays them no mind. The little girl fits the rest of the rat in her mouth and swallows. Sucks in the tail like a spaghetti noodle. She's disgusted, but nourished. She looks to her mother for more, but there is none. There's a city full of rats, but none for her to eat. Her mother tells her if she wants to eat, she must catch her own rats. She's almost an adult now, catch your own rats.

Sour-faced, the girl bids her mother good-day and goes on her way. She pushes through the throng of people in the streets, some peddling merchandise, others trying to find safe passage from Point A to Point B. Everyone acts with haste. The girl spots a rat in the gutter, but it disappears behind the army of moving feet. She pursues the rat like Alice and the White Rabbit.

The man with the knife hidden beneath his black cloak follows too.

The girl squeezes between two people haggling over fruit. Apples. Apples are her favorite, but they cost too much and rats cost nothing. So, rats it is.

The rat bounces behind a stand selling firecrackers. The man operating the stand has one eye and two fingers. He smiles at the girl oddly, and the girl thinks there are other rats in the world, and decides not to go anywhere near the man or his stand. The man waves his stunted hand at her, and she runs in the opposite direction.

She doesn't know it, but girls go missing frequently in the city of rats.

She comes to a clearing and there's a single rat in the middle of the street, nibbling on a slice of bread. She creeps forward, careful not to alert it. I'll get you, rat, she thinks. You'll be the tastiest rat I've ever had!

The dreamer wishes to warn the girl, tell her she's the rat, but it's too late. The man in the cloak draws his knife and his shadow falls over her unnoticed. The city is bathed in shadows, and the shadows come and go as they please. The little girl sneaks behind the rat and crouches, ready to pounce. A man in the cloak reaches, grabs the girl by her hair and yanks her back. The rat hears her scream and flees, finding safety in the closest sewer. The man in the cloak puts the blade to her throat and whispers, "You've been a bad little girl," in her ear. She tries to scream again but the man clamps his hand over her mouth. He digs the blade into her back, careful not to break her skin. "Quiet."

The dreamer watches. The man turns to the dreamer and smiles.

He'll never forget the face.

He never forgets a rat.

-2-

The convoy of vehicles four strong weaved between the permanent congestion on I-295 as the drivers scanned the green roadside signs for their exit. Soren looked in the rearview mirror and saw Shondra staring back at him. It had been like this much of the way; he could feel her gaze on the back of his neck and every time he looked in the mirror her eyes stared back. Soren guided the SUV around some wreckage and charred bodies strewn across the highway haphazardly. There had been instances over the past two days where they had to get out and move obstructions aside, but other than those few instances, the highway had been kind.

If I could only do something about those eyes...

Her stare never left him. He didn't trust her. Not for a moment. He didn't trust any of Sam's leftovers. He sensed Brian had a weak arm he could twist with ease. The Mouth talked a good game, but when it came down to it, he could be manipulated too. The girls were young and impressionable. Dana had already jumped the fence, and Becky wouldn't be too far behind once they realized their father was dead and no one was coming to rescue them. What purpose they would come to serve, Soren didn't exactly know. But they were pawns, and in a game where the stakes were high, in a world that demanded sacrifices, you could never have enough pawns. They'd come in handy, he was sure of it. They all would.

He glanced at Susan in the mirror. She ran her fingers through Dana's hair, curling the ends. Dana didn't seem to mind, but wasn't overly joyed about being her pet either. Susan could muck this situation up. He knew it. She had *that* potential. So did Shondra. They both needed to go. Susan had done well back at the store, played her part perfectly, but since Soren's great *unveiling,* she changed. More confrontational. He didn't like it. He didn't need people to ask questions, he needed people to listen for answers.

Soren glanced over at Brian. He was out cold, had been for the last twenty miles or so. He had been up most of the day, keeping lookout while they hunkered down in an empty office building several miles ago. *Couldn't sleep,* he remembered Brian saying, and there was something odd about the way he said it. Like not sleeping had been a regular occurrence. Soren hadn't thought much of it until now. The man's lips moved in his sleep, like he was having a casual conversation with someone. Eyebrows twitched. Nose wrinkled. A smile, a frown. The occasional whispered word, cryptic and labored.

Soren faced the road, wondering if he missed the exit.

"Stay on 295," Shondra said, "over the bridge. We'll merge with 95 and it's straight all the way through."

Soren eyed her warily. She exchanged a similar look, continuing to bore into him. He checked the gas gauge and noticed it hovered above the big E.

"We're going to need to stop for gas," he said.

"Brian has the map," Shondra said. "If I remember correctly, there should be a rest stop on the highway up ahead before the bridge."

Soren didn't want to wake Brian, but with the map tucked under his right thigh and out of reach, he had no choice. He nudged Brian's shoulder.

"Wake up," he said softly.

Brian didn't budge.

Soren pushed him harder.

"The rats will get us," Brian muttered, barely audible.

"What?" Soren said, whipping his head toward the unconscious man.

"The rats are here," he said, louder this time. *"And they will get us."*

Brian's body twitched. Once. Twice. Three times. Then a series of spastic thrashing. His arms flailed and legs kicked wildly, slamming into the dashboard. Foam sputtered from his lips. His eyes opened, but his pupils disappeared behind clouds of pure white. Shondra reached over the seat and tried to subdue him, to prevent him from hurting himself. Soren reached over him as well while trying to keep his eyes on the road, swerving past the abandoned obstacles scattered before them. He turned to Brian in time to catch him cough up a foamy white substance. It ran down the man's chin, staining the Hawaiian shirt he had stolen from Waldo-Mart.

"I got him!" Shondra said, pointing toward the road.

"Soren!" Dana yelled. "Look out!"

Soren whipped his head forward and gripped the wheel. A deer flashed in front of the SUV and Soren reacted, yanking the wheel to the right. It was too late. The deer stopped, gawking at the headlights, seemingly open to impact. Instead of jamming on the brakes and losing control, Soren stomped on the gas pedal. The SUV surged forward. The deer mewled as the bumper leveled it, its bones snapping underneath the weight of the tires. The SUV jerked violently as they rolled over Bambi

THUD THUD

and once the ruined cadaver was behind them, nothing more than a bloody tumbling shadow in the rearview mirror, they resumed normal speed.

Soren's heart slowly climbed down to its usual beat. He watched Mouth guide his vehicle around the carcass effortlessly. Deciding he should check to see if there was any substantial damage to the SUV, Soren pulled over and parked on a clear stretch of highway.

Shondra slapped Brian's cheek as Soren pulled the SUV to a complete stop.

"Wake up," she said. "Wake up!"

The fog in his eyes finally lifted and Brian returned to the conscious world.

It skipped across the pavement in front of them, tossing bloody gobbets in the air as it tumbled. Mouth saw the accident unfold and slowed. "Christ on a Christmas tree!" he shouted as he careened the car around the mutilated animal. Becky pushed her face against the window and looked down at the squirming creature as it lived out its last agonizing moments. By the time Mouth stopped and climbed out, the deer was dead. "Un-fucking-real."

He jogged over to the carcass. Becky opened the passenger's

door and stood up, her nose and mouth reaching for each other, pulling her face tight. She wanted to puke. Death controlled the air and she found it difficult to breathe. Putting a hand over her nose, she stepped away from the vehicle they had stolen back at the old folk's community.

"Dead," Mouth said, standing over it.

The other two vehicles stopped behind them. One of the drivers stuck his head out of the window and asked Mouth what the hell was going on. He pointed down at the deer and explained.

"You guys hold tight," he told them. "I'm going to check on the others."

Mouth walked toward Soren's SUV and Becky trailed him, keeping his pace.

"Why don't you stay back."

"No," Becky replied.

He rolled his eyes."You ever going to listen to me?"

"Not likely."

Ain't that the truth.

"Fine," Mouth said sharply; a battle not worth the fight. "But keep a safe distance."

"I want to make sure Dana is okay."

Mouth understood. "Me too."

When they reached the SUV, Soren was standing outside the open passenger's side door. He was yelling and Mouth couldn't make out exactly what had his cock in a knot. Whatever it was had him concerned and breathing heavily. Standing on the backseat floor, Shondra leaned over the door, hovering above Soren. She was calling Brian's name and Mouth didn't hear him answer.

"What's going on?" he asked.

No one answered.

"Brian," he heard Soren say. "Wake up you bastard."

"Come on, Bri," Shondra called. Mouth saw her eyes twinkle in the moonlight. "Please wake up."

Unable to see over Soren's lanky figure, Mouth stood on his toes and peered over his shoulder. Brian rested in the reclined passenger's seat, and he knew something was wrong. The man was unconscious. Breathing, but unconscious.

"He woke up before we stopped," Shondra told Mouth and Becky.

Soren slapped Brian's cheek.

Nothing.

"What the hell happened to him?" Mouth asked.

Soren rotated slowly, his movement lacking enthusiasm. "Your friend decided he wanted to go on a little dreamwalk and not return."

"The fuck?"

Soren stepped aside, allowing Mouth an unobstructed gander at his friend. Mouth didn't care for the smirk tugging Soren's lips to one side of his face. Instead of dishing out another smart-ass remark, Mouth looked past him and eyed Brian's unconscious body. He didn't look dead or injured and Mouth couldn't spot any visible wounds. Brian looked...

Asleep.

"He said 'the rats' are coming," Soren said. "Any clue what that means?"

Dreamwalk.

"Zero." Mouth approached his sleeping friend and placed his hand on Brian's forehead. A little warm to the touch, but not enough to suggest a fever. "He doesn't look sick."

"He started foaming at the mouth and had a seizure."

Mouth glanced at Shondra, who disputed nothing. He rotated, pulling back from Brian's forehead.

"So, let me get this straight—one minute he's dreaming, the next he's going all Linda Blair on you?"

Soren didn't find Mouth humorous, and wasn't ashamed to show it. He bared his teeth like some primal savage, and Mouth—for a second—thought Soren might strike him with a closed fist.

"I don't remember saying he was possessed."

"He was mumbling nonsense and spitting foam at'cha?" Mouth asked, counting the number of weird things on his fingers. "Sounds like possession to me."

"He wasn't mumbling nonsense." Soren suddenly appeared

haunted, his complexion matching the moon above, which worried Mouth because Soren didn't seem like a guy who scared easy. "He said, 'the rats will get us.'"

"Well, you got a goddamn rodent problem? Maybe we should pull off the next exit and find our neighborhood exterminator."

Soren placed his hands on his hips. "We don't have time for this. The bridge is up ahead. We need to cover as many miles as we can while it's still dark. Besides..." He glanced at the trees off the highway. "We don't know what might be out there."

"*What* might be out there?" Mouth asked. "You expecting werewolves or something, fucknuts?"

"No. Flesh-eating maniacs maybe. Or animals. Bears. Packs of wild dogs. God knows." Soren looked to Shondra. She continued to stare down at Brian, worried and wishing he'd wake up soon. "I'll put him in the back for now. He's not dead, so he'll wake up eventually." He didn't sound convinced of this last bit. "Susan, help me get him in the back."

Susan walked past Mouth, brushing shoulders with him. He knew her intent, but he didn't allow himself to fall into the trap. She wanted him to react harshly and he wouldn't give her the satisfaction. He smiled at her, hoping to plant himself deeper beneath her skin. She wrinkled her nose and Mouth won the small battle in what he knew would be a long war.

As Mouth walked away, heading back toward the other vehicles so he could inform the others, he heard Soren ask Dana if she wanted to be his "little navigator."

Emphatically, she answered, "Yes."

-3-

"**Everything okay?**" **Becky asked,** standing between the car and the passenger's door. Mouth shuffled back, his eyes fixed on the pavement. Although she hadn't known Mouth long, she could tell something was bothering him. He bit his lower lip feverishly. His eyebrows created waves on his forehead. Rubbing his chin, he glanced up when Becky repeated her question; "Everything okay?"

"Yeah," he said, trying to play it cool. "Life is fucking peachy."

"You don't look like everything's okay."

He rolled his eyes, and Becky found the role reversal comedic and sad all at once. "Brian passed out and mumbled some nonsense, had a seizure, and everyone has their cocks in a knot. Other than that, everything is cream and sugar, baby, cream and sugar."

"Do you think Dana's okay?" She had decided to hang back and let Mouth investigate after all.

"She's doing great. I think she got promoted to Satan's Little Helper."

"Huh?"

"Nothing." Mouth climbed back in the driver's seat and Becky plopped down on the warm seat. "SUV's fine. Bumper has a few dents and a splash of blood. I think there might be some damage below, but nothing to keep the bastard from running. We'll see though. Won't really know until we start moving."

Nodding her head, she pretended to care. In that moment she wanted to get out, run over to the SUV, and wrap her arms around her sister, tell her everything was okay, and to stop following Soren and Susan around like the brainless follower of some suicidal cult. Instead, she listened to roar of the SUV's engine and sat in the crimson glow of its brake lights. The SUV lurched forward and before Becky could decide, Mouth cranked the engine into existence and followed the SUV toward the bridge.

Becky remembered what it was like the day of The Burn. How chaotic it had been. She recalled her father driving like a maniac, swerving in and out of traffic, almost killing them in the process. Now she was thankful for his aggressive driving skills; if he hadn't been daring, someone would find *their* bodies on the side of the highway, toasted pickings for famished night critters. As they drove, Becky spotted glowing eyes in the darkness to her right and wondered what creature they belonged to. Wolves? Bears? Mountain lions?

Her thoughts pulled away from what might be lurking in the wilderness and she found herself thinking about Dana again. Poor Dana. Had the whole Soren/Susan problem been her fault? She guessed she could have been a little easier on her. Not so... *bitchy.* If her father was here he might have slapped her. She shook her head. It wasn't right to think that way. The slap had been a mistake, and he apologized for his actions. Although she forgave him, she still couldn't shake the memory. Even after everything, the countless bodies she had seen, the massacre at Costbusters, *Chris Atkins,* she still couldn't let that moment go. Her father hit her. Across the face. With his hand. On purpose. In front of her siblings. If she thought about it long enough she could still feel the burn on her cheek. *I have issues.* In the time she should have spent mourning the loss of her make-out buddy, she couldn't shake the awful memory from her thoughts. Her father's hand and her face becoming one and the mark it left. *Yup,* she thought, *major issues.*

"What the hell is wrong with you?" Mouth asked.

Becky snapped out of her reverie and looked ahead, toward the bridge, its magnitude taking up the entire windshield.

"Just thinking."

"About..."

"Dana."

"She's fine. Other than being trapped with Captain Insane-O and the Evil Mistress, that is."

Becky wanted to smile, but her emotions would not allow it. Instead, she gave the bridge her catatonic attention and hoped Mouth would uncharacteristically keep his face-hole shut, an event unlikely to happen.

"You know, Becky, if you ever want to talk, get anything off your chest, I'm here to listen." He snorted. "I mean, hell, I have nothing else to do." Other than Mouth, the drive had been extremely quiet. The only thing occupying the radio waves was static. They found a sleeve of compact discs above the sun visor, but whoever previously owned the Hyundai only listened to Bluegrass and Smooth Jazz and if it wasn't Led Zeppelin or Motorhead, Mouth didn't want anything to do with it. A saxophone sounded like dying geese and he preferred silence over that ruckus. "So, if you want to share your feelings, or talk about your little boyfriend—"

"I don't want to talk about him," she snapped. "Ever again. Understand?"

"Yeah, sure. I get it."

"I'm sure you do."

He flinched as if her sarcasm cut him. He parted his lips, thought better of it, then decided to open them again. "I know I come off as smooth as sandpaper and about as warm as a mausoleum, but I've been through some shit. Like *real life* shit."

She continued concentrating on the bridge, unimpressed with Mouth's encouraging tone.

"I never bothered to tell anyone this—mostly because no one fucking asked—but I lost my wife in The Burn." Mouth watched her twitch, his story clearly striking a chord. "She was home when it happened. On Hospice. Cancer got a hold of her, really fucking bad. Danced around her body for a decade. First it was in her tits and she beat that shit. Few years later, the bastard came back with vengeance and got into a place inappropriate to tell you, but you're a smart girl and I'm sure you can figure it out. Beat that shit, too. She was cancer free for over five years when it came back again, roaring like a hound from Hell, spreading faster than the Clap at an Atlantic City motel. They said it got into her spine this time, deep into her bones. Doctors—pssh, doctors, what a fuckin' joke—the doctors said she didn't have much time, gave her six months to cross out the last remaining things on her bucket list." The tears came unexpectedly. He had gotten through his tale smoothly until that moment. They all came at once, streaming down his face. Becky was staring at him now, engrossed, her face begging for more. "Sorry. Didn't expect this to happen. Anyway," he continued, wiping the tears away, "she loved to have the shades open so she could stare out the guest room window. The view faced a grassy meadow and a children's playground. She liked to watch the kids play because it brought her back to a positive time in her life, or some shit like that. The day of The Burn, I opened up the blinds, let the warm sun on her face, kissed her on the forehead, and headed down to your Dad's store to grab a few items. And I..." He stopped staring out the window, the massive bridge looming before him. Becky wondered if he was still paying attention to the road and before she could say something, he said, "And I wanted to take my sweet time." A touch of guilt grabbed his vocal chords, squeezing his words. "When you're in that situation, and you spend every waking minute waiting on someone hand and foot, you don't get a lot of time to yourself. Fuckin' rare I got to get out of the house. Even when the nurses were there, taking care of my baby every step of the way. How could I leave her? I couldn't. I felt bad taking ten minute trips to the pharmacy, because I knew she was home, suffering, and I wasn't there to hold her hand, kiss her forehead, tell her everything was A-fucking-okay. But not on that day. That day, for whatever reason, I had enough. I wanted... some time. For me. I fuckin' deserved it, didn't I? I spent every waking minute catering to that woman, being the best damned husband I could. But I couldn't do it any longer. A part of me wanted to run away. Sure I loved her, loved more than most men love their wives, I'd wager. But I couldn't... couldn't do it anymore. Couldn't watch her die the slow death. The cancer ate my spirit the way it ate her bones. So I went to Costbusters, and turned a twenty-minute trip into two hours. I talked. And talked. Talked to every fuckin' person I could find. I talked to some old lady about cat litter for ten minutes and I never owned a cat in my fuckin' life. Talked to Brian about the bathrooms and how dirty they were, even though I never stepped foot in them. I even smoked a cigarette with Chris—um, one of the employees— and I haven't touched tobacco since 1989. Fuck..."

Becky couldn't speak, although she wanted to. Tears brimmed her eyes, and she wiped them away with the back of her hand.

"Anyway, I left her. Left her for the sun." He shook his head, suddenly wishing he hadn't exposed his dark secret. It was meant to unburden him, but the admission left him feeling like the biggest piece of shit who had survived The Burn. "The sun didn't kill my wife though. Wasn't the cancer either." He looked to Becky, expecting her to agree with his logic. *"I did.* I killed her." He sobbed, trapping loud outbursts in his throat. "I was her family," he moaned, "and I was supposed to be by her side to protect her and make her feel safe, and I abandoned her."

She placed her hand on his shoulder and cried with him.

-4-

The bridge was no less crowded than the roads before it. Slowly, the caravan slithered along, squeaking between the gaps left by abandoned cars and trucks. Shondra's most pressing concern was discovering the road blocked with downed vehicles and no possible way around. There were so many obstacles on the road it shouldn't have surprised her. But a blocked road meant they'd either have to travel back and waste precious gas or hoof it, and Shondra was in no mood to walk across the country. She didn't know how long before the preferred method of transport ran its course, but she figured it wouldn't be long before they found themselves on foot again. She wanted to enjoy the time in the car, catch up on sleep, and relax. Think about nothing for a good long while, but she couldn't help staring at the eyes in the rearview mirror. Those dark eyes harbored secrets she wanted—no, needed—to know.

(How exactly did he survive that stunt back at the Costbusters?)

She watched the crow's feet under his eyes jiggle as his lips stretched into a subtle smirk.

You proud bastard, she thought, hating Soren and what he was doing to Sam's youngest. Dana sat in the passenger's seat, running her little finger along the map, calling out possible routes and nearby towns where there might be gas and food. She had gotten as far as Kentucky when Soren laughed and told her not to get too far ahead of herself. He rubbed Dana's head and messed up her hair, but the girl didn't seem to mind. Soren chuckled like a father proud of his daughter's attempt at something beyond her capabilities. As he did this, he glared at Shondra in the mirror. And winked.

A thought percolated: Shondra could remove her belt and wrap it around Soren's throat and strangle him to death before his faithful servant could react. Susan was long and slender, like a snake in a woman's body. Compared to Susan, Shondra was a horse. She figured in a fight to the death, she would snap the skinny bitch's neck with relative ease. Unless she deceived her in some way, like any good snake was prone to do.

She fingered her belt buckle. She released the prong from its notch when Soren slowed the SUV like he meant to stop.

They parked on the bridge's apex and looked down at the crowded declination. Just after the bridge where the road was flat again, several cars blocked free passage to the city beyond. They couldn't see exactly what caused the vehicles to congregate there, but a huge circle formed in the middle of the pileup.

"What happened?" Dana asked.

"Look's like a... sinkhole?" Susan replied, although she too was uncertain of the sight before them.

Soren slipped the SUV into gear and rolled toward it. "I don't know. But let's get a closer look. There might be another way around."

Sinkhole, Shondra thought. She didn't like the idea of getting closer to it. They had a great vantage point from atop the bridge; even from the backseat she could see there was no way around it. "Maybe we should find another way around," Shondra suggested. She didn't mean for the fear to bleed into her words, but they had and now Soren and Susan knew she was afraid. More ammo for them to sling.

Soren glanced at her in the mirror. "Frightened?"

"No," she snapped. "But there's no need to get closer if we don't have to. I mean we all saw—"

"We don't know what we saw. We were too far away. A closer look will tell us what to do next." He spoke confidently, although for some reason Shondra thought his answer had been for show, a mask over his true intentions.

Her thoughts turned to the belt again.

"Don't you agree?" Soren asked, the tone of his voice uncharacteristically high.

Mockery.

Before she could protest, her eyes fell on Dana, the girl's head appearing between the two front seats.

"Relax, Shondra," she said. "Soren's got this."

Shondra faked a smile. The muscles around her lips ached.

They parked twenty feet from the fifty-car smashup. Soren stepped out first and Mouth was right behind him, waving his hands in the air like someone trying to pump up the crowd at a football game.

"What the fuck are we stopping for now?" he asked, his voice shaky and lacking the intensity of his usual self. "Another piss break? You all got the bladders of a bunch of pregnant broads!"

Soren ignored him and walked forward. He sensed Susan and Shondra following him and put his hand up. He waved them off and they obeyed his command. Squeezing between two vehicles extremely close to touching, Soren looked ahead, trying to seek a way through. He didn't locate any. He climbed an F-150 and hopped on top of the cab. He looked over the crowded mess and determined there was no way around. He knew there wouldn't be from their view from the bridge, but still, he had to see what had caused the obstruction. Soren hopped onto the hood of a burgundy Explorer. From there he jumped on top of a yellow Corvette, sandwiched between a gray Sonata and an old pale-green Impala. He made his way across the roofs of a few more vehicles until the giant hole in the ground became visible. He heard Susan call to him, yelling, "Be careful!" but he ignored her. He barely heard her over his own thoughts.

Keeping a safe distance in case the sinkhole wanted to swallow more of the world, Soren stood on his toes and looked down into the dark, endless void. After he satisfied his curiosity, he turned to his followers. Almost all of them were out of their vehicles, watching him with anticipation. Some of them feared for his safety, while others wished the sinkhole would open and gobble him up like the mouth of some mythical monster. He carefully made his way back, being careful not to lose his footing on the vehicles' rooftops. Once he was safely across, he jumped back on the pavement and glanced at his following.

"Just as we thought," he said. "No way through or around."

"No fucking shit," Mouth said. "I thought the sinkhole was pretty fucking apparent."

"'Watch your mouth, Mouth," Dana snapped.

"Dana," Becky grunted.

Mouth put his hand on her shoulder. "No... she's right."

Dana jerked her head and wrinkled her nose at Becky.

Something was off about Mouth, Soren thought. He couldn't place his finger on it. Had he been crying? Soren saw the moonlight twinkle in Mouth's glossy eyes. Yes. The man had recently shed tears.

"We need an alternate route," Soren announced. "Little miss," he said to Dana. "Would you do us the honor?"

She smiled. Unfolding the map, she took one last glance at her sister before returning to her duties. Becky wasn't happy, but Dana didn't seem to care much. She looked pleased with the ugly look on her sister's face.

"We'll have to head back over the bridge," she said, "and head... *south.*"

"South?" Soren asked. "You sure?"

"Yes. We'll head south for a little before making our way west again." She showed the map to Soren. "See. We'll take this road. It might not be as crowded as the highway."

Impressed, Soren's mouth fell into a unique, pleased smile. "South it is," he agreed, patting the girl on the back.

-5-

"Great!" Mouth yelled, slamming the car door shut. His sadness had melted away and anger settled in its place. Becky had watched his face grow rosy on the walk back to the car. "Now we're being led by the psychopath's twelve-year old protegé!"

With her attention adrift, Becky faced the window. The brake lights on the SUV painted her face in a faint red glow. She watched the vehicle head in reverse, back over the bridge. Mouth sighed and pushed the car in first gear. They sped after them.

"Sorry, honey," Mouth said. "Didn't mean any offense toward your sister."

"Yeah, I get it," she replied, continuing to stare outside. The ocean of dead cars and trucks zipped past her and nausea set in. Her brain ached, as if melting into a gelatinous ooze inside her skull. Her stomach somersaulted. Bile crept up the back of her throat. She closed her eyes, hoping the feeling would soon subside.

She thought malnutrition was the culprit of her motion sickness. She longed for a Caesar salad with tender, juicy grilled chicken strips sprinkled with Parmesan cheese. Or a turkey club sub sandwich topped with extra pickles. Her mouth watered as she thought of food she'd never eat again. She needed something, anything, and soon. She was sick of eating canned beans (or canned anything for that matter) and stale potato chips. She wanted shrimp and scallops. Filet mignon. Tuna steaks. Something tasty and savory. Something filling.

"Whatcha thinking about?" Mouth guided the car to avoid a collision with a truck and a minivan. Glass littered the road and Becky thought it was pure dumb luck the Hyundai's tires survived; loud popping noises interrupted the silence as they rolled over the sparkling lake of glass. Mouth winced, waiting for the inevitable hiss of escaping air, but it never happened and the car rolled on untouched. He turned back to Becky, her eyelids clenched together like angry fists. She gripped the armrest as if she were falling. "You okay?"

"Don't feel well." Her stomach crawled up her throat. She

opened the door without giving much thought. Luckily there was enough room between their car and the closest disabled vehicle. She stuck her head out and vomited. Mouth slowed the car down and eventually stopped. The two cars behind them followed their lead. Soren noticed they weren't being followed and parked in the middle of the bridge. Becky continued her sickly assault on the pavement, tossing her stomach's contents until there was nothing left but acidic bile. Although it burned coming up, she already felt better.

Mouth turned away. He hated puke. The sight of it made him want to join. The sound of the slop smacking the pavement didn't help matters. His stomach rotated and he thought about anything and everything to take his mind off it. He thought about Sundays in September in the old world; football, Sam Adams, chicken wings, and pumpkin pie. To block out the sour stench of vomit, he imagined the wood-smoke scented nights in chilly October. He breathed it deep into his lungs like the cigarettes he used to smoke back in his Navy days.

Becky closed the door while wiping her mouth on her sleeve. She faced the windshield, her skin as pale as moonlight.

"You gonna be okay there?" he asked, the smell of autumn fading away.

"Yes."

"Good."

"I think it was the way I was looking at the cars when you were driving."

"Uh-huh."

A tear rolled down the side of her face. She tried to stifle the whimper, but failed.

"There, there," he said, patting her shoulder. "Getting sick happens. I used to get motion sickness all the time when I was a kid. My mother—"

"It's not that. I can't do this anymore."

"Do what?"

"Live like this," she said, wiping her nose. She sniveled and her lips trembled softly. A tear leaked from her eye, ran down the side of her face, and dribbled off her chin, disappearing in the darkness below.

"Don't say that."

"I miss my family. I miss..." she breathed deeply and exhaled slowly. "The way things used to be."

"We all do, honey. But we gotta deal. Things'll get better. They always do."

"When?"

Mouth didn't know exactly. He nodded as if to say *well, you got me.*

"When we reach Alaska?"

"I guess so. Won't really know until we get there."

"I can't do this." She slammed her head back against the headrest. "And I feel horrible for having those thoughts when..." She paused and grabbed her mouth as if she might puke again.

"When what?"

She blocked an outburst with the back of her hand. "When so many have died trying to survive."

"You're not a bad person for having those thoughts," he said.

"I feel guilty. But I don't want to live like this anymore. I feel like... like ending it." Her body shuddered as she cried harder.

"It's natural to feel this way."

"No it isn't," she argued. "I should want to live."

"I can think of at least twenty people who disagree with you." He threw his arm around her shoulder. One of the cars behind him beeped the horn, but Mouth ignored it. "Remember Sherry? The gal who fixed your father up when he got that arrow stuck in his leg."

Of course she remembered.

"Soren promised he'd bring her husband back, but that never happened. The cannibals, they killed him. Maurice, I think his name was."

"I remember."

"Sherry killed herself on the first night. Never told no one except for Brian and Shondra, mostly because I don't think anyone else gave much a shit. I found her hanging from an oak tree about fifty feet from camp. She was as blue as the sky. She was still swaying back and forth, so I couldn't have missed her by more than a few minutes. Even if I had found her in time, what would I have done? She wanted to die, and who the fuck was I to deny her?"

"You're not making me feel any better, Mouth."

"Shit, I never was one for motivational speeches." He sighed deeply, slowly resting his back against the soft leather. Another horn sounded, followed quickly by two more. The convoy was growing impatient. "The point I'm trying to make here is your feelings are natural. The world is in the fuckin' shitter and the future is fuckin' bleak. But I'm not checkin' out yet and neither are you. I promised your father I'd look after your sister and you and that's exactly what I'm-a-fuckin' do. And if you..." He stopped himself. He had her attention now, her glossy eyes fixed on his. "If you kill yourself, Missy, I'll be a fuckin' wreck. You got your father out there somewhere looking for you, and when he catches up I don't want to be the one to tell him I found you with your wrists slashed open or hanging like Sherry." He shook his head. "Uh-uh. No way. So listen to my idea. We stick together. We survive. We look after your sister, and keep an eye on this Soren character and his mindless robots and we beat this game together. As a team. You and me. Whaddya say?"

She looked at him, the beginnings of a smirk finding her face.

"When you put it like that, it doesn't seem so bad."

"Guess I'm better at speeches than I fuckin' thought."

The tears evaporated and her lips stretched, curling at the corners. She even chuckled. Mouth rubbed her shoulder again, reassuring her even though the world was a complete clusterfuck and the chances of surviving dwindled each day.

"Just gotta stay fuckin' positive," he said.

With her mind stuck in negative muck, she couldn't promise anything. Every time she thought about how lucky she was to be alive, she thought of Chris Atkins and his dead, bleeding corpse. Sometimes he came to her when she closed her eyes, his dead eyes staring at her, his mouth twitching to life. She told herself the nightmares would die with time, and she believed herself too, but she didn't know how long it would take, and how much she could take of them.

"Positive," she said, nodding again.

A horn blared behind them. Mouth rolled down the window and shouted, "All right you fuckwads! I'm fuckin' going! Jesus's Balls!"

Mouth put the car in gear and trundled forward.

-6-

Two hours later, the convoy passed a sign welcoming them to Arthur, Maryland. After the detour, Soren urged the group to push themselves as far as they could before dawn hit. He told them via walkie-talkie they wouldn't stop and when they did, he'd find them shelter from the dangerous daylight.

They took the back routes like Dana had suggested, and as predicted, the two-lane roads were clean and free from abandoned vehicles, homeless drifters, and desperate, animals willing to give human flesh a try in order to prevent starvation. He told the group above everything, packs of wild dogs scared him most. They were no longer man's best friend and he urged his following to steer clear of all animals, but especially dogs. Dana thought it was silly, but promised Soren she'd listen to his orders. She had always loved dogs, *puppies* specifically, but never had one growing up. She always asked for a puppy for Christmas, but her father always said they were too much work and her mother never cared much for pets. When her mother remarried, she tried to get Bob to take on the added responsibility, but he seemed to share her father's opinion on the matter. They compromised and told her she could have a cat, but cats were "stupid" and not as fun as puppies.

As the group passed another ransacked shopping plaza, Susan shifted uncomfortably in her seat. She knew Soren was leading the charge and wouldn't dare speak against his decisions—not in front of the others—but the decision to press on with dawn quickly approaching had her in jitters. Sweat dribbled down her forehead; she thought if she were to die, it wouldn't be on someone else's folly. She leaned forward, sticking her head between the front seats.

"Um, Soren," she said timidly. "We passed another strip mall. Seemed empty. Safe. You think we should double back before the sun comes up? It's been getting light awful quick these last few days."

For a second, Soren didn't acknowledge her. He looked in the rearview and stared directly at her. Then to Shondra, who sat next to an awake, yet relaxed Brian. The man had awoken about an hour ago, and the group had to explain to him what had happened. He laughed it off, admitted he got occasional seizures, and promised it was no big deal. He didn't elaborate any further, and Soren sensed the man was hiding something, and with good reason. When it came to the words he muttered unconsciously, Brian said he didn't know, told him it was only a dream. Soren didn't believe him, not for a single second.

"Sit back," he commanded. "Your face is hogging up the mirror."

She dropped the act and her smile ran like wet paint. Susan leaned back slowly, her eyes never drifting from Soren's. He ignored her, and stepped on the gas, propelling the SUV toward wherever he had mapped in his mind.

Dana grinned. She didn't like Susan, finding the way Soren spoke to her enjoyable. She giggled beneath her hand as her eyes fell back on the map.

Brian sat up. Shondra pushed on his shoulder, trying to ease him back down, but he waved her off, and mouthed the words, "I'm fine."

His movement caught Soren's eyes. "Are you all right, Mr. Waters?" Soren asked.

Brian rubbed his right eye with the heel of his palm. "I feel great," he said. "But I have to ask; where exactly are we headed?" When Soren didn't respond, Brian asked, "What was wrong with that strip mall back there? Isn't the sun coming up?"

"Why don't you lie down and take another nap. You seem to be good at that."

"Yeah," Dana said, "and talking in your sleep like a weirdo."

Susan made a clicking noise with her mouth and tongue. "Now, Dana, it's not nice to call people names."

"Indeed, young lady." Soren's words came attached with a grin, telling Dana not to take them seriously.

Brian pushed his shaggy hair aside. His head felt empty, the world around him foggy, like a piece of his mind remained inside a dream; he usually knew the difference between the waking world and the one his mind sometimes visited, but today was different. Today the visions clung to him like dogshit to a shoe.

Why can't I have good ones, he thought. *Like hitting the lottery or sleeping with that hot cashier,* he used to think. But no, they were never good. It was always something terrible. A fatal accident. A robbery. A house fire. In the past, when he was a kid, the nightmares were vague, resembling nothing of reality, and he never thought about them much. It wasn't until his teen years he made sense of them. They never happened frequently. Once a year. Seldom twice. He remembered the first time he knew they were more than dreams. He had envisioned a priest inviting an alter boy to the back room for snacks and juice. The rest of the nightmare made him sick to his stomach, but the images burned themselves into his mind for eternity. A week after the dream he opened the newspaper and found a story on the altar boy from his dream. He didn't know it was the same boy for sure because his picture and name had been withheld, but he knew. He knew and there was no denying it. The boy had made the press, not for what happened to him in the backroom, but for what had happened to the priest years after the abuse. One lazy afternoon, the boy stumbled upon the priest taking a nap in the confessional and decided to take a kitchen knife to the holy man's throat. Another priest found him later that night, his throat slashed wide ope

n, puddles of red covering the seat and floor.

After that night, Brian hated the dark.

He looked out the window. A tall green sign stated "Chesapeake Bay Bridge and Tunnel/1 Mile" and an eerie chill cut through him. Shondra must have caught his reaction because she placed her hand on his shoulder and asked if he was okay.

"Fine," he said. "Just a little chilly."

The rats are coming...

He looked at Soren's seedy eyes in the rearview mirror and realized they were already here.

-7-

The first of two tunnels loomed before them. Soren rolled the SUV to a stop. The sun threatened the horizon behind them, but the sky above was dark, full of stars refusing to scatter. Soren glanced at his passenger, his little navigator. She smiled back at him, approving their direction.

"What are we waiting for?" Brian asked.

Soren didn't answer. Instead, he took his foot off the brakes and stepped on the gas. The SUV zoomed forward. He clicked on the brights and the tunnel walls illuminated. The road looked clear and free of debris, which immediately threw Soren into a state of suspicion. Sure, the back and side roads had been relatively clean, but the major highways and interstates had been like a parking lot. The Chesapeake Tunnel and Bridge was a major road, and its unblocked entry seemed too good to be true. With the orange beast rising behind them, there was no time to double back.

The SUV led the way, and the other three vehicles followed closely behind. The first quarter of the tunnel was dark, the power around these parts no longer operable. There was no one left to man the power grids. The fact that the power was still on in some areas surprised him. It was only a matter of time before all the lights went off, and *stayed* off.

The second half of the tunnel split three lanes wide. Mouth pulled up next to the SUV, the other two vehicles hanging back. Soren glanced over, saw him motioning to roll down the window. Soren obliged.

"A little fucking creepy, ain't it?" Mouth yelled. They had slowed to about five miles per hour. "I mean, not a single fucking car?"

"Maybe God has graced us with safe passage after all."

"Ah, boo-fuck!" Mouth said. "I don't like a single thing about this. The others are having second thoughts." He jerked his thumb at the vehicles behind him.

"And how would you know that?" Soren asked.

Becky held up the walkie-talkie.

"Maybe you should try channel two once in a while," Mouth said, slowing to fall back in line.

Soren maintained his speed. *Channel two?* He glanced at the walkie-talkie Dana had stuffed between the seats. He snatched it from its resting place and did as Mouth suggested.

"(crackle crackle) fucking scared, man (crackle crackle) crazy. It's so dark in here (crackle crackle) deathtrap."

"Calm down, dude. I can barely he—(crackle crackle) tunnel sucks for (crackle)—municating. Just calm—"

"—urning around."

"No, don't—"

(crackle crackle)

"Bad feeling—"

"Dude, don't—"

"Fuck this—"

(crackle crackle)

"Come on, goddammit—"

"Sorry, bro—"

(crackle crackle)

The rest of the conversation was a steady mixture of static and lost syllables. Soren looked into the rearview in time to see one of the cars slam on the brakes. The tires squealed as the driver cut the wheel. The other car slowed to a stop and the driver scrambled out. He waved his hands at the other car, trying to talk sense into the driver, but he had already made up his mind. The passengers seemed to agree because no one hopped out when they had the chance. The car zoomed toward the exit, toward the approaching dawn.

"Idiots," Susan muttered. "They'll die."

What began as a band of forty, had dwindled to almost a quarter that number. Between the suicides and the ones who thought they had a better chance of surviving by *not* traveling across the country, and now a car carrying five once-loyal followers, they were left with fourteen people. Mouth and Becky in the car behind them. Susan, Brian, Shondra, Dana, and himself in the SUV. And the eight people in the minivan. That was it. His inventory was running low.

The world is never short on pawns, he thought, stepping on the gas.

Brian braced himself for a huge let down. Shondra squeezed his hand; she could feel it too. Things had been too smooth for something not to go terribly wrong. He closed his eyes and envisioned a massive pile up at the end of the tunnel, fifty or sixty cars strong. Brian offered Shondra a quick smile, and she returned it with one of her own; both smiles were given by two people good at faking smiles. On the inside they were both kicking and screaming, wanting to get as far from this situation as possible.

"It'll be okay," Shondra whispered, giving his hand another comforting squeeze.

Brian smirked. "How do you know? You psychic?"

Silent laughter.

Soren must have heard them, because he immediately became alert, staring at them in the mirror.

"Something you two want to share?" he asked.

"Not really," Brian said. He didn't like the way their self-appointed leader glared at him. Did he suspect something? *Did I say something crazy in my sleep?* They told him he rambled about rats, but that was as far as it went. Or did it? He suspected Soren was holding out on him. Like he knew something. Something about him and the intense nightmares stalking his dream life.

We all have our secrets, Brian thought. He thought a man who could withstand the sun's destructive rays was more intriguing than a man with strange dreams. *I should be looking at him like that. Not the other way around.*

In the distance, a faint light lit up the end of the tunnel. It was dawn. As they traveled, the sun had stretched over the horizon, basking the morning in a pale purple glow. Soren gunned the SUV toward the mouth of the tunnel. The entrance to Tunnel Two was less than five miles away. With the sun over the horizon, there was no way they could safely make it across without becoming human toast.

At least I was wrong about the tunnel being clogged.
Soren stomped on the gas.
"There's no way we can make it!" Susan shouted. "We'll burn if we try!"
He ignored her.
"Soren..."
The SUV sped forth, Soren pushing the pedal to the floor.
"Soren!" Susan screamed.
"Oh, Christ," Shondra said, realizing the crazy bastard was going for it.
"You may be immune to the sun, but we are not!" Susan screamed.
He heard the walkie-talkie crackle. *"Soren, what the fuck are you doing?"* It was Mouth. He sounded pissed, which wasn't much different from any other time.
Brian grabbed the walkie-talkie from where it rested between the seats. "Mouth, it's Brian. We're going for it. We're going for Tunnel Two."
"(crackle crackle) Why the hell for?"
Brian paused. "Mouth," he whispered. "Just trust me."
"(crackle crackle) Fuckin' (crackle crackle) ball sack! (crackle crackle) fucknut (crackle crackle) dick-skin licker! (crackle crackle) bunch of fu—(crackle crackle) tards, dickless, re —(crackle crackle)."
Brian clicked the walkie-talkie off and sat back, holding the oh-shit bar with one hand and Shondra's hand with the other, praying to a god he no longer believed existed.

Dana was scared, but she never showed it. When the car zoomed out of Tunnel One, her eyes drifted toward the odometer. The gauge hovered over the 100MPH tick. She quickly did the math in her head and quickly determined the ride across would take precisely three minutes. Three. Long. Minutes.
The sun wasn't as high in the sky as they had previously

believed. It hung halfway over the horizon, the bruised-purple sky still holding onto night. Still, it was more than enough light to burn the flesh off their bones. Dana rolled herself into a ball on the front seat. She hid her nervousness behind her knees. The others ducked, keeping away from the windows. Soren continued driving, speeding toward Tunnel Two, which an overhead highway sign told them was called the "Thimble Shoal Channel Tunnel." Dana thought the name was funny, like it had come from a fantasy epic like *Lord of the Rings* or *Game of Thrones.*

"Almost there," Soren told them.

Dana peeked over her knees. Soren was right. They were more than halfway there. She looked in the side-view mirror and saw Mouth and Becky chugging along behind them, the minivan bringing up the rear. He wasn't pushing the car nearly as fast as Soren was driving the SUV. The minivan had no balls whatsoever and was falling behind with each passing second. Those were precious seconds; the sun was ascending the sky with a pace Dana had never seen before. She'd never been this close to being trapped outside since that first confusing day at the water park.

The second Soren crossed the finish line, he slammed on the brakes and gently turned the wheel. The wheels screeched below them, an effect he seemed to be aiming for. The car spun, but stopped on a ninety-degree angle.

"You're a fucking asshole," Shondra blurted.

"You're alive aren't you?"

She placed her palm on the center of her chest. "For the moment."

"Susan? You okay?"

Susan swallowed a lump in her throat.

Soren turned his attention to the girl on his right. "You okay, Dana? I know that was scary."

Dana put on her game face. "Nah. I knew you had it all along."

Soren smiled, but the smile told her he didn't believe a word. He patted the girl's shoulder and turned, opening the door and stepping out. He waited for the other cars to follow his lead, and didn't have to wait long. Mouth cruised into the tunnel, parked about twenty feet away from them, and scrambled out of the car. He was already cursing when the door opened.

"You sonuvabitch!" he screamed. "I'll kill you!"

Soren folded his arms across his chest, watching the man make a hilarious fool out of himself.

Becky stepped in front of him, trying to talk some sense into the foul-mouthed maniac. Soren turned away from them and concentrated on the approaching minivan. The van finally crossed over and escaped the dangerous territory. Once underneath the safety of the tunnel, the driver of the van threw open the door and jumped out like someone had stocked the van with explosives.

"Help!" the driver screamed, waving the others over.

Soren sprinted forward. The driver, Hugh, ripped open the passenger's door and grabbed one of the passengers, removing him from his seat with little struggle. He smelled the acrid stench of burning flesh once Hugh hauled the man into the open.

Dana jogged along side of him.

"What happened?" Dana asked.

"Go back to the SUV," Soren told her. There was no gentleness in his voice.

"But—"

"Go."

She didn't listen, but she stopped following him. She stood back and watched the drama unfold from a safe distance.

Soren knelt next to the victim. He was rolling on the asphalt, screaming, kicking his feet, trying to escape the torture. The victim's name was Dustin, a man in his mid-thirties, although he looked a hell of a lot older. The sun had toasted most of his scalp, burning away the little hair he had left. Several layers of skin had been erased from his face, the old acne scars from his youth replaced by yellow oozing burns. Badly drawn and faded tattoos covered most of his arms and legs, some of them gone, charred over from the sun's touch. Skin hung from his triceps like a fleshy hammock, runny like egg yolk. Several of the van's passengers were around him now, holding him down, telling him to keep still.

Shondra had joined the party, holding a brown bottle of peroxide. She unscrewed the cap and poured the liquid on the burns. Dana watched the man thrash as the medicine bubbled into a froth over the wounds. He screamed as if he was passing kidney stones the size of grapefruits. Dana turned away when Shondra poured the peroxide on him once again.

There was only so much a little girl could take.

"You could have gotten us all killed, motherfucker!" Hugh shouted as he shoved Soren. He was smaller than Soren, although most men were. Hugh's blonde hair shimmered even in the tunnel's dimness. His mustache didn't exactly match the shade atop his head, and Soren wondered if the man dyed his hair to make it brighter. It was a question for another time, when things were less tense, and the man didn't want to punch his face in. "Are you fucking nuts?"

"I'm sorry."

"You're sorry?" Hugh said. "Oh, hey everybody, it's all good. Soren's sorry. Don't worry about it! It's all okay! The Grand Poo-Bah said he's sorry!"

A woman, younger than Hugh and Dustin, placed her hand on Hugh's shoulder. Tied back in a ponytail, her red hair swung back and forth as she shook her head, telling him to let it go. Her verdant eyes fixed on Hugh, her stare immediately washing his anger away.

"Calm down," she said.

"I'm sorry, Jo," he said. "It's just... fuck, babe. He could've gotten us all killed."

"I know," Johanna said, wrapping her arms around him. "Just take it easy. Don't stress. God is with us. He is on our side."

"You're right," Hugh said, hugging her back. "I love you so much."

Soren wanted to roll his eyes, but Jo's glaring eyeballs made him think twice.

"It's okay," she told Hugh, rubbing his back. "God's on our side. Isn't that right?" The question was meant to be rhetorical, but Soren got the sense she expected him to answer.

Hugh bit his lower lip and gave a single nod. He turned to Shondra, and asked, "How is he?"

Shondra had finished wrapping Dustin's arm in a giant ace bandage. "Pretty bad. I think he's mostly in shock. I think he'll be okay. The burns are really bad. Never seen anything like it. I'm no nurse, but I think we should keep an eye on it so doesn't get infected."

Soren agreed.

"So what's next, oh Great One?" Hugh spat.

He drew a deep breath. "We press—"

"Do you smell that?" Dana interrupted.

The group dropped their conversation a moment and sniffed the air. There was something there, something no one could put their finger on.

"It smells like..." Something tickled her nose.

"Fire," Brian finished for her. "It smells like fire."

-8-

A black garbage can sat in the middle of the road, spitting flames and small embers. A figure wearing a hooded cape glanced over his shoulder, shielding his eyes from the headlights belonging to three vehicles. His other hand hovered over the flames.

Beyond the man and his fire, a dozen cars and trucks blocked the tunnel, only allowing access for those on foot. Soren drove within twenty feet of the man and parked the SUV. He looked to Dana, turning to Brian, Shondra, and Susan next. "I'll go out first. Susan, why don't you hop in the driver's seat in case we need to make a speedy retreat." He turned back to Dana, gave her a wink, unlocked the door, and let himself out.

She opened her mouth to protest, but Soren stepped away before she could.

"I don't like a goddamn thing about this," Shondra said. Susan eyed her dirty when the word "goddamn" rolled off her tongue, but she chose to ignore the woman's hard glare.

"Me neither," Brian added.

They watched Soren approach the homeless man and his flaming garbage can. Brian leaned forward, sticking his head between the front seats. Susan hustled around the SUV and into the driver's seat.

"It's okay," Brian said, noticing the trepidation leaking into Dana's features. "It's all going to be okay." He didn't know this for sure, not exactly. He wasn't psychic after all; his dreams only showed him snippets of the future, and most of the time they were masked within vexing riddles. Some were impossible to unravel, so convoluted only someone insane could solve. *Maybe I am in insane.* Things might have been easier if he believed that.

Soren pantomimed back to the vehicles as he spoke to the stranger. During their exchange, Brian noticed how unclean the tunnel man was. His face was covered in dirt and grease; he looked like the mechanic who used to fix his car at the local Hyundai dealership. Bloody rags were wrapped around the man's wrists. They were old, stained the color of rust. His clothes were ripped and torn, revealing cuts and bruises on the man's body. Someone had either kicked the shit out of him or he lost a fight with a forest.

As the seconds passed, Brian grew nervous. "This isn't good. It's taking too long."

"Maybe you should go out and help," Susan suggested.

Brian looked around the tunnel, saw only shadows. Shadows of the cars in the firelight. Shadows belonging to Soren and the Tunnel Man. Shadows of...

"Shit," Brian said.

It was too late to help Soren.

The shadows twisted toward him.

Toward them all.

"Howdy there," Soren said. He approached the man cautiously, keeping his hands where the man could see them. "I was wondering if we could, perhaps, with your permission of course, pass on through."

The man grunted. He wasn't a pretty-looking bastard, and he smelled worse than he looked. Soren inched closer and thought the stench wasn't coming from him, but the tunnel itself. Nope, it was him. He backed away when he reached striking distance. The man flinched. Maybe the smell permeated his clothing, the gag-worthy result of collected aromas from his apocalyptic journey.

"I'm not here to hurt you," Soren said, putting up his hands. "Just the opposite. In fact, I can help you."

"Help," the man rasped, as if he hadn't spoken in months. For some reason Soren got the sense the man was putting him on, that this was all for show—and a good one. Very believable. "Help?"

"Yes, help. I want to help you. My friends and I," he waved back to the convoy, "we are on a long journey. There's this sanctuary beneath the surface in Northern Alaska. It's a secret place, but it's safe and not too many people know about it. And we're headed there. Now. Today. Well, we won't get there today, but—" He was rambling and he knew it. He watched the man's eyes shift back and forth. Something was happening behind him. He sensed movement, but it was too late to react. "But we will get there. And we will be safe. And free. And we won't need anyone to come and save us because we'll have everything we need to live out the rest of our lives."

"Help," the man said again.

"Yes," Soren said, following the man's eyes. He found himself surrounded by sixty men, all armed to the teeth with pistols, rifles, swords, baseball bats, hockey sticks, meat cleavers, makeshift cudgels with round spiky ends, and he even spotted one man with a lasso. They were equally unclean and bandaged as the half-wit standing next to the fire. "Help."

The man smiled, displaying a mouth that hadn't seen a dentist since 1975. His blackened gums trembled as a laugh crawled from his mouth. An awful odor intensified when the man spoke, spitting saliva down his chin.

"Help," the man uttered, introducing Soren to his friends.

They weren't gentle; not even with Dana. They ripped the girl from the front seat like an old Band-Aid. Brian tried fending two of them off, but they sucker-punched him in the gut and he collapsed to his knees. A throbbing pain entered his testicles as they dragged him away from the SUV. He heard Mouth shouting expletives making little and no sense. Shondra went willingly and they pushed her along like she had committed some unspeakable crime.

The rats are here...

In the dream, the circumstances were different. There were actual rats sweeping through the city. The city in his dream had been replaced by a tunnel in reality. No, that didn't seem right. The city should have been a city. The rats should have been rats. Had his dreams failed him? *No,* he thought. *This isn't what I was dreaming about.*

They gathered everyone together and circled them like sharks. They turned their weapons on them, pointing their blades at their faces. The men grumbled and shouted, cursing and saying things no man should ever say to a lady, or anyone else for that matter. They reeked of trash and sewage pulp. Some gritted their teeth and said things like "I'm going to fucking gut you!" and "I'm going to have fun with your lady parts!" Some simply spat on their captives, laughing and singing like lunatics.

This was absolute Hell.

Someone whistled over the noise and the cacophony of vile insults and bestial groans abruptly came to an end. A single figure pushed through the throng of dirty men. He had long, raven-black hair that fell on his shoulders, a bandage taped over his right eye, dried blood caked around it. Dirt stained the skin under his eyes like warpaint, surrounding his hawk-like nose. His beard, which matched the color of his hair, was months old, streaked with grime and food from who-knew how long ago. Brian's eyes migrated and found the sheathed machete hidden in his leather-mahogany hip scabbard. He found everything about the man unsettling, because he'd seen him before.

In a dream.

Bad boys. Bad, little boys.

"Welcome to Thimble Shoal," the man said, after giving the group a slow once over. "This is a toll road, and to pass safely, you must pay it."

Soren stood up defiantly. A few of Hawk-Nose's people motioned like they were going to sit him back down, but the leader of the group raised a single fist and ended that idea. He extended his hand diplomatically.

"My name is Soren Nygaard. My people and I mean no harm to your... community."

For a second no one said a word. Then, all at once, every single filthy mouth in the tunnel erupted with raucous laughter. Their gut-busting outburst deafened the tunnel like the roll of thunder. Hawk-Nose let the laughter drag on for far too long before raising his fist again.

"We are aware of that," Hawk-Nose said. "To us, you're like flies on the wall. And we have plenty of swatters to go around."

One man dropped the end of his Louisville Slugger on the

ground, the hallow thud of the barrel hitting the pavement grabbing their attention.

"What is it you want with us?" Soren asked.

Hawk-Nose smiled, displaying five teeth, the rest blackened with acidic erosion and rot. "It's simple: we want your cars, your coats, and your cunts."

The dirty boys cheered in agreement.

-9-

Hawk-Nose smiled, and the sixty-seven men behind him grinned and giggled, clearly enjoying the look on their prisoners' faces. Catching Shondra reaching for the pistol tucked in her jeans, Soren put his hand up. If she drew on them, their journey would end in gun smoke and bloodshed. He gave her the squint-eyes and her hand drifted away from the weapon and fell at her side.

"I realize what I said may have disturbed you," Hawk-Nose said. The psychotic grin never seemed to leave his face. "For that I'm sorry. You must understand—this tunnel has been home to these men since the purification."

"Purification?" Shondra asked.

Hawk-Nose dropped his smile and glanced at Shondra, his lips quivering with disgust. "Who gave you permission to speak, cunt?" the man snapped.

Shondra resisted the urge to reach for the gun again.

"It's all right," Soren said, stepping in front of her. "She didn't mean any... disrespect."

"You let your women speak freely?" Hawk-Nose asked him.

Soren couldn't tell if the man was kidding or not. "Yes. Of course." He surveyed the crowd of dirty faces. "Speaking of which, I don't see any women among you. Are there any?"

"Why?" Hawk-Nose asked, insulted.

"No reason. I find it odd not a single woman is present among you."

"What are you trying to say?" one of The Dirty asked. Grime had been worked into his cheeks, forever staining them black. A gash above his left eye had been stitched shut. "That we're a bunch of butt-fucking queers?"

"No, not all. Just—"

"You don't know anything about us," the man growled.

"You're right. I'm sorry—"

This wasn't going particularly well. Soren wished he had a rewind button and could start over. Hawk-Nose glared at him like a prospective meal. The women continued receiving threatening stares. Eyes wandered over their bodies. The men licked their teeth as they examined their quarry. If it weren't for Soren and the other men of the group, who knows what would have happened already. One thing was certain: they couldn't stay in the tunnel. Not a second longer than necessary. Soren knew he had to get them through, and quickly. Whatever the cost.

But where was there to go? The sun had already hoisted itself above the clouds. They were trapped in here, at least for the duration of the day.

"Not sure I like your tone, partner," Hawk-Nose said, with a southern twang that sounded phony to Soren's ear.

"I do apologize, gentlemen. Just simply making conversation. I'm interested in your arrangements here."

"Why's that?"

He nibbled his lower lip. "I'm curious how sixty-seven men survived almost half a calendar year underneath a tunnel, secluded from civilization. I've always been interested in humanity's struggles. Please. Enlighten me."

Hawk-Nose furrowed his brow and wiped his mouth with the back of his hand. "Hasn't been easy," he said solemnly. "But you do what's necessary to survive. Ain't that right, boys!"

The Dirty cheered again, raising their fists in the air like a band of guerrilla warriors.

"Well, I'm astonished. What have you done for food?" Soren asked, trying to buy time. There was no way he could keep the conversation going for the next twelve hours, but every minute they were talking about nonsense was one more minute The Dirty weren't trying to figure out which way to flay them.

"We go shopping once a week. Closest market is about an hour from here. Most of the town is dried up. Plus, there are folks like you."

Soren squinted. "Folks like us?"

The Dirty laughed collectively.

"Relax," Hawk-Nose said. "We don't eat people. We're not desperate. Not yet."

Laughter again.

"We make trades with people. Food, water, whatever they got in exchange for free passage. Works for us. Works for them. And most of the time everyone is real nice about it."

"Most of the time?" Mouth asked.

Hawk-Nose glared at him, opposing the tone of his voice. "Yes. Most of the time. There have been incidents. But if you want to talk business and be on your way peacefully, then we won't have any repeats."

Soren cleared his throat. "Why wait? Let's talk about business now."

"Sure thing," Hawk-Nose said. "But business is usually discussed with The Boss."

"The Boss?" Soren asked. "You're not him?"

The group laughed, but Hawk-Nose silenced them, thrusting his fist in the air. Soren could tell their laughter insulted him, the idea of him being their leader a joke he did not care for.

"No," he said, his lips twitching. "I'm not."

"Then who are you?"

"I'm Spencer. I collect the tolls."

"Of course."

"Let's get one thing straight—I don't like you or your friends. You don't fit in here. So I want to send you on your way as quickly as possible. Got it? Good. Now you pay the toll, or we're going to have ourselves a problem, and trust me, you won't like how problems get solved around here."

"We haven't discussed terms."

Spencer blew a wad of snot through his nose. "As I said: we want your cars, your coats," he looked at Johanna like she were Little Red Riding Hood, and he were the Big Bad Wolf "and your cunts." No one spoke. No one dared. "You have one minute to get your shit together."

From the shadows, a robed figure watched Spencer. He watched with a grin and a twinkle in his eye. He liked when Spencer commenced his collections. It was fun for him. Fun for the group. Fun for all. Things were seldom fun around here. Except for the nightly brawls, the only action they had was with travelers. Travelers never lasted long and that was okay.

They made great use of short time.

"Allow me a minute to discuss this with my group," Soren said. When no one moved, he gritted his teeth. "Privately."

Spencer waved The Dirty back. They took a few steps away and although it wasn't as private as Soren would have liked, he knew it was all they'd give.

"Okay, folks," he said quietly. "Looks like we don't have much of a choice here. We have to comply."

"Fuck that!" Shondra said. She practically growled the words. Her eyes were wild, a side Soren hadn't seen from her before. "I'm not going anywhere with these... savages!"

"Calm down," Soren demanded.

Susan put a hand on her shoulder, but Shondra only shrugged her off, shooting her a sour glance. She turned back to Soren as if she had expected Shondra to react that way.

"What are you thinking, Soren?" Susan asked. "There's no way you can hand us over. You know what they want from us."

Soren knew. He knew exactly what they wanted. That's why he had to give it to them.

"I know what they want. And I don't like it any better than you do, trust me."

"Trust you?" Shondra asked. "Are you fucking kidding me?"

"I'm not going with these freaks," Johanna spoke up, her voice cracking.

Becky gripped Mouth's hand. "I'm not going either," she said.

Trisha, the quiet bookworm type, backed away from the group. "Fuck this shit," she said. She took off, streaking toward the minivan. David, another traveler who had been in the van with her, reached out, trying to grab her hand.

"Trisha, no!" David yelled.

One of The Dirty stepped away from the group, raised a small pistol in his hand, aimed, and pulled the trigger. A bloody firework exploded from the girl's head, painting the side of the van with gory splatter. Her body hit the ground hard, the sound of her skull cracking against the pavement echoing throughout the tunnel.

"What a waste of a good cunt," Spencer spat.

"You bastards," David said, standing up. He stuck his chest out defiantly. He was a big man who had hit the gym hard every day of his life since his seventeenth birthday, but no amount of muscle and creatine supplements would help him take on the The Dirty alone. Individually, not one of them stood a chance against him, but he couldn't take on the entire army, not by himself. "You motherfuckers!"

Spencer pulled a handgun from his black cloak. He aimed it at David's head. "Sit the fuck down, before I put you down. Permanently."

David's veins bulged on his neck and forehead, however he wasn't rage blind. He knew what would come next. Slowly, he found his seat on the pavement, his lips quivering with hate and fear.

"What the fuck are we going to do?" Mouth asked Soren. "You can't possibly be considering this!"

"We have no choice."

"We can all make a run for it," Johanna said. "Back to the cars. They can't kill us all."

"Yes," Dana said, tears sticking to her eyelids. "They can."

"Well it beats being raped by these savages!"

"Even if we made it to the cars," Soren said, "where would we go? They have the tunnel blocked off."

"We can get the SUV up to speed," Hugh said. "Run right through the fuckers."

"I'm trying to work our way out of this with the least amount of bloodshed."

"Three... two... one..." Spencer checked his watch. "Time's up, kiddos. Guess you fuckholes want to do this the hard way. Boys, line up the men for the firing squad, and take the women back to Mole."

Soren shot up like a spring. "I want to see Mole."

Giggling, Spencer said, "You do, do you?"

"Yes."

The man said, "Mole doesn't get seen. Mole sees you."

"I want to strike a bargain with him."

Spencer's face immediately twisted, his lips wrenching into a bestial snarl. His brows arched and eyes blazed with fervent rage. "I AM THE TOLL COLLECTOR!" he screamed, his voice going off like a gunshot. "I am the one you bargain with. I am in charge of the tolls and I will decide who passes..." He looked to the women. "And who does not."

"We want to comply with your demands," Soren said.

"Oh...?"

"But I have some demands of my own."

"Forget the women," **Soren** said. He looked Spencer directly in the eyes. Before he spoke the next few words, he glanced over his shoulder. His group was pacing around nervously, wondering what he and the toll collector were discussing. Shondra's look worried him the most. Something incredibly stupid occupied her thoughts, he was sure of it. "What if I told you I could give you immunity to the sun?"

Spencer scoffed. "You don't really expect me to buy that nonsense, do you?" He laughed through his nose and patted Soren's shoulder. "Nice try, asshole."

Soren grabbed Spencer by the collar and hoisted him off the ground. He heard the shuffling of weapons and knew he was about three seconds away from eating a bullet sandwich. "I'm not fucking around."

Spencer waved The Dirty down. As instructed, they lowered their weapons.

"Get your filthy paws off me," Spencer said through his teeth.

Soren almost laughed at the irony, and did as Spencer requested.

"You better talk, and fast. I'm not having fun anymore,"

Spencer told him, fixing his bent collar.

"Immunity," Soren said, ignoring his offer. "To the sun. I have it."

He snorted. "You think you can tell me lies in exchange for passage. That's not how this is playing out."

"I can prove it."

Spencer sneered. "You take me for a fool."

Soren produced a vial from his inner jacket, full of turquoise liquid. He shook it, and the liquid within sloshed, bubbling with anticipation.

"This is the antidote. I'll give you two vials; that's a month's worth. In exchange you let us go. All of us."

Spencer studied him. "If what you say is true, I'll let you pass, but I'm taking two cunts and two vials. That's a fair price to pay."

"Two vials and one girl of your choosing."

A grin slithered across Spencer's face.

"But not the young one," Soren said. "You won't lay a finger on her."

Disappointed, Spencer wriggled his lips and thought about how he could include Dana in the deal. Before he could renegotiate, a shadow appeared on the wall behind them. Soren noticed Spencer's eyes shift and he turned. A figure in a long, hooded black robe stood ten feet away. The tunnel's shadows hid him well, and neither Spencer nor Soren knew how long he was listening to their secluded conversation. The figure stepped into the dim light provided by The Dirty's battery-operated lanterns which hung from the walls every twenty feet.

"Sir..." Spencer said, fear tugging his vocal chords.

"That's all right, Spencer. I'll handle it from here," the figure said.

"Mole, I was about—"

"I said all right, didn't I?" Mole said. Under the hood, he glared at his associate. "Didn't I?"

"Yes, sir."

"Good." He turned and waved Soren on. "Come with me. And bring your magic elixir."

-10-

The frail man in the long robe looked more like a monk than a depraved psychopath. He didn't speak like Spencer; he was articulate and precise and didn't seem to have the same interests in mind. There was an overwhelming sense of practicality to him, which Soren admired. Men like Mole had been lost in The Burn's aftermath, replaced by savages and simpletons relying too heavily on their primal instincts; the need to eat, kill, and fuck. Mole had other ambitions, a brighter future planned for him and his people. And Soren had what they needed to get there.

Or so he hoped.

"How does it work?" Mole asked. They were standing on the other side of the barrier, the long row of working vehicles separating Soren from the rest of his group. They were about as far away from them without being out of sight. Mole shook the vial and watched the turquoise liquid bubble as if he were expecting the contents to give away the lie. "Is it ingested, or it taken intravenously?"

"Ingested. Works fast. Will grant you immunity for several weeks." He kept looking back, making sure The Dirty were treating his people with respect. "As I was telling Spencer, I think two vials in exchange for passage is more than fair."

Mole smiled pleasantly. He pushed back the hood and revealed a bald head, purple burn marks marring the landscape from where hair would never grow again. The skin hadn't healed properly, becoming lumpy and freakishly uneven during the process. Some of the flesh had blackened over, a crusty reminder of the evil outdoors, unless dark. The marks occurred not so long ago.

"Do I repulse you?"

"I've seen worse."

"Usually people gasp when they see my disfigurement. They cover their mouths or swallow their condolences. The polite ones will stay stone-faced and say nothing about it, change the subject when I ask." Mole studied him. "But not you."

"Life's too short to be polite. Want my opinion? You look like a freak."

Mole erupted with laughter. "I like you, Mr. Soren. You entertain me. You and your... elixir. Tell me, how did you come about it?"

"I manufactured it. In a lab."

"You're a scientist?"

"I was." Soren sensed Mole didn't believe everything he was saying, even though he'd been more truthful with Mole than any one of his followers.

"How much do you have?"

He thought about it. There was a game being played; Soren couldn't put his cards on the table yet, not all of them.

"A few."

"How many is a few?" Mole asked with a shifty smirk.

"Four."

"And you're willing to give up half of your inventory in order to pass through Thimble Shoal?"

"Where we're headed, I'll have the ability to make more."

"And where are you headed?"

"Alaska," Soren said. "There's an underground research facility there. We plan to... claim it as our own."

"Ambitious." Mole looked toward the tunnel's exit, hidden behind a bend in the road. "Alaska is a long way from here. Think you'll make it? Winter months are approaching. I thought the blazing sun would put an end to winter altogether, but the temperature keeps dropping. Got down in the 50's last night. Can you believe it?"

"It's quite the anomaly."

Mole squinted and searched Soren's eyes for answers. "Can I be frank with you?"

"Please."

"I don't think you're lying, but I know you're not telling the truth."

"Interesting observation."

"I can't tell which parts of your story are true and which are not," Mole said, turning away from him. He walked over to the wall where a small cooler sat on the ground. He opened it, removed two bottles of water and a turkey sandwich. He tossed Soren a water bottle, unwrapped the sandwich, and handed him half.

Soren waited for Mole to take the first bite.

"Please," Mole said, a hearty laugh escaping his mouth, "if I wanted to kill you, you'd be dead already."

Soren couldn't argue. He put the sandwich in his mouth and bit into it anxiously. It had been weeks since he had eaten something substantial.

"Where do you live?" Soren asked. "Where do you sleep? I don't see much of a camp."

"In the walls," Mole said. *"Like rats."*

Mole thought it was a funny thing to say, but Soren didn't find it as amusing. He remembered what Brian had said in his sleep; *the rats are coming.* Was it a sign? Despite imitating a preacher at Costbusters, Soren stopped believing in fate and divine influences a long time ago.

But...

He couldn't shake the feeling Brian had seen something. The whole event had been too weird to explain. The seizure. The rambling. Something odd had happened, something Soren—and anyone else in the group for that matter—couldn't rationalize, couldn't make sense of.

A coincidence. Had to be.

But was it?

He was having a dream. He was having a vision. He saw this happen.

Soren grew paranoid, and it must have shown because Mole glanced at him suspiciously. Soren snapped free from it when a strip of turkey fell from his sandwich and landed on the cracked pavement.

"Did I say something wrong?"

"No," Soren said, trying to recover. He handed him back the half eaten sandwich. "I'm sorry. Not hungry."

"Let's take a walk," Mole said. "You have something to show me."

Mole walked beside Soren, two of The Dirty trailing them every inch of the way. Ahead, sunlight waited for them at the end of the tunnel. Even though the light was half a mile away, it still put a strain on their eyes. Soren didn't shield his eyes from the bright yellow glow. He welcomed the warmth, his blood heating with each step forward. A breeze blew, and he inhaled a breath of fresh air. In that moment, he couldn't smell the stomach-twisting stench The Dirty so prominently emanated, instead only scenting the burnt-leaf fragrance of late-October.

"Was everyone inside the tunnel when it happened?" Soren asked.

"Mostly. A few joined after. We're always accepting new members."

Soren snorted. "I think I'll pass."

"Most of them came from the Virginia Beach area, some farther south. Some were looking for a new place to call home, figuring the farther north, the cooler the climate. They thought cooler weather would protect them. But as we know it doesn't really matter how cool things are." They reached a safe distance from the sun's light, and stopped. Mole put his palm out like a gorgeous woman displaying a prize to a game show audience. "We had to learn this the hard way."

A dozen bodies lay crumpled in the middle of the road, charred to a crisp, frozen in death. A few of them had been holding each other when the sunlight reached them, the ash-ridden corpses gripped in an affectionate pose. One body had been kneeling when the sun burnt him black, his knees bent to their breaking point, exposing bone, his legs tucked underneath his back. A woman had been crawling toward a much smaller corpse. She had been reaching when she died, and the smaller body had been reaching back.

"A shame. We've been trying to think of less dangerous ways to test the sun. We're hoping one day it'll *blow over* and we'll be able to travel outside once again."

"Don't hold your breath."

"And what makes you say that?" Mole asked. "You know something I don't?"

"This world will never be safe again."

Mole grimaced as if he only half-believed.

"So about this toll..." Soren said as he turned to face him. "Spencer said he wanted our vehicles, our clothing, and our women. Seems like a lot." He glanced at the two guards, each holding weapons designed to bash his brains in. "I think we can both agree on that."

"I think we can agree I have the upper hand here."

"Can't argue there. But I disagree with the terms and want to renegotiate."

Mole threw Soren a contemplative glance, placing one hand on his chin, resting his elbow on the arm tucked inside his robe. A moment later, the cordial grin reappeared. "We're not monsters," he said finally.

"No?" Soren asked. "One of your men shot a woman in the head."

"That was unfortunate and I'll punish the man responsible, you have my word."

"Right," Soren said, his eyes looking elsewhere as if the conversation bored him and the tunnel walls held greater interests. "Honestly, I don't care much about that. I care about moving on from this place and getting to where I need to go. And to do that I need to get out of this goddamn tunnel. So what will it cost? The agreement I worked out with Spencer was two vials and a woman of his choosing. I'm willing to give you three vials in exchange for everyone's safety."

Stroking his chin, Mole thought it over. "You know, the truth is I abhor violence. Yes, I let my men hold daily bare-knuckle fights, because it keeps them entertained and quiet and calm, and those three things allow me to do what I do."

"And what might that be?"

"Like you, I have a vision. A plan. An end game. In my vision, we rebuild society. I don't know how many men, women, and children are left alive out there, but evidence suggests not many. We're an endangered species, Mr. Soren." Mole thought Soren would protest, tell him there are many people alive out there, waiting for someone to come along and save them, to tell them exactly how to live. Instead, Soren said nothing and looked toward the exit. "You know where I'm headed with this, don't you?"

"Yes."

"So you know what I'll need." It wasn't a question.

Soren clenched his jaw. As a result, the muscles in his neck flexed, and Mole knew he had gotten to him.

"Yes," Soren said in a hushed voice. "But the vials—"

"Don't mean as much to me as a place to plant my seeds."

Spencer paced back and forth, side to side, repeating the same three words over and over again, changing the order in which they were said, not realizing he was speaking aloud and everyone in the tunnel could hear him. *"Coats, cunts, cars,"* he said. "No. *Cars, coats, cunts."* It was as if he couldn't decide which sounded better, more perfect. He stopped and thought he should change his wording for the next group of wanderers, maybe to something more threatening, something that meant business. *"Nah,"* he whispered, then shouted, *"Cunts, cars, coats!"*

"Excuse me," Susan said. "Can you mind your mouth, mister? Dana is a child and you should refrain from using that potty language in front of her." She had attempted to put "earmuffs" on the sides of Dana's head, but the girl had slapped her hands away.

"I've heard curse words before," Dana said.

"That doesn't make it okay for the man to say them."

Spencer approached them with a twinkle in his eye, one Susan viewed as a warning. Dana glanced at him oddly, not enjoying the attention. Mouth had moseyed his way over, watching Spencer carefully, itching for a reason to knock the man on his ass.

"Little girl?" Spencer asked, as if the words were alien. "Yes, you are a little girl, aren't you?"

"Dude," Becky said, turning her nose. Her throat clenched

and she almost gagged. "You kidding me?"

Mouth stepped between Spencer and Dana. He jabbed his finger into the man's chest. "Son, you're going to take ten giant fucking steps back and let someone else pretend they're in charge, or I'm going to rip your fucking throat out."

Spencer guffawed heinously. Shrill and cold, a serial killer's touch. He gripped his belly as if to contain his outburst, but the laughter continued to slice through the tunnel like a police siren. He silenced himself abruptly, and stepped to Mouth like he meant to strike him.

Mouth's reaction was lightning quick. No one saw his fist coming, only the result: Spencer bending over, his hand over his nose, catching copious globs of blood that spilled from his nostrils. Crimson leaked through his fingers, pooling on the road below. Mouth rushed to where Spencer had hunched over, ready to make good on his throat-ripping threat, when several of The Dirty intervened. One of them took the butt of his rifle and clocked Mouth on the back of the head. Mouth's vision went dark, but not black, and he kept control of his consciousness. He dropped to one knee and looked back as his chin met a powerful fist. The impact snapped his head sideways, and Mouth's vision dropped out. He lost a few seconds and found himself face-to-face with the pavement. Feet pummeled his ribs, and he could feel them breaking against the force.

He heard Dana scream, pleading with The Dirty to stop, but they didn't negotiate with little girls. He heard Shondra's voice too, but his neck ached too much to move it. After a while, his ribs went numb.

Something cold pressed against his temple.

A gun screamed in his ear.

Blackness whisked him away from the world.

Soren stood in the sun, rotating, making sure to demonstrate that this was not a game, not a trick, but the real-fucking-deal. He displayed his product like a QVC special, minus the smiles. When he was sure they had had enough, he turned to them and stretched his arms, as if offering a hug.

"Satisfied?"

The two men standing behind Mole watched, jaws agape, unable to speak. Mole folded his arms across his chest, as if unimpressed, although he truly was. Deep down, he didn't believe a word Soren had said about the contents within the vial. But now, watching the sun sparkle in the man's eyes, he had no choice but to accept Soren for what he was—a man of integrity, a man of power.

Soren held the vial in the air and shook the elixir inside. He dripped with sweat. Warmth tingled his neck. *Damn,* he thought. It had been weeks since he had taken his last dose. Was it starting to wear off, or was his mind playing him for a fool? He assumed his subconscious imagined the nerve-pricking sensation and he was in no real danger. But the feeling further manifested itself as time dragged on.

"I can give you this power." A bead of sweat dribbled down the side of his face. "This will make your body impervious to the diseased rays of the sun. With women you can offer them hope, yes. But with this they'll fear you. And once you are feared, you will have their undivided attention and their respect. Something more important than the prospect of rebuilding society."

"I guess we can strike ourselves a deal," Mole said.

Soren didn't waste a precious second. He practically sprinted back into the shade the tunnel provided. Mole clamped a hand on his shoulder, squeezing it hard.

"I never doubted you," he said.

Sure you didn't, Soren thought.

"Your people don't know about this?" Mole pointed to the vial. "The elixir, I mean."

"No. And it's important that trend continues. Include that in the bargain."

Mole flashed an approving grin. "Your secret is safe with me."

Soren bowed his head graciously.

"Two vials. And two girls," Mole announced, speaking like

negotiations were no longer needed.

"Three vials. One woman. You can have Shondra. I think she'll make a great addition here."

Mole curled his mouth and narrowed his eyes. "Which one is Shondra?"

"Short hair."

"No." Mole slapped the air as if a fly had buzzed near. "She's too old and not attractive. The men won't *want* to impregnate her. I'm also certain men aren't her flavor." Mole squinted as if he had a terrible headache. "No, we need someone younger. And there has to be more than one. You know how long it would take to repopulate with one womb?"

"You're forgetting what's important here. You're forgetting about the serum."

"I haven't forgotten, Mr. Soren. I just don't value the power associated with your elixir as much as you do. I don't need my people to fear me. I don't need them to wonder about my intentions. I don't need secrets to get what I want. See, I surround myself with people that have common goals. Common wants. Common needs."

"Doesn't everyone just want to survive?" Soren asked. "Isn't that the goal that unites us all?"

"Sometimes survival isn't enough. We're human. We need more than to merely survive. We need to thrive. And your elixir can't grant us what those cunts back there can."

Soren was beginning to see the man for the monster he was. He knew what he'd have to do, but he was struggling to keep his temper in check.

"In fact, the more I speak about it, the more I've decided to take three women. The three *youngest.*"

Soren lunged forth and grabbed the man by the throat. His two associates drew their weapons, hands so tightly gripped their knuckles went white. They didn't swing their bludgeons, not yet, and waited for Mole to give the word. He couldn't speak with Soren's fingers clasped on his vocal chords, but waved them off instead.

"If you think I can't snap your fucking neck before they bash my skull in, I beg you to test me," Soren whispered. Rivulets of sweat leaked down his forehead. Some droplets ended in his eye and he fended off the stinging sensation and concentrated on the task at hand. He loosened his grip as Mole choked.

"Two cunts it is," he squeaked.

A gunshot boomed, echoing through the tunnel.

The men took one look at each other and ran. Soren followed Mole and his men back to the heart of the tunnel where screams of confusion and women crying out for help ruled over the day.

-11-

Pain hammered Brian's shoulder, feeling like a heavy punch at first, but seconds passed and something hot flared where the bullet entered and migrated down his arm, numbing his fingers. What felt like glass shards swam through his veins. He looked down and saw blood leaking from a tiny tear in his shirt. He tore his sleeve off at the shoulder and inspected the wound. Smoke rose from the bullet hole, little silver wisps that reeked worse than death. Placing his hand over the wound, he watched blood trickle through his fingers.

Just a flesh wound, he thought and almost laughed. If the pain didn't feel like shark's teeth shredding his arm apart, he might have. He sat down and rested against the wall. Over the commotion, he swore he heard rats scurrying behind the tunnel's brick wall. The pain held back a laugh, but it finally broke free, and there, alone, sitting on the dirty ground with a wounded arm that wouldn't kill him unless left untreated, he cackled uncharacteristically loud.

Exhaustion controlled his thoughts. Closing his eyes, he let the pain drift away with everything else.

Mouth opened his eyes, surprised to find his head intact, and his brains where he last left them. He heard shouting and looked up with one eye. Mole and Soren had returned from their little discussion, along with those mopey guards Mouth knew he could kick the shit out of in a fair fight. Mole was shouting, demanding an answer for what had happened. As Mole approached, the men who had used Mouth's ribs for soccer practice backed away. It was a struggle, but he lugged himself to his knees. Shondra and Becky helped him the rest of the way.

"He started it," Spencer said, wiping his nose on his sleeve. The bleeding had stopped, but the red smears covering the lower half of his face told Mouth he had bled a lot. "Motherfucker tried to kill me."

Soren glared at Mouth. "This true?"

Who the fuck does this guy think he is? My father?
"He was giving Dana funny looks. I thought there was something wrong with his face so I tried to fix it for him."

"Fuck you, asshole!" Spencer screamed. He tried lunging for Mouth, but several of The Dirty held him back.

"What a fuckin' jerk," Mouth said. "Bet Dana can kick harder than you!"

Soren grabbed Mouth by his chin. He went to slap him away, but Soren caught his wrist with his other hand. He squeezed and Mouth let out an agonizing grunt.

"You shut your fucking mouth right now," Soren whispered. "Get the stuff out of the SUV and throw it in the minivan. At dusk, we're all taking the van out of here. We'll camp near the exit and leave the second the sun drops." He let go of Mouth's wrist and pushed him away. "Get going."

"Are we all going to fit in that fucking thing?" Mouth asked, rubbing his wrist.

Soren growled at him. "Just. Fucking. Do. It."

The second Soren turned, Shondra was in his face. Her concerned features rubbed Soren the wrong way, and he wished he could tell her the truth. He'd see her reaction to their arrangement soon enough.

"So women aren't part of the deal, right?" Shondra asked. "Tell me we aren't."

From the corner of his eye, Soren noticed Mole's sly grin.

"You aren't part of the toll." It wasn't a lie. Not completely. "I gave them something else."

He pushed past her and continued walking, heading over to the car Mouth had been driving.

"What?" she yelled after him.

Power, he thought, leaving Shondra to wonder.

A city in the clouds, a city below the streets. Two cities. One king over them both. A ruler of rulers. A king of kings. The rats are here, and they scurry about, creating mischief and carrying diseases; diseases that melted people's faces off and forced amputation of vital extremities. He walks through the crowd of people as they stroll through the city below the streets. He looks up and sees the city in the clouds and wonders how to get there, which way to meet the king. He taps the man closest to him on the shoulder and asks for directions. The man turns and half of his face is missing, burnt away by the day or consumed by rat bites. His face looks like a pizza minus the cheese, raw and bleeding, infected and oozing. The man tries to speak, but his voice malfunctions. Maybe the sun stole his vocal chords along with his appearance. He turns to a woman walking her child, hand in hand. He says, "Pardon me, miss, but how can I see the City in the Clouds?" She and the kid turn, their faces as hideous as Pizza-Face's. The woman's eyeball melted right out of its socket. The left half of the kid's face is scaly and yellow with dried pus. The right side had been burnt down to the bone. Brian didn't turn away, couldn't—the dream forced him to look. Everyone in the street turns to face him, and he finds himself the center of attention. They look at him with their eyes—those who had eyes remaining—and point to the same indiscernible object he can't see without turning his back to them. He rotates slowly, relieved to look elsewhere, viewing something other than the walking burn victims. He looks down and sees train tracks glowing underneath his feet. He turns back to the dead and they are gone. A train station replaced them. It's dusk and misty and the only light shines from a few flood lights near the end of the boarding platform. A conductor steps off the train. He tips his cap and bids Brian hello, revealing a black crusty dome that once grew long flowing curls of gold. The conductor tells him the train is leaving for the City in the Clouds in two minutes and how he needs to hustle and bustle or else he'll be left behind. The conductor's face is mutilated, baked to a bloody mess. Brian hates looking at him, but again, the dream has its way and the conductor's face fills his vision. A moment later, he is sitting on the train, surrounded by more of the sun's victims. It was getting old, the faces of the damned, their blackened skin, their smoking corpses. Brian's dream-self is resilient however, and makes it all the way to the next stop without puking once. When the train rolls into the next station, the conductor announces they have arrived at their destination, The City in the Clouds, informing all those who wish to enter to disembark. Brian stands and faces the door. When it opens, golden light fills his eyes and he feels the warmth on his face.

Then pain.

He starts to burn.

Shondra fixed him up the best she could. She told him the bullet didn't need extraction because it had gone clean through, missing his collarbone by less than an inch. He asked her who had fired at him, but she didn't know. "The whole thing is hazy. There was a lot going on and it all happened fast," she told him. It was the truth. She never saw the smoking barrel.

"How are we doing with the locals?" Brian asked, taking a sip from a bottle of water. A cottony feeling ruled his mouth. He was dehydrated, he was sure of it. His piss had been bumblebee yellow. While he sipped, he saw Soren unpacking the car, hurriedly grabbing the bags of food and tossing them toward the minivan. "We getting out of here or what?"

"Yeah, hopefully," she said, less than pleased with the situation. "I don't know what Soren worked out with them, but I don't like it."

"Why don't you ask him?"

"I did," she said. "Bastard shoved me off."

"Shit." He took another sip, enjoying the refreshing chill running down his throat. "That can't be a good sign."

"He did say no women were involved, but forgive me for not believing him."

"Well," Brian said, shrugging. "You know my opinion. Haven't trusted him since day one. We'll keep our eyes open."

"You look like you could use a long nap."

He waved her away playfully. "Got enough sleep. Although it

hardly feels like it."

"Dreams?"

"You know it."

"Anything enlightening?"

Recalling the weirdness, Brian shook his head. "Something about a city in the sky. And a train."

"City in the sky? Man..." she said, grinning. "How much acid did you take in your life?"

Brian smirked, although he didn't find the dream sequences particularly amusing. Chills crawled across his neck as he thought of them. Scared to close his eyes, he sat back and wished he could enjoy a normal night's sleep for once. Had a mirror been handy, he would've barely recognized the man staring back at him.

"Guess we'll be leaving at sundown," Shondra said apprehensively.

"Well, I'm just glad we're getting out of here in one piece."

"Yeah, well..." She motioned to the body fifty feet away. Someone had thrown a bed sheet over it. "Not all of us."

"Shit." He wished things turned out differently. Shit happened, but at least most of them were alive. *For now.* He wondered if the City in the Clouds was Heaven, and death was the direction they were headed. *Doesn't matter,* he thought, *we're all going to die in the end anyway.* The world was too dangerous, too savage. If they had any chance of surviving the journey to Alaska they'd have to change their mindset and drop their scruples. They'd have to adapt. Adapt or die. The world was ugly now; no need for makeup.

"Something bad is coming, Shondra," Brian said, staring off into the space behind her. "Something that's going to change everything."

She swung her head back and forth slowly, befuddled.

"I don't know what it is, and I can't even begin to speculate, but... I don't know. I feel something in the pit of my stomach. Something bad is headed in our direction and we need to get out of its way; or it could kill us all."

"We need to find your Cloud City?"

"No, I think we need to avoid it."

The day took its sweet time changing into dusk. For Brian and Shondra and the others, it couldn't come soon enough. They had enough of the The Dirty's seedy eyes glaring at them, their malignant smiles hiding their sordid intentions. Shondra had come close several times to taking one of their craniums and smashing it against her knee. If given the choice, she'd prefer a bed of spiders over the touch of their fingers. After a while, she looked away from them and found something else to pass the minutes; she counted the bricks on the tunnel wall.

As soon as the sun settled on the horizon, Soren informed them it was time to roll out. "Mouth, Shondra, Becky, Dana, Susan, Kyle, and David will ride with me in the minivan. The rest of you will take the SUV."

"Whoa, whoa," Shondra said. "Hold up."

Soren stopped and turned to her, seething.

"I think Brian should ride with us in the minivan. Dustin, too. You packed most of the medical supplies in there, and since I've inherited the duties of nurse since Sherry offed herself, I think Brian should be with me. And there's more room in—"

"You want them to have some medical supplies?" he asked.

"Well, yes—"

"Fine." Soren stormed his way over to the minivan, tore open the passenger's door, reached inside, grabbed the bag full of medical essentials, and flung it in Shondra's direction. The bag landed at her feet, some of its contents sent tumbling across the pavement. "Allocate them to your liking."

Shondra glowered at him, not realizing her lips had pulled back like an attack dog. She bent down as Soren turned, grabbing the fallen medical supplies. She collected the roll of medical tape and slipped it into her pocket. The bandages and antiseptics she tossed back in the bag and swung the strap over her shoulder. Then she helped Brian to his feet.

"What a fucking asshole," she said.

"Don't worry about him. Let's get through these next few minutes without incident," Brian said.

Together they walked over to the SUV. Dustin was already inside, wincing as the pain raked through his body. Shondra asked if he was okay and if there was anything she could do to make him more comfortable. He replied with, "A bullet to the head." Hugh helped Johanna into the back, and the two of them held hands, interlocking their fingers so they couldn't let go unless the decision was mutual. Shondra placed the medical supplies on the floor, next to Brian's feet. Jaime smiled at Shondra from the backseat; she told Shondra she wished she was coming with them.

"I'm not going to start a war with Soren over this. There will be plenty of time for that later," Shondra told her. She faced Brian. "Ready, soldier?"

"Yeah," he said. "Take care of yourself. And take care of Becky and Dana, too. Sam would appreciate it."

"You're acting like I'm never going to see you again." She patted his cheek. "Don't be so dramatic. I'm only a car away. And we have walkie-talkies."

"Yeah," Brian said, smiling. "Yeah, we do."

Ahead, the minivan's brake lights glowed. The sea consisting of sixty-seven dirty men parted as the van trundled forward. Hugh sighed and turned the key in the ignition.

Nothing happened.

He tried again and listened to the engine crank, but not turn over. Desperately, he twisted the key, giving the gas pedal a gentle push simultaneously. Nothing again. *This isn't fucking happening.* He looked to Brian, whose expression remained unchanged, no sense of panic, as if he expected this to happen.

"What the hell is going on?" Jaime asked.

"I don't know. Won't start," Hugh said.

He tried again. The engine coughed, struggled, and died.

"Well, why are they leaving?" Johanna asked, pointing to the van, which was almost out of sight. "They'll realize it and come back, right?"

Just before the van vanished past where their eyes could see, Hugh knew what had happened. "Motherfucker," he muttered.

The Dirty converged on the SUV, ripping open the doors while screaming and howling like the filthy animals they were.

"Something's off," Mouth said, looking over his shoulder. "They're not following."

Shondra eyed Soren warily from the seat behind him, the worst possible scenario crossing her thoughts.

Soren ignored them and stomped on the gas pedal. The van's engine growled, propelling them toward the tunnel's exit.

"I think you should stop, Soren," Mouth said, concern growing in his voice.

"Shut up," he hissed.

"Excuse me, motherfucker?"

Soren handed Dana the map and told her, "Find us the quickest way west."

She grabbed the map hastily and unfolded it, spreading it across her lap.

Mouth nearly jumped out of his seat. "Hey! Pull over! Right the fuck now!"

A forearm slipped under his chin and yanked him back. He choked as his neck squeezed between the seat and his assailant's bony arm. He flailed around the back seat, grabbing for whoever had him in a rear naked choke-hold. He breathed through his nose, but the asshole behind him applied more pressure, cutting off his air flow.

Soren slammed on the brakes and the van skidded to a stop a few feet before the tunnel's exit. He whipped his head back, staring Mouth directly in the eyes. Susan and David watched as Kyle continued to choke him. Shondra watched helplessly.

"Listen to me, you loudmouth fuck," Soren spat. "I did what I had to so we'd get out alive. If you don't understand or don't like it, then I'll be more than happy to let you out."

Kyle loosened his death-hold.

Soren pursed his lips. "Do we have an understanding?"

Mouth grumbled something Soren understood as "yes."

"Now sit down and shut up." Soren smiled.

"You're a real motherfucker," Shondra muttered.

"You're a fucking monster..." Mouth spat through his teeth. There were worse things on the tip of his tongue, but the look on Becky's face begged him not to make matters worse.

"We're all monsters now," Soren said. "Deal with it."

Soren turned, slipping the gear in DRIVE. The van rocketed out of the tunnel, onto the bridge, and beneath a fading purple sky.

THE TASTE OF POWER IS MINTY
(An Epilogue)

Mole sniffed the magic elixir and found its fragrance somewhat familiar, a remnant of the old world. It burned the nostrils a little, the way Scotch used to, sweet and tangy. He looked to Spencer with disappointment.

"What am I going to do with you, Spencer?" He looked at his loyal servant, wondering where he had gone wrong. Had he been too lax? Too easy on him? Too care-free? He could change of course, become the leader Soren had suggested. It wasn't his style and the idea didn't sit well with him, but he could pull it off. He could put himself in charge of the tolls from here on out, let Spencer lead the troops into the neighboring cities for plunder and supplies. "You're starting to frustrate me."

Spencer leaned against the tunnel wall, folded his arms, and scowled.

"You know we need women to repopulate. To start a society here," Mole said. "We don't need to go outside during the day. It doesn't do us any good."

"I just thought—"

"That's your problem. Don't think, Spencer. It's not your style. You listen. To me. And my directions. And that's it."

"You put *me* in charge of the tolls." He bounced himself off the tunnel wall and stood chest-to-chest with his leader. *"Me."*

"And I could put you in charge of cleaning out the shit cans. If you prefer that duty."

Spencer bared his teeth. His breath reeked of week-old seafood and sour milk. Mole would have found it repulsive in the old world, but now it was commonplace. Mole didn't smell like a bar of Dove either, and most rotten stenches he had gotten used to, even found some of them strangely pleasant.

Mole placed the vial on his chest. Spencer wrenched it away from him, and held it before him like a long lost artifact.

"I want you to test it," Mole said.

Proudly, Spencer said, "I'd be more than happy to." The way he figured it, once he became unaffected by the sun's deathly attributes, he could dethrone Mole and claim The Dirty's crown for himself. An easy task once the others witnessed his power. In their eyes, he'd be a god amongst men. They'd have no choice but to bow down before him, worship his almighty power. Drunk on his own potential, he downed the vial in one gulp. The liquid burned all the way down, but it was nothing he couldn't handle. A minty aftertaste stuck to the inside of his mouth, thick and syrupy.

Mole smiled and said, "Soren said it would take two hours to work." Dawn was only an hour away. "We'll wait here until you're ready."

Spencer expected for the serum to fill him with vigor, to enhance him in some way. He didn't feel anything except stomach-wrenching cramps. *That's just the elixir working its magic,* he thought. Mole ushered him to the end of the tunnel, stopping on the brink of sunlight flooding the road before them.

"Off you go," Mole said, after the two hours were up.

Spencer flipped him the bird and stepped onto the bridge. The smell of salt water crept up his nose and ran down his throat as the warmth of day buried itself in his pores. A strong breeze brushed his hair to the side, pelting his face with ocean droplets. Rays of sunlight licked his skin, a glorious sensation he never thought he'd experience again. He turned and looked directly at the burning orange globe in the sky. His eyes were weak; the brightness hammered his eyelids like fists. Shielding himself from the sun, he continued to walk, farther from the tunnel, farther from safety. He spun around in circles, arms outstretched, laughing like a love-sick teenager. Outside, the air was pure. He could breathe again, his nose needing a break from sweaty armpits, stale piss, and unhealthy fecal matter. He never wanted to step in that tunnel again. He debated making a run for it, turning his back on Mole and the rest of The Dirty and starting a new life, a life allowing him to spend his days outside, and his nights sleeping. The way humans were meant to live.

"This is the greatest day of my life!" Spencer cried out,

forgetting the other great days of his life all at once: the first time he got laid, his wedding day, the birth of his son, Spencer Jr.'s first word *(Daddy)*, their first ball-game together, all forgotten underneath the warmth of the sun. He laughed and hollered and stomped his feet in wonderment.

Then, without warning, it came. The pain. Sharp and stabbing. His skin boiled and blistered. He looked up and saw a shadowy figure standing on top of the tunnel, garbed in black from head to toe. Who was this devil garbed in black? The sun had no effect, whoever it was. The figure stood there, watching tongues of fire spread across Spencer's body, melting away the flesh on his fingers down to the bone. The moment the excruciating pain seared his face, he knew it was the Angel of Death, here to collect his soul.

Soul.

Toll.

Who was the collector now?

No, he thought. *No! No! NOOOOOOOOOOOO!*

Flames flared on his arms. Quickly, he stripped off his clothes, hoping it would help, but it didn't. The last thought he had before his own screams powered off his thoughts was how strangely the magic elixir tasted like mouthwash.

"ONE ANGRY MAN"

EPISODE TEN

-1-

The officer had his pistol drawn as he kicked them toward the station house. He reminded them to comply, no funny business, no sudden movements whatsoever. He said, "Yous wouldn't want to make me nervous now, would ya?" No one answered him and he took their silence as, *"Of course not, officer, we want to comply with everything you say and be good, obedient citizens, and oh, did we mention we're sorry for causing this mess, well, we are, extremely sorry. If you let us go we'll never cause a fuss again, honest, we'll be good citizens, role models for the kiddies. You believe us don't you, officer?"* The officer smiled and said, "We'll leave it for The Judge."

"What Judge?" Chuck asked, turning around.

The officer curled his mouth to one side of his face. "Son, you're a stupid sonuvabitch, ain't cha?"

Chuck looked to Jarvis. "What the hell is wrong with this guy?" he said under his breath so only they could hear him.

"Don't antagonize him," Sam whispered back.

"What yous saying up there?" the officer asked. "No one likes secrets, 'specially me."

"We were commenting on your lovely décor," Jarvis said, nodding to the light poles. The bodies swayed back and forth, an October wind pushing them gently. He stared closely at one in particular. The body's features had been blackened with gristle, erasing any human resemblance. The smell the wind pushed in their direction told them some of the deaths had been recent. Some were old, most of the skin and bones deteriorated, now ash, most of which nature carried off during the change of season. "Love what you've done with the place."

The officer stopped about twenty feet from the station's front door. He put his hands on his hips and looked around, admiring his handiwork. "Well, that's what you get for breaking the law. Don't worry though, friends. Perhaps The Judge will have a bigger heart for yous. Never seen him hang a man for jaywalking." He frowned as if he remembered something unsettling. "Though, possession of narcotics he might not care too much for. Might earn yous a firm spanking for that."

"Sir, for the last time—" Jarvis argued, but Sam grabbed his arm, cutting him off.

Despite the chill in the air, Chuck was sweating. His heart drummed, making his whole body vibrate. He looked to his surroundings for a way out of this riddle, avoiding the hanged blackened bodies, but his curious eyes fell on them anyway. He forced himself to look elsewhere and settled on the edge of a forest, not more than two football fields away. He wondered how good of a shot the cop was, if he was a cop at all. The more the officer stood there admiring his gruesome display, the more Chuck sensed he could safely make a run for it. Even though the sun was due up shortly, he'd take his chances hiding from the sun in the forest over the insane man holding a pistol in his hand. He looked to his friends, tried mouthing the words *I'm running for it,* and turned to speed off toward the forest. As he rotated, his right leg went one way, his ankle the other, and the maneuver sent him sprawling to the concrete.

The officer guffawed obnoxiously, his doughnut-loving belly shaking like a dog leg. His shadow fell over Chuck, who rolled around the parking lot, holding his ankle with both hands, hollering in agony.

"Well, where the fuck did you think you were going?"

Chuck was in too much pain to reply. He grunted as the officer bent down. In one lightning quick strike, the officer smashed the butt of the pistol into the center of Chuck's face. His nose busted, streams of blood squirting from his nostrils like caterpillar guts from under a boot. Jarvis and Sam rushed forward to his rescue, but they were greeted with a pistol.

"You just hold the fuck on, right there," the officer said.

"Guess we'll add resisting arrest and assaulting an officer to the charges." He grabbed Chuck by the throat and hoisted him to his feet. He shoved him toward his friends, who caught him as he stumbled. "Get inside the station. Now."

Sam and Jarvis helped Chuck hobble forward. He winced, the pain too much to risk pressure on his foot.

"And the next time one of you decides you want to get rowdy, I'll put a bullet in your fuckin' head."

With their backs to him, they couldn't see his face, but they could tell from the sound of his voice he spoke through a broad grin.

Brenda knelt next to Lilah and offered her a wet cloth. She smiled and took the rag, arched herself back on the pullout they found in the pharmacy's break room, and placed it on her forehead. She closed her eyes. Brenda rubbed the girl's shoulder and asked her if there was anything else she could get her.

"Is there anything to eat?"

"What would you like?"

Lilah's eyes shifted. "Is there... any meat? I know I shouldn't. A day ago I couldn't even think about meat. But I'm so hungry."

"I don't... I don't think so. There's whatever we grabbed from the store and I spotted a vending machine by the checkout counter."

"Oh." Her disappointment almost broke Brenda's heart. "I guess, crackers or potato chips, whatever they have."

"Is that enough to fill you up?"

"Not sure. I haven't eaten any real food in a long while. I'm scared I might get sick again."

Brenda didn't know exactly what the girl meant by "real food", but it frightened her. Surely she couldn't have survived only on human flesh over the past few months. She had to have eaten other things... *right?*

"Thank you for taking care of me," Lilah said, closing her eyes. "I know it must be hard, considering how my brother treated you back at the zoo. If I were you, I wouldn't have been so nice."

"Well, I'm usually a good judge of people. And you don't seem anything like your brother."

"He brainwashed me, you know. He was like... a disease. He infected me."

"You weren't the only one. He had a whole army of kids that bought into his psychotic escapades."

Lilah scrunched her lips together. "That's because they were as crazy as him. I look back on it and I can't believe how I went along with it."

"Maybe you feared what he'd do to you if you didn't comply."

"Maybe." She opened her eyes and faced Brenda, a sick grin briefly overpowering her face. "Maybe I liked it."

Brenda's heart wriggled. This was the girl her son fell in love with? A girl who participated in cannibalism and used hard drugs? *She's changing. She's not that way any more. You can tell. You could always tell about people.* She wanted to believe it, but it took a special kind of crazy to get involved in that lunacy. *They twisted her, HE twisted her. Malek. He brainwashed her and pumped her full of drugs and she had no idea what she was doing. Matty only wants to help her. Help her get better. Help her be the person he sees on the inside.* Brenda thought she saw glimpses of that person too, but in that moment she doubted whether that person existed at all.

"I don't believe that," Brenda said, hiding her disbelief behind a smile. "I think deep down inside you're a wonderful person who cares about people. I think your brother did some very disturbing things that altered your perception. I think once the sickness is purged from your body, the real rehabilitation can begin."

"Rehabilitation?" Lilah asked. "You sound like a psychiatrist. And I would know. I've seen my fair share of them."

Brenda chuckled softly. "Before I became a full-time mother, I studied psychology at Rutgers. Night school. That's where I met my first husband. He was going to school to become a nurse, and working at Costbusters part-time. We shared a few classes, went on a few dates, and voilà. The next thing you know, they offered Sam a management job and he quit college to make a career in retail, and it all went downhill from there. Three kids, one divorce, one second marriage, and here we are."

Lilah managed a smile, but it hurt. Even the most insignificant muscle ached.

"But, that's boring stuff you don't want to hear," Brenda said.

"No, I like it. Sounds... normal," Lilah told her.

"Your family wasn't normal?"

"Sure. If you consider your brother murdering your parents normal, then yes."

"Oh..."

"He claimed the sun did it. That's what he told Carp and I. But we knew better. Maybe if they had lived, we wouldn't be where we are today."

Brenda put her hand back on Lilah's bare shoulder. Her skin was clammy and cold. "I'm sorry about your parents."

"It's okay. They were assholes anyway."

"Huh." Brenda had expected her to break down, mourn them in some way. Maybe the drugs she had taken still numbed her true feelings. The shit continued working its way through her, tearing her apart from the inside out. It was possible she wouldn't be herself for some time.

Rehabilitated.

Maybe she's permanently fucked, her inside voice spoke up. *Maybe she's every bit a killer her brother was.*

She couldn't think like that. She had to see the good in people, the person on the inside. For Matty's sake, she hoped so. But once the girl was better and on the mend, if she doubted Lilah for a second, thought she was as twisted as Malek, she'd do whatever it'd take to protect her son.

Anything?

Anything.

"Brenda?" Lilah asked, her voice sugary sweet. Her eyes slipped behind her fluttering lids. "Could you find me a blanket? I want to sleep."

Brenda put a hand on her forehead, feeling the heat escaping Lilah's pores as she made contact.

"Jesus, you're burning up."

"No, Mark. *I won't eat it,*" Lilah whispered. Her arms and legs twitched. Lips quivered. *"I'm not a killer, Mark. I'm... not... like... you."*

Brenda kissed her forehead before calling her husband, telling him to scrounge up all the blankets and towels he could find.

The officer locked them in the holding cell and pretended to swallow the key. "Just kiddin'. I'm such a prankster."

They weren't amused by the officer's antics.

Sam read the small engraved tin tag on the big man's chest. "Officer Mickey?"

"That's Sargent Mickey. Sargent James Mickey," he told them sternly, the words rehearsed.

"Okay," Sam said. *"Sargent* Mickey. Come on. What are you doing here?" He figured the best way out was to reason with the man, find out what he wanted, give it to him, and be on their merry way, assuming the man wanted something. The bodies outside suggested he wanted to watch them burn. *No,* Sam thought. *If he wanted us to burn, we'd be out there already.* "I get it. We were jaywalking. Shame on us. We shouldn't have done it and I'm truly sorry, but this—" He pointed to the jail and everything around him with a wavy finger. "This is a little much, don't you think? Is there a fine we can pay and be done with it? There's a family member we need to get back to. She's very sick and needs the medicine—"

"Oh, right," Mickey said. He stretched his fingers in the air and wiggled them, making air quotes. Sam hated when people used air quotes. Especially when he was the one being quoted. *"The medicine."*

"It is medicine!" Chuck shouted. His face was a mess. Between the pounding he took back at the rehab center and the one suffered outside, he looked like he had survived ten rounds with Tyson and lost badly. "It is medicine, you fucking bastard!"

"You watch your goddamn mouth, you insufferable little shit!" Mickey shouted back. "I swear to God, you will not await trial and I will blow your goddamn brains out all over the fucking place. Then I'll take your skull and fuck the exit wound with my twelve-inch cock."

This shut everyone up.

"Goddammit," Mickey said, chuckling, the redness on his cheeks fading. "I almost lost my cool there. Whatta mistake that woulda been, right?" He bent over and slapped his knee. Laughter escaped his mouth, throaty and strange. "Whew, doggie!"

Sam opened his mouth, but thought better of speaking. He succumbed to the notion it was best to wait this thing out, see where it would go. He couldn't keep them here forever.

"So, I wish I could stay and shoot the shit with you gentlemen, but I have a helluva lot of paperwork to attend to. But don't worry your heads, you'll get your due process and if The Judge wants to slap you with a fine and send you on your way, then so be it. You'll be outta here without further deliberation, you have my word." Mickey's demeanor shifted. "But if he doesn't—and I have to say, possession of narcotics, resisting arrest, and assault on an officer are serious in these parts—then you boys better buckle up and start making amends with your maker. Catch my meaning?"

Mickey's wide grin sunk their hearts.

-2-

After Bob handed his wife a few blankets for Lilah, he strolled down the pain relief aisle to see what he could take for the drum beating in his temples over the past two hours. He scanned the shelves and picked up a bottle of ibuprofen. His mind wandered away from the pulsing needle in the epicenter of his brain, into the past where he'd been enjoying a wonderful life, pre-apocalypse. He had it all: a beautiful wife whose love and support were parallel to none, three nearly-flawless stepchildren who accepted him into their hearts, the ideal home, a job he enjoyed and patients he loved even more. His life had been complete. Perfect.

And it all ended when the sun tried to wipe out humanity.

Tried.

Popping two pills in his mouth, he thought about how worse things could be. Would things go back the way they were? Would he ever enjoy a long afternoon of jogging and tennis? Would the Gaines family spend another Friday night on the couch watching movies and eating popcorn until their bellies sagged?

Things could be worse, he reminded himself. He had Brenda by his side and the kids were still alive, and even though they weren't all here, they had no reason to suggest otherwise. He thought about what he would do if one of them died. They weren't his children, but he had been around long enough to watch them grow, take them to ballet, dance recitals, and science fairs. One might argue he had been more of a father to them than Sam, but he was too good of a man to suggest something like that. He never saw spending time with them a competition like their father. And unlike their mother, Bob had never badmouthed Sam in front of the kids, and seldom agreed with his wife when she did so privately. Although he didn't care for Sam as a person, he didn't hate him, and often sparked cordial conversations. One time, several years back, he suggested they become friends, grab a beer sometime and have a talk. The idea went over like a lead canoe. Sam had never been outright mean, but there had always been this indignation bubbling beneath the surface.

Now that the world was over and the real struggle began, it no longer mattered if they existed on good terms. Reality set in like storm clouds on a sunny afternoon, and after nearly a decade of putting up with Sam's shit, suffering through his tantrums and Type A personality, it was time for Bob to stick his chest out and set him straight. No more dancing around sensitive subjects, no more being treated like a "welcome" mat. It was time to step up to the plate and swing for the fences.

As he popped two more pills into his mouth and swallowed, he heard Brenda scream, "She's having another seizure!"

He took off down the aisle with speed he never knew he had. His foot slipped while making the sharp turn around a spin-rack holding postcards, but he was able to keep himself from falling. He sprinted toward the sound of his frantic wife, rolling his sleeves past his elbows. When he turned down the last aisle, he spotted Brenda kneeling beside Lilah, holding the girl's hand with both of her own. Lilah convulsed rapidly, gagging on air. He scrambled toward them and slid on his knees like a flashy rock star.

"What happened?" Bob asked.

"I don't know," Brenda said, her voice shaky and full of panic. "I was sitting next to her, holding her hand while she slept. Next thing I know she's having a seizure."

Bob looked in her mouth. He could see Lilah's tongue rolling back and forth between her teeth. Quickly, he unfastened his belt buckle.

"What are you doing?" Brenda asked.

He didn't have time to answer. With one rip the belt was off his waist. He wrapped his hands with each end and gently placed the leather between her lips.

"I need you to hold her mouth steady," he told his wife. "But be careful. Don't put your fingers where she can bite you."

Brenda carefully did as she was asked and opened the girl's mouth wide enough so Bob could slip the belt inside. Once the belt was in place, Brenda let go and backed away. He continued to hold the belt until her bout was over. The second she stopped, he removed the belt from her mouth and tapped her cheek, praying to

God the child would wake.

Foam erupted from her mouth, sputtered on her lips. Bob turned Lilah sideways. The frothy mixture of stomach bile and cracker fragments exploded forth, collecting in a small puddle on the floor. A few chunks splattered Brenda's pants, but she didn't seem to mind. She held Lilah's hair back, allowing her to concentrate on purging her stomach.

Brenda shot her husband a grave look, and he stared back, dread forging wrinkles on his forehead. He had forgotten about his headache, but once he remembered, the pain returned with a vengeance.

"I'm worried," Brenda said. "They should be back by now."

"They better get here soon." Whatever maleficent substance pumped through the girl's system was killing her, slowly and violently. He didn't voice his opinion, but Brenda saw his eyes shift, and she knew exactly what her husband was thinking.

Lilah was going to die.

Sargent Mickey was carrying a cardboard box overflowing with paper-packed files when Chuck awoke from his cat nap. Sam and Jarvis were sitting in opposite corners of the holding cell, watching the man closely as he made several trips back and forth. There was simply nothing else to look at.

"How come no one fills the Keurig around here?" Sargent Mickey asked. "They always leave it for me. You know how much that pisses me off?"

No one answered him.

"Golly," he muttered, disappearing back the way he came. A few minutes later he emerged with another box in his hand, equally full as the last one. "Be a cop, they said. It'll be a shitload of paperwork, they said." He stopped and placed a finger on his lip. "Oh wait. They didn't say that!" He raised the box of folders above his head and smashed it against the floor like a cavemen bringing a rock down on the head of his injured quarry. Stewing, Mickey placed his hands on his hips, looked down at the mess he had created, and sucked wind like he had run a marathon. His face wrinkled like a throwaway dress shirt. He turned to his prisoners and stared at them as if their presence made him want to vomit.

"Fuck are you bozos lookin' at?"

Sam looked at his feet, feeling the cop's eyes fall on him. He couldn't believe the man was still carrying out his duties as if the world hadn't ended. Society was no longer civil. There was chaos all around them, the echelons of a stable social order had crumbled. There were no more cops. No more law. No judicial system in place. No one to prosecute the guilty. They were all guilty of one thing or another, a part of living now. *No one survives this world without doing something dishonest or unjust.*

"I know what you're thinking," Sargent Mickey said. Sam didn't look, but he could tell the cop was staring directly at him. "You think I'm crazy. You think all of this is one big bowl of nutzo soup. Ain't that right?"

Bingo, Sam thought.

"Well allow me to drop a little knowledge on you. I have a family. I have people who care about me. People who need me in a time like this. But you know who needs me more? The United States of America. That's who. And I'll be damned if I let this great country go to waste."

"Sir, we appreciate everything you're doing," Jarvis said. "But you need to let us go."

"Let you go?" Mickey asked. "Just let you go. So, what—you could break the law all over again? Do you know the statistics on repeat offenders in this country? It's sickening! We need harsher punishments for first offenders and I will take this all the way to the Supreme Court!"

"Sir, there are people out there doing worse things than jaywalking," Jarvis said. He banged the wall with his fist. "Like killing people!"

"And they will be dealt with!" Mickey pressed his face against the bars. "I will bring them in and they will be judged like every other lawbreaker!"

Jarvis looked to Sam with a *how-the-fuck-do-I-get-through-*

to-him face. Sam grimaced. Jarvis backed off. He slammed himself against the wall, cupped his hands over his face, and slid down until he was seated on the cool concrete floor.

Chuck cleared his throat. "What can I do to get out of here?" Chuck asked. "I don't wanna die. I want to get out of here. I'll do anything, I just don't wanna die."

His words brought a smile to Sargent Mickey's face.

"Son, you should have thought about that before you broke the law," Mickey said with the voice of a pastor giving a light sermon. "Should have thought about that good and hard. Hopefully good ol' Judge Murphy Fayden will have mercy on your soul. Whether you believe in the Good Lord or not, I'd start prayin' if I was you." With a few steps to his left, Mickey disappeared out of sight, although no one in the holding cell truly believed he was gone.

"What do we do?" Chuck asked. Sweat poured down his forehead in several rivulets. His lips were shaking as if he were cold, but the temperature in the cell was far from frigid. He tapped the sides of his head with his fists as if trying to shake loose an idea. "What the fuck do we do?"

"I don't know—" Sam said, but Chuck screamed, "You don't know? How could you not know!"

Sam turned and faced him, kneeling down to his level. "Look, you can't freak out—"

"I can't freak out! I can't freak out! What the fuck are you talking about, man! That crazy bastard is going to kill us! Why would I not freak out!"

Sam glanced over at Jarvis with pleading eyes. He put his hands up as if to tell him, "You're all on your own with this one." As Sam turned back, Chuck smashed his fists against his head, breaking away from the harmless gentle taps. Sam grabbed his wrists, trying prevent the man from hurting himself. Chuck screamed, "Get the fuck away from me!" and wrestled for control of himself. A second later, they heard the loud clang of metal swinging against metal behind them. They stopped and faced the hallway.

Sargent Mickey had his baton out, an exasperated mug on his face. He sucked in deep breaths, glaring at the three prisoners as if they had called his mother a fat pig. "That's enough, you motherfuckers!" With his free hand he reached over and grabbed three pairs of manacles off the wall next to their cell. He smiled when he read their expression. "That's right. Stand up, put your hands against the wall. No funny business. You know I don't tolerate no funny business."

Chuck cried as Sam helped him to his feet.

"Where should we start?" Tina asked Matty once they were inside the sporting goods store. She had gone in alone and made sure there weren't any squatters waiting to attack them once their guard was down. She did this aisle by aisle, checking the back stockroom and employee lounge. She was quick about it, not wanting to leave Matty out of her sight for more than a few minutes. "I noticed they have a lot high quality rifles behind the counter over there."

"Mmm," Matty said, his eyes darting away from the weapons counter. "How about camping supplies?"

In the same moment, Tina winced and smirked. "Thought a young boy like you would love to hold a gun. You know, because of all the *Call of Duty* you play."

"Yeah," Matty said, not sounding the least bit interested. "Guess I'm weird like that." Shuffling toward the camping section, he grabbed the backpack closest to him. He opened it and glanced inside, determining how much stuff he could cram in there.

"It's not weird," Tina said. "Different. But not weird."

"Most kids my age would love to hold a gun. Fire one, too."

"Yeah, I bet. Look, I know it's dangerous and all, but you don't have to be afraid of guns. If you use them right, respect them, know what they're capable of, there's nothing to fear. If used properly, guns could be a good thing. Especially..."

He glanced over at her. "Especially since what?"

"You know. Now that you have someone you want to protect.

Someone you care about."

"I care about lots of people," he told her, setting the backpack down and reaching for the sky blue 32.5L Marmont Daypack. It was the most expensive pack on the shelf and he could see why; it had plenty of compartments for water, zippered pockets for fitting phones and other hand-held devices, not to mention the cushioned laptop sleeve. It was everything Matty could have wanted in a companion pack. He slipped it over his shoulders. It was a little loose so he tightened the straps until it fit snug.

"You know what I'm talking about."

"Yeah, I know."

"I can teach you."

His head snapped toward her. "Teach me what?"

"How to shoot?" She narrowed her eyes. "What did you think I was talking about?"

"Nothing." He returned his attention back to the shelf and sorted through the hip holsters. "I don't think I need to shoot a gun to protect Lilah."

Tina placed her hands on her hips and tapped her foot on the linoleum-tiled floor. "Oh yeah? What if we run into a gang like the cannibals again? What if instead of baseball bats and spiked clubs, they have shotguns. How will you protect her from that?"

Matty stood in awkward silence, wishing the uncomfortable moment away.

"Matty?"

"What?"

"Do you have an answer?"

"Not really."

"Why?"

He turned to her. "I guess, because, I don't think we'll run into anyone like that again."

Tina wrinkled her forehead. "Matty, I hate to break it to you, but the world has changed. You know that. Better than anyone." He knew she was talking about the scar on the side of his face. He touched it gently as she asked, "Why are you playing dumb with me?"

He dropped the hip bag at his side. "I don't know..."

"I remember what it was like to hold my first gun," she said with a childish smirk. "I was eight. My father taught me. I remember he told me to never aim it at somebody or something unless I was going to pull the trigger and wanted them to go away and never come back. I know you're scared, but I promise you, it will be a good thing."

He wasn't so sure.

Turning to the gun counter, she said, "Come. It won't take long."

-3-

Sargent Mickey pushed the three men along with the barrel of his .38 Special. They headed down a long corridor, an elevator waiting for them at the finish. The fluorescent lights in the hallway flickered, buzzing like busy bees.

"Power sucks," Mickey said, glancing at the long bulbs above. "Got enough gas to keep the generator running for years. Problem is, the generator ain't big enough to keep the entire station running at once." They were five feet from the elevator when Mickey said, "I sure hope the elevator don't get stuck."

The way the cop laughed at this unsettled them.

The elevator opened with a ding. Sam stepped on first, not his own choice; Mickey had shoved him in the back, propelling him forward. He didn't push Jarvis or Chuck, and Sam sensed Mickey had singled him out. Sam wasn't exactly sure what he did to piss the brawny man off. The cop's deranged eyes settled on him the entire duration of their walk.

After all four men entered the elevator and the door closed behind them, Mickey punched the GROUND LEVEL button and their electronic casket descended. "Here we go."

A few seconds later the elevator slowed turbulently, bouncing like a puppeteer yanked on the cables above, until finally they reached their destination.

"Not the smoothest ride..." Mickey admitted. The elevator doors retracted, and Mickey ushered them out like the place was on fire. "Hurry up," he grumbled.

Down another long hallway with flickering florescent bulbs, the tall wooden courtroom doors stood, stained chocolate mahogany. Mickey rushed ahead with child-like excitement. He grabbed the satin nickel door handle and pulled it open, waving the three men inside, his face glowing with demented excitement.

"Destiny awaits," he said, doing a terrible impersonation of a daytime game-show host.

Sam led the three of them inside. The second they entered the courtroom, the familiar odor hit them, its potency on a level they never experienced before. The miasma held the room hostage, causing Chuck to cough and gag, the heavy odor creeping down his throat.

Sam surveyed the room, barely able to stomach the putrid smoky stench; it didn't take long to spot the offender. *Offenders,* he thought. The jury box was occupied by twelve corpses, all of whom suffered a recent encounter with the sun. The exposure had baked their bodies, and if Sam didn't already know they were once human, they could have been mistaken for tree branches covered in dark sap. Sargent Mickey hadn't gone through great lengths to undress them, and most of the jurors sat with tattered garments. A woman in her forties, gristle hanging from the temples of her glasses. A man in his fifties sat, his mouth agape as if in his final moments he had made amends with his maker. A kid, no older than twenty, had clenched his eyes shut, unable to watch his own demise as the flames surrounded him, liquefied the flesh on his arms, neck, and face. A little girl, her pig tails caked and stiff with cooked fat and blood, sat in the front row, a confused expression forever planted on her little face, her lips twisted, forehead scrunched, and brow raised above her empty sockets. The rest of the jurors had no distinct traits detailing their last moments alive.

Sam dropped to his knees. Chuck puked behind the flagpole stand, unloading bile and other rank stomach fluids onto the faded blue carpet. Jarvis found it hard to keep his balance and placed a hand on the bench next to him.

The officer prodded the three men toward the defendant's box. Chuck, trembling with fear, stumbled and fell to the floor.

"Oh, Jesus-fucking-Christ," Mickey said. He picked the man up with one hand, the other hand tightly gripping his .38, ready to blast away if Sam or Jarvis so much as flinched.

After getting his prisoners settled in the box, he turned and faced them, sticking his chest out proudly. "Let us face the flag," he said, spinning on his heels to face the American flag Chuck had almost soiled. He put a hand over his chest and looked at Sam, Jarvis, and Chuck out of the corner of his eye, making sure they were following his lead. They did so after they noticed Mickey was still watching. "I pledge allegiance..."

After The Pledge was finished, he twirled back, glaring at them as if they were on trial for murder.

"I'll get Judge Murphy Fayden," he said, his lips barely moving. "Yous be nice now."

The second Mickey left the courtroom, Chuck screamed, "We need to get the fuck outta here, man!"

"Are you fucking nuts?" Jarvis whispered. "If he hears you, he'll kill us."

Sam leaned over. "I have to go with Chuck on this one. Obviously this asshole isn't going to let us waltz out of here."

"No shit." Jarvis thought for a beat. Without warning, his eyes bulged and he snapped his fingers. "Guys, trust me."

"Trust you how?"

Jarvis grinned and arched his brow. "No one knows crazy like I know crazy."

The rifle felt alien in his hand, as if it had come from another dimension. He did as Tina instructed, everything except wrapping his finger around the trigger. He wouldn't do that unless he was ready to fire and Tina applauded his interest in safety. The last thing she wanted was the kid blowing his own hand off, or worse. Matty held the gun like it weighed thirty pounds, the barrel dipping as he aligned his eye with the receiver.

"No," she said, shaking her head. "Like this." She took the gun from him. "The stock goes under your arm like so." She wedged the stock in her armpit and readied herself to aim. "Then take your left hand and place it on the forestock. Not too far down, not too far up. In the middle. It'll give you the best support." She closed her right eye and held the .22 caliber Henry Golden Boy to her left. "You can rest your finger on the trigger guard until you're ready to fire, if you don't trust yourself keeping it on the actual trigger."

"I don't trust myself."

She grinned while wondering if this had been a mistake, if

teaching him would cause more harm than good. Even though she was an expert, accidents happened. She saw them almost everyday at work. The gun freaks used to argue guns never killed people, *people* with guns killed people, but that wasn't always true. Guns killed people, too. Maybe not as much as people with guns, but there were always incidents. She had once responded to a six-year old who found his father's Glock and didn't know the difference between the actual weapon and the water gun he had been given on his fourth birthday. The kid killed his mother, pumping two bullets square in her chest and severely injured daddy. The local NRA chapter had a field day with the story, blaming the father for being a careless gun owner, and maybe that was true, but Tina—while being a gun supporter all her life—thought the gun had been the guilty party that day.

"You don't trust me either, do you?" Matty asked.

The memory of walking on the scene and seeing the kid's mother bleeding on the carpet while the six-year old slapped her face in desperation faded from Tina's thoughts. "No, it's not that. It's..."

"You can say it. I'm a klutz. I get it."

"Matty, you're not a klutz. Just—I feel bad not asking your mother for permission."

He chuckled. "Permission? Oh, jeez. I'll be sixteen next year. I don't think she needs to give me permission—"

"Still," she interrupted. "You're her son. And I know if you were my child, I'd like a say in whether or not my kid is learning how to handle a gun."

"Whatever. We need to gather more stuff and head back anyway. I want to grab some headlamps, backpacks for the rest of the group, some Carhartts, and as many MREs we can pack in those shopping carts."

"MREs?" Tina asked. The acronym sounded familiar, but she couldn't place it.

"Meal Ready to Eat," he explained.

Survival training, she remembered the second the words fell from his lips.

"They have a ton of them," Matty said. "All of them are freeze-dried and will last up to twenty-five years. Soren said they have rooms full of them in Alaska."

"Yeah, well, Soren said a lot of things. Not all of them are true."

Matty didn't argue with her, although he wanted to. "Whatever. Help me?"

"Sure thing, kid." Her attention turned back to the rack of guns. "But first..." She yanked a 12 gauge off the wall and presented it to him."I want to show you how to load this puppy."

He looked at the gun, then to her, seemingly unimpressed. "I thought we were over this. Thought you needed to ask my mom for permission."

Ask for permission or for forgiveness?

"Well... it's the apocalypse. I don't see her having much of a problem with it."

It was always better to ask for forgiveness.

-4-

The door leading to the judge's chambers opened, and The Honorable Murphy Fayden strolled through, shutting the door behind him with authority. "All rise," Judge Fayden announced, although the only three men in the room—alive—were already standing. The Judge saluted the American flag and took a seat on the bench. He waved at the others, commanding them to do the same.

Sam, Chuck, and Jarvis exchanged identical glances: *Is this guy fucking kidding me?*

Judge Fayden wore a long black judicial robe, embroidered gold seams outlining the entire garment. Atop his head rested a bench wig, something Sam had only seen in European History books, Halloween stores, and *Pirates of the Caribbean* movies. The curly stark-white hair fell at his shoulders. Fayden glowered at the three offenders over glasses several sizes too small for his head. The whole look didn't fit, and Sam thought he looked more like a cartoon character than a Magistrate.

Jarvis almost lost it, subduing his laughter the moment before it left his mouth.

"Um, Sargent Mickey?" he asked. "I think—"

"It's Judge Fayden, boy. Sargent Mickey left to attend to some other important matters and will only be called upon for emergency situations."

"Yeah..." Jarvis said, losing his wide smile. "Yeah, okay. That makes sense."

The Judge shuffled through the papers on his desk, stopping to examine one. Sam doubted there was anything important written on it, or anything at all, but Judge Fayden stared at it like it contained something enlightening. He wondered about Sargent Mickey, if he was truly an officer of the law or some deranged psychopath who stumbled across an empty police station and took on the role. *Or several roles,* in this bizarre case.

Sam glanced over at Jarvis. He was breathing differently, deeper, like an athlete about to step on the field for the biggest game of his career. He lowered his head, whispered silently to himself, prepping himself for what was to come. What exactly, Sam didn't know. On one hand Jarvis's "idea" scared the shit out of him. On the other, Sam didn't think Jarvis could say or do anything that would make their situation worse.

Trust me, Jarvis had said.

There really was no other choice.

"Court is now in session," Judge Fayden said, smacking the bench with his gavel aggressively. "Case number 5607 dash 201, let's get started. The defendants," he glared at the three of them contemptuously, "that's you three fucknuts—stand accused of ONE COUNT each, Jaywalking; ONE COUNT each, Breaking and Entering; ONE COUNT each, Possession of a Controlled Dangerous Substance; ONE COUNT each, Resisting Arrest; ONE COUNT each, Aggravated Assault on a Police Officer." Fayden exhaled as if announcing the charges stole his breath away.

Hearing the charges aloud brought back dispiriting memories for Jarvis. Memories of sitting alone in the exact spot he was now, his good-for-nothing court-appointed lawyer seated next to him, telling him lies while Jarvis stared at the empty space in the audience where his parents should have been. A ghostly pain had slithered through his guts when the judge—a *real* judge—told him he was going to jail—a *real* jail—for what seemed like a long time, but not really in the grand scheme of things. *I killed a child and only served fifty months in state prison,* he thought. It was like he had gotten away with murder.

Jarvis gazed at the bronzed Bald Eagle mounted on the wall behind the judge's bench. He glanced over at the empty stenographer's seat. He forced himself to look at the jurors, mouths that would never speak again and decide nothing today.

This wasn't a courtroom.

It was a fucking joke.

And Jarvis decided it was time to get funny.

"Gentlemen," Judge Fayden began, "at this time I will commence with your arraignments. The charges will be reread to you individually and I will then ask you to enter a plea of guilty or not guilty. Understood?"

Jarvis rose, scooted past Chuck, and let himself out of the defendant's box. It was Sargent Mickey's eyes glaring at him, not Judge Fayden's.

"Boy..." Fayden said.

"Your Honor," Jarvis said, bowing like Fayden were the King of England. "If I may..."

Fayden said nothing.

"If it pleases the Court," Jarvis said, "I'd like to act as Counsel for myself and my co-defendants." Judge Fayden glowered over his glasses, but remained silent. Jarvis couldn't tell if his little stunt was working or sentencing them to a fiery death. "If it further pleases the Court," he continued, "and his eminence, I have prepared an opening statement which I'd like to submit to the bench and jury."

The Judge leaned back in his seat, rolled his eyes, and waved at them lazily, a gentle flick of the wrist.

"Thank you, Your Honor." Jarvis noticed Sam and Chuck's expression, the look of pure terror rendering their skin colorless. "Your Honor, ladies and gentleman of the jury, citizens of this fine town, my co-defendants stand before you accused of crimes we did not commit. Mind you, this is not to say we did not commit those specific acts—because we did—but what I will prove today is these actions were without criminal intent, and in these uncertain and changing times, I daresay they could not even be considered crimes. How can one be 'jaywalking' if there is no traffic to avoid, or traffic signals to advise when it is safe to cross? I submit this was a misapplication of an obsolete law. 'Breaking and Entering?' Yes. I must confess, we did forcibly enter a private establishment after operating hours. However, as we made plainly clear to the arresting officer, we were obtaining medical supplies for our gravely ill friend, who is still waiting for treatment a few miles from here. Her life depends on us, and so, yes, we broke into a facility where this medicine was stored. If you call that breaking the law, then ask yourself if you would feel the same knowing it saved a life. Was Oskar Schindler a criminal? He broke laws that saved thousands. Or how about John Stuart Mill's *The Greatest Good for the Greatest Many?* Doesn't this, without a doubt, serve The Greater Good?" Jarvis strolled closer and closer to the jury box, fighting his way through the emanating stink. The closer he became, the worse the smell, the putrid stench of twelve hot deaths. He had gotten so close he could touch the jurors in the first row, had his hands not been cuffed behind him. "And lastly, we stand accused of possession of a controlled dangerous substance. Well, let me be the first to tell you, ladies and gentleman of the jury, that stuff ain't gonna get you high. Oh, and the resisting arrest and assaulting an officer charge? Laughable. HA!" He pointed at one of the jurors, the blackened statue resembling a woman, and laughed along as if she had been laughing too. "We complied with Sargent Mickey's request all the way to the bitter end. Never stepped outside the boundaries once.

"So, the question here isn't 'were we guilty of possessing narcotics,' because lab results, which I can only assume the prosecution conveniently *lost* prior to these proceedings, will show no narcotics were in our possession. Boom. Not guilty. That is, unless you choose to take the word of the arresting officer, Sargent Mickey as gospel. No. The question is, 'why would he assume we had narcotics?' Is it because of how we looked? The color of our skin perhaps?" He paced back and forth with a troubled look on his face. Glancing at Judge Fayden out of his peripherals, he could tell the man wasn't biting. He was going to have to kick it up a notch. "Have we not learned to stop judging others by their outsides? Did the Civil Rights Movement accomplish nothing? Did Dr. King fail us?" The more he spoke, the louder he spoke. He made sure to amp up the intensity, hoping to grab Fayden's attention and hold it.

He turned to the juror's box for his next (and final) act. "You ma'am," he said, facing the burnt woman. He leaned over the oak railing and stood nose to nose with her. He could taste her smoky flesh in the back of his throat. His stomach somersaulted. "Do you wish the times of 'separate but equal' still reigned? Would you have war veterans like John Rambo ousted from your small town because he wore a uniform with which you did not agree?"

He heard Sam whisper, *"Oh Jesus Christ."*

"John Rambo? What the fuck is he talking about?" Chuck asked Sam under his breath.

Judge Fayden clearly had his fill of nonsense and tapped his gavel on the striking plate. "I think we've had enough—"

"You haven't had nearly enough, good sir!" Jarvis yelled, snapping his head toward the bench. "You haven't had nearly enough at all!"

Judge Fayden looked at Jarvis as if the man had stabbed him. "That's it! You are out of order—"

"You're out of fucking order!" Jarvis screamed, cackling uncontrollably. He composed himself quickly, before Fayden could open his mouth again and attempt to restore order. "Would you attack a simple boy because his maker gave him scissors for hands instead of fingers?" He turned from Fayden and hopped over the railing, landing inside the juror's box. He bent over and leaned in one of the corpse's ears. "Would you discriminate against the moon? The stars? It's not our fault the sun is one big giant orange asshole!" He rubbed his backside against the woman. "How does that suit your fancy? Whoo-hoo!"

"That's enough!" Fayden screamed, veins popping in his neck and forehead. He removed himself from the bench and stormed over to the juror's box. Jarvis didn't run. He stood, frozen, waiting for the judge to pull out his .38 Special from under his long black robe and blow his brains clean out of his skull. Instead, Fayden grabbed him by the collar and yanked him over the railing, planting him on the ground. "Get up you crazy son of a bitch!"

Jarvis complied, pushing himself to his feet. Fayden ushered him back over to the defendant's box, shoved him in, and closed the hip-high door behind him. Pleased with himself, Jarvis turned to the others, watched them shake their heads with clear disappointment. A wry grin settled on Jarvis's face, and he winked at them. Sam glared at him, wanting to punch his mouth off; Jarvis's stunt could have cost them their lives. Jarvis leaned forward and looked over his shoulder, nodding for the others to follow his eyes.

Sam and Chuck's eyes lit up like Christmas morning. They immediately straightened their backs, correcting their posture, and looked back to the bench. Judge Fayden had still been walking when Jarvis showed them the result of his loony actions.

Sam smiled as Fayden climbed back onto his seat and tapped the gavel three times in rapid succession.

"Thank you, counsel," Judge Fayden said, his eyes piercing, "for those opening remarks. Now, the prosecution has decided to rely upon the observations of the officer, and as a result the court will now make its ruling."

The first thing Jarvis noticed was the brooch on the woman's tattered suit. It was covered in sticky remnants of burnt flesh, blackened with human decay, but it was sharp and he was experienced with picking locks with safety pins, especially handcuffs. It had been somewhat of a hobby of his back in the day, but this was the first time he ever needed to put his talent to use in a timely matter. The "opening remarks" routine had been staged so he could nab the brooch, and Jarvis figured the crazier he acted, the better chance he had at masking his true intentions. He didn't want to call himself a genius—not yet—but he took a moment and a deep breath and congratulated himself on a job well done. He took the brooch and went to work.

"Is the defense ready to hear its ruling?" Judge Fayden asked, clearly bored with this whole charade.

Jarvis pleaded for more time with his eyes. He needed a minute, maybe two. The cuffs were tougher than he expected and he hoped they weren't a new model, impossible to pick. He stood while he fiddled with the lock, trying to figure out how to buy himself more time.

"The defense would like to further question the arresting officer," Jarvis said. "Sargent James Mickey."

Judge Fayden's eyes bugged as if he had been defeated in some way. "Sargent Mickey is unavailable at the moment," Fayden countered. "Call your next witness or I will have no choice but to move forward with the ruling."

"Um, b-but," Jarvis said, stammering. "How's about recess, Your Honor?" Jarvis asked.

"Recess?"

"A discovery period? Right? That comes next, I think."

"That's enough, counselor. Take a seat. I think you've made enough mockery of this Court for one day."

Jarvis sat down slowly, fiddling with the lock one last time.

Fayden sighed, raised a paper closer to his eyes, and said, "After careful consideration, this Court finds you guilty on all counts. The three of you are hereby sentenced to death by hanging."

Chuck screamed and nearly fainted.

-5-

Chuck's blood pounded so furiously he thought his organs might fail. His chest burned, his heart pumping liquid glass through his extremities. It was hard to breathe, so he stopped trying and let his body do whatever it wanted. Lightheaded, Chuck climbed to his feet and stumbled. Jarvis caught his arm before he fell out of the defendant's box.

God, help me! Chuck thought. He'd never been a devout Christian, but the last thing he wanted was to die, and who better to help him now than the almighty deity. He managed to escape his fate on more than once occasion since the apocalypse started, which he attributed to the good grace of the Big Man Upstairs. That, and he was beginning to get a handle on this whole survival thing. Somehow he had managed to keep it together, kept his wits about him when Malek and his bloodthirsty buddies had him locked away in that cage—but now, seeing Sargent Mickey approach them in that ridiculous judge's costume, he sensed the inevitable. And for some strange reason, God was nowhere to be found. He felt alone. Abandoned.

Mickey strolled over to the defendant's box and reached for Chuck first. He grabbed him by the back of his scrawny neck and ripped him from Jarvis's grasp. Chuck tumbled to the floor, unable to keep his balance. He tried crawling away, but Mickey brought his boot down on his ankle. It sounded like a twig snapping over the knee of some burly lumberjack. Chuck screamed, cried, and begged for mercy he would never receive. While continuing to apply pressure to Chuck's ankle, Mickey turned back to Sam and Jarvis, wagging his finger.

"Don't you boys try any funny business while I'm gone," Mickey said. He held up a key. "I'm gonna lock you fuckers in. No escaping, so don't bother trying."

"Don't do this, man!" Chuck hollered. "Please, for the love of God, don't do this!"

Mickey glanced down at the groveling nitwit, laughter emanating from the bowels of his throat. "You disgust me," he said.

Chuck pushed himself to his knees, clasping his hands together in prayer. "Let me go!"

Mickey took the back of Chuck's head and held it firm while he smashed his knee into the beggar's face. Chuck dropped to the floor, unconscious, blood leaking from the hole in his lip where his front teeth pushed through. He turned back to Jarvis and Sam. "I'll be keeping an eye on yous." He pointed to the far corner of the room where a camera roosted on the ceiling. "Make one move I don't like, and I'll make sure you fuckers roast slowly."

He picked Chuck up with both hands and flung the lightweight man over his shoulder. He carried him out of the room, making sure to lock the door behind him. There was only one door out of the courthouse, and hope abandoned them when the audible click of the lock slipping into place echoed throughout the room.

"I killed him," **Jarvis** said, his eyes fixed on the door, their only means to freedom. "I got him killed."

"He was going to kill us all anyway. Decided it the moment he put us in the car."

"How is he going to hang him?" Jarvis asked. "It's light out. He can't go outside without burning himself up."

"I don't know. I don't want to know." Sam looked behind Jarvis's back. "How are you doing with the lock?"

Jarvis brought his hands to his face. Free hands.

"Good job."

"Doesn't matter."

"Sure it does. Do me."

Without much excitement, Jarvis picked the lock on Sam's cuffs in less than thirty seconds. Sam flung them across the room and stood up, rubbing his wrists.

"You might want to act for the camera," Jarvis suggested.

"He's not watching shit." Sam hopped out of the defendant's box. "He's preoccupied. Are you coming?" Sam asked.

Jarvis continued to sit, staring at his own lap. "What's the point?"

Sam sighed and placed his hands on his hips. "I know you think it's your fault, but it's not. Yeah, I mean you picked *that* rehab facility in *that* town, and maybe if we went elsewhere, we wouldn't be here. You can't change the past and you sure as shit can't keep continuing to blame yourself. You did the best you could given the circumstances. We would have never gotten what we needed if it weren't for you. No one in our group would've known how sick Lilah was if it weren't for you."

"Lotta good I'm doing her, here on death row." His eyes sparkled in the dim light the courtroom provided. "I'm a fucking failure."

Sam approached the defendant's box. "You are not a failure. Not in the least."

"I failed my family. My friends. You people."

"You don't think we've all made mistakes? You don't think we'd all like a rewind button and do our lives over again?" He remembered slapping Becky on the day of The Burn and how he wished to have that moment over again. "Trust me, Jarvis, we've all done things we regret. That's life, my friend. Life is a series of regrets. I don't want to bore you with stories you don't give a shit about, but I almost lost my kids before The Burn. I almost lost them because, well, for one I was an asshole. And two, I was never there for them. But now I realize what's important and what I have to do to get them back. And *I will* get them back. Just like you'll save Lilah."

Jarvis looked up, staring Sam on. His mood shifted, the poor-poor-pitiful-me face vanquished. He stood up, his head bouncing like a bobble-head doll. "Yeah..." he said, a faint smile spreading across his face.

"Yeah?"

"Yeah," he said confidently.

"Good." Sam jerked his thumb at the door. "Now, I believe we have an escape to plan."

Lilah's eyes shot open, and for a long while she stared up at the white-tiled ceiling, counting their crater-like freckles, concentrating on something else besides the beating drum that was her heart. The adrenaline rush came on strong and lasted longer than any good high she ever had. After counting craters became tiresome, she looked at Brenda, who held her hand the entire time. Bob hovered over her, pushing a bottle of water in her face. She drank slowly, careful not to overindulge and choke.

"How are you feeling?" Bob asked, touching her forehead. The fever was still running strong, but at least the girl was conscious.

"Like a hundred bucks," she replied groggily.

"Just a hundred?" Brenda asked.

"Maybe two?" She tried to smile but it hurt and made her want to puke. "Honestly, I feel like shit. I'm hot and cold all at once. I'm hungry and full. I'm sleepy and full of energy."

"You take it easy. It'll all be over soon."

"I'm going to die, aren't I?"

Bob wiped her forehead and forced a grin, although it came off like a grimace. "No, sweetheart. You're fine. Sam, Jarvis, and Chuck went to fetch some medicine to help with the withdrawals. They should be back..." He glanced at the clock on the wall, and knew it couldn't be correct. No way it was five o'clock. According to time's ticking hands, the sun would set in about an hour. "Soon. They should be back soon."

"You don't believe that, do you?"

Bob chewed on his tongue. "Yes, I do. We have no reason to believe otherwise."

"They left last night?" Lilah asked, holding her stomach as it bubbled and burned.

"Uh-huh."

"And they didn't return before sunup?"

"No."

Disappointment marked her face. "They're dead, aren't they?" Brenda said emphatically, "No."

"Lilah!" Matty said from down the aisle. He had a rifle slung over his back and pushed a shopping cart full of lifted merchandise.

"You're awake!"

She smiled at the sight of Matty's glowing face, but her expression suddenly changed, her mouth forming an O and blowing out a series of coughs. Foam bubbled on her lips and Brenda wiped her mouth with a fresh rag.

"How was your trip?" Brenda asked, trying to change the subject. She turned back to face her son, instantly setting eyes on the weapon strapped to his back. Her heart descended. Something changed; reality shifted. "Matty?" she asked.

"Great, Mom," he said. "We got a lot of cool stuff. Check out these MREs—"

"Matty, what is that?"

"It's... it's..."

Tina stepped in front of him. "It's my fault. We were in the store, looking for supplies, and they had a gun section. I used to be a cop so I showed him a few things, how to *safely* operate—"

"You taught my son how to fire a gun?"

Matty recognized the tone and backed away as if his mother were rabid.

"No," Tina said. "I would never do that. I only instructed him how to handle it. How to be safe."

"Oh," she said, wrinkling her brow, "well, that's much better."

Tina folded her arms across her chest. "Look, I know. I should have asked first."

"Yes, you should have."

"But, I think we could use a few more people in our group who can handle a gun. We don't know what we're going to face out there."

"So you chose my fifteen year old son to be your militant?"

Tina rolled her eyes. "Mrs. Gaines, look—"

"No, you look." Brenda rose to her feet, glaring at Tina, surveying her mistrustful eyes. "I don't care what you think this group needs, the next time you put a killing machine in my son's hands, you ask me first."

Several seconds of silence caused everyone to shift uncomfortably. Lilah coughed, not because she had to, but because the awkward moment needed to die.

"You got it," Tina said through strained lips.

"Matty," Brenda said, "get that thing off your back and give it to Tina."

"But, Mom—"

"Now."

Slowly, he did as his mother commanded. He handed Tina the rifle. She took it, mouthing the words, "I'm sorry." Matty looked to his mother, then to Lilah, who pretended to count the ceiling tile craters again, for the tenth time. Embarrassed, he ran down the aisle and disappeared around the bend. Brenda called after him, but it was useless; he was gone.

"Now look what you did," she said, storming past Tina and down the aisle after her son.

Mickey removed his hood and the goalie mask protecting him against the harmful rays of the sun. The winter jacket came off next, along with the snow gloves. He was sweating profusely and wiped his forehead with his knuckles. He kicked free his boots and tore off the snow pants he had stolen from one of the officer's lockers. Slipping into a pair of worn Nikes, Mickey announced, "All right, you law-breaking tugjobs," and unlocked the door to the courtroom. "It's time to pay for your sins!"

He pushed open the doors and found an empty courtroom, the defendant's box where Sam and Jarvis should have been, but now weren't. He quickly searched the courtroom, hands clamped to the sides of head, squeezing as if it were a over-sized pimple he meant to pop.

How is this possible?

There was no way the men escaped. They were handcuffed, for one. Two, there was only one door in and out of the courtroom and it was locked, he was sure of it. He irrationally thought they dug themselves out like a dog under the neighbor's fence, and searched the floor for evidence. He didn't find any secret tunnels, but he found the opened handcuffs, with the dead woman's brooch resting a few feet away.

He pieced it all together.

Jarvis and his silly act. It had been a distraction. A ruse. First-grade trickery. And...

It had worked.

"Motherfuckers!" Mickey shouted. He was more pissed off at himself than he was at Jarvis. He fell for it. Dumb bastard fell for the whole gag. "You dumb son of a bitch! You couldn't see it coming?" Mickey asked.

Judge Fayden frowned. "I couldn't see it. I only thought..."

"You only thought..." Mickey repeated childishly. "You only thought what?"

"Just thought he was fucking nuts!" Fayden cried.

"You stupid asshole."

"Fuck you, shit-for-brains! Where were you during the whole trial? Whacking off in the back again! Your pecker must be raw from all the abuse!"

"I don't hear you complaining!"

Fayden closed his eyes, breathing in through his nose and out through his mouth. "All right. Let's take a deep breath and calm the hell down. They couldn't have gone far. It's not dusk yet and they don't have any protective gear. They could still be in the station somewhere, waiting it out. All we have to do is wait for them to come out and boom. We got 'em."

"They could head for the woods. The trees would protect them."

Fayden scrunched his nose. "Risky play. Sometimes the trees aren't enough. Remember last week? Found those kids in the middle of the forest? Toasted."

Mickey slapped himself in the head. "Duh. Almost forgot."

Fayden smiled. "We'll search the station. If we don't find them by sundown, we'll take to the road. They wouldn't have gotten far."

"Plus..." Mickey said, giggling. "We know where they're going."

"Bet your ass we do. Help that little girl they keep yammering on about."

"Think we'll find more criminals once we get there?"

Fayden laughed. "You goddamn right we will. And they'll burn like the rest, until the earth is pure and free from the filth that stains it."

Mickey and Fayden left the courtroom, a sinister smile plastered to their shared surface.

Under the desk in the Judge's quarters, the small room behind the bench, they hid for an hour. They waited for Mickey to enter, prepared to attack the bastard if he found their secret spot. For some reason, the schizophrenic cop never thought to look there, the most obvious place in the whole municipal building. They listened through the paper-thin walls as the Sargent Mickey destroyed the place searching for them, cursing and yelling about how the entire mess was his fault and how his stupidity was going to ruin everything. If the cop hadn't scared them shitless, they would have shared a good laugh at his expense.

Jarvis peeked through the blinds and into the parking lot. The sun had ducked behind the horizon and he deemed it safe to travel outside again.

They opened the door and poked their heads into the courtroom, making sure it was free from their friend, the psychopath. When they were sure it was clear, they bolted. The doors to the courtroom were wide open and they sprinted down the hall until they reached a fork. Jarvis glanced at the hallway on his left, found it clear, and waved Sam on.

"How do you know where we're going?" Sam asked, still whispering.

"I don't. Keep moving."

They jogged about halfway down the hall when they heard footsteps ahead and watched a shadow form on the long wall. Jarvis grabbed Sam by the neck and yanked him into an office on their right. They slipped inside undetected. The footsteps grew closer. They could hear Mickey mumbling to himself, something about "killing the fuck out of those motherfuckers."

Jarvis looked around, his heart smacking against the walls of his chest. The office might have belonged to the chief of police, a secretary, or it may have been Sargent Mickey's. On the desk stood a framed family photo, a close group of a dozen strangers. Next to it sat a wedding photo, and sure enough, a young Sargent Mickey smiled back at him wearing a black tuxedo, his bride garbed in a long white dress, the veil pushed back revealing her smiley face. She wasn't Jarvis's type, but she wasn't bad-looking either. A better catch than what Jarvis thought Mickey deserved. The cop was a lot younger in the photo, more hair and less stress lines in his face, less crazy in his eyes. It was what he looked like before Judge Fayden entered his life.

Jarvis looked away from the photo and found a gun rack mounted on the wall, harboring two rifles and a shotgun. Jarvis stood and reached for one, but before he could make contact, Sam grabbed him by his shirt and pulled him across the room, into a small closet stocked with boxes of stationary goods.

Sam shut the closet door and placed a finger over his lips.

"Motherfuckers," they heard Mickey grumble. He was outside the door. They could hear him breathing. "No one escapes from me! No one!" They heard the desk flip, crash against the far wall, the picture-frame glass shattering into shards and specks.

Jarvis squinted and peered through the tiny crack between the closet doors. He watched Mickey hunch over to regain his breath. Standing up straight, the officer's face fixed in a ferocious snarl, reminding him of the feral cats in the back alley behind a restaurant he worked at in high school. Mickey turned to the gun rack, rubbing his hands together like a twisty-mustached villain in some black and white cartoon from the 1950's. He stole the rifle off the top rack, and immediately checked the cartridge. Finding it unloaded, he opened the sliding drawer beneath lowest rack and removed a box of ammo. As if he had no time left in the world, he shoved the bullets into the gun's belly, and rushed out of the room.

Sam and Jarvis waited until they couldn't hear "motherfucker" anymore.

Five minutes of interrupted silence seemed like more than enough time, and they opened the closet door.

"Think he's gone?" Jarvis asked. He hurried behind the overturned desk and rummaged through the drawers.

"God, I hope so," Sam replied, heading over to the gun rack.

"We have to hurry. He knows where we're going."

"He knows there's a sick girl and she's in a pharmacy

somewhere," Sam said, not seeming too concerned.

"No," Jarvis said, locating a pair of keys with "Cruiser #3" written on a piece of tape wrapped around the key ring. "No, you told him the name of the town."

Sam turned to him as if Jarvis was the Ghost of Christmas Past. "What?"

"You told him the name of the town when he arrested us."

"My son is there," Sam said. "Tina. Brenda. Bob."

"Then like I said." Jarvis jiggled the keys in the air. "We better fucking hurry."

They made certain Sargent Mickey's cruiser was gone before they rushed out into the parking lot like the building behind them was about to explode. Jarvis spotted Cruiser #3 almost immediately and rushed over to it, slipped the key into the lock, and watched as the button popped on the inside of the door. He ripped open the door, jammed the key into the ignition, recited a prayer he had heard in Narcotics Anonymous six-billion times, and cranked the fucker over. The engine roared, the power of eight-cylinders vibrating the seat beneath him. *Thank God,* he said, although God had nothing to do with anything that had happened over the last twenty-four hours, Jarvis was sure of it.

Sam sprinted over, opened the passenger's door, and hopped inside. "Gun it!"

Jarvis hammered the gas pedal.

As they peeled out of the parking space, they noticed a fresh cadaver swaying from a light pole in the gentle October wind, his face burnt beyond recognition. If it weren't for the man's flame-frayed attire, they would have never known it was Chuck. Scaly pink and oozing yellow scabs masked his face, looking more like a fresh cheese pizza than a man in his mid-thirties. Wisps of smoke rose off his raw flesh and tattered clothing; dusk had saved him from becoming the blackened brisket the two of them were accustomed to seeing.

Jarvis punched the gas and the cruiser sped out of the parking lot, leaving him and the other twelve hanged bodies behind, forever. They didn't look back and neither Sam nor Jarvis mentioned Chuck, the man who died so they could live, the whole way back to Havencrest and if they had it their way, they'd never speak his name again.

-7-

Sargent Mickey idled in the handicap space in front of Havencrest's one and only pharmacy. He killed the cruiser's brights and stared through the twelve-foot long picture window running across the entire length of the building's facade. Cones of light waved back and forth in a fury. People were inside, he confirmed it. The only thing left to do was bust them for illegal dope-smoking and harboring fugitives.

Mickey knew the sick-girl story was a goddamn lie conjured by a group of drug addicts, habitual offenders, and unlawful citizens trying to get one over on him. He wasn't stupid; he'd seen and heard it all before. Sargent Mickey promised himself he'd never be fooled by criminals again, not after what those savages did to his wife and kids a week after The Burn. He and some co-workers, all of whom survived the terrible tragedy that had claimed the lives of many others, let a pair of seedy characters stay at the police station, letting them live among their families. The two middle-aged men, no older than the three looters he found at that rehab facility, stumbled into the parking lot late one night, hurt and bleeding from a violent altercation taking place several hours earlier. They needed a place to crash for a few days to lay low from the people who were after them. They seemed weird and untrustworthy (he noted their quirks and distrusted the authenticity of their story), but the cops were good cops and good people and so were their family members, so they invited the two men indoors without asking many questions. The first couple of days were cordial, and the cops had barely spoken to their new mates, leaving them to their lonesome down in the holding cells, while the cops' families remained upstairs in the offices they had converted into bedrooms. Two days later, Sargent Mickey left to grab some snacks from a local convenience store—it was a Tuesday and Tuesday meant it was his turn to scavenge—and when he returned, he found his family along with the other cops and their families butchered, their body parts scattered across the station house like a macabre treasure hunt. It took damn near a month to clean up the mess and eradicate the smell, but Judge Fayden helped, putting in long hours while Sargent Mickey mourned the loss of his loved ones and hunted for their killers, which he later found and executed in the same manner they had exacted on his wife and children, only slower and more calculated. James Mickey Jr. was only eight and Ben Mickey was only four, and he thought of their miniature parts scattered like the toys in their playroom when he hacked their killers to pieces. After he satiated his hunger for vengeance, Mickey returned to work with full force and a new zest for law enforcement, scouring the county and beyond for offenders of all types, vowing to never let what happened to him happen to others. He found loads of lawbreakers, all shapes and sizes, sexes and age. Judge Fayden helped him lay down the law of the land, and punish those guilty, (which had been all of them) no exceptions. Everyone was guilty of something and Mickey always found it.

Damn skippy.

He pushed open the cruiser's door and stepped out, one size-twelve at a time. Despite being unable to look the sun in the eye, Mickey continued to rock his Big Texas sunglasses. Once out of the car, he leaned one arm on the open door, using his other hand to work the bullhorn. He watched shadows stir in the window as he brought the megaphone to his mouth.

"CITIZENS OF HAVENCREST," his voice boomed through the speaker. "IT HAS COME TO MY ATTENTION THAT YOU ARE HARBORING FUGITIVES IN THAT PHARMACY, AND TO ENSURE NO ONE GETS HURT, I ASK YOU ALL TO COME OUT WITH YOUR HANDS ABOVE YOUR HEAD, EVERY LAST SINGLE ONE OF YOU."

Shadows shifted within the pharmacy, but no one approached the window or complied with his demands.

Want to play hardball, huh? Mickey thought, shaking his head, but loving the adrenaline rush associated with busting criminals. He lived for this.

"I SAID COME OUT WITH YOUR HANDS UP!"

A shadow walked toward the picture window, a flashlight wavering in its hand. Light bounced everywhere, pissing Mickey off when the beam caught his eyes.

"PUT DOWN THE GODDAMN FLASHLIGHT AND COME OUT WITH YOUR HANDS UP!"

The figure skulked toward the front door. Another shadowy outline marched behind it and grabbed the figure, stopping it dead in its tracks.

"Oh, what in the hell!"

The second figure signaled for the first to stay and disobey Mickey's orders. The first figure shook its head, disagreeing.

Ain't this sweet, Fayden whispered in his ear. *Mercy for Lawbreaker Number One for complying. Number Two, however, will be prosecuted to the fullest extent.*

"THAT'S IT," Mickey said, grinning. "COME ON OUT. ALL OF YOU. GIVE UP THE WRONGDOERS AND YOU SHALL GO FREE."

The front door opened and a man appeared, waving amiably. He neglected to turn off the flashlight and the bright light continued to find its way into Mickey's eyes.

"SON, IF YOU DON'T DROP THAT DAMN FLASHLIGHT YOU'RE GONNA DINE ON A NICE, TASTY BULLET FOR SUPPER."

The man killed the flashlight at once.

"Sorry about that, officer," he said, waving his hand in the air as if to mean *I come in peace.*

Mickey drew on him. "Stay the fuck still!" he yelled, dropping the megaphone. "Or I will drop you like the sack of shit you are!"

The man nearly jumped out of his skin. His hands shot into the air. The flashlight fell from his trembling fingers and hit the sidewalk, small pieces of black plastic shooting in opposite directions. The man's face changed, the sense of relief associated with being rescued melting, turning to fear and terror. The man tried to speak, but couldn't locate his voice.

"You gotta problem, buddy?" Mickey asked.

"I t-think, t-think, there's a m-misunderstanding," the man managed to say.

"Only misunderstanding is you don't seem to want to fucking

listen to a goddamn thing I say." Mickey flashed him a sardonic grin. The man was on the verge of shitting himself. "Tell all your drug-abusing buddies to rally up and come on out here. Especially the fugitives. I got business to settle with them, right here and now."

"What fugitives?"

"What fugitives?" he asked as if the man had called him a pecker head. "Don't you play stupid with me. I know what I know, and I know you got two fugitives that escaped my jail cell, and if you don't give them up right this instant, you're gonna be in a world of hurt."

The man closed his eyes. Mickey thought he saw tears glistening under them, but couldn't be so sure. His sunglasses made it impossibly dark.

"Sir, please. There's a sick girl inside—"

"Up!" Sargent Mickey cried. "There we go again, yammering on about a sick girl. What is it with you dope fiends? Yous make up the same damn story together? Does that story really fly in these parts? Bout the craziest bunch of bullshit I've ever heard."

The man seemed at a loss, and Mickey took the man's sullen glance as he was considering a peaceful surrender, but still on the fence. He thought a bullet might settle things, tie up a few loose ends, illustrate a few points his words clearly weren't making. He raised his gun again, gently flexing his finger on the trigger. The man gulped, loud enough for Mickey to hear it.

"S-sir," the man said. "Y-you've m-misread the situation here. P-please, put down the gun."

"Misread this, motherfucker." Mickey pulled the trigger and the man flew backward, landing hard on his back. His head ricocheted off the sidewalk. Air whooshed from his lungs.

Clamping his hand over the bullet hole, Bob screamed.

Brenda told her husband to stay inside; something was off about the way the cop was speaking to them. It didn't sound right. *He* didn't sound right. And although Bob didn't exactly disagree, he left anyway.

"It'll be fine, honey," he had said. "He's a cop. Maybe he's here to help."

It was wishful thinking on his part and if he had been locked in Malek's cage with her, he might have read the situation differently.

"We can't trust strangers," she had told him. "Not even cops."

He waved her off and told her, "trust me" and now he was shot, writhing on the sidewalk, bleeding out through a hole in his shoulder. If he survived, she vowed to never let him talk her out of a gut feeling again.

She slammed through the front door and sprinted to his side, screaming his name and ignoring the cop's request to "stay the fuck back." Quickly, she located the bullet hole, above his right clavicle. The bullet went straight through, and Bob wasn't bleeding too badly. Nothing cotton and tape couldn't fix.

She glanced up at the cop, who hadn't moved from behind the cruiser's door.

"What the fuck is wrong with you?" she said, her voice strained with anger.

"Ma'am, you need to get the fuck away from that man, and put your hands where I can see them, or I will open fire on both of your candy asses!"

He didn't act like a cop. At least no cop Brenda ever met. He acted more like a cop on television or "reality" TV. Society's version of the ultimate bad-ass police officer. For Christ's sake, the man was wearing sunglasses at night.

"Ma'am? Don't test me."

She rose to her feet, her upper lip trembling. Her contemptuous lip motion pleased the officer, and he let her know this with a sly grin. She could almost hear his voice: *Damn right, bitch. I'm in charge here and you will obey.*

Brenda didn't have much of a choice other than to meet his demands. Her son was inside the pharmacy, along with his girlfriend, and the only other person she could rely on was Tina, who wasn't her biggest fan, nor she of her. In that moment, she pictured Tina on the rooftop, peering at the officer through the scope of a sniper rifle, readying herself to peel back the cop's scalp with one trigger pull. But Brenda waited and waited and the officer's head remained intact, not peeled, exploded, or disappeared behind a firework of blood and brains like she imagined. The man simply laughed as he stepped away from the car door, pointing the gun at her head.

"Now," the officer said, capturing high-pitched giggles in his throat. "Why don't you go ahead and call out those renegade fugitives?"

Before she could speak, bright blinding lights filled her eyes. Brenda threw her arm over her head, protecting her eyes from the burn. Blind from the action around her, she heard honking, sounding far away at first, but closer as the seconds ticked. Another gunshot sounded and she expected to feel her own head explode before finding herself in Heaven or Hell, or wherever her soul was destined to reside. Glass shattered behind her and she knew the brights had caused the cop to miss. She had the driver to thank when this was all over, whoever he was.

Brenda heard the cop yell, "Oh fuck!" before the tires squealed and the metal on metal collision deafened her ears, and bits of glass showered her face.

-8-

"Fuck!" **Sam** **yelled,** **smashing** his fist against the dashboard. His wrist throbbed, his hand half-numb from the adrenaline kick. Mickey stood several football fields away, outside his car, gun in hand. Bob stood less than twenty feet from the psycho cop, shoving his hands in the air, surrendering peacefully. Whatever words the two men exchanged went unheard, and Sam watched the gun buck in Mickey's hand, a sudden thunderous boom joining the moment. Bob's body whipped backward and he landed on the sidewalk, back first, feet up in the air. A second later, Bob was writhing around the sidewalk, his eyes clenched together, screaming in agony.

Jarvis accelerated.

"What are you doing?" Sam asked.

"Driving," Jarvis said, concentrating on the road. Cruiser #3 gained speed as he slammed his foot on the pedal. Sam didn't like the look in Jarvis's eyes; it reminded him too much of Sargent Mickey's.

Sam spotted Brenda. She dropped to her knees next to her husband. Once she realized he was going to live, she turned on the cop, screamed at him, pointing her finger vehemently, a lot like how Sam remembered. He didn't need to open the window to hear her shout; Sam witnessed this particular rage a thousand times before, and had committed her wide range of insults to memory. He waited for the cop to exceed his boiling point, and for Brenda's head to explode in a cloudy mist of blood, for her body to hit the sidewalk lifelessly while remnant brain matter splashed the street. Sam knew she was asking for it, pushing the man to his limit. Each second the cop's finger remained off the trigger was a blessing.

Mickey's face twisted. His eyebrows climbed higher, stretching toward his forehead. His bullshit meter neared capacity. His finger squeezed the trigger.

Sam reached over and pounded the center of the steering wheel, over and over again until he snagged the bastard's attention. Mickey whipped his head toward the noise, and Jarvis clicked on the high beams, lighting the pharmacy parking lot up like a Broadway show. They watched the cop shield his face with his arm. He fired blindly at Brenda and the two shots sailed past her head, shattering the pharmacy's glass facade behind her, reducing them to dancing, glittering granules.

"Slow down," Sam said to Jarvis.

"No," he replied. He continued to accelerate, pushing the cruiser above sixty-five.

"You're going to crash into—"

"Exactly!" Jarvis yelled, white-knuckling the steering wheel. "Buckle up!"

Sam nearly ripped the seat belt out of its home, buckling himself in record time. Grabbing the *oh-shit* bar, he tucked his knees against his chest and braced for impact.

The crash was worse than he imagined. The airbags deployed, preventing their heads from smashing against the dashboard and keeping their brains inside their skulls, but the experience was far from pleasant. Sam immediately ached all over, his neck taking the worst of it. He'd feel like death tomorrow, stiff and unable to flex a muscle.

He'd deal with that later.

Now, he had a family to save.

Jarvis scrambled out of the cruiser first, looking like the crash had zero effect on him. How he felt was a different matter, one Jarvis didn't pay much attention to. His focus was on the cop, the evil bastard who had already found his feet and his .38 Special. It seemed like crashing the car had been an unnecessary risk, one that had played out better in his mind.

Sargent Mickey stumbled. Blood poured from a gash above his right eye. He fired his .38 and missed whatever he was aiming at. The bullet sailed into a brick building behind him, kicking up red chalky dust on impact. He pulled the trigger again and obtained similar results. A leaky cut above his eye impaired his vision and the crash had damaged his right leg, throwing off his balance. He limped toward Jarvis, pulling the trigger, the gun roaring with each vicious squeeze. Bullets sailed past Jarvis and the brick storefronts absorbed them. The last bullet came close to finding its intended target; Jarvis felt the breeze brush against his ear.

"Someone needs practice."

Mickey wiped the blood away from his eye. He aimed at Jarvis, steadying his hand, summoning his complete concentration. Jarvis stared into the insane man's eyes, and the cold gaze told him he wouldn't miss again.

Oh shit, Jarvis thought. *This is it. This is game over, man.*

"Wait!" Sam shouted.

The cop froze. His eyes shifted toward the sound of his voice.

"It's me you want," Sam told him. "I'm the drug kingpin here."

Mickey chewed the inside of his mouth while he tried piecing the information together. None of it seemed to make much sense, and he didn't enjoy the struggle his brain was giving him. "Explain," he said, keeping the gun on Jarvis, waiting for Sam to give him a good reason not to blow the back of his skull out.

"You're right. We raided the rehab facility for drugs and we fully intended to sell every last pill, and make a bank load off our discovery. Until you came around and fucked everything up."

Mickey still wasn't convinced. Things weren't adding up. He didn't know exactly what Sam was talking about, but to his ears it sounded like trickery. He kept his attention on Jarvis, the gun steady in his hand.

"See, I'm like... Heisenberg," Sam said. "And he is my Pinkman. And the pharmacy is our lab. There's a ton of drugs in there!" A panicky laugh escaped through Sam's lips. "And you found it! You're a hero. All you gotta do is bust us. Rally us up, take us down to the station, book us—"

Jarvis mouthed the words, *What the fuck are you doing?*

"Judge Fayden will sentence us to a nice long trip up at the statehouse, with no parole mind you—hell, he might even issue us death by fire? Wouldn't that be nice?" Sam asked, grinning as wide as his mouth would travel.

"Fuck Fayden," Mickey said.

"Huh?" Sam asked.

"Sargent Mickey is in charge. And I will do the sentencing from here on out." His eyes narrowed to slits. "And I'll start with you," he said to Jarvis. "Guilty. Sentence: death by firing squad."

The gun roared and everybody gasped.

Sargent Mickey's calf muscle exploded into a glob of blood and shredded sinew, splattering against Cruiser #3 passenger side door in rough Rorschach fashion. Crying out, the man crumbled to his knees. He abandoned the .38 and used both hands to cover the gory mess once part of the leg he worked out every morning at the precinct's gym. Mickey winced in agony and rolled on his back, cursing the "motherfuckers" and "cocksuckers", wishing they'd all "burn in hell" with the rest of the drug-abusing sinners.

Sam looked up from Mickey and saw his son standing a good thirty feet away, lowering the rifle away from his eye, wisps of smoke unfurling from the muzzle.

"Holy shit," Matty said. "I shot him."

Tina rushed down the street, stopping at Matty's side, her stone-cold face hiding her true feelings about what had just happened. Together they walked closer to the injured man, stride for stride. Tina aimed her handgun, ready to blow him away if he reached for the .38 on the ground next to him.

Jarvis approached cautiously. Sam grabbed the rifle he had nabbed from the office and directed it at Mickey's head. With the others he approached, until the foursome formed a tight square around him. Brenda tended to Bob; the bleeding had stopped, the ebbing pain reduced to a dull throb. Bob watched the crazed cop's actions along with his wife, asking her with his eyes to leave the wound alone until after Sam resolved the situation and guaranteed their safety.

"Holy shit," Matty said again, watching the gore dangle from the cavity his rifle created.

"It's okay, Matty," Tina said, grabbing his shoulder, pulling him close. She could feel Brenda's eyes burning a hole in the back of her neck, but she didn't care. "It's okay." She turned to Sam. "Where's Chuck?"

"This fucker killed him," Jarvis answered.

"And I'll fucking kill you too, boy!" Mickey cried. "I'll kill all you motherfuckers!"

Jarvis kicked the man as hard as he could in the head. His jaw snapped, twisting to the side of his face. Matty turned away. Tina put a hand on his back and ushered him over to his mother. He sat down and lowered his reddening face into his palms, refusing to look his mother in the eye.

"Take that, bitch!"

With his jaw rearranged, the cop would never say another word. He squirmed around, trying to worm his way out of the situation, but Sam placed his foot on Mickey's back, squashing the feeble escape attempt.

Sam glanced over his shoulder; Matty was crying into his hands, his mother rubbing his back and whispering into his ear, trying to comfort him, ensuring him everything was okay, that he didn't do anything wrong. He wasn't sure she believed it herself, but it seemed to help. Matty's loud sobs diminished, replaced by quiet sniffles. He looked to Tina next; she fixed him with that *what-choice-do-we-have* expression he came to adore. He shrugged and turned back to Jarvis, who continued kicking Sargent Mickey in the head, but with less force than before. The cop had lost his fight, lazily punching the space between them. Matty's aim left Mickey's leg a mangled mess and if ignored, he'd die of infection; or the smell would attract a pack of carnivorous animals, happy to finish him off; or he'd survive the night and the day would take care of him, end his suffering in fire and smoke. Either way, it'd be the slow death he deserved.

Sam knew they couldn't take a chance. Suppose another group came along. Suppose they were nice people; good people; *innocent* people. Suppose they took good care of Sargent Mickey, nursed him back to full strength. He'd be back to his tricks in no time, slaughtering people who simply want to survive. He couldn't risk it. He wouldn't be able to sleep knowing that plausible scenario existed.

Sargent Mickey reached out for Jarvis's leg, one last effort.

Sam put the rifle to the back of Mickey's head.

"Sam, don't."

The plea came from Brenda, but it was too late.

He pulled the trigger and Mickey's brains spewed through the exit wound, splashing across the pavement like a broken jar of raspberry jam.

"WESTWARD"

EPISODE ELEVEN

-1-

The world before The Burn would always be remembered. Mouth was sure of it. Television, movies, the Internet, hand-held artificial intelligence, new music, PS4; all the things humanity loved to occupy their dull minds were lost in the past, artifacts future generations would one day marvel over. He didn't like to think the old world was extinct. Life could continue the way it was before. Humanity just needed some time to figure it all out. Sort through the madness. Take a few steps back. Recollect. Get back on the horse again. It would work out. Humanity would rise above it. They always did, didn't they?

It was wishful thinking. The sad truth was the world had gone to shit, and there simply wasn't enough forward-thinking people to pull it out of the toilet. Humanity now relied heavily on its primal instincts, the hopes and dreams of a stable and structured society abandoned. Mouth couldn't see why people weren't rallying together, trying to reestablish government and law and order, organizational methods of any kind. The world had simply given up. Waved the white flag. Cried uncle. It was easier to live like animals and become the primal, savage beasts everyone was, deep down.

As he drove down the coast, the tranquil black ocean waters to the east of him, he thought about Soren's Alaska and what it'd mean to them. He thought about the potential dangers and what might happen once they arrived. If there were people surviving beneath the surface, who was to say they'd let them in? Suppose they were crazy as the rest of the world. Suppose Soren couldn't guarantee everyone a safe place inside. Would it snow in Alaska now that the sun had obtained the unique ability to wipe out the human race? The sun seemingly had little to no effect on Mother

Earth's climate. Mouth could see the evidence on the trees, their green hands being granted the autumn effect, curling in death and falling to the tall weeds below. He marveled over how unruly nature had become; weeds sprouted everywhere, some growing almost as tall as Dana. It was a wonder what six months could do to an unkempt world.

Everyone slept while he drove, thinking about the world and how much it had changed in a relatively short period of time. Sometimes it seemed like he and few others were the only sane people left. Soren was smart, but Mouth sensed he was a few tools short in the shed. Dana and Becky were still too young and easily influenced by their environment. He could see Dana drifting toward what he called "The Dark Side" and sadly, there wasn't much he could do or say to stop her. He'd watch over her like he promised Sam, but if she wanted to follow Soren like a lovesick puppy, that was her prerogative. Shondra was perhaps the only person he trusted as much as himself. Susan was a full-blown basket case, and the end of times seemed to have brought out the worst in her, religious fervency fueling her bitter presence. He didn't know David well, but the guy seemed decent. He had been a victim of volatile emotions during Costbusters' early days, but he attributed those moments to the steroids he had abused, and as time progressed, so did he. He mellowed out. A few weeks ago, Mouth had struck up a conversation about sports and David joined in, arguing amiably about the future of the Mets' franchise, and what great shape their pitching was in. Mouth, a die-hard Yankee fan since ten years old, told him the Mets would always be the second best baseball team in New York, and no amount of solid pitching could change that. The conversation slowly died off when they realized they'd never see those young arms in action again. Never see them develop into the legends the experts had predicted. Never see them win the Amazin's a title. Saddened, they ended their sports talk and discussed things that mattered now. Food. Water. A safe place to stay while the sun reigned over them.

Soren stirred in his sleep. Mouth watched him closely, switching back and forth between the road and the man he wished he could kick out of the moving van. After about ten minutes of mumbling in his sleep, Soren's eyes shot open.

"Bad dream?" Mouth asked.

"How'd you know?" He rubbed his temples. They ached like hell.

"You were crying like a fucking baby."

Soren narrowed his eyes.

"Just fucking with you." Mouth was still bitter about what had happened in the tunnel and his expression showed. Anger seeped into his words. "I wouldn't expect you to cry over spilt milk. Because that's all Brian and the others were, right? Just a small tragedy? I hope you heard their screams in your nightmares, you son of a bitch."

Soren rolled his eyes. "Mouth, please. It's too early for this."

"It's never too early!" he said, pounding the dashboard. Shondra and the others shifted in their sleep, the noise not enough to wake them. Mouth adjusted his volume. "You sent those people to die," he whispered.

Soren tilted his head to the side. "And what would you have me do? If I didn't give them what they wanted, we'd all be dead."

Mouth kept his eyes on the road, pretending the conversation never happened.

"I realized what needed to be done and I did it. And I'd do it again, a thousand times over. Compassion is a weakness and this world no longer awards the weak. You have to realize that. Everyone in this van needs to, or we're not going to make it to Alaska."

Mouth chuckled without opening his mouth. "Alaska. You ever gonna tell us how we plan on getting there? Or, you know, what to expect once we get there?"

"I don't know exactly how we're going to get there and I already told you what to expect. Everything we need to survive."

"What do you mean you don't know how we're getting there?"'

It was Soren's turn to keep silent.

"Holy fuck. You ain't got a fucking clue where this place is.

Do you?"

"Of course I do," Soren said. "And I don't need you second guessing me. You either trust me, or get out."

Mouth leaned forward and looked up. "Well, chiefy; if we don't find cover soon, we're going to end up a nice smoked brisket."

Soren checked the dashboard behind the steering wheel. "We need gas before we find a place to rest. Coming up on empty."

"Won't be any need for gas if we're fucking barbecue."

The drive down the coast had been surprisingly therapeutic; the silence; the clear roads free from apocalyptic congestion; watching small waves ripple across the black ocean tide under night's authority; Mouth experiencing a moment to himself, alone with his thoughts. Since Soren woke, everything went to hell. No more silence. Aggravation. The roads had become more difficult to navigate, abandoned vehicles populating the highway once again. A small crack of light lit up the horizon, killing the comfort the night sky provided.

"Just drive, Mouth." Soren said. "And for once in your life, try to stay quiet." He massaged his forehead, his fingertips applying firm pressure. "You're not helping my headache."

February 2nd, 1985

Sandborough seated himself in the far corner of the cafeteria. He ate his greasy cheeseburger and french fries as if he had all the time in the world. He eyed the table seating six security guards, no more than thirty feet from him. They laughed haughtily at a joke Sandborough couldn't hear, but wouldn't have joined even if he heard it; he wasn't laughing much those days.

"Whatever you're thinking, forget it," Aldo Hood said, sitting down across from him. He immediately grabbed a fork and went to work on the fluffy white mashed potatoes and crispy green string beans, shoveling the meal into his mouth as if it were the first in many days.

"I wasn't thinking anything," Sandborough told him.

"Mm-hm." Aldo wiped a pasty potato smear off his lips. "You have that look about you. That I'm-going-to-do-something-terribly-stupid look."

"Oh really?"

"Yes, sir."

"I wasn't thinking that at all."

"What were you thinking about?"

Sandborough glanced down at his half-eaten cheeseburger as if it were the one speaking. "Your sister."

The answer Aldo expected.

"I think you two should keep a low profile. I don't know for sure, but your relationship is gaining notoriety with the wrong people."

"Elias?"

Aldo snorted in an obnoxious way only his closest friends could stand. "Of course, Elias. He speaks of you differently these days. Not as enthusiastic as before."

"Doesn't mean anything."

"I've known the man for a long time, Alan. Longer than you. You've gotten inside his head somehow. Mixed him all up. Like he... knows."

"I told you, I expected him to be suspicious. He'd be a fool not to. He can't possibly still believe she loves him."

"Not what I was talking about."

Sandborough abandoned the thought of taking another bite of his burger and pushed the tray aside. "I'm all ears, Aldo. Enlighten me."

"I think he knows you plan to sabotage his little operation here."

Sandborough rolled his eyes. "I don't see how. We haven't really discussed it further than the other night."

"You know these walls have ears. Shit, I wouldn't be surprised if he had the entire facility bugged. Our rooms included. You know what a control freak Elias is. Man needs to have his finger on everything."

Solid points, but none that sat well with Sandborough. Elias couldn't possibly know the plans; Sandborough barely knew them himself. The plan was in its early stages, only a few ideas being kicked around between interested parties. Nothing concrete, nothing in place. But, Aldo was right. Elias Wheeler had resources and hated being out of the loop. In all probability, Sandborough's room was bugged, his phones tapped the second he suspected Kyra's affair.

Aldo shoved half of his steak in his mouth. He chewed on it for a few seconds before swallowing. If Sandborough cared about such things, Aldo's eating methods would have embarrassed him. It was a spectacle to furrow your brow at. Within sixty seconds, Aldo had consumed the entire meal and licked the plate clean.

"You're a disgusting person to eat with," Sandborough said.

"Yeah, I get that a lot. It's mostly why I eat alone." Aldo turned, and scanned the cafeteria. "Where's our buddy Joe?"

"Back in the lab. Working on a chemical that reverses the effects of Project Sunfall." Sandborough thought about polishing off the rest of the burger, looked at it wistfully, deciding it was better not to indulge. The grease hadn't sat well in his stomach and he could feel it clawing its way through his intestines. He'd grab a banana on the way out and eat it later. "It's kicking our ass, but I think we're almost there."

Aldo waved him off like Sandborough had told him a story he had heard a thousand times before. "Not like any of these machines are ever going to get used. Waste of time, if you ask me."

Sandborough narrowed his eyes. "How do you know?"

Aldo smirked. "Come on! No one is going to unleash these weapons on the public. You'd be crazy to do such a thing."

"You don't think Elias is crazy?"

Aldo smacked his lips together. This particular conversation had grown tiresome. "I know you hate the guy and I'm right there with you, especially the way he treats my sis, but the guy isn't *that* crazy. Not, I'm-going-to-end-the-world crazy."

"I hope I'm there to tell you 'I told you so.'"

"Do you know what Sunfall would mean if someone launched it? If they found a way to somehow localize the effect to a specific region, the results would be catastrophic. You take away the ability to exist during the day, and the world will go mad. Think about it. It's crazy."

Sandborough did think about it. A lot.

"What am I preaching to you for?" Aldo asked, flicking his wrist. "You know damn well what that machine is capable of. You helped design it."

Sandborough smiled.

"Just listen to me," Aldo said, leaning across the table as he lowered his voice. "Stay off the radar for a bit. With my sister, I mean. Key and I don't need you dying on us. Or worse."

"What's worse than death?"

"Montana. Mexico. A ton of places. Just promise me. You two won't see each other until I think Elias is off your back. Promise?"

He stared him down for what seemed like an hour. "I'll see you later, Aldo. I have to go back to work."

As he stood up to leave, Aldo stretched out and grabbed his wrist.

"I'm serious. Trust me on this one. Elias is saying some really weird shit, and I think he might do something you might not like if your relationship becomes a little more noticeable. You have other lives and feelings to consider. Not just your own."

Sandborough broke free of Aldo's grasp. The advice had soured his already-crusty mood and he wanted nothing more than to head back to the lab, finish his work, and think about something else other than Elias Wheeler and the power he held over him.

"I'll take it under careful consideration," Sandborough said, turning and heading toward the cafeteria's exit. As he shuffled past the security guards' table, he couldn't help but notice their heads craning in his direction.

"Where'd you blast off to, spaceman?" Mouth asked.

The others were still sleeping. Soren didn't realized he had lost himself within the reverie until Mouth spoke. He didn't know how much time he had dedicated to the memory, but it couldn't have been long; the sun kept itself hidden behind the horizon, although the sky above had turned a moody black.

"Nowhere," Soren said, resting his head against the window, looking out into the shrinking night sky. "Nowhere at all."

"You seem different since we left the tunnel. Your conscious getting the best of you?" Mouth navigated around some dead traffic, cursing as he almost clipped an abandoned Explorer. "Seeing ghosts in your thoughts?"

"I see many ghosts," he replied, closing his eyes again. "None of them from this life."

"You're a weird fucker, Nygaard. Guess you already know this, but it doesn't hurt to say I fucking hate you. Brian was my friend. The others were good people, too. You left them with monsters. But I guess it's all for the greater good," Mouth mumbled. "Ain't that right?"

Soren opened one eye to the world. "The greater good," he agreed.

-2-

Matty reached for the switches on the cruiser's dashboard, but Brenda grabbed his hand, deterring him from flipping on the lights or a siren that would attract unwanted attention. She shook her head, and Matty's eyes fell.

It had been an awkward commute, no one really knowing how to carry on from what had happened outside the pharmacy. They needed to talk about sensitive subjects, but with the seven of them crammed into the squad car, it was neither the time nor the place. Tina took the wheel while Matty, Brenda, and Sam squeezed into the front bench. Bob and Jarvis sat in the back, Lilah resting between them, unconscious and getting valuable rest.

After Matty's mother turned his attention away from the dashboard, he glanced over his shoulder, watching Lilah's chest rise and fall, the only clue she remained among the living. The pink returned to her lips, but her complexion continued its milky-white campaign.

"She okay?" he asked. The group agreed to head westward, thinking the others would do the same, but Matty lost interest in their travels after they left the pharmacy.

"She seems stable," Bob answered. "I think the Flumezanil is working, but we should seek a second opinion."

Tina tried to contain the small laugh, but couldn't. "Well, let me pull up to the nearest emergency room." She looked into the rearview and found Bob's eyes. "Not exactly possible at the moment."

Jarvis looked over his shoulder, out the back window. "Looks like we got bigger problems—the big orange is about to rise and shine."

Tina returned her eyes to the road, hoping to find a safe place to pull over. The stretch of road offered little except tall oaks and disorderly weeds.

Sam placed his hand on his son's knee, giving it three comforting pats. "It's out of our hands, Matty. We'll have to wait and see what happens. Lilah seems like a strong girl. She'll pull through."

"I'm worried about her," Matty said.

"We all are." He looked over his son's head and found himself locking eyes with his ex-wife. The slightest curls on the end of her lips told him she wanted to smile, and he wanted to smile too, although nothing about their situation implied happiness. "You know, Matty, when you were born, there were serious complications with the pregnancy. Something happened to the umbilical cord and they had to perform an emergency C-section, which the doctors didn't really want to do, because your mother was a higher risk for blood clots. But, the priority was the baby, so you had to come out, regardless of the risk to your mom. We were really nervous, your mom and I. I mean, more so me. Your mom was tough; she kept telling me everything was okay, it'll all work out, but I was a wreck, worrying about what would happen if something went wrong, and I was left alone to raise you and your sister by myself. And not in a selfish way—I only saw the way your mom was with Becky, how she was destined to become this super mom, and how my 'dad skills' were nowhere up to par.

"Anyway the surgery went fine and out you came, small and beautiful, with no complications. Easy as pie, the doctor said. They kept warmers on your mother for three days to keep her blood flowing, and she never had a clot. But those three days were absolute hell for me. All I could think about was how something had to go wrong and my worst nightmare would come to life—how I'd never be able to raise two kids on my own and how shitty of a single father I'd be. It was all I could think about.

"But I'll never forget that day. When your mom woke up, she asked how you were doing and I told her the doctors said you were doing fine. I told her how nervous I'd been, how I hadn't left her side the entire time she was sleeping and resting up. I told her how the blood clots scared the shit out of me and how I don't know what I'd do without her.

"Your mom looked at me and said, 'the worst is over now,'" Sam said, smiling. "And—"

"The rest is out of our hands," Brenda said, gripping her son's hand.

Sam squeezed Matty's knee. "That's right. The rest is out of our hands."

Matty smiled like he knew what they were talking about, but the story still didn't quell his worries.

Behind the cruiser, a splash of lavender soaked the horizon.

Mouth stared at the gas pump like it had kicked him in the balls. *Son of a bitch,* he thought. He turned, facing the dreary, yet tranquil, world behind them. They were somewhere outside of Richmond, the city towering over a small cluster of trees. The road they had chosen ran parallel with the major highway intersecting with the city. They avoided major interstates due to the amount of traffic they had seen. Plus, the incident in the tunnel demonstrated that the better option was avoiding human interaction when possible.

The gas station's property was overgrown with hip-high weeds and grass and dangling tree foliage from neighboring stretches of woods. He couldn't make out the road through nature's unruly behavior, and turned to the convenience store where Soren and the others had gone "shopping." There was something desolate about the way the world looked now, and Mouth's spirits dampened as he examined the apocalyptic scenery. His mind couldn't help but return to hopeless thoughts, succumb to the notion that the old world was dead with no resurrection in sight.

Soren exited the convenience store first, gripping a map of Richmond with both hands. He looked at Mouth as if he expected an immediate report.

"No power," Mouth said simply, jerking his thumb at the gas pump.

"What are you saying?"

"Unless they have a backup generator somewhere, we're completely fucked."

The answer didn't seem to jibe with Soren. "I took some plastic tubing from Costbusters. It should be in the red duffel bag in the back."

"So?"

"Siphon the gas out."

Furiously, Mouth shook his head. "No, no. Not from the pump. I'd have to get underneath and tap into the tank directly. Which is a lot of work, not to mention dangerous and dirty."

"What choice do we have?"

Mouth pointed toward the city. "I'm sure there's a lot of abandoned vehicles on the highway. If I can find a way to transport the gas—a can or something—I can siphon some from another vehicle." He glared at Soren, biting his tongue. He didn't want to start an argument, but he needed to vent. "You know, you could have told me you had a hose. We must have passed six-hundred cars over the last two hours. We could have avoided this whole mess."

Soren's eyes narrowed. "I forgot about it until now."

Mouth breathed deeply. "Bullshit, Nygaard. You don't forget a thing like that. You wanted to stop here. Why?"

Soren flared his nostrils.

"You know," Mouth continued, stepping away from the pump. "If we're gonna be traveling buddies, you better start cluing us in on some fucking answers. I know you're lying. Hiding stuff from us. What's the harm in spilling the beans, telling us everything you know? We're going with you no matter what."

Slowly, Soren reached into his pocket and retrieved the key he had taken from Joe's garden.

"Fuck is that?" Mouth asked. "A key?"

"A key that unlocks a PO box."

Mouth's brow dipped. "Fuck's that got to do with anything?"

"The PO box is right around the corner from here. Within walking distance. Fifteen minutes by my estimation. Inside, waits our next direction."

"Oh yeah?"

"Yes."

"Why do I get the feeling I'm in a seriously fucked-up version of *National Treasure?*"

"I don't know what that is."

"The movie? With Nic Cage? Forget it," Mouth grumbled, swatting the air. "Okay, here's the deal. I'll get the fucking gas. But it's going to take some time, cutting it close to sunrise. We got about an hour before that big orange bastard rears its ugly head. I'll try to get it done, but I'm not risking my skin if I don't think I'll be back in time."

Soren agreed.

"Head to your precious post office. I'll meet up with you fuckers before day breaks."

Mouth walked away, toward the highway, flipping Soren the finger before turning around.

Soren yanked the handle, but the door wouldn't budge. As if he had expected to find the tall glass door locked, he unzipped his shoulder bag and removed a hammer. Taking two steps away, he cocked the tool back and thrust it forward, the words "United States Postal Service" breaking apart, falling to the ground in hundreds of glittery grains. Soren walked toward the door, shards squeaking beneath his rubber soles, and reached past where the glass stood moments before. He turned the lock and pushed the door open with his foot.

He didn't hold the door for Susan, Shondra, David, or Kyle who followed him, surveying the area for other desperate survivors as they walked. Susan was next to enter the unoccupied post office, following Soren like a puppy, abandoning her duties of lookout. Kyle followed closely behind her, wearing the same dumb grin he had always worn while making mischief. Shondra followed them inside, hovering near the door with an eye on the road. David breezed by her, following Soren's lead.

Near the horizon, light brightened the bruised sky. Watching shades of purple coalesce with full dark didn't sit well with Shondra. If Soren didn't stop taking his sweet time, they'd be forced to hold up in the post office, separate from Mouth, Becky, and Dana for a whole twelve hours. That also didn't sit well with her.

"You should hurry it up," Shondra said. "We're losing dark."

Soren searched each box, running his finger along the numbers. He stopped when he found the box whose number matched the key. Without wasting time, he slipped the key into its home and listened as it clicked into place. He opened the door and reached inside the box, rushing to retrieve its contents.

Shondra looked over her shoulder to see what the hold up was. Soren tore open an envelope, paper shavings falling to the floor like large snow flurries. He removed what Shondra thought was four golden tickets.

"What is it?" Shondra asked.

Ignoring her, Soren and Susan exchanged glances.

"I don't get it," Susan said, turning her attention to the tickets. "Is it another clue?"

Soren didn't respond; didn't need to. His eyes widened like a knowledge bomb had exploded inside his brain. He held the four golden tickets in front of his eyes, studying them, like he had seen them before in a fantasy or distant memory.

"Yes," Soren said, almost dreamily. "Of course."

"What is it?" Shondra snapped. With her patience depleted, she had about all the mysticism she could take.

His eyes slowly rose from the tickets and settled on Shondra's unpleasant face.

"You going to talk to us, or are you going to stand there and admire yourself?"

"How dare you talk to him like that," Susan said, stepping in front of Soren as if taking a bullet for him. "Soren's done a lot for us. Show some respect."

Although difficult, Shondra kept herself from exploding with laughter; or from doing what she really wanted—bashing Susan's witch-like face into the wall. "Susan," she said, displaying a false smirk for her enemy. "With all due respect—you need to shut your trap."

Susan glowered at her, undoubtedly wishing Shondra would go tanning.

Resting a hand on Susan's shoulder, Soren whispered into her ear, "Everything's okay. Why don't you let me handle this one."

Kyle folded his arms across his chest, a self-satisfying grin stamping its trademark across his face. David's eyes shifted between both sides; Shondra sensed the man didn't know which team to settle on. She didn't have much of a case for hers. Soren had the glam; he had followers, and the ability to shield himself from the sun's death rays.

Not much of a choice at all, she thought.

"They're tickets," Soren said proudly.

"Tickets for what?" Shondra asked, gasping as if their conversation had physically worn her out.

"The train."

She balled her hands into fists. She imagined tackling Soren to the ground, wrapping her hands around his throat, squeezing, watching his skin turn blueberry blue. "What train?" she asked, the words squeezing between her teeth.

"Yeah, Soren," Susan said, the confidence in her voice fading. "What train?"

"We are taking a train, and that's all I can say. Anyone else want to waste more time and darkness asking questions, or do we want to head back to the gas station before light? It seems our friend Mouth isn't coming to pick—"

Something moved. They all sensed it, their eyes shifting back and forth, experiencing the same unsteady behavior of their surroundings.

Shondra lost her balance and stumbled. David crouched, holding on to the small table in the corner. Kyle planted his backside on the chipped linoleum floor, his legs unable to keep him upright. Soren stood, his arms outstretched, as if surfing a giant wave. Susan slipped and fell to the floor, her head bouncing off the linoleum like a rubber ball.

The floor swayed beneath them, shifting side to side. They heard a rumble—like thunder—only it came from below, not above. A deep reverberating groan, as if the earth was having a stomach ache. The walls shook, pictures and other old-world knickknacks falling like melted icicles on a warm December day. Shondra crawled across the floor, toward Susan. The back of her head opened like a budding flower, blood already beginning to puddle beneath her.

"Help!" Shondra shouted as the world continued to tremor.

As David turned his attention to Shondra, who had applied her hand over Susan's wound, the table he held for support shimmied away from him. Seeing the blood pour from the woman's head, David ripped his shirt off and scrambled across the floor and crouched next to Susan. He wrapped his torn shirt around her head. Immediately, blood bloomed in a big red blotch, staining what was once a nice white dark crimson.

"It's not enough," Shondra said, looking around the vibrating room for another method. "Check the room back there!" She pointed to the door marked "Private", a word which held little meaning these days.

David struggled to his feet, but managed, fighting the unsteady ground beneath him. The world shook like it wanted to rid everything and everyone clinging to it, and start anew. He stumbled like a seasoned drunk, the quake pushing him left and right, backward and forward. Once he reached the door, he turned the knob and threw his shoulder into the heavy oak barrier. Shondra continued applying pressure with David's shirt, but by the time he reached the door, the shirt was wetter than a pair of used swim trunks. She wrung the shirt out, blood splashing like drain water. She pressed the shirt against the crack in Susan's head again, hoping David would hurry.

He returned as soon as the earth's mood changed, transforming from a turbulent tremor into a gentle feeling of unbalance. Two rolls of paper towels tucked under his arms, David sat beside Shondra, handing her fistfuls of absorbents.

The quake had ended. Soren, who had kept himself standing during the violent vibrations, glanced around nervously, as if he expected the floor to open up and swallow him into the darkness below. Kyle slowly guided himself to his feet, using the wall of PO boxes behind him as leverage. He looked to Soren for answers, the expression on his face suggesting he may have some.

"No," he said, his voice hushed. "It can't..."

"What is it?" Shondra asked, tossing another blood-soaked towel aside.

Susan was conscious, but in a state of shock. The gash in the back of her head looked a lot worse than it was. Bled worse too. Once Shondra stopped the bleeding and a clot formed, she'd be fine.

"Quakefall..." Soren said thoughtlessly.

"Quakefall?" David repeated, wiping sweat off his nose with the back of hand. "What the hell is Quakefall?"

Soren's head shook like a wet dog. "Nothing."

"You just said—"

"Doesn't matter what I said," Soren said, the old him returning. "How is she?"

"She'll live," Shondra told him. "No thanks to you."

He flinched. "What do you mean?"

"I mean you could have helped get something for her instead of standing there all high and mighty."

A wave of relief cleared his suspicions. "Yes. Of course."

"You're acting weird," she said. "Mouth is right. You better start providing us with some damn answers or you're gonna—"

"I'm gonna what?" Soren asked, gritting his teeth. "What am I gonna have? Hm?"

"My foot up your ass for one."

David snickered behind his hand. Kyle didn't seem to find it so funny.

But Soren surprised everyone and kept quiet.

"Two," Shondra said, motioning to a stable Susan, "Little Miss Sunshine here will be mighty upset with you, not sharing your secrets. Can't imagine she'll want to continue following you much longer after that."

Soren seemed to take this under consideration.

"Which brings me to my next point," Shondra continued, throwing her index finger in the air. "Why do you want us to follow you so badly? Seems to me, more people means more mouths to feed once you get to this sanctuary in Alaska. Doesn't add up." Her eyes drilled into him, expecting answers. She'd get nothing from him. "I think you need us for something. Not sure what. But something. Otherwise you wouldn't have kept us around this long. That's what you told us, right? That we may be useful? Hmpf. Yeah, right. That's all we are to you. Tools. Items in a cache. Ready to use at your disposal."

"You think you have it all figured out, do you?" Soren asked, his mouth tight as he spoke. Veins formed on his forehead as his jaw flexed. "You think you know it all?"

"No, but I have a good idea."

"Very well. Believe what you want." He stormed past them, not bothering to look over Susan's injury. He planted his foot in the scarlet puddle and bloody footprints followed him to the door. "But I have a train to catch. And unless you plan on being left behind, I suggest you keep up with me."

-3-

When the quake ended, Becky examined her face and checked for her pulse, making sure she was still alive. She had ducked behind the convenience store's counter when the ground shifted, tucking herself into a ball in the corner. The bathroom was the ideal place to hide—no merchandise to fall on top of her—but she thought it was too risky to move about the store while the quake was happening. She had heard the collision of metal shelving, rows of candy bars and potato chips crashing into one another, the soda case doors opening and slamming shut, and Dana screaming—

Dana.

She had almost forgotten about her sister.

"Dana!" she called, remaining on the floor behind the counter, knees tucked tightly against her chest. "Dana, are you okay?"

No answer.

Slowly, Becky stretched her fear-stiff legs. Once her blood began to circulate and the pins and needles sensation subsided, she used the counter to pull herself to her feet. She gasped when she saw the damage, the place looking looted a thousand times over. Candy bars littered the floor. Stacks of newspapers had spilled, their string bindings broken, millions of words scattered about. Coffee pots had danced off the counter and onto the floor, several jagged fragments sitting in dark mocha puddles.

"Dana!"

A small groan floated from somewhere on the other side of the store. She limped off toward her sister's groggy response. Invisible needles stabbed her feet, her nerves swimming in puddles of pain. She made it around the counter quickly, and searched the first aisle; no sign of her sister.

"Dana?" she called again, less panicky this time around.

"Here," the small voice answered, her tone above a whisper.

The second aisle was no longer an aisle; two stacks of merchandise—beef jerky products and 2-liter soda bottles—collided against each other, leaving no part of the cheaply-tiled floor visible. Becky walked over the mound of merchandise, plastic packaging crinkling and crackling beneath the weight of her footfalls. She called her sister's name again and listened for her response.

"Over here, Beck," Dana said, raising her voice this time.

In the back of the store she heard rustling. Becky jumped off the small hill of jerky products and rushed to where she heard Dana. She hopped over some fallen racking and found herself in the back aisle. To her left, the spin-rack with five dollar sunglasses had tumbled, spreading its shades across the floor, most of them broken beyond repair. To her right, pet products covered the floor. Beneath the heap of Kibbles 'n Bits and bags of kitty litter lay Dana, looking up at the ceiling, absorbed by the nothing resting there.

"You okay?" Becky asked.

"Oh, fine," she replied, continuing to gaze at the nondescript features above.

"You hurt?"

Dana pushed some of the products off her. "No."

"Good. Come on out of there."

"I like it down here."

"Well, you can't lay on the floor forever, so—"

"Why not?"

"Because you can't."

"But it's safe down here. No one dies down here."

"Dana, what are you talking about?"

"No one's ever died staring at a ceiling."

"Dana, stop being weird and let's go. We have to find the others."

"What's the point?"

The question stumped Becky.

Dana rose, boxes of Milk-bones falling off her, tumbling to the messy floor. "I mean, really," she said, turning to Becky. "What's the point? Everywhere we go, people die. Everywhere we go something bad happens. If we stay here nothing bad will happen."

Becky wanted to smack some sense into her. "We have to go to Alaska. Mom and Dad will be looking for us there."

"How do you know?"

"I just do."

"You don't know anything."

Feeling her patience slip, Becky gritted her teeth. "Dana, stop fooling around."

"I'm not. Mom and Dad are probably dead. Matty, too."

"Stop it."

"No."

Becky folded her arms over her abs. "What about Soren?"

"What about him?"

"You like him don't you?"

"He's cool, I guess."

"You think he'll be disappointed if you don't go to Alaska?"

Dana lowered her head. "Yeah... I guess."

"So, do it for Soren. Since you're sooooooooo in love with him."

Dana snapped her head toward her sister. "Becky, you're so gross!"

Laughing, Becky dropped to one knee. "Come on, sprout." She offered Dana her right hand. She wiggled her fingers, inviting her up. "Come with us. I'll keep you safe. I won't let you out of my sight. And Mom and Dad are alive, for the record. Matty, too. I can feel it. Can't you?"

With a twinkle in her eye, Dana said, "Yeah, I kinda can." She grabbed her sister's hand and Becky yanked her up. Her knees, weak from the quake, barely held her weight.

"We'll see them again. I promise."

"Don't make promises you can't keep."

Becky extended her smallest finger. "Pinky swear?"

Slowly, Dana curled her finger around her sister's. "Pinky swear."

Before they could bury the past, they heard a grown man cry out for help, sounding like a witness to his own murder.

The world blurred before him, a kaleidoscope of gray and black, shades of dark lilac jockeying for space among the morning lights. Mouth tried to move, but couldn't; the muscles in his arms and legs twitched, but did nothing to motor his limbs. It was like being frozen inside himself, cocooned in his own skin. He screamed out, but heard nothing. Had he screamed or imagined it? The world slowly focused, the battered exterior belonging to the convenience store starting to take shape. He looked down and his nose met the concrete parking lot. A sprouted weed tickled his neck. He moved his head in other directions, but something stopped him. He couldn't tell if the pressure on top of his body was a physical object pressing down on him or something internal broke, disallowing control over his motor skills. He didn't feel anything. No pain, no discomfort. Just the feeling of being trapped, a prisoner in his own frame.

He screamed again and two blurs appeared in the convenience store's entrance. At first he thought they were ghosts, reapers sent from Hell to escort him to the underworld, but he realized how ridiculous that sounded, even under the current spell of dizziness and the barrage of fragmented thoughts. He called out to the bleary smears, hoping they came with smiles and good news. They approached slowly and stopped outside his line of sight, no more than six feet away from him. One of them shrieked, although Mouth only heard a warbled version of it.

What? he thought he asked. *What is it?*

One of them replied, but he couldn't hear the words.

He glanced down and saw a small river of blood flowing beneath him. *My blood?* He didn't understand. He didn't feel pain. He didn't feel anything. *Can't be mine.*

Then whose? an internal voice asked.

I don't know.

Look at the facts: you can't move; you can't feel anything; you don't remember the last ten minutes of what happened.

Sure I do.

Then what happened?

I came back from the highway with a few gallons of gasoline —

He could smell gasoline. It was strong, as if he swallowed

some and exhaled the fumes.

And?

And that's it.

You don't remember the earthquake?

Earthquake?

See? You don't remember.

I was filling the tank. Then...

Then what?

Then I don't know.

Exactly. You're hurt. Bleeding. Dying.

No...

Yes. I hate to be the one to tell you. But...

You aren't real. This is a dream.

Is it? the voice asked.

No, it wasn't. Mouth could distinguish the difference between dreams and reality. Whatever was happening to him *was* happening to him.

"He's talking to himself," he heard a girl say with perfect clarity.

His vision continued to show him cloudy swirls of dark tones, but at least he had his ears to help guide him through this muddled reality.

"He's bleeding, Beck," he heard Dana cry.

"Dana? That you?" he heard himself say, although his voice was barely recognizable. "Dana, help me. I don't know what's happened."

She bent on one knee. He could make out her face clearly; fog bordered the area around her head. In the corner of her eyes, he saw tears taking shape, preparing for the fall.

"Why are you crying?" He didn't understand.

"Mouth..."

"Yes?"

"You're hurt."

He looked down. "My blood?"

A tear spilled down her rosy cheek.

Mouth pieced it all together. It was coming back to him. An

earthquake. He vaguely remembered the earth shaking and something hitting him. A piece of the canopy? He couldn't remember. Yes, he could. Something metal and solid, something with a lot of weight, had smashed him in the face and that's the last thing he remembered before waking up numb.

"What happened?" he asked Dana.

Becky entered his view. She wiped his forehead with her fingers, drawing back thick syrupy smears of red.

"Your head is cut," she said.

"Bad?"

"Bad enough." She pointed beyond where his vision could go. "Looks like a piece of the canopy came loose in the earthquake. Must have knocked you right out."

"Damn." The feeling in his arms and legs returned gradually. Except for the throbbing pain in his right ankle, nothing hurt. He'd be sore in the morning and the cut on his forehead would need special attention, but otherwise he counted his blessings.

He tried to stand, pushing himself up on his knees, but something inhibited his movement. Pressure on his ankle. A scalding pain grabbed hold, ebbing up his leg, stabbing his thigh with force.

"The hell?" he asked, trying to peek over his shoulder. His neck was rigid from the blow to his head. To top it all off, he had been concussed.

"There's another problem," Becky said in a *oh-I-forgot-to-tell-you* tone. She glanced around, looking for something specific. Her eyebrows flared when she found it. After jogging over to where a small cubicle containing a register and other useful supplies used to sit—now a heap of bowed metal and fragmented junk—Becky bent down, picked up the small shiny object, and sprinted back to where Mouth lay helplessly.

"Fuck's that?" he asked.

"A mirror," Becky said. "Sort of." She took the broken mirror, mindful of its sharp corrugated edges, and placed it in front of Mouth so he could see without straining.

"Fuuuuuck me."

Pinned to the parking lot, a mound of—what used to be—the gas station's canopy lay on his ankle, squished beneath the wreckage. The structure had collapsed, and luckily Mouth wasn't completely under it when it fell.

He stared at his ankle. Broken. Snapped like a thin twig.

"Can't lift it I suppose?" Mouth asked.

Becky stared at the daunting task, knowing their strength wouldn't be enough. "We can try."

The two girls hustled over to the wreckage and tried lifting the beam, but to no avail. The long metal structural rod didn't budge, didn't wiggle an inch. It was simply too heavy for the girls, easily outweighing them by several hundred pounds.

"No dice," Becky said.

"Fuck a duck." Mouth planted his head on the concrete, sucking in deep breaths. Panic rose in his chest, kicking his heart around like a soccer ball. He tried to steady his breathing, hoping to prevent a full-blown panic attack, but he could feel the adrenaline rush taking over his body; face down on the ground, he felt like he was falling.

"And that's not the least of our worries," Becky said, in a voice that nearly sent Mouth into a frenzy.

"The sun is coming," Dana said, pointing to the tangerine smudge spreading above the horizon.

-4-

They looked at Johanna and Jaime like five-star meals as they backed them against the tunnel wall, forming a half-circle around them, leaving no room for escape. Some of The Dirty giggled with delight while others groaned brutishly, savoring the moment before their nasty assault. They pushed each other around, fighting for firsts, forcing themselves to the front of the line. There was no order, no predetermined arrangement, no dibs, no desire for civility. Whoever wanted it more.

Mole watched from a safe distance, refusing to partake in the devilish activities.

"You're sick," Hugh said, trying to shake himself free from the two savages locking his arms behind his back. "You're a goddamn psycho and if you let them do this I'll fucking kill you! Those are innocent women! You hear me? Innocent!"

Mole refused to look Hugh in the eye. "No one survives innocently. I'm sure you've done things you're not proud of. Lie. Cheat. Steal. Kill. These things are immoral, yes—but necessary for survival."

"Raping women? That's necessary?" Hugh had worked himself into a fury. Kicking and thrashing around, the two men struggled to contain him, despite their physical advantage.

"To repopulate Mother Earth and secure the survival of mankind? Absolutely." Pacing back and forth, Mole continued to watch the horror unfold.

Hugh sensed the bastard enjoyed watching, living vicariously through his followers' filthy actions.

"You cannot do this!" Hugh struggled to move his arms against his captors' combined strength.

"One day, humanity will look back and thank me for the sacrifices we've made here today. You're women should consider themselves lucky."

"Lucky?" The word enraged Hugh further, instigating thrashing that got him nowhere.

"Yes, *lucky*. They will be mothers of the children who will piece this world back together. And I'll be their fathers. Teach them the tools they'll need to carry the human race back to existence, rebuild society—not the way it was—but better. Teach them the ways of a brighter future."

Whether a momentary lapse in effort or the amount of perspiration slicking his arms caused the two men to lose their grasp, Hugh didn't know, but he slipped free and immediately took full advantage of their blunder. The two men reached for him, attempting to haul him back, but the moment he sensed freedom his legs were propelling him toward the rabid throng of savages. He sprinted like death itself followed, slamming into the small gap between two cheering Dirty. He wedged his way through the crowd and made it without anyone stopping him. He rushed forward, placing himself between Johanna and Jaime and the encroaching savages. He waved his arms frantically, begging them to reconsider.

"Stop!" Hugh shouted over their lewd outbursts. "Stop, for the love of God! What is wrong with you people?"

In reply, a member of The Dirty stepped forward and wrapped his arms around Hugh's waist, suplexing him to the ground. Within seconds the crowd hovered over him, kicking and stomping, bending and breaking him. They rolled him over, face up. A large man with no shirt raised a sledgehammer over his head as high as he could stretch, and brought it down on Hugh's forehead. The momentum of the first blow wasn't enough to kill him, but the sound of his skull splitting went off like a firecracker. He struggled to stay conscious, although (if he had been in the right frame of mind to think about it) crawling toward that bright light would have been better.

Before the shirtless man brought the sledgehammer down on his head again, he heard Johanna scream as the bastards ripped the shirt off her back.

From a locked car not too far away, Brian watched the unspeakable acts occur. They had secured him inside a blue Toyota on Mole's command, parking two other cars against the doors so he couldn't open them. As Hugh's head became nothing more than crimson soup, he turned away, unable to watch another second. He found Mole staring back at him, proud of his own accomplishment. His grin told Brian more; mostly how he needed to get the hell out of the tunnel before he matched Hugh's current status. He hadn't seen Dustin in some time, but Brian assumed they put the poor bastard out of his misery.

Brian wondered why they kept him around. What did they need him for? Surely there was no great use for him. If repopulating the earth was priority number one, Mole had plenty of male donors, ready and willing to help the cause. Why wasn't he with the others? Did Mole know something about him? Did he know about his unique ability?

Soren.

He must have told him something. That he had visions. Premonitions. Soren could have told Mole a thousand different things to save his own skin, but for some reason Brian thought Soren had unearthed his talent.

Talent, Brian thought. *Hardly the word for it.* Curse was more accurate. His visions had brought him nothing but misery and mystery. Nothing good had come from his visions.

He couldn't take Mole's eyes any longer. He turned away, the thoughts of what Mole had in store for him causing imaginary spiders to borrow his spine.

Bad little boy, a voice rasped in his head.

A dark figure stood at the opposite end of the tunnel. Crouching. Waiting. The figure didn't resemble any of The Dirty. Another traveler perhaps? Or one of The Dirty's outcasts, a former member banished for their refusal to participate in family functions? Brian didn't know. The figure didn't act like one of them. It crept along the wall, hugging close, using the shadows as an ally. Stalking The Dirty like a jungle cat seeking a fresh kill from the branches above, the shadow crept, utilizing caution, clearly not wanting to draw attention to himself. Suddenly, he stopped. Had he spotted Brian? He didn't think so. He had been still and quiet, careful.

The shadow stopped and waited. For what, Brian was eager to find out.

"Will she survive?" Soren asked.

"Yes," Shondra said, refusing to take her eyes off the wound. Susan could walk fine, but David and Shondra walked on opposite sides of her in case the dizziness returned. "The bleeding has stopped."

Soren glanced over his shoulder, toward the horizon. The sun would ascend soon and as much as he didn't want to wait out the day, the train station would have to wait.

Unless you leave them...

He considered the option as he toyed with the vials in his pocket, running the glass between his fingers. Thanks to Joe's stash, he had plenty to get himself to Alaska. Traveling by day meant he'd arrive faster, but it meant having no companions, and in his experience, companions meant pawns, and pawns helped him out of sticky situations. Day travel was dangerous; if seen by the wrong eyes, it could cause serious complications he wanted no part of. The potential interrogators would demand explanations and answers to questions they wouldn't understand, even if Soren laid things out simply.

Leaving them behind and traveling alone was not an option. He'd wait out the day; they could use the convenience store as shelter, and set off the second the sun dropped behind the western horizon.

He needed to figure out how to dispose of Shondra.

The woman had become a pest. A nagging pest, good for nothing unless headaches were your thing, and Soren experienced enough headaches for one lifetime. He mused with ways to destroy her, everything from bashing her head in with a pipe wrench to pushing her out into the daylight. She had to go; there were no if, ands, or buts about it. The only thing worrying him was resistance from the others. Shondra could eat a bullet for all Susan and Kyle cared, but what about Mouth and David? Mouth would throw a tantrum, but he got over leaving Brian behind quickly, and figured he'd do the same if something happened to Shondra, especially if he believed it was an accident. Mouth seemed to care more about the girls than anyone else, and as long as they were okay, Mouth could deal. The girls were partly the reason Soren hadn't dispatched Mouth; the three of them had a bond, and Soren, although hardly sentimental about that stuff, thought it shouldn't be broken, not yet, not unless it was for something he could capitalize on, use to his advantage. And David? He couldn't tell how much he cared for the others, but figured he operated with his own safety in mind. He'd go along with anything he told him, as long as his own skin was safe.

Shondra. She was the one who could really fuck this thing up.

As they saw the gas station in the distance, Soren plotted.

"**Never thought I'd** say it," Mouth said, as David and the others pitched in, lifting the steel beam high enough for him to slide his foot out, "but, I'm glad to see you."

"Wish I could say the same," Soren said, the only one besides Susan who refrained from lending a hand in rescuing Mouth. Instead of worrying about the stability of Mouth's ankle, he surveyed the damage to the minivan. The canopy had collapsed on the roof, rendering the van unusable. A metal rod, smaller than the one that had nearly crushed Mouth, had pierced the windshield and sent webbed cracks throughout its entirety. It would have been better if the glass shattered. "Looks like we're walking to the train station."

"Is it far?" Dana asked.

Soren referred to the map. "No. Not at all."

David helped Mouth over to the convenience store.

"We better get inside," Mouth warned. "Sunfall is coming."

Soren twitched at the word, as if a bee buzzed too close to his ear. *Sunfall*.

Everyone headed toward the door, except Soren, who stood and faced the rising sun, memories of The Dish and what had happened there floating in the back of his thoughts.

"This train of yours better work," Shondra said, jabbing his chest with her finger as she passed.

Memories of the past ended and thoughts about how he should dispatch her rushed to the forefront.

He followed her inside.

They had settled into the previously unoccupied Old Moon Motel when the earthquake hit, causing everything around them to shimmy and shake. Sam had been in Room 6 with Brenda, Bob, and Matty, checking on Lilah, who lay on the bed, hopefully dreaming of unicorns and rainbows and not half-eaten hearts and buckets of blood. Bob was rambling on about how the fever should break soon when the ground rumbled beneath them and thunder rolled from below. Matty knew what it was instantly; a seismic shift of tectonic plates, which was odd, because the eastern side of the country had no such plates to compliment the size of the quake. If it had happened in California or Mexico, he might have been able to buy it, but the earthquake certainly didn't make sense here.

Nevertheless, he warned the others, rolled himself into a ball, tucking his head between his knees, and waited it out. When it was over, he unrolled himself and found everyone fine. Lilah woke, grabbing the ruffled sheets as if falling down a mountainside. A lamp took a dive off the nightstand, a bulky television set from the late 80's wriggled its way to the edge of the dresser, and a painting depicting the English countryside jumped off the wall; other than those minor things, their surroundings remained unchanged.

Tina and Jarvis, both of whom took to separate rooms and planned on retiring for the day, rushed into Room 6, making sure everyone was okay.

"What the hell was that?" Tina asked, once everyone had caught their breath.

"An earthquake. Although its existence is perplexing to say the least."

"What do you mean, Matty?" Bob asked.

"A seismic shift of that nature doesn't make sense on the east coast. It's not uncommon to have a small earthquake, but not that aggressive."

"I don't understand, little man," Jarvis said. "What are you trying to say? Like, the world is ending? Because newsflash: I think it already has."

"I don't know what it means. It could make sense that whatever is happening to the sun could cause other environmental changes, although..." He ran over to a backpack he had lifted from the sporting goods store. Removing a notebook and flipping through it, he said, "I've been doing experiments. Little stuff. Small sample sizes and whatnot. Nothing major."

"And?"

"Back in July, shortly after The Big Burn, I could put my

hand into the sunlight for an average of sixty seconds before I felt a tingling sensation. The temperature averaged the upper 90's."

Sam and Brenda exchanged glances. Neither of them looked happy to hear that their son risked his flesh for the sake of an experiment.

But it was Jarvis who voiced their concerns. "Pretty risky, little man."

Matty continued, putting one finger in the air, still concentrating on the notebook and the recorded data within its pages. "As of a week ago, the average time was down to forty-three seconds, the temperature averaging in the 60's. That's an average of seventeen seconds in almost six months. It's getting cooler, but our tolerance is diminishing."

Jarvis squinted, the information giving him a slight headache. "So, what you're saying is, the sun is getting stronger?"

Matty put down his notebook. "I don't know. Evidence would suggest that, or the environment is weakening, a rapid digression of the ozone layer. There are countless possibilities, none of which can be proven. I plan to collect as much data—"

"Matty," Sam interrupted. "I don't think it's a good idea risking yourself for a science experiment. You've seen first hand what happens out there."

Brenda placed a hand across her ex-husband's chest as if she expected him to rush forward and shake the common sense into their son. "Now, now. Let's not discourage him. There might be valuable information we can use—"

"Brenda." He grabbed handfuls of hair from the sides of his head. "It's dangerous. This is our son we're talking about here."

Everyone in the room shifted uncomfortably. *Here we go again,* the looks on their faces suggested, as the mood shifted from person to person.

"Sam, I'm not saying it's not dangerous. Matty should be supervised." She gave Matty the tilted-head glance that wasn't scolding, but not all that encouraging either. "Right, honey?"

Matty nodded enthusiastically. "Yes, ma'am."

"I'll see to it we experiment safely from here on out."

Sam wanted to ask Matty why he didn't come to him with these experiments before, but feared the answers, *"Because you didn't have time for me"* or *"You never listen to what I have to say anyway, so what's the point?"* There were other appropriate responses, all of which would cast Sam in bad light, and he didn't need anymore negative publicity thrown his way. Instead of opening his mouth, he smiled at his ex-wife, handing her the win begrudgingly.

"It's late," Bob said, interrupting the silence. "Sun's due up any moment. I suggest we sleep as much as we can."

No one disagreed.

-6-

Soren didn't sleep much. He watched Shondra most of the day. She didn't sleep much either. When she took her two-hour nap, he watched, wanting to go for the knife in his pocket, run the blade across her throat and call it a day. That was too obvious. He needed a subtle touch. Something the group wouldn't immediately notice.

He tapped Kyle's shoulder, waking him from an enjoyable dream, the one where he bent Becky Wright over and fucked her against Chris Atkins's tombstone.

"What?" he asked groggily. Only one eye opened. "What is it?"

"I need a favor," Soren said.

"Oh, Jesus. What?"

"It's Shondra."

"What about her?"

"I think you know what."

Kyle nodded and closed both eyes, hoping the previous dream was not too far out of reach.

Once the sun hid from the night and twilight reigned, Soren clapped his hands several times, waking the remaining sleepers. David shot out of his dream like being launched from a cannon. Shondra twitched on the floor and immediately pushed herself to her knees. Mouth was already awake, limping his way around the coffee station; he had made a fresh pot by boiling water and running it through the machine manually. The girls stirred awake, neither one of them rushing to join the waking world.

"We're moving out in five," Soren informed them.

Shondra and David checked on Susan. She was awake and the gash on the back of her head looked ten times better than it had twelve hours ago. Susan thanked Shondra for her concern, and nothing more. Shondra didn't regret saving her life; she wasn't vindictive, and never saw Susan as a true threat. The real threat was Soren.

"Shondra," Soren said, approaching the three of them.

"Yes?" She refused to look him in the eye.

"A word."

He walked her to the other side of the room where Kyle waited behind the counter, helping himself to a pack of cigarettes and an expired Tastykake. Kyle handed Soren a cigarette and the two of them lit up, inhaling clouds of smoke and puffing them out in rapid succession.

"What is it?" Shondra asked, staying far enough away so the smoke wouldn't bother her. A non-smoker all her life, she hated everything about it: the strong present odor, the taste, the never-fading stench that clung to her clothing, the harmful effects. Everything.

"I need you to help Kyle with something."

"What's *something?*"

"I don't want to discuss it much, because I don't want the others to hear."

She folded her arms across her midsection. "And why is that?"

"Because... it's important."

Shondra glared at him.

"Please," Kyle said. "I can't do it myself."

"I'm not doing anything unless you tell me what it is."

Soren sucked on his cigarette. The lit end glowed bright orange. "I think Susan needs more rest."

"She's fine. It wasn't as bad as it looked."

His head wavered as if to say *maybe yes, maybe no.* "Regardless, I think she could use the extra time to relax. I, however, cannot wait. I'll press on with Mouth, David, and the girls, you and Kyle stay back with Susan. You'll let her sleep for a few more hours, then meet us at the station."

Shondra turned to Kyle. "Can't handle it by yourself?"

Soren answered for him. "I'd feel better if there were two able-bodied people watching over her."

"What about David? He's able."

"You seem like you were taking good care of her."

"What—"

"Enough," Soren snapped.

Shondra rolled her eyes. "Fine." Her eyes settled on the map tucked under his arm. "How far away is the train station on foot?"

He hesitated. "Less than an hour. West."

"We'll see you in a few hours."

No, you won't, Soren thought.

Mouth hated everything about their journey from the second they left the gas station. He hated that David had to help him walk. His ankle wasn't broken; it had purpled over the last twelve hours to the point where it would have been better if the bone *had* snapped. He couldn't put a lot of pressure on it. He didn't like leaving Shondra behind; his gut told him it was a bad idea. Along the walk, he and David fell behind about thirty feet, not nearly far enough for Soren to consider stopping. Dana bounced alongside him, and Mouth couldn't decipher what the two of them were talking about. Becky strolled between the two parties, occasionally checking over her shoulder to see if Mouth and David had fallen past the imaginary distance that would warrant a break.

They saw many dead bodies along the way. The sun had blackened them beyond the point of recognition, heaps of tar and ash, black dust in an already dark world. Crows picked at their remains, digging through the crispy exterior and removing the warm gobbets beneath. They cawed to their brethren and a dozen more circled above, waiting for Mouth and the rest of the travelers to experience a similar outcome. Against the black sky it was hard to make out their appearance, but he heard the flapping of their wings and eager cries for expired flesh. He wondered what other scavengers the darkness harbored, how many eyes were watching them from nearby fields and forests. The thought injected a shiver through his veins, which made its rounds quickly, dying in the base of his spine.

On the steps leading to the train station, several dead collected, their bodies picked cleanly by the hungry buzzards, whose world—six months ago—became an expansive buffet that would occupy their bellies for a long time. An old-fashioned clock stood a few feet from the entrance. Ivy arms told them when the power went out; the big arm settled on the three, the little on the eleven. A murder collected on the clock, continuing to watch them, biding their time, waiting for a meal fresh off the grill.

Soren pushed through the revolving glass door and Dana

jumped into the next opening. Becky followed a few spaces behind, while David and Mouth followed a few minutes later. Lugging Mouth up the stairs populated with rotten bodies had been a challenge. Mouth wasn't fat or what most would consider chunky, but he did carry some extra weight he hoped the post-apocalyptic lifestyle would correct.

Once through the doors, Soren stopped in the lobby, looking up at the departures board, yellow letters and numbers against an ashen background, displaying times for trains that never arrived. The group stood behind him, hoping to spot whatever it was they needed to find. Soren directed his flashlight at the board, reading every single departure and train number, unable to find the necessary information to continue.

"Mouth," Soren said, turning to him.

"Yeah?"

"You have the tickets."

Scrunching his face while trying to remember, he rummaged the inner pocket of a denim jacket he had taken from a dead man weeks ago. In the pockets rested the four glittery-gold tickets and Mouth produced them quickly, placing them in Soren's grabbing hand.

Soren turned the tickets over and read the back. "Sub-Level 5. Solar Bay," he read aloud. He checked the departures board and couldn't find any mention of Sub-Level 5, nor could he locate a space for the words "Solar Bay."

"Looks like you've led us on a wild-fucking goose chase," Mouth said. "Wait til Shondra gets here. She's going to love tearing you a new asshole—"

"Shondra didn't make it," Kyle said, appearing behind them. He assisted Susan through the revolving door. "We were attacked. They... took her."

Mouth turned on his good ankle, keeping the bad one elevated. "Fuck you mean she didn't make it? Who attacked you?"

Kyle's eyes dodged Mouth's hard gaze. "I don't know. A gang. They had weapons. We were lucky to get out of there alive."

Mouth furrowed his brow, his nose crinkling from the strong

scent of bullshit. "Wait a minute. You mean to tell me a gang took Shondra and you two dumbasses managed to escape? Doesn't make a whole helluva lot sense to me."

"Well," Kyle said, "that's what happened."

"Yeah, sure it is, slimdick."

"You don't believe me?"

"Son, I'm more apt to believe Pinocchio."

"I'm not lying."

"Yeah? How many gang members were there?"

"I don't know. It was dark. Maybe four?"

"Four? You managed to escape four attackers and Shondra couldn't?"

"Yes."

Mouth glared at the sweaty kid. "Did you help her?"

"I tried, but..."

"You didn't, did you?"

"It was dark..."

"You fucking pansy."

"It was dark and we were scared. We ran."

"I don't fucking believe it."

Soren stepped between them. "That's enough. What happened, happened. We can't go back and fix it."

"The hell we can't!" Mouth shouted. "We can go back and get her!"

"No point," Kyle said. "They killed her."

Mouth hobbled over and pushed Kyle's chest with a firm finger. "You just said you ran."

"I did. I mean, we did."

Heat leaked through the pores on Mouth's face. "How do you know she's dead?"

"Because I know. I saw it. As I was running."

"How'd they do it?" Mouth kept calm, fighting the urge to grab the little cretin by the throat and squeeze until his windpipe splintered under his rage.

"I... I... I think a pipe. I think I saw a pipe."

"You lying little shit."

"Okay, enough," Soren said, muscling his way between them again. "We have to find the train. It's clearly not above ground. I suggest we head to the stairs and take a look below. The train we're looking for is solar-powered, so it should be under a charging station, isolated from the rest."

"What makes you think I want to go anywhere with you?" Mouth asked.

"No one says you have to," Soren told him. "You're more than happy to stay here by yourself."

"Becky, Dana—let's go. We'll go back and find Shondra and find your father some other way." Becky and Dana didn't move as he had expected them to. "Girls? What's the matter?"

"I want to go with Soren," Dana said.

"Dana, he's dangerous. He'll sell you to the highest bidder if that means his survival. He's a trickster. The whole walking out in the sun thing is a gag. An illusion. He has no real powers, Dana. I call smoke and mirrors."

She stood her ground.

"Don't listen to this fool, Dana," Soren said, staring into the hobbled man's eyes. "He knows nothing."

"I want to go with Soren, too," Becky said.

Mouth's face contorted like she had punched him in the balls. "Becky... why?"

"Because..." She averted her eyes. Dana stood next to her, putting an arm around her sister's waist. "Alaska is safe. That's where our father will be looking for us. It's too risky to travel the way we came. Plus... I trust Soren."

"Becky, you can't—"

"Enough, Mouth," Soren said. "We've heard enough. If you want to go, go. If you want to help us achieve the common goal, then come. No one will force you either way." Soren turned and walked toward the steps leading down to the lower level platforms. He waved to the others to do the same.

Dana followed Soren immediately with a bouncy gait. Before following her sister, Becky glanced at Mouth like she knew what she had said was wrong. Susan and Kyle bustled past Mouth, refusing to look at him. David put his hand on Mouth's shoulder.

"Don't let them get to you," he said.

Mouth spat on the glass tile floor, as if purging a bad taste. "They're liars."

"You can't do anything about it. Not now."

David was right. What else was he going to do? Leave? Break his promise to Sam? No. He made a promise he intended to keep, whatever the cost. He didn't know if Shondra was really dead or how much of Kyle's Swiss-cheese story was true, but he couldn't risk doubling back. He had to stick with Dana and Becky, no matter what.

"You're right," Mouth said.

"Just keep cool. I don't trust him any more than you do." David draped Mouth's arm over his neck. "Now let's go. Before *we* get left behind."

The stairs led to a basement area that offered little, except bland concrete walls and empty platforms where there were no trains left to board. They searched for an area marked "Solar Bay" but no one found anything like it. Discouraged, Soren paced up and down the long platforms, looking across the tracks where another long row of platforms sat, equally hopeless.

He kicked rocks off the edge of the platform and the group listened to them ricochet off the rusty metal train tracks. Placing his hands on his hips, he cursed and kicked more pebbles and pieces of trash into the darkness below. After his tantrum was over, he turned back to the others, popping another cigarette between his lips. He lit up and inhaled, taking several long puffs, savoring every ashy moment.

"I don't see a Solar Bay," Mouth said. "I don't see any train whatsoever."

"No shit," he replied. "It's here somewhere. We have to find it."

"Soren," Kyle said, helping Susan to the ground. She found a nice corner to rest against, taking her jacket off and using it as padding between her and the concrete wall. "Maybe Mouth is right. Maybe there's another way?"

"There's no other way. This is where we were told to go. This is where it is."

"Who told you to go?" Kyle asked. Soren's eyes threatened him and he felt compelled to elaborate. "I only ask because this place is freaky, man. It's dark. Abandoned. There are dead bodies on the steps out front. I mean, of all places you could have picked..."

"I didn't pick it. It was chosen for me."

"By who?"

"Doesn't matter."

"Just doesn't make sense."

Soren sucked the last inches of his cigarette away and tossed the remains into the darkness below. "It's here," he repeated. "I know it is. We just have to find it."

Above them they heard movement, a noise sounding vaguely like footfalls accompanied by the sound of two rusty metals grinding against each other.

"I don't think we're alone," Susan said.

Soren squinted, making out elevators in the near distance. "Then we better hurry." He walked along the edge of the platform. "This way."

As soon as the elevator doors parted, a strong moldy odor hit them like a slap in the face. Painted on the gray concrete wall before them in safety yellow were the words SUB-LEVEL 1. The group hurried out of the elevator. Susan put her hand over her nose and mouth, trying to block the toxic odor from carrying harmful spores into her lungs. Soren marched forward—only the mission in mind—without care. Susan placed her hand over the lower half of Dana's face, but she pushed the woman away and protected herself. She hustled after Soren, leaving Susan by her lonesome.

"Maybe it'd do you best to leave the little lady be," Mouth chimed in her ear.

"Screw you, pal," Susan muttered.

"Screw me! Well, that doesn't sound very Christian-like of you." Mouth chuckled as he spoke. "Tell you what? Once this is all over, I'll let you screw me all you want. I mean, you wouldn't be my first choice—a bit too old, sagging in parts that—"

"You're a filthy creature," Susan snapped. Her lower lip quivered and Mouth enjoyed every subtle movement. "Filthy, disgusting monster. How dare you talk to me like that."

"Listen, Sister Crazypants. You came on to me." Mouth smiled and limped away, leaving Susan behind, ignoring her mindless murmurs and hushed prayers.

SUB-LEVEL 5 had no train parked in its bay. Soren stood on the edge of the boarding platform, facing the space where a train ought to be. He lowered his head and cursed the world, replaying the last few hours over, trying to figure out where he had gone wrong. Did he misinterpret the golden tickets? He had looked them over thoroughly, read the words typed on the back in big bold letters several times. SUB-LEVEL 5. They were here and their transit was not.

"What are you thinking?" Mouth asked.

Soren surveyed his surroundings. "This doesn't add up."

"Told you we should head back," Kyle said.

He glared at his minion, disapproving of the young man's tone.

"Look!" Dana shouted, pointing down at the tracks. Between the two rails, a manhole cover lay next to a small opening.

Soren directed his flashlight at the hole, but from their vantage point it was too dark to see down.

"Where do you think it leads?" Dana asked. "I mean, we're already below ground."

Searching the ceiling, Becky pointed up. A ton of electronic equipment covered the ceiling. The alien structure reminded her of something she saw in *Alien*. "That's where the solar panels must be." She followed the cables running from a giant circuit board down the walls and into the ground. "The solar panels must charge on the surface and transfer the power down below."

"Why the fuck wouldn't the train be here," Mouth said, directing his finger at the empty space before them. "I mean, seems sort of unnecessary to have all this space, and no fucking train in it."

"Of course," Soren said. Jumping from the boarding platform and onto the tracks below. Soren's happy face returned. He jogged over to the open manhole and gazed down into the dark abyss. He shone his flashlight down; a faint glow at the end of the descent caused his heart to leap. "It must use its own set of tracks."

"Well that fucking explains it!" Mouth said, smacking his own head as if to knock the sense into himself. "Well, let's go jump into the black hole everybody! Nothing bad can come of it, I'm sure!"

Ignoring Mouth, Soren put his right foot on the first rusty rung. "If you're coming, I suggest we hurry. Whoever is down here with us won't be far behind."

"Wait!" Becky said, before he could put a second foot on the thin metal step. "Take these flares. Found them in the convenience store's emergency kit." She shimmied her way off the boarding platform to the tracks below. Becky jogged over to Soren and gave him the package containing four flares. She lit one with the butane lighter Chris Atkins had coveted, the one she took from his pocket after his death.

"Clever girl," Soren said, taking the flare and dropping it into the darkness below.

The solar-powered train sat below SUB-LEVEL 5 in a special bay all to itself. It was the only train in the entire station, and if anyone in the group still had an iPhone with Internet access, quick research would tell them it was the only solar-powered train in the entire country, abandoned in the late stages of development, but ready for its inaugural test launch. Almost a thousand feet in length, the station's charging dock was simply not long enough to contain it. So its designers gave the first train of its kind the unique ability to flex and bend, utilizing short cars instead of long ones. It rested in the charging dock like a snake, coiled when not in use. The train itself looked like a long bullet; the head cab's dome-shaped exterior provided the project with the futuristic appeal early concept artists, investors, engineers, and government overseers agreed upon. Atop each car sat long solar panels, giving the train the ability to hold longer charges between stations. They were forged into the frame, molded to fit the design and avoid the clunky appearance that marred most homes' curbside appeal. It was the one "necessity" the project needed. Bulky panels across the top of the train were bad for two reasons: one, the aerodynamic aspect—giant, conspicuous panels limited the train's speed and efficiency rating—and two, it looked fucking ugly and no self-respecting Eco-friendly traveler would pay the amount of money charged to sit inside an unattractive speed machine.

The endgame had the train running across the country, east coast to west, an environmentally friendly (and cheaper) alternative to flying, that would eventually expand to many destinations. As with many dreams and aspirations, the project died when the world died, and the train sat in its charging station outside the city of Richmond, Virginia, unused and never once operated, outside of powering the monster up during initial quality testing.

It never left the station until Soren and his group stumbled upon it.

-8-

Soren ran his fingers over the train's smooth metal exterior, his eyes lost in the battleship gray paint job. He could taste the Alaskan snow on the tip of his tongue. The distance was great, a problem the train would solve easily, transporting him very close to the place beneath the heavenly terrain: *The Dish*. His return was long overdue. Though thirty years had passed, Soren never felt right being on the outside; like an inmate granted parole after serving most of his sentence. His flesh became riddled with bumps when he reminisced about those days. Sitting in the lab, analyzing the genetic makeup of unknown death-dealing diseases. The Launch Room, where an array of civilization-ending weaponry awaited the push of a button, the ability to wipe the map clean. His small chamber, the one he used to plot and plan against Elias Wheeler, the man responsible for the world's current state of chaos. His bed, where he and Kyra spent many nights, losing hours while exploring each other's bodies, examining every naughty detail.

Behind him, the rest of the group climbed down the access ladder. Mouth brought up the rear, hopping down the ladder one-legged, making sure the ground was clear in case he lost his footing and fell. Once he jumped off the last rung—with David easing him back on his feet—and everyone huddled inside the solar train's bay, Soren turned to them. He opened his mouth to speak, but thought better of it after hearing movement above. Instead, he waved them toward the front car, the one shaped like a nuclear warhead. Hearing the echo of footfalls above them, they hurried after Soren, occasionally looking over their shoulders, expecting knife-wielding maniacs to appear, eager to flay their flesh.

In front of the windowless door, Soren stood and inserted the golden tickets into the automatic redeemer, solar-powered as with the rest of the train's features. The redeemer swallowed each ticket as fast as he could feed it. Once the train digested all four, the door hissed and slid open. A robotic female voice welcomed them. "THANK YOU FOR CHOOSING SUN-TRAC. AN ELIAS WHEELER COMPANY."

Hearing his former boss's name aloud soured Soren's mood. Nevertheless, he stepped inside the train's welcoming platform, turned, and waved his six followers on, acting as the train's conductor. Once everyone filed in, he pressed the small red button next to gliding door confidently. The door whooshed shut. Soren turned, heading directly for the door marked "OPERATOR CABIN."

Unlocked, the door glided open smoothly. Soren poked his head into the room, making sure it was vacant and not harboring street scum or squatters, threats of any kind. It looked empty so he headed inside, leaving the rest of the group to wait in the first car. For a few seconds he stared at the controls, a smorgasbord of buttons, dials, levers, and pulsating lights, none of which had names or labels. Not knowing where to start, he glanced around the cabin, hoping to find an operator's manual, instructions on how to get the beast powered on and the wheels turning. Unable to find anything useful, he turned back to the door and headed into the first cab, where the rest of the group waited nervously.

"Nothing," he said, leaving the operator's cabin.

He found the looks on their faces disturbing. They looked confused, uneasy, like they expected something terrible to happen. Their attention shifted toward the door to his right, the one he had thought he locked behind them. Susan pointed toward something and cried out, but—

A blur flashed through the air. Something smashed against his head, sending him sprawling to the ground. Pain exploded across the right side of his face. He pressed his hand against his cheek and checked for blood. Scarlet decorated his palm, a concerning amount. Soren crawled until his back was against the train's beach-beige interior. He looked up at the hooded figure as it prepared to swing once again. Kyle advanced on the figure, but the attacker sensed his movement, turned, squared its shoulders, and swung for the fences. Blood and spittle squirted from Kyle's mouth like a fresh bottle of ketchup as the bat connected with his jaw. The blow sent the kid to the ground, unconscious and bleeding. The figure turned back to Soren, pointing the end of the barrel at him. Promptly, the figure peeled back the hood.

"You left me for dead, motherfucker," she said, her face bloodied and broken. Her nose dipped slightly to the left. Her lower lip had split against her teeth. Gashes had bloomed on her forehead, near her hairline. Crimson rivulets leaked down the side of her face. Murderous intentions burned within her eyes. Soren swallowed hard, hoping one of the others—specifically Susan—would stop her from pounding his face into mush.

"Shondra..." he tried to say, but it came out in a hoarse whisper no one could understand.

"Sent your goons to kill me? Leave me to die out there? Well, let's see how impervious you are to this baseball bat." Shondra cocked her arms, the bat wavering behind her head, harnessing as much power as she could conjure. The real power came from her legs and as she planted her feet, put pressure on the thick muscles in her thighs, and swiveled her hips, she remembered her high school softball coach's lessons. *Swing through the ball,* he had said. She pictured Soren's head as a white leather grapefruit she planned on cranking over the left field wall. As the bat gained momentum, as she focused on her target, she heard Susan scream. The scream was music to her ears, a delightful score that soothed her soul.

It all ended when a crack of thunder sounded. A hole opened on the side of Shondra's head, a chunky splash of red spraying the cabin door. The bat fell from her hands and crashed on the floor; her lifeless body along with it.

"Do not be alarmed," the shooter said, making his way down the aisle. The end of the pistol continued to smoke, ashy billowing wisps. He wore a winter jacket, the hood pulled over his head, ready for northern weather. Despite the darkness, he wore sunglasses that blacked out his eyes. A chest-long beard with autumn tones covered the lower half of his face. His short stature and appearance made Mouth think of a garden gnome. "I am here to harm no one."

Mouth stared at Shondra's dead body and the crimson puddle underneath her head as it flooded outward. Her eyes were open wide, capturing that last moment of absolute fear, that momentary glimpse into a world beyond the living. Looking at her lifeless stare pained him—as did all dead eyes, as they reminded him of the woman he left behind. He liked Shondra. Always had. The resistance against Soren, a man as dangerous as any post-Burn encounter, just decreased by one number.

"Could have fucking fooled me," he said, looking away from Shondra's body, promising himself he wouldn't look down again.

The shooter glared at him as he strolled past, continuing to hold the pistol out, suggesting his work wasn't finished. Mouth raised his hands, letting the gunman know he was no Clint Eastwood and he'd receive no more lip.

After he made his way past the group, he stopped at Shondra's body. He tapped her corpse with his toe, making sure the woman was gone.

"You okay... old friend?" the shooter asked Soren.

Soren rose to his feet, squinting at the man, digging through his memories.

"It's good to see you, too," the shooter said. He pushed back his hood. "What do you say we grab a coffee, get this monster rolling, and catch up on old times?"

"PLAN B"

EPISODE TWELVE

-1-

August 22nd, 1985

Sandborough was sitting in the cafeteria, a cheeseburger occupying the hole below his nose, when Aldo sat down across from him, giving him those sad puppy eyes. The look had meant to alter Sandborough's mood, but he stared at his friend and felt nothing. No change in mood, not even slightly.

"If you're going to continue to be pissed off at me," Aldo said, swirling a french fry in the ocean of ketchup before him, "might I suggest you make it less obvious."

Alan said nothing, continuing to rip off huge chunks of beef with his teeth. He swallowed slowly, gazing hard into Aldo's beady eyes.

"I know you're upset. I get it. But I told you to trust me. I have a Plan B, and someday, Sandborough, you're going to thank the shit out of me. If things go wrong that is."

"If things go wrong," Sandborough said.

"Yes. *If.* " Aldo bit his lip. "Alan, you don't think Plan B is a replacement for Plan A, do you?"

"I don't know, Aldo. Is it?"

Aldo raised his hand as if Sandborough lunged at him. "You've got the wrong idea."

"Do I?"

"Yes. You do."

"Why do I get the sneaking suspicion you hate Plan A, think it's suicidal, and convinced everyone that Plan B is better?"

"For the record—Plan A *is* suicidal. But still, I'm your friend, and you dragged me into this, so it's your plan we're sticking with, much to my chagrin. Plan B is exactly that. A backup plan."

Sandborough wasn't convinced. Aldo was avoiding eye contact, staring down at the french fries, greedily shoving them into his mouth.

"Okay, Aldo. Say I believe you. What happens after you get me out?"

"I told you. I have connections on the outside. It's taken care of."

Sandborough pounded the table with his fist. *"Tell me."*

Aldo sighed deeply. He glanced at the ceiling and scratched the stubble on his chin. "It's better you know less."

"Why is that?"

"Trust me."

"I trust no one."

"You better start." Aldo stood up from the table, abandoning the fries on his plate. "If you're going to get anywhere in this life, you're going to have to trust a few people along the way."

Sandborough disagreed.

NOW

Soren gripped the man's throat, cutting off his air supply. The man struggled, thrashing wildly. He kicked Soren's shins, but he didn't flinch. He reached for Soren's throat, but he fell a few finger lengths short. Finally, he resorted to words, hoping to talk his way out of the situation.

"Sandborough.... stop," the bearded man rasped.

"Plan B? Plan B? *This was your Plan B?*" Soren tightened his grip. "You fucked me. You fucked everything up, Aldo! I trusted you! Your own sister, trusted you!"

"Mistaken... all... big... mistake..."

"The only mistake was listening to you and your half-cocked Plan B!"

With his conscious slipping, Aldo's eyes rolled behind his lids. "Alive..."

"What?" He relaxed enough so Aldo could breathe.

"She's... alive."

"Who is alive?" Soren let go. He pinned Aldo's shoulders to the vacant space next to the brain-splattered cabin door. "Who is alive?" he repeated through his teeth.

Aldo put a finger up, struggling to catch his breath.

"Kyra." he said, wheezing. "My sister. She's still alive."

Sam glared out the window, watching the sun take its seat behind the horizon. Surveying the parking lot. His eyes following the extensive damage to the concrete, his stomach grumbled. He turned to Matty who lay next to Lilah on one of two full-sized beds. The girl had fallen back to sleep some time after the earthquake ended. Jarvis, who sat on the second bed—closest to the window—reading *The Holy Bible*, predicted as much. He told them she'd drift in and out until "the shit" was out of her system. "The best thing she can do is get as much rest as possible." That wasn't likely to happen with orbit-altering earthquakes, but the disaster seemed like an isolated incident and wouldn't repeat itself. At least, according to Matthew Wright.

"I'm going to find a vending machine," Sam announced, turning from the window. "Maybe check a few things out. Make sure it's safe." He walked to the foot of Matty's bed. "You want to come with?"

Matty, barely making eye contact with his father, slowly swung his head from side to side.

"Jarvis? You want anything?"

Jarvis hoisted the Bible in the air. "I'll pass. I'm getting to the good part."

Sam smiled, unable to tell if Jarvis was kidding or being serious. He looked at his son before leaving. "I'll be back in a few. Bob and your mother are in the next room."

Once his old man was gone, Matty returned to facing Lilah. He watched her sleep, wondering if she was dreaming, and if so—what about. Sweat bubbled on her forehead. Her body fought off the fever and Jarvis had said the counteractions were performing as expected. She was in good shape. Or, as good as one recovering from withdrawals could be.

"The second is this," Jarvis said, reading from the Bible. "'Love your neighbor as much as yourself.'"

"What?" Matty said, continuing to watch Lilah. He wondered if she'd find his affection creepy or sweet, or somewhere in between.

"Just reading out loud. 'Love thy neighbor as much as yourself. There is no commandment greater than these.'"

Matty ignored him the second time around.

"That's a bold statement by Mark, don't you think, little man?" Jarvis asked. He closed the Bible on his finger, marking his page. "I mean, for one, he's saying other than loving God, loving your neighbor is the most important commandment. More important than not killing, not stealing, not saying using the Lord's name in vain. But that's because—and here's where it gets deeper—every other commandment is an elaboration of loving your neighbor; don't steal from him; don't think about banging his wife; don't kill him. Instead, love him. Hell, honor your mother and father is the same thing, only they're the neighbors that gave birth to you. There could really be *two* commandments: love God, and love other people. I think about how relevant it is now. The outside world—it's pure danger. Chaos. We've reverted back to primitive times. If it's not the thing giving this planet life trying to kill you, it's the misguided survivors bent on evil. All this madness out there, and if we could just honor each other—love each other—then maybe we could all survive. Together. Because that's what it's all about. Unity." Watching Matty continue to focus on Lilah, Jarvis smiled. "It's easy to forget how powerful a book can be."

Matty turned to him. "Especially when used for the wrong reasons?"

Jarvis narrowed his eyes.

"You never met Soren."

"No, I never did."

"You might have a different opinion of that book if you had." Matty turned back to Lilah. Her color had changed, her skin more pallid than before.

Jarvis also took notice. Swinging his legs off the bed, he peered over Matty's shoulder.

"I don't understand," Matty said. "I thought she'd be better by now."

"These things take time, little man." He placed a hand on his shoulder. "I know it sounds cliché, but you'll see. She'll be better in no time. No time at all. In fact, she'll be better before you can say strawberry-banana pancakes."

"Strawberry-banana pancakes," Lilah whispered. Her eyes remained closed, her body still.

Matty's mouth curled at both ends. He tried to hide his joy, but his eyes stung and he knew tears were taking form. Slowly— trying not to make it glaringly obvious—he slipped his finger into her hand as if to test their relationship, to see how far they had come. Her fingers curled around his and his heart fluttered like a cage of drunk butterflies.

"It's kinda hard to sleep next to your Bible-thumping ass," she said, her tone rising above a whisper. Her eyes opened to slits and a goofy smirk fixed her dry lips.

"Well, shit. I guess my days as Reverend Jarvis are over."

Matty jumped off the bed and headed for the door.

"Where you going, little man?" Jarvis asked.

"Going to find my dad. I need to ask him something."

-2-

The second Brian opened his eyes, he heard shouting. At first he thought Mole's rabble was outside his door, ready to string him up, cut him open, and harvest his innards. But when the world focused, he found himself in the same position he fell asleep; locked in the car, his future grim. The arguments were coming from farther away, around the tunnel's slight bend. Shadows on the wall danced in the flickering candlelight. Things were growing loud and angry and it was only a matter of time before the argument would make its way to him.

Something is happening.

But what?

A coup? Mole is being overthrown?

No. Makes no sense.

Mole appeared in the distance, his two loyal guards in tow. He ran toward Brian, the two guards attempting to keep pace. Once Mole rolled the car blocking his door aside, he scrambled over to Brian's four-wheel prison and ripped the door open like the vehicle was on fire and valued the life inside. He grabbed Brian by his neck and heaved him to the ground. He tumbled several times before landing on his back, staring at the three troubled faces crowding his vision.

"Who is it?" Mole asked.

"I don't understand. Who is what?"

Mole bent to one knee and grabbed Brian's collar. "Don't lie to me, you shit. Soren told me all about you and your unique ability. And although his word doesn't mean a lick of shit, I've seen the way you dream. He's right about you. You have something special about you, boy. Something powerful."

"I... I..."

"Tell me who is butchering my men!"

Brian looked around uneasily. Red covered the interrogators' hands. Droplets fell from their fingers, a steady stream that pooled on the asphalt. Unable to piece together the puzzle, Brian said, "I don't know."

"Is it one of your men? Has Soren come back to rescue the rest of his people? Are they coming back for you?"

"I have no idea!" Brian shouted.

"You lie, you die," Mole said, his lips fixed in a feral snarl.

Behind them, they heard screams. The shadows on the wall moved about frantically. The screams were cut short, replaced with throaty gurgles. Brian watched a splash of red decorate the far wall, replacing the area where the shadows had been. A man's head rolled across the asphalt into his view, a trail of crimson following in its wake. Streaked with blood, eyes wide with terror, the head faced them, forever depicting the man's final moment.

"Holy shit," Brian muttered.

Mole steadied himself. He held his two men back as they charged forth. "We can run. Right now. We might make it if we run."

"But, boss," a guard said.

Mole stopped him, putting a finger over the man's lips. "We can run."

"It's almost daylight," the other guard said. "We can't go far."

From behind them, something hissed like a broken gas pipe. They whipped around, facing the noise and watched a cloud of smoke tumble toward them.

"What the hell is that?"

"I don't know," Mole answered, huddling the two men close. "Stay together. We stand a better chance together."

The attacker moved silently, stalking his prey like a trained ninja warrior. Even if Brian had wanted to warn Mole and his two henchmen, there was no time. The attacker appeared like a shadow behind them, swinging the katana with both hands. The blade—already slick with blood—sliced into one guard's neck. Dull from overuse, the blade wasn't sharp enough to complete the job and the man's head tilted to the side, still attached to his neck by skin and sinew. Scarlet squirted from the laceration like a geyser, bathing the attacker in blood. The other guard raised the gun in his left hand, but before he could fire, his hand disappeared along with the weapon it held. The guard looked at his bloody stump and screamed, but his vocal outburst ended when the ninja took the tip of the katana and inserted it into his throat, far enough so half of the blade exited out the back of his neck. The ninja retracted the weapon easily and the guard dropped to the asphalt next to his buddy.

Mole turned and ran.

The ninja took two long strides and was already in striking distance. The blade became a blur in the ninja's hand, the force directed at Mole's feet. The blade tore through his ankle, severing Mole's foot, sending the frantic leader to the ground. He flipped over, spouting nonsensical promises. He offered money, women, men, power, everything he no longer had. The blade zipped across Mole's stomach, opening his belly. Viscera ruptured from the wide gash, spilling onto the pavement. He screamed as his guts slip through his fingers. He cried, begged for the ninja to cut his throat. Brian watched Mole scoop his innards up and try to mend himself, stuffing what looked like wet purple hoses back into his midsection's crimson cavity. It was a messy task and every time he managed to fill himself, the intestines tumbled out, landing on the pavement. The wet sound of his innards splashing on the road echoed throughout the tunnel.

Brian opened his mouth to beg, but he knew it was useless. The ninja had already made up his mind.

The shadow warrior readied the blade.

Aldo sipped coffee from a *Star Wars* mug he had found next to the Keurig machine. He sat atop a small table in the center of the first car, opposite Soren and the other passengers. With his eyes locked on Soren's, and Soren's on his, Aldo searched for the right words. For what seemed like several eternities, they glared at each other, as if hearing a riveting tale full of peril and wonder.

"You have a lot of explaining to do," Soren said.

"Fucking-A-right you do," Mouth said. "I'd like to know exactly what's going on, and right fucking now."

"Is he always like this?" Aldo asked.

"You have no idea," said Soren. He plucked a cigarette from the pack Kyle had given him. He wrapped his lips around the tan end and lit up.

"See you haven't kicked the habit."

"My health has not concerned me since I was betrayed by my best friend and banished from my lover."

Mouth laughed. "Lover! Ha! Who the fuck would ever love you, you heartless bastard."

Soren ignored him and continued smoking. "I want answers, Aldo. Right now."

"How much do they know?" Aldo asked, nodding to the others.

"Not much." Soren rolled his eyes and turned to them. "Long story short—the facility underneath the Alaskan surface was a government-funded research project. I worked there. They wrongfully accused me of some unflattering things and I was—more or less—fired. The end."

"Fired?" Aldo asked. "That's a funny way of putting it." He sipped his hot coffee through a grin.

"What kind of research facility?" Becky asked.

"Hold all questions until after I interrogate this little bastard," answered Soren.

"I respectfully disagree," Mouth said. "I say you answer our questions now."

Soren shot him a glance. "Mouth, I swear to God. If you don't quit running your goddamn trap, I'm going to close it for you. Permanently."

"I'd like to see you fucking try, Soren, or Alan, or whatever the fuck your name is."

Soren rose to his feet, smoke billowing out of his nose. "Don't fucking test me."

Susan stood between them, glaring at Soren as if he were the devil disguised in human flesh. "I can't believe I trusted you. Put my faith in you. You're nothing more than a savage. No different than any other Godless man."

"Shut up," he told her, disgusted. "I'm sick of you. I'm sick of all of you."

"What the hell did I do?" Kyle asked.

Ignoring him, Soren scrunched his face together as if he had bitten into something unexpectedly sour. "You're all weak. Not built for this world. You ask questions instead of seeking out answers. You search for a leader; why not take the reigns yourselves? Because you're followers. And this world *eats* followers. You feel like pawns on a chessboard? That's because you are pawns. This world is full of them."

Aldo laughed incredulously. "You're still the same Sandborough I remember."

Soren rushed forward and grabbed Aldo by his throat. He yanked him off his feet. The *Star Wars* mug fell to the ground and the ceramic scattered into several pieces on impact.

"We're going to have a conversation, you and I," Soren growled into his Aldo's ear. "A *private* conversation."

He dragged him into the second car, the automatic door closing behind them with a cobra's hiss.

Bob curled up into the fetal position next to her and found sleep almost immediately. He snored, a habit which she hated before The Burn, but now cherished. She counted themselves lucky Bob wasn't seriously injured. She didn't know what she'd do if something terrible happened to him. They had been through so much—the church, the zoo, the pharmacy—and in a world where death was commonplace, she thanked God or whatever ethereal force ruled the universe for each day they spent together, alive and well. She kissed his forehead, gentle not to wake him.

Two knuckles rapping on the door startled her. Bob stirred, but remained dreaming. The door cracked open and Sam's face appeared. After seeing Bob asleep, he whispered, "Sorry," and ducked back out.

"Wait!" Brenda whispered. She looked down at Bob, who remained trapped in his dreams. "He's out. It's fine." She wasn't whispering anymore, but kept her volume low.

"Sorry," Sam said again.

She waved. *No big deal,* her hand said. "What's up?"

"Heading to the vending machine. Want to see if I can steal you anything?"

She smiled. "No, I'm good. But thanks for the offer."

"You sure? You're looking like you could use a snack." He twitched his brow in rapid succession and returned the cozy smile.

She stifled a laugh. "What's that supposed to mean?"

"Ah, nothing." He looked over his shoulder as if he heard a noise. Brenda didn't hear anything and his face returned to the doorway a second later. "Hey, have you seen Tina?"

Hearing the name, Brenda's smile unintentionally faded. Sam perceived this as an act of concern, but it was something else. "No."

"Hm. Weird. She wasn't in her room."

"Maybe she went for a walk."

"Yeah, maybe."

"Do you like her?" She knew she shouldn't have asked once the words left her mouth, but it was too late. She waited for his answer, unsure if she wanted one.

Just when she opened her mouth to tell him to forget it, he grinned and said, "I don't know. Would it bother you if I did?"

She didn't smile back as he expected.

"I don't know. Maybe."

Confusion wrinkled his forehead. "Maybe?"

"I don't know, Sam. That's a complicated question."

"Not that complicated."

"I know we haven't been together in a long time, but it's still hard for me to imagine you with someone else." She glanced down at Bob sleeping, wondering if he was truly asleep or if he was pretending, listening to every word. "You know what I mean?"

"Not really. Besides, you asked me—"

"I know. It was dumb. It's just..."

"What?" he asked, and not in his usual irritated tone.

"I don't trust her."

"Don't trust her?" Sam tilted his head. "Brenda, if there's anyone I trust, it's Tina. She's helped us out of many tough situations."

"She taught our son how to fire a weapon, Sam. Behind our backs."

"And look what happened. Matty saved your husband from getting his head blown off by that psychopath."

"I know, but..." Brenda searched for the right words. "There's something I don't like about her, Sam. I have a bad feeling about her and I don't know what. I just..."

"Just..."

"Just don't want to see you get hurt."

"You don't have to worry about my feelings, Brenda."

"I'm sorry. I worry about you sometimes."

"I appreciate it."

They sighed in their own way, as if trying to recover lost air.

"Okay. Guess I'll be off. Sure I can't get you anything?"

Brenda winced.

"Fair enough." Sam forced a faint smile and said, "Get some sleep," before closing the door and heading down the hall, toward the small vending machine enclave.

-3-

"I apologize for what happened," Aldo said, sitting in the third row. With tired eyes, he looked up at Soren who stood in front the door separating the two cars, arms folded across his chest, a fresh cigarette smoking between his lips. "I didn't mean for it to go down like that. The whole objective of Plan B was so no one got hurt."

"A lot of people were hurt," Soren said. "I watched Kyra die. Do you understand me? I watched her die."

Aldo raised his brow. "She didn't die, Alan."

"I watched..." The picture of her squirming in a sea of her own red interrupted his train of thought. "There was so much blood. She couldn't have..."

"They couldn't save the baby. While we were getting you out of there, another team rushed her to the hospital wing. The doctors were able to save her, but the baby, I'm told, never had a chance."

"She's... alive," Soren said between puffs. "Kyra's alive."

"Yes, Alan. She's alive. But she's in trouble. We all are. No thanks to you."

The muscles in Soren's jaw flexed.

"A lot has happened in thirty years. Not all of it was bad, mind you. To make a really long story short, after they patched Kyra up, she reconciled with Elias. Promised to be a devoted housewife, keeping him happy and keeping *you* safe."

"Keep me safe?" Soren glared at him. "I thought that was your job?"

"It was. But my connections only go so far. With Elias happy, it kept the attention off you."

"Doesn't he think I'm dead?"

Aldo laughed through his nose. "Come on. This is Elias Wheeler we're talking about here. He doesn't think you're dead. He never saw a body. I mean, he saw *a* body, but it barely resembled yours. We took a dead guard's corpse and burnt it beyond recognition. He was about your height and build. Genetics came back inconclusive, though we didn't have half the tests we do today.

Elias wasn't satisfied, but Kyra convinced him to quit pursuing the matter. She told him..." Seeing the tears build in Soren's eyes, he stopped. After a moment, he decided he must continue. "She told her husband that you were a mistake. He believed her. Despite being a bastard, Elias really loves her."

Soren winced, Aldo's last four words feeling like a dagger through his ribs.

"Don't take it to heart. Take comfort in knowing it was a lie to save your ass. Sure, I have connections on the outside, but Elias— he had a small army on speed dial. If he wanted to, he could have found you. Whatever my sister did to stop him from looking, well... I don't want to think about it and I'm sure neither do you."

Soren sucked in a cloud of smoke, then released it through his nostrils. "Get to the part that doesn't make me want to kill you."

"Right. Plan B was designed to get you out. But it was also designed to get you back in."

"Get me back in?"

"After you left, things went back to normal. Elias culled everyone he thought you infected with your lies and deceit, and replaced them with mindless robots he could control with ease. Things were good and there were no incidents. I mean zero. Everyone worked together and the government enjoyed what we were doing and everyone was happy, until..."

"Until what?"

"Elias lost what little mind he had left." He twirled his forefinger near his temple. "I don't know all the details, but Kyra kept me informed when she could. I seldom saw her after you left. We spoke briefly once a month. Sometimes less. About ten years ago she said he was starting 'to lose it.' I'm not sure what that meant, but rumor had it Elias had been diagnosed with some rare form of osteoarthritis and it appeared the disease ate away more than his joint tissue. He started acting irrational and paranoid. Much like you had acted, now that I remember. Recently, it had gotten so bad that his eighteen year old son—"

"Son?" Soren interrupted.

"Shit. Yeah, forgot to mention that, didn't I? One of the

conditions to whatever arrangement Kyra made with him was that she promised to birth his child. Kid's name is Wallace. Wallace Wheeler. Catchy. Anyway, some people dubbed him 'Damien' because of that movie. Spawned in Hell, and all that. Personally, I don't know how my sister dealt with it. Wasn't easy I assure you. It's bad enough living with someone you hate, your entire existence wasted on appeasing their every wish and desire—but, to add that little monster on top on things." Aldo bit his lip and shook his head, his sister's struggles delaying his thoughts. "Yeesh. The kid is a carbon copy of his father. Chip off the old block and then some. He's twenty-eight now, and his father's disease has taken a turn for the worst. The government keeps trying to step in, threatening to cut back funding, claiming the existence of this sort of weaponry is too dangerous. The Bush Administration extended the contracts another fifteen years after the attacks on 9/11. But this new administration is threatening to shut it all down, and of course Elias is stressed and pissed and has started taking it out on the world. Of course he can't do much now. The disease has crippled him. Wallace is practically running things now and—"

"How long have you been out?" Soren cut in.

"The second someone pushed the button."

"Sunfall?"

"You know it."

"Was it Elias?" Soren asked.

"Either him or his demon spawn. The government wanted to test Sunfall in a localized area, somewhere in Afghanistan. A ten mile radius. To see if what they were sinking millions into was worth it. But someone cranked the fucking thing up to full power. Next thing we know, we're watching the world burn. Not literally, of course."

"Why'd you leave?"

"I told you. Plan B."

"Joe came to me," Soren said.

"I know. I sent him."

"He knew someone would turn on the machine. He supplied me with the antidote."

"We all knew about it," Aldo said. "However, we didn't know exactly what would happen when they threw the switch. I had to prepare for the worst."

Stamping his cigarette out on the ground, Soren squinted at his old friend. "Why do I get the sense you aren't being truthful with me?"

"Alan, look at me. This was all part of Plan B. We knew it was a matter of time before something happened. Sunfall, Quakefall, Stormfa—"

"We experienced a serious earthquake earlier today. Know anything about that?"

Aldo waved his hands in the air. "I lost all communication with The Dish since I left. I don't know what the hell is going on there. Chaos, I presume. Which is why what I say next is very important and time sensitive."

"What's that?"

Aldo leaned forward as if there were other ears in the room. "Once the switch was thrown, The Dish entered lock-down mode. It was a precautionary approach Elias made me design after you tried killing him and everyone else in the world. I guess it was my punishment. No one can get in or out once someone activates the system. I managed to get myself and a few others out before the doors closed for good."

"How resourceful you are."

Aldo ignored him. "I accounted for this. After all, you're speaking with the man who designed the fucking system. To get back in, we need a key code."

"A key code?" Soren asked. "Am I to assume you have this key code?"

Aldo clenched his eyes and sucked air through his teeth. "Actually I don't."

Soren eyed him warily. He reached for his cigarettes and found his pocket empty. He had left them in the other room.

"There's a young woman in Chicago. She's the only one on the entire planet who can access The Dish's security system. We'll need her."

"She still alive?"

"God, I hope so. Be a shame, wouldn't it? A real wrinkle in our sheets if we got all the way there and found her dead."

Soren bit his tongue. "I'm having a hard time believing you."

"I figured you might. Who could blame you? I only saved your life after you risked ours—for what again? Oh, right. So you could live happily ever after with the love your life."

Soren ground his teeth together. "I did what I did to protect all of us from a madman."

"You talked a good game, but once the dust settled, things became clear. The only thing you ever cared about was her. And yourself. You *used* us. You made us believe that Elias was a madman—and maybe he was—but only because you *made* him that way. You're as responsible for this mess as much as he is."

Soren had no words.

"So, it will be my word we trust from here on out. Got it?" Aldo asked, glaring. "Now I suggest we get this train moving. Time is wasting and judging from the ten-point-oh earthquake we all experienced, we don't have much of it."

With his arm halfway up the vending machine's skirt, the package of sourdough pretzels on the tips of his fingers, Sam heard his stomach growl. *Okay,* he told his belly, *I'm working on it.* He pushed harder, working for the extra inch or two that would allow him a good grasp on the plastic packaging. *Just a little more.* The security flap designed specifically for situations such as this stopped him from getting that much-needed inch. After a painful ten minutes of struggling and altering his approach, Sam threw in the towel. He sat with his back against the motel's snack cubicle, opposite the three vending machines. Lazily kicking the ice machine, he cursed to himself.

"There's an easier way to do that."

Sam turned to the open doorway and saw Tina standing there, her forearms resting on the jambs. The hunting rifle strapped to her back made her look like an outlaw, and he found it strangely attractive. Loose strands of hair dangled over her eyes, almost seductively. She smiled, amused by Sam's effort.

"How long have you been watching?"

"Long enough."

She pressed her back against the wall and readied herself. "I've always wanted to do this." She took one step and kicked the thick glass protecting many full rows of candy bars and potato chips. The glass cracked on the first attempt, but didn't break. Two more, and the glass separated into several pieces and fell to the ground, granting them access to whatever treat they desired. Sam immediately went for the pretzels, tore the bag open and shoveled the small crunchy bites into his mouth.

"Hungry?" Tina asked, grinning. She went for the Crunch on the second shelf.

"Just a little," he said, his mouth full. "Where'd you go?"

"What do you mean?"

"Was looking for you before. Couldn't find you."

"I was around," she said, chewing her chocolate bar. "Can't a girl go to the bathroom in peace?"

Sam rolled his eyes. "I was worried about you."

Her chewing slowed. "Worried about me?"

"Yeah... you know."

She eyed him warily, her lips forming a flattered smile. "No, I don't. Tell me."

Sam swallowed the half-chewed pretzels in his mouth and leaned in. Tina stayed where she was, refusing to meet him halfway. She could have stopped him or tilted her head sideways or told him no, but she did none of those things. Sam pressed his lips against hers and kissed. She kissed back, softly at first, as if she wasn't sure she should, but the longer the moment carried on, the more passionate pressure she put into it. After a short fifteen seconds, they parted. Tina's eyes darted to the ground while Sam wiped excess saliva off his lips with his sleeve.

"I'm sorry," he said.

"No, it's fine."

"I don't know what got into me."

"You don't have to apologize."

"It's the whole apocalypse thing: I'm hungry, my stomach was going nuts—you come in with the gun on your back, looking all sexy—then you put your foot through the machine and I lost it—"

"Sam?" Tina said, still grinning, but only looking half as happy as she was moments ago.

"Yeah?"

"Shut up." The grin remained. "Don't ruin it."

"I understand. Play it cool."

She rolled her eyes. Several seconds passed. They shared them in silence, childish smiles claiming their faces. Sam felt like a teenager who had secretly kissed his best friend's hot sister in the coat closet. A pang of giddiness spelled his mood.

"So.... you want to do it again?" he asked.

Tina started to laugh when the sound of glass shattering came from the center of the parking lot. They looked at each other and thought the same thing: *the cruiser.*

-4-

Soren, Mouth, and the remaining passengers sat in silence as the train powered on and began its journey north-west. Mouth stared at Soren, hating the cryptic man for making him leave Shondra's body on the boarding platform like an emaciated dog in a grungy back alley. Soren ignored his gaze, his mind swimming in pools of more concerning thoughts. After the train uncoiled and left the station, Aldo opened the cabin door and stood before them, looking satisfied.

"Gotta love technology. We're on automatic pilot from here to Pittsburgh," he told them, tossing his conductor's hat on the first empty seat available.

"Pittsburgh?" Becky asked.

"Yes, my lady. We're going to need the charging station there. We'll spend the day. The station won't give us a full charge, but it'll be enough to get us to the next station in Chicago. There are five charging stations in all. Once we get to Chicago, we're going to have to spend a few days there. One, to let the train get a full charge, the other because I have some business to attend."

"What fucking business?" Mouth asked.

Aldo raised his eyebrows. "Need to find someone. Won't be easy. Chicago has become an... interesting place since..."

"The Burn?" Dana asked.

"The Burn," Aldo repeated, amused. "Yes, that's it. I've heard other names for it, but The Burn—so far—is my favorite."

"I don't understand why we have to stop at all," Becky said. "Aren't there panels on top of the train? I saw panels."

"Yes, there are. But they only help hold the charge. Our designers preferred aesthetics over efficiency. We didn't have our current situation in mind when we engineered her."

"You say 'we' like you had something to do with this," Mouth said.

"Aldo Hood, lead engineer for SUN-TRAC. Pleasure to make your acquaintance."

Mouth muttered, "Fuck you" under his breath.

"I'd like to apologize for your friend. I didn't know the situation. I saw my old pal about to get his head smashed in and I reacted hastily. If there's one thing I've learned from this scary new world, it's shoot first, ask for forgiveness later. I've seen many people die who believed the contrary."

No one forgave Aldo. They turned their heads away from him, looking out their designated windows and into near darkness, scanning the faded city outline under a pale moon and star-studded sky.

"You should consider yourselves lucky. You're the first people to put this train to the test. She's been sitting in The Snake—that's what we called the charging station back in Virginia—for two years, awaiting its initial launch. However, SUN-TRAC was a project the Wheeler Corporation wasn't too eager to finish. No money in it yet, and too many other projects required all hands on deck—"

"I don't think we give much a shit about your history lesson, chiefy," Mouth said. "I myself would like to know how you two knucklefuckers know each other and exactly what kind of shit-storm we have coming our way."

Aldo stood, staring Mouth in the eyes. "Alan—I mean, Soren —and I used to work together. Nothing more than a couple of colleagues. Isn't that right, old pal?"

Soren nodded subtly.

"And I wouldn't call what lies ahead a shit-storm. Rough times? Maybe. Perilous territory? Sure. But keep your wits about you, and you'll be fine. Hell, you might even fit in."

"I don't think Chicago is safe for a couple of teenage girls. I didn't go into Richmond, but I heard a lot of noises. Shouting. People. Sounded chaotic. I think we should avoid big cities." He jerked his head at Becky and Dana. "Maybe you can drop us off somewhere beforehand and come back and get us when you're finished with your giant circle jerk."

Aldo almost laughed. "What's your name again?"

"Fuck you, that's my name."

"Mouth," Soren answered for him.

"Fitting." Aldo chuckled. "Mouth, with that kind of attitude—

and that manner of speaking—you're going to find yourself in a world of trouble. I suggest you be a little more like the rest of your fellow passengers." He walked over to Soren and placed a hand on his shoulder. "The company you keep nowadays," he said, whispering into his ear.

The ninja put the tip of the blade to his throat. Brian swallowed, closing his eyes, unable to watch his own execution. He thought about all the good times he had. It was true what they said —in your final moments you remember everything at once, an entire life experienced in a nanosecond. Tears squeezed out of his clenched eyes. He sniffled and whispered, "I'm ready."

"Stand up," a woman's voice said.

The sharp tip on his trachea receded. Opening his eyes, he saw the ninja had unmasked herself. Long black hair flowed past her shoulders, flaring in the faint breeze that hustled through the tunnel. Her toffee-colored skin was smooth, free from age-related cracks and crevices. She was younger than Brian by nearly a decade.

"Stand," she repeated.

Slowly, he pulled himself to his feet, using the car for support. "Who are you?"

"What's it to you?" she asked, continuing to point her sword at him.

"I'm not one of them."

"I know."

"You've been watching them. Haven't you?"

He took her silence as "Yes."

"Thank you," Brian said. "For rescuing me."

"I wasn't rescuing you." She lowered her blade. "I was killing monsters."

"There was more of my group. Two—"

"Dead."

Brian froze in horror.

"They killed them. Not me."

"I'm Brian."

"I know."

Confused, Brian tilted his head.

"I've been listening and watching for quite some time. Planning carefully." She pointed back the way she came, to the severed head sitting in the middle of the tunnel. "They've been at it for months. Taking people. Raping them. Killing them. I had to stop it. No one else would. I've watched dozens of parties pass through here, eager to give up their women for safe passage. This one," she said, looking down at Mole's bloody corpse, kicking him in the head. "This one promises he wants to build a better world, repopulate, but the women never make it through the rapings. I had to do something."

"You did the right thing."

"You should leave. There's nothing left here but death and it reeks of decadence."

"Where are we going?"

Wriggling her brow, she asked, "We?"

"I'm alone. I won't make it by myself. Neither will you."

Silence.

"At least tell me your name."

She sighed deeply.

"Please."

"Rachel."

"Thank you, Rachel, for all you've done."

She turned and he reached out, grabbing the hand not carrying the katana. She whirled, placing the blade across his throat.

"Whoa!" Brian cried.

"Who said you could touch me?"

"I... wanted..."

"What?"

"Nothing. I'm sorry."

"You should find a safe place, Brian."

He kicked a pebble across the pavement, losing it in the shadows ahead. "I don't know if such a place exists anymore."

"Sure it does," Rachel said. "You just haven't found it yet."

Matty drew the shades shut. He backed into the bed and sat down. Behind him, Bob and Jarvis helped Lilah into the bathroom. Her body was shaking and her skin remained pale, the fever holding strong. Matty heard his mother whispering in his ear, telling him to come, but he ignored her and stared at the blinds. His mother's fingers interlocked with his own. She squeezed. Ignoring her, he thought about the policeman. Had he somehow survived? Tracked them to this motel? No, it was impossible. Bob had turned Matty's head, preventing him from witnessing the man die at his father's hands, but he was dead with a capital "D." The psychotic man was likely where they left him, unless it was the officer's vengeful spirit outside.

"Matty, come," Brenda said, tugging his hand.

Slowly, he turned to his mother. "Who's outside?"

"I don't know, sweetheart."

"We need guns. To protect ourselves."

She squeezed his hand, harder than she meant to. "No, Matty. We don't. We need to hide. They've likely come to raid the rooms for supplies and food and whatever else they can find. And we don't know if they're friendly or not."

"They're not."

Confused, Brenda rubbed his arm. "Why do you say that?"

"No good people are left."

She didn't disagree. "Get inside the bathroom. We need to make sure Lilah is comfortable in there."

Dreamily, he walked with his mother across the room, past Bob and into the bathroom.

Once the four of them settled inside, Bob said, "I'll stay out here."

"No," Brenda said. "Stay with us."

He wiped layers of sweat from his brow. "Somebody has to stay by the front door. To run interference in case they're after more than food and supplies."

"Interference?" Brenda scoffed.

"I can draw them away from here."

"Bob, no. You need to stay here, with us." She reached for his hand. "To protect us."

"Jarvis can protect you in here." Taking a step back, he dodged her hand. "Odds are they're a couple of kids looking to make a little trouble. But if not... I'll need to get them away from this room. So you can escape."

Hating the idea and Bob's sudden courage, she sniffled. "Okay... fine. If you have to."

Bob rolled his eyes, recognizing her tone, knowing it well. "God, Brenda, please don't be like that. Not over this. I'm only doing this to keep you and Matty safe. If there was another way—"

"There is. Stay with us, and let them pass."

Bob pointed at the front door. "Sam and Tina are out there."

"I don't give a shit about them. They can take care of themselves. We are in here, and we don't have any weapons. And —"

"Actually," Jarvis said, pulling out the .38 Special he had tucked in his pants. "I got this off our friendly-neighborhood police officer back there. Figured it might come in handy."

Brenda turned back to Bob. He was already moving toward the front door.

"Jarvis will protect you," he said, already at the window, splitting the shades apart with his fingers.

"I count six men," Sam said, peeking through the wrought-iron railing. Tina looked over his shoulder, keeping invisible from their mystery guests' eyes. All four of the cruiser's doors were open, and three of the men were ransacking the interior. Two others popped the trunk and rummaged through, tossing unwanted materials over their shoulders, littering the parking lot with traffic cones, first aid kits, and wads of paperwork. Another man with a black bandanna covering everything from his nose down sat on the hood, staring up at the rooms. He peeled up the bottom of his bandanna and bit into an apple he'd been tossing in his hand. He chewed slowly and swallowed. Occasionally, he checked on his fellow hoodlums, watching them much like a guard over a group of prisoners cleaning the side of the road. Sam noticed they all wore the same black bandannas, but each had their own distinct clothing. The man on the hood wore a white T-shirt, a rippling American flag printed on the chest. The others wore nondescript clothing of various dark colors. Sam watched American-Flag eat his apple down to the core and toss it onto the pavement. As his cronies finished digging through the car—one of them removing the shotgun nestled between the front seats—American-Flag stood on the cruiser's hood and cupped his hands over his mouth.

"WE KNOW YOU'RE IN THERE!" he shouted. "Come out and say hello! We won't bite!"

The five men snickered behind him. Each of them had stripped something useful from the cruiser and were holding the items in their hands. Food, camping gear, and weapons were among the things they found, and apparently, they weren't satisfied with their discovery. They wanted more. Much more.

"I'll go out there," Sam whispered to Tina.

"What?" she said, keeping her voice equally low. "No. You're not."

"Maybe I can settle things peacefully. I'll try to talk them out of whatever they came here to do and send them on their way. If they don't leave, I'll yell..." He spotted the apple core on the ground. "Apple."

"Apple?"

"If you hear the word apple, I'm in trouble and need back up."

"Fine." She pulled a semiautomatic pistol from the back of her jeans. "Take this."

Reluctantly, he took the gun and stuffed it into his jeans. Sam started to push himself to his feet when Tina grabbed the back of his head, turned him to face her, and smushed her lips against his. "Come back to me in one piece, goddammit."

Sam crept down the hallway, moving in the shadows, making sure the six men in the parking lot didn't see him. He thought about getting back to Tina alive. And that meant not dying at the hands of these intruders. He thought about his encounters in the past. Malek (nut job), Officer Mickey (raging psychopath), and Soren (megalomaniac). With the apocalypse rearing its ugly head, the world had lost its sanity; why would these masked intruders be any different?

As he made his way to the end of the catwalk, he heard footfalls ascending the staircase ahead. Sam ducked underneath the small overhang above one of the rooms. He put his back against the door, flattening himself, appearing invisible until they were at the door. *What am I doing?* He had told Tina he'd try to settle things peacefully, but the more he considered it, the more it sounded like a death sentence. He had been through much over the last few weeks, escaped death on more than one occasion. Did he really want to put himself back in death's cold grasp? Or did he want to adopt the *shoot first, ask questions later,* Wild-Wild West mentality the world had become so smitten with over the past six months. Sam knew one thing: he had to survive, whatever the cost, by whatever means necessary. If that meant stooping to the level of others, changing the way he thought, becoming a savage in a savage land, then so be it. *I have to do what I have to do. For my family,* he thought, as two shadows appeared on the concrete walkway before him.

The shadows stopped.

"What? What is it?" one of the men asked.

"Yo, I heard something," the second man answered.

"Shit, what?"

"I dunno. Something. Fuck. You didn't hear it?"

"Hell no. What do you think it is?"

"People?"

"Shit, son. Think they got guns and shit?"

"Shit, man, of course they do. Be careful. We don't want to —"

He abandoned his hiding spot and rushed forward, throwing his shoulder into the man closest to him. The impact knocked the intruder backward, into the railing. Sam pushed him again, forcing the man over the railing. He fell thirty feet and hit the parking lot head first, the sound of his head splitting on the concrete echoing through the still, silent night.

"Holy shit!" the man's partner said.

The man's hand moved speedily toward his inner pocket. Sam drew the semiautomatic pistol and fired two shots into the masked man's chest. Less than ten feet way, he saw two red holes blossom on his chest, flowers of blood blooming, and the man stumbled back, into the door marked 10. He slid down the door, leaving two crimson streaks in his wake.

Sam turned. Two men—American-Flag one of them—looked up from the parking lot, catching his eyes. Sam looked across the lot to the other side of the motel. Two men were on the walkway parallel to his position. They had been creeping toward Brenda and Bob's room when they heard the gun clatter. They were facing him now, their priorities changed. He glanced down and spotted the corpse of the man who had toppled over the railing, a crawling red pool beneath his lifeless body. His head had split open like an overripe melon; brains leaked out of the crimson crevice, spilled across the pavement, reminding Sam of raw hamburger meat. He glanced up at the two men next to the cruiser. The one who had removed the shotgun was now pointing it at him, steadying his aim. Sam ducked as the shotgun thundered. Too far away, the shots scattered, not a single fragment coming anywhere close to him. Without hesitation, without thinking himself through the next few moments, Sam booked it toward the stairs. He flew down the steps three at a time. He cupped his hands over his mouth and yelled, "APPLE" as loud as he could. Then he took aim at the two men near the cruiser and fired three shots, all of which missed. The two men took cover behind the cruiser as the bullets sailed into the driver's side door.

He approached with caution, gun drawn, waiting for the two men to either give up or grant him a clean shot. As he started forward, he waited for the men to make their move, being mindful of the men on the second floor across the way.

"One of you go around!" American-Flag shouted to his men on the balcony. "Surround him!"

One of the men took off down the hall, hustling, moving like a gazelle on the African plain. *Shit,* he thought. *They'll have me cornered.* He'd have no choice but to surrender at that point, or fire until he ran out of bullets. He didn't know how many bullets he had left to spend, but knew his ammo was limited. He kept his eye on the cruiser, the gun pointed at the area over the hood where he last saw the shotgun-wielder.

"APPLE!" he shouted again.

As the running man turned the corner and approached Room 6, Sam saw the door crack open.

Shit. She was going to walk right into him. Unless...

The man spotted her too late. He tried to stop, draw his weapon, but Tina had the drop on him. She stuck the rifle in his face and pulled the trigger. Blood and brains misted into the air, a burgundy cloud of death vanishing as quickly as it appeared. The man's body collapsed on the floor while electrical synapses misfired and caused his arms and legs to twitch violently. Tina wasted no time before aiming at the other man on the second floor, who stood diagonally from her. He was armed with a compact handgun and fired at her. The bullets sparked against the motel's metal exterior. She ducked back into the room before getting a shot off. The man with the shotgun fired in her direction also, but again, the weapon had no range and the round was wasted. Sparks from the shotgun blasts sizzled in the air like a dud firework.

Sam sprinted to his right, hoping to get the drop on them while their attention continued on Tina. As he rounded the cruiser, he saw the man with the shotgun waiting for him, looking down the barrel, expecting him to appear. This time, he was in the shotgun's comfort zone. Scared, he fired quickly, no time wasted on aiming. The shotgun roared and Sam felt thunder in his knees. Pain entered his chest, but it wasn't terrible, and Sam couldn't immediately figure out if he had been shot or his chest was aching from his thumping heart. A red puncture opened on the shotgun-wielder's throat. His hands abandoned the weapon and immediately clasped over the hole. He choked and gurgled, blood shooting through his fingers in wild spurts. The next thing he knew they were both on the ground. Sam looked away from the writhing man, unable to watch his suffering and inevitable death, and up at the man on the second floor. Tina had dropped him to his knees by putting a bullet in each leg. She rounded the corner and called to the man, demanding he drop his weapon. The man yelled some obscenity back to her and she ended his rant with a swift tug on the trigger. She ran past the man as he crumbled to the ground, bleeding profusely from the new orifice in his head.

Sam looked down at his chest and saw a lot of red that hadn't been there earlier. On his back, he looked up at the stars as they twinkled against the black sky. The pain had come in waves at first, but once his adrenaline rush faded, the pain became constant and sharp, like someone had set fire to his heart and the arteries surrounding it. He ripped open his shirt and surveyed the damage. Two red holes in his chest drooled scarlet. He touched the wounds and immediately regretted it, the pain fiery and unforgiving. He glanced up from where his rash actions got him and his eyes settled on the black bandanna and an American flag T-shirt standing over him.

"You fucked up, bro," American-Flag said, holding the same shotgun that had already done enough damage to Sam's body. American-Flag aimed and placed his finger on the trigger. "Night-night, motherf—"

The thunderous clap caused Sam to flinch, and for a second he thought he was dead and ready for that sprint toward the celestial white light. Scarlet flecks pattered his face, although he barely felt their gentle touch. He uncovered his eyes and watched American-Flag drop weightlessly to the parking lot.

Tina appeared where the man had stood moments before. She knelt over him, surveying the bullet holes in his chest. After she deemed them minor and of no immediate threat, she shook her head at Sam, no sign of jest in her features.

"What happened to talking to them?" she asked, patting his injuries with a rag torn from Sam's shirt.

Despite the searing pain, he smiled.

It was the middle of the day when SUN-TRAC pulled into the Pittsburgh charging station. Aldo informed them the train needed a good six-hour charge to make it to Chicago. He left the car and under the safety of a massive awning, hooked the train to the dangling equipment. The pleasant woman's voice announced the train was "CHARGING" and how long it would take until the battery reached capacity. It was a long six hours and the train left the charging station promptly, as Aldo promised.

Mouth grew nervous about Chicago, and his concerns fell on deaf ears, or at least ears that gave zero shits. Chicago loomed over his thoughts like black clouds on the perfect beach day.

Twenty minutes after leaving Pittsburgh, Soren excused himself from the rest of the group and headed to the back of train. Four cars down, he opened the door and stood on the platform separating the two cars, welcoming the fresh air. The train was moving at high speeds through the fall night, but he greeted the roaring wind as it pelted his face and ruffled his hair. He closed his eyes and thought about the past, the present, and the future. Kyra being alive changed things. Revenge no longer mattered. What mattered was finding her and dispatching Elias Wheeler, his demon spawn, and whoever else stood in his way.

Since he left The Dish his heart had been missing an important piece, and where it lay empty, hatred and misanthropy found a home. The world bored him. People annoyed him. He saw them as ants scurrying about the earth, unaware there were more important matters taking place, unaware of their own insignificance. Unaware they were specks in the universe's map. How their course of history influenced the universe's ultimate scheme as much as one deciding where to dine.

Soren drew in a deep breath. He thought back to Thoreau's book, how much nature influenced his existential thinking, and realized how important the earth's survival truly was to *him*, and not the universe. He knew what weapons The Dish had, how much potential damage it could inflict on the earth and its atmosphere.

Maybe it wasn't wise to destroy the world after all. Maybe he needed the world. Maybe the world needed him.

He suddenly imagined himself living in the mountains with Kyra, two little ones playing at their feet while they huddled in front of the fireplace in their log cabin. He smiled at the dream, and although it'd never come to fruition, it filled his insides with warmth despite the chilly night around him.

Hours later, he headed back inside the car, the door sliding behind him with a forceful hiss, sealing off the strong earthly currents. Thoughts of her occupied his mind as he walked from car to car, until he reached the first car, the place they found comfortable and suitable for the journey.

The first thing Soren noticed upon entering the cab was Aldo kneeling on the floor, looking over his shoulder at him, and the gash above his right eye. The cut ran a scarlet dribble down the side of his face. Mouth was facing him, pointing the gun Aldo used to kill Shondra at Aldo's cheek. Mouth gripped the weapon, his knuckles white with anger. Soren took note of the madness in his eyes, and chose to tread carefully. Aldo's life held little value in Soren's eyes, but Aldo knew the individual in Chicago, the one with The Dish's codes.

Plan B.

"Stop the train," Mouth said to no one specific. "Stop the train and let me, David, and the girls go."

"Mouth, what are you doing?" Becky asked. "This isn't helping anything!"

"I told your father I'd protect you, little lady, and that's precisely what I'm doing."

Soren watched Kyle skulk ahead, but Mouth must have heard him coming or sensed it. He whipped around, turning the gun on the twenty-something year old. The kid froze instantly, waiting a moment before backing away. Mouth returned his aim to Aldo's bleeding head.

"I don't want to shoot you, even though you fucking deserve it," Mouth said, stepping forward. "But I will if I have to."

"We can't stop. It's too dangerous."

"Boy, it'll be more dangerous if you don't."

Soren stepped forward. "Aldo, listen to him."

"But, stopping the train at this speed could—"

"Just do it," Soren snapped. "Do what he says and let them off."

Aldo rose to his feet, wincing in pain as if every muscle in his body ached. He started toward the cabin, but paused after one step. He parted his lips to plead with him, but Mouth waved him on with the pistol. Aldo continued forward, reaching the cabin in the matter of seconds.

"You follow him," Mouth said to Soren. "I trust you about as far as I could chuck your lanky ass."

Soren followed Aldo into the cabin. Mouth kept the gun on them, steady and ready.

"This is a bad idea," Aldo said, looking back at Mouth. "Very bad indeed."

"Just fucking do it, short stuff."

Aldo pulled the lever and the train rumbled like they were caught in another earthquake. The car shook and shifted, tossing its passengers left and right. Mouth lost his balance and fell to the ground. He watched Dana slide across the floor. Becky held the seat to prevent herself from slipping. Susan had fallen and rolled down the main aisle. Kyle was in the back of the car, gripping the seat closest to the back door.

Aldo held the wall as the car rocked back and forth turbulently. "Everyone!" he said. "Hold on to something!"

What sounded like the world ripping in half filled their ears. Over the deafening noise, Aldo shouted, "We're going to crash!" but no one heard a single word as the car flipped, tossing the passengers in the air like paper shreds at a ticker tape parade.

Tina extracted the second fragment with a pair of tweezers Bob had retrieved from a first aid kit he found in the parking lot. Sam winced and cried out. Jarvis gave him the open bottle of Jack Daniel's he had stripped off an intruder's corpse. Sam took a swig, hoping to numb the pain. The golden liquor did nothing but burn his throat and the pain in his chest raged like the sun.

"Not bad. Thought you'd cry more," Tina said.

"Me too," Sam grumbled. He took two more gulps of whiskey and handed the bottle back to Jarvis.

Tina dropped the metal shards on a bloody paper towel.

"You okay, Dad?" Matty asked.

"I'll be fine, kiddo."

"You were awesome out there! Like James Bond!"

"I was doing what I had to. To protect us." He looked at his son, hating the joy in his eyes after witnessing his father's violent actions. "You understand that, right?"

As the smile faded, Matty said, "Yes."

"I didn't enjoy it."

"I understand."

Matty turned and sat on the other bed, the one Lilah rested on, propped up on one elbow, watching the family drama unfold. She looked away when the bloody shotgun shrapnel made an appearance. He asked her if she was okay, and she replied yes, quickly explaining how she couldn't stand the sight of blood, blaming the withdrawals for her weak stomach.

Tina stood. "Take it easy over the next day or two," she told Sam.

Throwing his feet on the bed and leaning back against the bed frame, Sam let out an overdue sigh. "We'll have to figure what to do next. Right, Bob?" he asked.

Bob turned to him as if he weren't expecting to hear his name.

"You have any plans for us?" Sam asked.

Bob looked to his wife. "Actually, Sam, we were hoping you could tell us."

"Me?"

"We had a discussion. You're different now."

"I am?"

"Yes. You understand."

"Understand what?"

Bob squinted.

Sam knew what they wanted hear. "I know I fucked up. I know that now. I thought the store was the best place to survive. It had everything we needed and it felt like home. I also had control. But I should have listened. I was stubborn and controlling and I'm sorry. It took that explosion for me to realize that."

Tina put a hand on Sam's lap. "It's okay." She noticed Matty staring at her. She knew he couldn't tell his father the truth, who really destroyed Costbusters.

Tina winked at Matty; *I was right.*

EPILOGUE

Morning broke through the clouds and his skin tingled, the serum's effects wearing thin. The ground was cold; he peeled his face from the damp earth, pushing himself to his knees. The world was out of focus, and while he gathered his senses, he reached inside his jacket for another vial of his magic juice. His pocket was empty and Soren's heart sunk. Over his shoulder, rays of sunlight streaked through broken clouds, and he was beginning to feel the orange globe's murderous touch.

Minutes passed; the world became clearer, although grainy. Disoriented, Soren glanced around and found himself in a wooded area, sparse with trees and other plant-life. Flames and embers danced around him, sporadically placed throughout, small sparks sailing through the air like drunken fireflies. In the near distance he could make out the tracks and ruined cars. The closest car was twenty yards away. Black smoke rose from the cabin, unfurling like the angry fingers of ghosts. The atmosphere reeked of burnt oil and death. He couldn't remember the details; the last thing he remembered was hitting his head on the control board. He reached for his face, finding it caked with dry blood.

How long was I out?

He had no idea. *Hours,* maybe more.

He tried walking over to the cabin, but his knees were too weak. Kneeling before the wreckage, he watched the flames flicker in chaotic fury. He squinted, looking for other survivors. He couldn't see any; they were still inside the cabin, either dead from the crash or being torched alive. Either way, day was upon them.

He crawled. Beyond the wreckage, he thought he saw movement. An animal? He wasn't sure. In the distance, over the sound of crackling fire, he thought he heard an engine. Then, he heard someone moan. Nearby. On the other side of the cabin, the one sweating black smoke.

Soren scrambled back to his feet. He put one foot in front of the other and found walking extremely difficult. It was like his legs had never learned the concept. His brain and feet weren't on the same page and he stumbled many times. More moans from the other side of the car, and the small groans coming from an injured man motivated Soren to kick-start his motor skills. It took several moments to travel twenty yards, but he arrived and spotted the source of the groaning.

Aldo lay next to a pile wreckage. Half of his face had been exposed to a ray of sunlight and his skin had crisped. Soren grabbed his old friend by his boots and yanked him into the shadows the battered cabin provided. Soren dropped to his knees and tapped Aldo's face, hoping to keep him conscious.

Over his shoulder, he saw a Jeep speeding in his direction. Voices. Shouting. Shadows were closing in.

"Aldo," Soren said, slapping him harder. "Aldo, can you hear me?"

"Blood," Aldo whispered. His eyes were closed, but his mouth hung open.

"I need you to tell me the name of the person in Chicago." He grabbed his old friend by the throat and shook him furiously. "The woman. I need her name. Do you understand?"

"Blood... Her... Blood."

"Whose blood, Aldo? Whose blood?"

"Sha.. Blood."

"Aldo. I need a name."

Aldo coughed. Blood spurted from his mouth, dripping down his chin. *"Blood... Shay."*

"Shay? Are you saying shade, or Shay?"

"Blood... Her... Blood."

Soren waited for more, but those were the last words Aldo Hood spoke. His eyes glazed over and when Soren checked for a pulse, he found nothing.

Behind him, shadows emerged. Men in full black. Covered from head to toe. They had weapons. Guns. Heavy artillery. They told Soren to stand, put his hands behind his head and make no sudden movements.

With no other options, he complied.

TO BE CONTINUED...

ABOUT THE AUTHORS

Tim Meyer is an author working on several upcoming projects. He currently resides in New Jersey, near the shore. When he's not writing, hunting ghoulish entities, or balling hard on the basketball court, he's usually annoying the crap out of his wife, the most amazing person in his life.

Chad Scanlon is a jack of all trades, master of none. Now he's pretending to be an author. When he's not outside running marathons, he's inside avoiding work.

Pete Draper is an author currently residing in Ocean County, NJ. He considers his literary influences to be Stephen King, George Orwell, J.R.R. Tolkien, Richard Matheson, and H.P. Lovecraft. When not lost in the worlds his mind tends to create, he is a practicing attorney and lover of cats. Actually, most animals. Except bears. They're scary.

Made in the USA
Charleston, SC
11 March 2016